Praise for Perv—a Love Story

"Dig it: *Perv—a Love Story* is a beautifully wrought and twisted ode to freaks, beatniks, hopheads, and the wild-assed and strange everywhere. Jerry Stahl is the American hipster bard."

—JAMES ELLROY

"Jerry Stahl's *Perv* is Philip Roth in a head-on collision with Harry Crews. Naked, ugly and funny. Hard to swallow, hard to put down."

—ERIC BOGOSIAN

"It is one thing, fine and rare, to write from the heart. It is another thing, finer and rarer, to write from the secret unutterable chambers of the heart. Jerry Stahl, whose words are as cool and deadly striking as a cottonmouth in the moonless dark night of the soul, does just that. No one who reads him will remain quite the same, for in that dangerous night, amid its horror and wicked laughter, lie the powers of a writer as brave as he is gifted. Jerry Stahl is the real thing."

—NICK TOSCHES

"Utterly charming! Surely the most registered evocation of youthful phalli and pudenda since George Eliot's *The Mill on the Floss*."

—MARK LEYNER

"This is a beautiful book. There are parts that had me laughing out loud, yet it is a tragic story of extraordinary tenderness. The prose is flawless whether he is relating what is happening at the moment or flowing through space and time, which he does with perfection."

—HUBERT SELBY, JR.

"Jerry Stahl's work fills the gap in American literature left void since the death of the late, great Terry Southern."

—JIM CARROLL

"Jerry Stahl is a dangerous man. His predilection for burrowing deep beneath the blistered pigskin surface of the American mind, his ability to puncture the distended bladder of the American libido, make him the kind of writer who speaks truths other writers wouldn't go near. *Perv* is nothing short of pure genius. It lays bare the sick-fuck underbelly of the peace-and-love era like no novel before it. Hysterical, disturbing, insanely funny, *Perv* blows the rest of American fiction out of the water."   —MARK MOTHERSBAUGH

perv—a love story

Also by Jerry Stahl

Permanent Midnight: A Memoir

perv—a love story

Jerry Stahl

Perennial

An Imprint of HarperCollins*Publishers*

For Monah Li and Ben Stiller

A hardcover edition of this book was published in 1999 by
William Morrow and Company, Inc.

HarperCollins books may be purchased for educational, business, or sales
promotional use. For information please write: Special Markets Department,
HarperCollins Publishers Inc., 10 East 53rd Street, New York, NY 10022.

First Perennial edition published 2001.

Designed by Chris Welch

The Library of Congress has catalogued the hardcover edition as follows:

Stahl, Jerry.
Perv—a love story : a novel / Jerry Stahl.—1st ed.
p.   cm.
ISBN 0-688-17094-3
I. Title.
PS3569.T3125P47   1999
813'.54—dc21   99-21960
                                            CIP

ISBN 0-688-17787-5 (pbk.)

01 02 03 04 05 WB / RRD 10 9 8 7 6 5 4 3 2 1

If six

turned out to be nine—

I don't mind

—Jimi Hendrix

perv—a love story

little trophy

I was third in line the first time I ever actually "did it." This was 1970. I was fifteen. The girl involved was a plump, freckled nursing student named Sharon Schmidlap, a ponytailed barber's daughter who lived with her parents three blocks from the small-town boarding school to which I'd been shipped and who had, apparently, been of special service to a select few of my schoolmates for a season or two before my own arrival in eleventh grade.

"Who's the nervous Nellie?" young Sharon giggled, gaping up at me through gapped teeth while Number Two in line, a carbuncled southern boy named Tennie Toad—on account of his Tennessee roots and his bumpy epidermis—humped away and turned his sizable head to wink repeatedly in my direction.

Number One was a boy named Farwell whose father'd been ambassador to Turkey until his mother found him hanging from a chandelier in the embassy banquet room. Rumor had it Daddy Farwell checked out in stockings and heels, and his mother'd slapped the body in a tux before the guards came. His son hadn't said one way or another.

On account of he'd only just come back from Ankara, where he met his bereaved Mom and waggled smelling salts at her nose on a State Department jet, Farwell got the leadoff slot with freckled Sharon. This seemed like the least we could do. It took no more than a minute for him to do his job, and he didn't take his khakis off.

As it happens, we were all of us fatherless sons. My father had stepped in front of a streetcar the previous spring, and Tennie's died in a boating mishap when he was nine and a half. "Before we could grab him, the sharks ate his calves," the toothy Memphis boy liked to say. "He was six-three in life, and five-two in the coffin. The bastard thought he was John Wayne, but we buried him like Mickey Rooney. . . ."

When Tennie was done, or when I *thought* he was done, he hopped onto his knees, reached under Sharon's ample hips and kind of flipped her onto her stomach on the wall-to-wall shag that covered the rec room floor. (A shade of purple, incidentally, that matched the nubby aureoles around her nipples, and the much chewed-upon, fruity gloss of her lips.) "This is what she *laks*," he giggled, in that half-screechy, half-cackling way he had, like Alfalfa from the Little Rascals, but grown up and nasty. "My gal laks a l'il bit o'spankin', donchu honeybutt?"

Before I knew what to make of that, Sharon gave a little coo. She adjusted her pillow-sized nether-globes upward for maximum impact, and Tennie let rip with a meaty thwack to her left buttock. I was amazed, horrified, nervous, and sort of in love. Sharon kept whipping her head from side to side. Her chocolate brown eyes rolled back, so that the whites showed down to the bottom, reminding me of pictures I'd seen of horses in barn fires. She looked scared. She looked like *she liked it.* I thought my brain would leak out of my ears. Even Farwell, sullen and bummed while the three of us slipped past the Schmidlaps' chained-up schnauzer and down the outside steps to their basement, perked up and raised his brows from his spot on the green-and-pink plaid sofa.

By the time Tennie rolled off of Sharon and onto the shag, her whole body had sprung a sheen, a glistening coat of sweat that made me think of supermarket chickens. Skinless and boneless.

I'd become so transfixed, when it was my turn I all but forgot I had to mount the girl myself.

Sharon wrapped a strand of mousy hair around her finger and ran it between her incisors, teasing. "Whatsa matter, Hercules, your pants glued on?"

I never even liked undressing in gym class, and now I had to de-pants in front of two older guys and a girl who looked like she could eat me on toast. But I had to do it. *I had to!*

Without letting myself think about it, I took a deep breath. I fixed my eyes on the rec room TV, a Motorola with tinfoil balls wadded on each rabbit ear and a one-armed brass bowling trophy plunked beside it. That trophy began to speak to me.

Weird but true. I knew the thing was just broken. I knew that Sharon's barber dad had probably gotten drunk after a tournament and dropped it stumbling out of his Pontiac. But *still* . . . It may have been the marijuana—we'd huffed a busload on the way over—but that trophy wouldn't let go. *Look at this little bowler,* I thought to myself, *he's got one arm, but he's not afraid! He's not ashamed! He probably gets heckled every time he steps up to the lane and slides his only hand around the ball to find the fingerholes. They probably laugh at him, but HE'S not going back to his room and sitting under a blanket. HE'S got a goddamn trophy! So what do I care if my penis under duress is the size of an acorn? What do I care if it shrinks up and people call me "Nugget" the rest of my life? I'm a brave guy—I CAN TAKE IT!*

By the time I finished my crippled-bowler meditation, I was loaded for bear. I was finally hard, though not so much from the sight of Sharon's spread pudenda as my own visions of handicapped ten-pin glory. The noble feelings it instilled. I must, however, have looked like I was dawdling, because Tennie Toad stepped up and shoved me hard between the shoulder blades, right into Sharon's saddle.

Amazing, the softness of her, the slightly tangy, slightly vinegary taste of her skin. When I tried to kiss her, she moved her head so I got just a lick, a slurpy smush from just below her chin up under her ear.

"Oh, a *romantic,*" she sneered, and I pulled back just enough to see her roll her eyes. "Cary Grant wants to smooch."

Still making a face, she reached between my legs with her left hand and grabbed me. Then she snapped her fingers with her right and Tennie tossed her a Trojan. She snagged it in midair, as if she'd been practicing for years. Sharon Schmidlap, Queen of the Condom Toss! I had a sudden vision of her naked on *The Ed Sullivan Show*, wowing them between Alan King and a troupe of plate-spinning, festive Romanians. Sunday nights always made me nervous.

I wasn't too sure what was happening, but Sharon made short work of it. She kept up the patter as she unwrapped the rubber. "One size fits all, lucky for you!" Right then, I remember thinking, *But I thought she was a cheerleader....* There was no time to muse, though—she was already wrapping me. "Okay, big boy, let's get dressed for church!"

At the same time Sharon was covering my hood ornament, Tennie was uncovering my behind. He grabbed me by the ankles and pulled my pants off over my shoes, then followed up with my undies.

"Viola!" he sang, and I found myself staring into the milky whites of my partner's eyes, wondering what to do with my arms, whether to actually *lay* on top of her or keep a respectful distance, as if we were strangers on a crowded bus.

Farwell chose that moment to put on a record—Mr. Schmidlap favored Perry Como—and Sharon plugged me in at the exact instant Perry asked the musical question, "How Much Is That Doggie in the Window" I actually *liked* that song. My father used to whistle it. That's how I knew when he was happy. I imagined Dad looking down from the sky, summoned from death by that cheery tune, watching his son fumble his way to Shameville atop the spongy Sharon.

Toad got me out of my reverie. "Newsflash for Bobby," he

perv—a love story

chided me. "You're supposed to move. Don't just stick it in and take a nap."

"I know," I cried back at him, adding inanely, "I'm just warming up."

More than what was happening in front, it was the action behind that had me squirming. I became, the second Tennie spoke, uncomfortably aware of him staring at my behind. I had never, to the best of my knowledge, showed my hindquarters to anyone before. Not, at any rate, for extended viewing. Self-consciousness burned my cheeks. I felt, with almost crippling intensity, split between two planes of reality: On one, I was timidly lunging into Sharon, poking her, or so it felt, like the fork my mother used to check if her cupcakes were done. On the other, the plane *I* couldn't see but the rest of the world could, my rear end was popping up, then popping down, popping up, then popping down again for Tennie Toad and Farwell to gawk at and mock.

I was so sure they were making fun of me I actually tried to crane my head all the way around, like an owl. Before I could get there, Sharon grabbed my face and held it.

"You pay attention, you little turd! *Pay attention!*"

My apathy, or whatever she thought it was, had the odd effect of making Sharon more passionate. And as much to my horror as my excitement, she began to mumble like someone half asleep. Or half alive.

"You don't give a hoot about me. . . . Oh no, you're not like my boyfriend, you're not like *Charlie*, with his *roses*, with his chocolate-covered *cherries*. . . . Ho no, you don't care. . . . You just want my *hole*. You just want to . . . Oh! You just want to . . . Oh!

Oh! You just want to . . . You little bastard, you little creep, you just want to fuh, wanna fuh . . . you just wanna *FUCK ME*, you wanna *FUCK MY GIRL-HOLE*, my *VA-GEE-NA*"—that's how she pronounced it, va-*GEE*-na, like Pasadena—"Oh yeah, that's what you want. . . . Oh God, oh goody God, that's what you want! *THAT'S WHAT YOU WANT . . . !*"

She went on like that, until I actually got scared. *Confused.* I kept feeling those eyes on the back of my skull. Finally I did turn around to find that Farwell had come out of his Turkish slouch. Tennie, too, wore a new look on his pitted face. An expression, I realized, of respect. I had just gotten the hang of it: the in-and-out, the shoulder-holding, the whole idea of nipple-squeezing, hair pulling, pawing—in a mild way—when Sharon went after my tongue. But no sooner did she start to kiss than she stopped. She pushed me off, called me a Communist, and repositioned her face on the woolly carpet.

"Now what?" I heard myself whimper. Toad made a swishing motion with his hand, as though signaling a runner home from third; then Farwell chimed in with a single clap. This was as animated as I'd seen him since the Ankara thing.

"Well?" Sharon angled her face sideways, so that I could see her tongue wiggle out of her lips. "Daddy don't wanna go fishin', Daddy shouldn't bait the hook."

"What?" I said.

"What do you mean 'what?' " Tennie leaped off the couch. He grabbed a book off the end table—a *Reader's Digest* condensed, including *Treasure Island, Gigi,* and *The Man in the Gray Flannel Suit*—and swung it off the back off my head.

"Ouch," I hollered. "What are you doing?"

perv—a love story

"What are *you* doing," he hissed back at me. "You silly fuck! Give it to her!"

At which point Sharon herself chimed in. "What do I gotta do, paint a bull's-eye?"

Her voice had gone all low and throaty. Tennie dropped the book. He backhanded me across my left ear, but not as hard this time. Then he leaned in so his breath tickled the back of my neck. I could smell the cheese steak he'd eaten earlier that afternoon, what seemed like a century ago, when I was still a virgin, as opposed to a half virgin, or a near non-virgin, or whatever I was now.

"I've been *bad*," Sharon cackled, with a low little laugh. "I've been so dirty-bad, you don't even know."

"Huh?"

"Jesus, you're a *feeb*!" Tennie whispered. Still leaning in, he reached over my shoulder and clapped one of Sharon's ample haunches, leaving a handprint the size of a pie-plate. "Didn't you *see* me before?" he asked. "Did you think that was *my* idea?" He was so close his lips grazed my earlobe. I wondered if I'd catch something. Lumps and rashes of one kind or another had plagued Toad as long as I'd known him. "It was *hers*, you retard. She *laks* that stuff!"

As if I were, indeed, too feeble to act on my own, my impromptu sex mentor grabbed my wrist. He drew my arm out to one side and swung it so my hand flapped off Sharon's buttock. "Git it?" he snapped at me. "You git it, stud-boy, or does Tennessee gotta slam the Spam in for you, too?"

"Okay," I protested. "*Okay!*"

But it wasn't okay. Not even close. I wasn't inside her now. I was just . . . *in the air*. Worse, so much time had passed, my organ had begun to sag. Panic grabbed me by the throat: What if the rubber slipped off? What if I just shrunk? What if I went back to acorn status? If I had to unpeel the Trojan and slink back to the dorm with Tennie and Farwell calling me Droopy, or Homo, or worse?

"Daddy, *spank!*" Sharon whispered, breaking my reverie. Perry was now singing "When You Wish upon a Star." No matter how I squinted, my dead father's face peered out from the blank TV screen. He was shadowy, but he was *there*, and he wasn't happy about it. The rec room air seemed to have gone electric, as if they'd dropped the Bomb on Slotzville, PA and nobody was left but us. My whole body began to shake. I was trying to decide if I was hot or cold, when Sharon reached around and slapped herself. She did it again, then slipped a finger under me, tickling beneath my testicles. The sensation was so strange I juked sideways and swatted her hand away.

"Cut it out!" I heard myself squeak, as if I'd been inhaling helium.

"Ooh, widdle girl make her poppa mad! Widdle girl do a baddie!"

"Cut it out!" I repeated, my voice still Jiminy Cricket–like, and cracked her across her goose-bumped caboose. I was suddenly tired, and I didn't know if she was making fun of me. I slapped her again before I could think about it and scare myself. To my surprise, I was re-erect. More surprising, each time I spanked her Sharon gave a tiny cry—a pouting little "Meanie!"—and wiggled her behind asking for more.

"Now you git it," Tennie hooted. "Now the cowboy's gittin' up to a gallop. That's what you're *s'posed* to do," he said, speaking very succinctly, as if teaching a Mongoloid to wait at the curb

perv—a love story

for the light to change. "That's what a girl wants, that's what a boy gives her. It's just po-lite-ness, son. It's just *na*-ture."

I didn't see it that way. But I didn't *not* see it that way, either. The fact was, I sensed that the best thing about this experience was that I didn't have to think about *anything*. That, for a few blessed seconds, maybe minutes, if I got lucky, my brain could just shut off. So that, against all odds, my dead father's frown, my mother's graveside crying, the echo of Farwell's shrieking at three A.M. when I heard him through the flimsy walls, *"Daddy don't! Daddy come down from the chandelier"*—all that pain-fuel that flew around inside my head would just *DISAPPEAR*. I could escape, or at least block out the Bad Thoughts for however long I could slap or fuck or just *hang on* to the willing local girl in front of me.

Which was fine, until I came, and came back out with my glazed and bare-topped unit at proverbial half-mast, absent the lubricated Trojan or any sign of where it might have gone.

"Oh, that was *magic*," Sharon sighed, rolling her eyes again. "That was heaven on earth." No doubt she would have gone on in that vein except that she saw Tennie's face—he'd already spotted my hatless apparatus—and looked down to see for herself that I'd lost the condom.

"What did you . . . ?" she sputtered. "Where did . . . ? What the . . ."

"Check inside," Tennie offered, going all professorial. Like he'd gone to Harvard and majored in rubbers.

Sharon just gasped and lifted a leg to peek inside herself. "Shit on a stick, I don't have my glasses!" When she got pissed off, I noticed, her freckles glowed. She looked up at me furiously. "You jerk!"

I didn't know what to say. I was grateful when Tennie kneeled closer, putting his face right up to her female orifice. "Calm down," he told her, his voice slightly muffled. "It's not like it's going to mate and have babies."

After a second Toad gave up and beckoned Farwell, who'd been chewing his lip on the couch. "Hey man, you're always shootin' them skeets, you got good eyes. Git over here and help snag Bobby's top hat."

"Somebody do *something!*" Sharon cried, her voice visiting the higher registers.

Soon the three of us kneeled on the shag in front of her while Sharon sat back on her hands, invoking Jesus, her blue-white thighs spread wide to fit us all in. The way we were kneeling, I kept thinking about pictures of Muslims in *National Geographic.* How they'd mash their faces on the mosque carpet and give praise to Allah. I wondered if I should pay Him a compliment or two, myself, while I was down there.

"Ali Baba," Tennie mugged, as if reading my mind, "I prostate myself before you!"

"That's pros-*trate,*" Farwell corrected, pressing one ear to her vagina as if listening for the ocean.

"A man can do both," Tennie said, aiming a little wink my way, "believe you me."

I was so glad he wasn't mad—wasn't making fun of me—that I smiled and nodded though I had no idea what he meant.

"Say 'Ahhh!'" Tennie said, leaning in and doing his best Dr. Kildare. Sharon gasped when he reached up and plucked one of her labia more or less open. Then he jerked his head for Farwell to grab hold of the other one. Once both boys had a love-lip in tow, Tennie, who'd taken charge of the whole operation, or-

perv—a love story

dered me in to have a look. "It's your wind sock, buddy boy. You planted it, you dig it up."

"Would you guys shut up!" Sharon squealed. "F.Y.I., this isn't *fun*! You asshole!" she added, for my benefit, as I was the only one who looked up from the job at hand to meet her eyes. Eye level with her genitalia, I felt like Lloyd Bridges on *Sea Hunt*, ready to strap on his tank and head down to the briny deep.

Mysteriously, I was not aroused so much as curious to be so close to an actual pussy. That vinegar scent intrigued me, but the texture had me transfixed: the soft, smushy-slick pink walls and deep purple interior; the moist flesh that, incredibly, seemed to give at my every probe. It kept expanding, which really terrified me, as if one wrong move and I'd tumble in, like some punch line in a dirty joke.

In went a single finger, then two, three, and finally my entire, trembling hand. At last I felt something rubbery—the words "eye of newt" came to mind—and managed to half snag the thing before realizing that Tennie and Farwell were no longer there. Sharon herself suddenly stiffened, but for reasons other than whatever sensations—a man can no more than imagine—were set off by my probing the wanton archaeology going on between her legs.

"Sharon!"

I heard the voice a second before the slam of the basement door and my companions scuttling up the outside steps. The rubber went flying.

"Jesus H. Fuck, what's going on down here?"

* * *

I wanted to look, but my head was at such an odd angle—half crunched in that grisly shag, half wedged in the fur of Sharon's slit—I felt like a man peeping through a mail slot to see if anyone was home. Besides which, with my fist inside her, I could not easily disengage and see who was there. While I'd had my fingers inside a girl before (fingering, in truth, marked the extent of my previous south-of-the-border experience), the whole-hand situation was uncharted territory. Despite my panic, I tried to extract my digits as gently as possible. I'd been such a buffoon, the least I could do was show a little finesse. Odd as it might sound, I *liked* this girl. I wanted her to be okay.

"Daddy," Sharon pleaded, and peeled herself off the carpet as I scrambled upright. A layer of purple shag-fuzz stuck to my mouth. Before I even looked at her father, I grabbed for my pants. Worse than me flapping naked, I felt awful that the man had to see his daughter in such shameless disarray. I felt awful for both of them. Sharon managed a choked whisper. "Daddy, it's not what you . . . Daddy, *NO!*"

I heard the whoosh of the belt before it actually caught me, a flaming lick across my back. When I turned, what I saw made me forget the pain. There was Sharon, doing a backward crab-walk toward her clothes. And there was Sharon's dad, shirtless, a stocky guy with a thick yoke of hair carpeting his back, shoulders, and slightly sagging pecs. More amazing, after my precoital bowling reverie, *he only had one arm.* The left bulged like a boxer's. The right hung in a kind of muscular flap, more like a puckered fin than a human extremity.

So he didn't drop the trophy! In the midst of everything—me panicking and trying to dress; Sharon weeping and struggling

perv—a love story

to squeeze into her culottes, even though her panties were AWOL—in the midst of all *that*, it hit me: *The man was probably in a one-armed bowling league.* This notion, despite the ongoing trauma of the situation, made me unaccountably glad.

"Sharon, *your room!*" father barked at daughter. He closed in with his right hand still clamped around his leather belt and his fin pointing ominously. In a doomed display of loyalty, Sharon peeped through her tears—*"Daddy, he's my friend!"*—then scooted upstairs clutching her jumper and underpants.

"Friend!" Mr. Schmidlap snorted, when the door banged behind her. "I'll show you a son-of-a-bitching friend."

Beneath his overhung belly, I noticed, my attacker sported a second belt, this one with a jumbo buckle that read SIR SNIPPY in raised letters over a crossed pair of scissors. He'd obviously tugged his pants on fast, and hadn't bothered with shoes or socks. But that buckle grabbed me.

"Sir Snippy?" I heard myself squeak. Under pressure, I was going Jiminy Cricket again.

"What of it, punk? A barber's daughter not good enough for you? It so happens that's the name of my shop."

By now he was right on me, raising the leather over his head, ready to swing. The hair bunched under Mr. Schmidlap's arms reminded me, disturbingly, of his daughter's bush. If, God forbid, he ever started to shed, he'd have no trouble replenishing his thatch from Sharon's pubes. And vice versa. I thought that and wondered, not for the first time, *Am I a normal person?*

"I asked you a question," snarled Sharon's dad, so close now I could inhale his aftershave. If I knew my cologne, it was English Leather. I'd received three bottles as bar mitzvah gifts and never worn a drop. I kept waiting till I had an actual date, and wasn't sure if standing third in line for Sharon counted. "Your father some kind of mucky-muck, is that it?"

"My father's dead," I said, which seemed to slow him down. The belt sagged in his hand. Even his flipper, which had been weirdly erect, drooped down below his tufted shoulder. He stood perfectly still, then let out a long sigh and turned toward the plastic turntable. "How Much Is That Doggie in the Window" had begun to skip. I remembered Farwell flipping it to "When You Wish upon a Star," but he must have flipped it back again. I'd been too wrapped up to notice.

"I like a little Como," Mr. Schmidlap confided, "but not now."

I watched him click off the record player, noticing how his stump moved whenever his arm did, as if waving encouragement. When he'd put away the record, he headed to the couch so recently vacated by Toad and Farwell. He plopped down with a heavy sigh. "Sit," he said, and patted the cushion beside him. "No, wait," he added, after giving it some thought, "grab some suds. There's a minifridge by the door."

I grabbed the beers—the fridge was fake wood-grain, its two shelves stocked with nothing but Rheingolds—and wondered whether he was softening me up before he killed me. For some reason I wasn't frightened. All I really felt was tired. That, plus simultaneously aroused and nauseated by the sticky scent of his daughter's sex still clinging to my upper lip.

"I was gonna pound you," he announced, producing an opener from between the couch cushions. He clamped the beer between his thighs and used his good hand to juke the top off. I tried not to stare, but it was like watching a circus act. If he'd balanced the beer on his nose or begun to juggle, I could not have been more enthralled. He burped softly before he swigged, then stared

perv—a love story

straight in front of him, at the velvet JFK framed over the television set. "Sharon's all I got," he began, still not looking at me. "There's nothing I can do. Her older sister's a bona fide slut. Lives with a bunch of bikers in Moon Township and calls herself Stormy. But Sharon—"

He choked back something that might have been tears, might have been Rheingold backing up on him.

"—Sharon was gonna be different. You understand? I come down here and see you three on her like ticks, what am I supposed to do? What would *you* do?"

"Kill me, I guess." He swung his head toward me and I forced a shrug. "I'm just saying, if I caught me, that's probably what I'd do."

I saw now how red his face was. How puffy. Like he'd either been crying or soaking facedown in a sink.

We sipped quietly for a moment, then he slammed his beer so hard on the coffee table it foamed out of the bottle.

"I'm not mad at you," he said, but very softly, in a way that made you think he might just as easily scream. "I'm just . . . *mad*. Can you wrap your pea-brain around that?"

I assured him I could. He nodded and gazed some more at the velvet Kennedy. When he finished his beer, he grabbed mine out of my hand and finished it.

"I used to have a tattoo parlor," he blurted, "but I drank. You don't want to be a drunken tattooist. Word gets around. You got any tattoos?"

"Not yet," I said.

"Well, don't start on your neck. That's my advice. Start out on your neck you're makin' a life choice that'll dog you forever. You wanna peddle insurance? Wanna go into dry goods? You got a goddamn loop of barbed wire 'round your throat people are gonna wonder. Had a kid come in, not much older'n you, wanted 100% PECKERWOOD right under his ducktail. Somethin' like that, you're gonna be explainin' till you're six feet under. Even then the damn embalmer's gonna wonder, but at least you won't have to hear him. That's one good thing. When you're dead, you're deaf. That's one of the benefits. One of what they call the hidden pluses."

He threw back his head to swallow the last drops, and I sat as still as I could. It was so *quiet* between his sentences. Just the humming minifridge. Footsteps upstairs. Running water. Between the pot, the beer, and my all-around panic in the man's presence, I felt like I could hear the shag growing out of the carpet.

"One of you'se I could see," he said, almost pleading now. "Say you wanted to sneak over and get a little somethin', I'm not sayin' I'm gonna throw a party, but I'm a man. I *understand*. You're just kids. But *three* of *you'se!* Three of you'se all over, between her legs. . . . *I ought to kill you!* I ought to chop you up and feed you to Scamper. That little mutt'll eat anything s'long as it's not dog food."

He stopped talking, then started up again in a completely different tone. "Grab a few more brewskis, wouldja?" He went straight from livid to matter-of-fact. "So how'd your daddy die? Heart attack?"

"No, streetcar."

I handed him the beer, unloaded five more on the table, and sat back down. Mr. Schmidlap gazed at me and blinked. "You wanna amplify?"

"Well," I began, figuring I'd just start in, "my mother sent him out for corned beef, like she did every Sunday, only instead of

perv—a love story

going to the butcher he just parked at the streetcar stop and got out. I guess he had to wait a long time, 'cause they only run once an hour on weekends. So he bought a *Newsweek*. Spiro Agnew was on the cover in golf togs. I know that 'cause the doctor at the hospital said they found it in his hand. One of the nurses gave it to me. Not his hand," I added, feeling a little dizzy. "They found that in a patch of poison oak by the tracks. I guess there were pieces of him everywhere. I mean, what she gave me was the magazine."

"The magazine. Jesus!"

Mr. Schmidlap shook his large head and gulped more Rheingold. He started to say something else, caught himself, and said "Jesus" again.

Before this, I'd never told the streetcar story to anyone but Farwell and Tennie. (In the Dead Fathers Club, the rule was include *every detail*. Epecially the bad ones, the ones you don't want to think about, let alone repeat out loud. When I first told my buddies how Dad's hand flew off, still holding the *Newsweek*, Tennie actually applauded. "Smart move just snaggin' the mag, pardner. Say you bag the hand, thinkin' to shellac it and pass it on, for an heirloom, like. You'd probably end up with poison oak, yourself. Then what? Trust me, you don't wanna catch an itch from a dead guy, especially your old man. . . . Every time you scratch yourself you'd be thinkin', 'My poor Daddy can't scratch nothin' anymore!' Imagine! Slap calamine on that rash, you're wipin' out the last thing your daddy left you. It'd be like killing the poor fuck all over again. . . .")

Still, there was some stuff I never told the club. Never told anyone. Until now. Mr. Schmidlap I told everything: how my mother hit me with her purse at the funeral, how her dress split up the back when she tried to climb on the coffin and, worst of all, how she screeched, in front of everybody, that she knew I wished it was her stuffed in that casket instead of my father.

I loved my father a lot, but he wasn't home much. When he was, and my mother wasn't screaming at him, we played pinochle or watched wrestling on TV. The thing is, though, once he died, I had to wonder if any of it, the wrestling and pinochle-playing, was real. Or if it was, if maybe he *hated* it the whole time, and that's why he hit the tracks. Why he checked himself out. Maybe the last thing he wanted to do on the planet was be in a house with me, his mopey offspring, watching Haystacks Calhoun bodyslam Killer Kowalski, or talking for hours about meld. None of this would have occurred to me if he'd stayed alive; but once somebody dies, because they *wanted* to, you can't help but wonder if maybe they did it because of you. Because of something you did, or didn't do. Because you just fucking existed and that was more than they could deal with and still walk around breathing and eating. I hated thinking about any of this Dad stuff, but when I finally stopped, *Mom* came into my brain. Which was worse.

All I had to do was think about that screeching, the foam-flecked lipstick, glittery eyes, the way she stared right at me and pointed: *"Walter, this child hates me. . . . This child wishes I was dead in a box. Make your son happy, Walter, make me die, too. . . ."* All I had to do was think of it and I was right back there: *She shrieks in my face, then drops down in the fresh dirt beside the grave. Her stockings rip at the knees and her girdle shows. Mud splotches her funeral dress. I don't know what else to do so I get down with her, try to budge her back up. My relatives turn away or glare at me like it's all my fault. I can smell their hate from five feet away.*

perv—a love story

What I didn't tell Tennie, what I never told a soul, was what I whispered to my mother when I was on my knees. With my face right next to hers, it seemed like the rest of the world had disappeared. Like there was nothing but the broken glass of her eyeballs, her clam cake skin, the tear-making stink of her White Shoulders, her hairspray, and her filter-tip Kents. The big empty space where my father used to be just swallowed us up. And somewhere, inside this hollow of grief, I listened to my mother's screams.

I listened, and then I leaned in as close as I could. I waved the smelling salts under her nose and whispered, so quietly I wasn't sure I was really talking, *"You're right, Mom. I hope you die. I hope that more than anything."* After that she stopped screaming. She just stared at me. She stayed quiet long enough for the rabbi to clear his throat and proceed with the funeral.

I'd mentioned none of this to Tennie or Farwell. But I told Mr. Schmidlap, without knowing I was going to. When I was done, he grunted and reached for two more beers. He one-handed the caps off both of them and held one out for me. It was like I'd been bursting to tell somebody, and once I did I wanted to tear my tongue out. I was crying and I wasn't even sure why: whether it was the thought of my father, bleeding in five pieces in the streetcar weeds, my mother damning me at his casket, or the savage fact that, less than an hour ago, I'd been leading a rubber expedition in Sharon's sex organs, and now I was pouring my heart out in her daddy's face. It seemed like everything horrible just kept happening, and I was bawling for all of it.

For a second more I buried my face in my hands, until I felt Mr. Schmidlap shift on the couch and slide closer. He mussed my hair and gave me a couple of pats on the back. It wasn't till I wiped my eyes and looked up again that I realized he'd been patting me with his stump. I thought, with a kind of panic, *contagious*. As if somehow I was going to break out in missing limbs. I should, I thought, be revolted. In fact, it was just the opposite. I felt like I'd gotten a gift. I'd never told anyone about saying *"die"* to my mom, and Mr. Schmidlap probably didn't get to give a lot of fin-pats. Between us, we had our own little club.

"I know about grief," he said thickly, while these thoughts lumbered through my brain. "I know about regret. I know all about that shit."

My head was spinning so much I was afraid to move. I'd toked up with Tennie and Farwell on the way over, but I knew it wasn't that. It wasn't the Rheingold, either. What had me swirling, I think, was this sudden intimacy, the strangers-in-the-night weirdness of confiding in a shirtless guy with fur on his shoulders and a missing arm, a guy I barely knew. A half hour ago Sharon's dad tried to myrtilize me. Now I felt closer to him than my own father, dead or alive.

"He say why he did it? Your old man."

I shrugged. "*His* father jumped off a bridge on the way to Auschwitz. *His* father died of mumps in Lithuania. Plus my mother nagged him all the time to get a better job. She was always yelling, '*A lawyer should not be poor! It's a crime against nature.*' But Dad liked defending the defenseless. That was his thing."

"Yeah, well." Mr. Schmidlap belched. "Who the fuck knows? One man's crap is another man's oatmeal."

"Wow," I said, but he just snorted and raised his eyes to the ceiling, speaking to whatever was up there.

perv—a love story

"I wanted a son and instead I got sluts. I got two slut-girls and a wife with acromegaly."

"Acro-what?"

I wasn't hearing anything right. Every word came coated in fuzz.

"*Megaly*," he sighed. "Acromegaly. The missus came down with it last Christmas. We pop a kid now, it could be some kind of monster. Like her. Let me show you."

Mr. Schmidlap reached in his pants and pulled out a snakeskin wallet. Even sans shirt, shoes, or socks, he still packed a wallet. I made a note of it. Now that I was dadless, I tried to observe these things, to study any reasonable grown man I encountered so I could pick up Manhood Tips. *Always carry wallet.* I dutifully filed this one away.

Sharon's dad flipped open the snakeskin and sighed. He waved it in front of me, and for a second I thought he might weep. "There she is, kiddo. The Sweetheart of Slotzville High."

"That's . . . I mean . . . She's beautiful," I murmured, and she really was. I don't know why I was stunned, or what I was expecting. The woman in the photograph smiled over her shoulder, like a movie star. She wore the same kind of flip as Betty Grable in those cheesecake paintings on the sides of bombers in World War II movies. Her teeth were pearly. They showed just a bit between slightly parted lips, as if she wanted to say something but thought the better of it. Even in black and white her skin seemed creamy. But the main thing was her eyes, the way they sparkled. Like there was some private joke, some happy surprise, something silly but personal that, just by looking at her, you felt you shared. Until you remembered that you didn't even know her, and suddenly felt lonely, left out of some perfect kind of love that, in my case, meant I had to settle on something nastier, some cruder buck-naked-on-the-basement-carpet version with her freckled daughter.

Young Sharon enjoyed the same, slight roundness in the cheeks as her mom. A semblance of that sparkle shone in her eyes, too, but in Sharon it suggested rank panic more than happy surprise, something so hurry-up mean and desperate you couldn't glance at her directly without thinking that, whatever she was so upset about, it was probably your fault.

I don't know how long I'd been staring before Mr. Schmidlap spoke up again. "That's her *Before*," he sighed. "You wanna see her *After*, come on with me."

I said, "Okay," and got up too fast. It had been so long since I'd moved, the couch felt like a part of my body. I couldn't extract myself from the cushion the first time I tried. I stood up and the rush hammered me down again, groping sideways to make sure there was something between me and the bottom of the world. So much blood rushed to my head, I thought it would spill out of my eyes.

"Easy, Simba," said Mr. Schmidlap. He grabbed hold of my shoulder and for a black second I froze, thinking: *Attack!* I took a feathery half-swing and he laughed through his teeth. "Drink much?"

"Not . . . used . . . to . . . Rheingold," I managed.

"That must be it. You'd probably do a lot better with Schlitz. Hold on and we'll get upstairs, meet the missus."

"Well . . ."

"Just do this for me, kid. You owe me that much. Come upstairs and see what I'm talking. It's not like she's a real monster," he said, sounding hurt, as if that were my objection: I did not

perv—a love story

want to see someone so afflicted. "I know she's no beauty," he went on, almost pleading, "not like she *was*, but Jesus Peanuts, buddy . . ."

He wheeled me around, so that we stood face-to-face. He clamped his hand on my right shoulder and propped his flipper atop my left. "You son of a bitch! Aren't you my *friend*?" he asked.

It struck me, staring into his bleary eyes, that he was as wrecked as I was.

"Upstairs, *please*! You won't have to stay long."

He loomed so close that his chapped lips grazed my cheek. I wondered, for one creepy instant, if he was going to kiss me. Take me upstairs and kiss me in a way his daughter hadn't, since Sharon said that kissing was for love, not "the other thing," the thing I'd waited my turn in line and done, more or less, for the first time, somewhere between ten minutes and a century ago.

Before I knew it, I was stumbling behind Mr. Schmidlap across the rec room. A bare bulb swung over the basement stairs. The light was watery, tainting the wood-paneled walls. I locked both hands on the banister, eased one foot and then the other onto the same step, and waited, reconcentrating, before attempting the step above it.

"First man to climb Everest," Mr. Schmidlap bellowed suddenly, catching and shushing himself before exploding in heaving cackles. "Sir Edmund Hillary and his Faithful Dog Pudbutter. If I ask for another Rheinie, hit me in the face."

I was too busy trying not to fall down the stairs to respond. We made it to the top and he pressed himself to the wall, as if expecting snipers. "Let your eyes adjust," he whispered, and I nodded okay. The air smelled like yellow mustard. I bumped into a Formica table and my guide swung around and clamped his hand on my mouth. "We're not waking her up. We're just going to look at her, understand? *Wake her up and I'll kill you.*"

I must have shown how scared I was. He hung his head and whispered, "Sorry." He turned away again, like he was going to keep going, then swung back and hugged me to his bare chest, squeezing me so tight his Brilloey pec-hair scratched my skin. I had not, I recalled in a flash of panic, even put my shirt back on. My underpants had vanished, too. Who knew where my shoes were, or my socks? In those days going shoeless was a defiant act, a statement, like wearing your hair long. *"You wanna walk barefoot? Fine!"* my mother used to tell me. *"Why not stick a rusty nail in your heel? Jam a tin can dipped in hepatitis into your toe, get it over with...."*

"Jesus, Mom," I snapped, as if she were standing in front of me, instead of lodged in my brain, and Mr. Schmidlap gave me a light crack across the face. "You're muttering," he said. "Take a tip from a pro. Never mutter. It makes people think you're drunk. Come on!"

"At least I'm wearing pants," I said, to no one in particular, but my guide either didn't hear or didn't choose to.

"With what you're packin'," he finally muttered, "I can't see as it really matters...."

"Excuse me?"

"Barbershop humor," he said, "occupational hazard. Watch the dog dish! Tramp in Scamper's Alpo, you'll stink up the house worse'n it stinks already."

"It doesn't stink," I told him. "Not that bad."

Mr. Schmidlap snorted. "Thank you, Emily Post." He stopped next to the sink and cursed. "Son of a B. What's it take to twist a goddamn spigot?" Still cursing, he fought with the faucet until

perv—a love story

it squeaked and wiped his hand on his pants. "Now come on, Mother's around the corner. We moved her downstairs, to the den. Got one of those motorized beds from the Home Care People. Costs an arm and a thigh, but she likes her *Million Dollar Movie* in the afternoon, and this way she can sit up on her own."

I followed him out of the kitchen and into the living room. With only one lamp on, a little Tensor in the corner, all I could make out was a giant TV cabinet with half a dozen framed photos arranged on top. Right away I spotted Sharon. It was too strange. When you're on top of a naked girl, when you're smelling her teeth and tongue-wrestling, you don't think about her smiling in her First Communion dress. The last thing on my mind was her squirming on Daddy's knee at the age of three. I felt my brain kind of curdle at the sight of Schoolgirl Sharon, at the knowledge this sweet child would turn into an eye-roller who did condom tricks. I wondered all over again why her father didn't just strangle me.

I didn't know he was standing next to me until he spoke. "She was cute as a pony," he sighed. "They both were. Sometimes I think life's nothin' but sittin' around watchin' pretty go bad."

Mr. Schmidlap guided me to a set of sliding doors. Squeezed the back of my neck. "Mother'll have her sleeping mask on, so don't let it spook you. It's kinda like the Lone Ranger's with the holes filled in. The light hurts." He lowered his face close to mine, locking eyes. "Just think of that picture I showed you. Remember that picture."

I said I'd remember. Then I told him how beautiful I thought she was, maybe the most beautiful woman I'd ever seen. Which was not all true but not all not-true, either. At any rate, I understood. After my father died, *my* mother created a shrine on top of our TV. She arranged a half-moon of mementoes and photos around the flag they'd wrapped the coffin in. Whatever her intention, that shrine, to me, just made missing him permanent. It preserved his absence. Those solemn knickknacks had nothing to do with Dad. They just reminded you he was dead, like having a tombstone in the living room. It was almost like Mom knew she'd driven him over the edge, and wanted to butter him up, wherever he was, just in case he was checking in.

But still. . . . The flag was folded in a tight triangle, and more than once I found myself pressing it to my face late at night, even kissing it, as if contact with the last object to have contact with my father would bestow some kind of power. Or at least offer *relief*. But neither came. It was like touching the toenails of a dead saint. (On the plus side, once I found out my mother was going through my stuff, I started hiding joints in Old Glory's folds. It was one place I knew she wouldn't rifle.)

"My mom put pictures of my old man on our tube, too," I confided, and Mr. Schmidlap nodded like it was understandable.

"It's the logical place," he said.

I said I agreed, but the truth was I didn't. The biggest item in Mom's Dad-altar was a blown-up wedding picture. Mommy-bride was beaming, but Daddy-groom was staring off. He looked like he'd spotted something he thought he'd gotten rid of, and wasn't thrilled to see that whatever it was was still around. I couldn't watch TV without my father watching me back, looking bummed. His moody gaze made it hard to get into the Three Stooges. I ended up staying in my room listening to FM radio till I got sent away.

perv—a love story

Sharon's dad talked some more about his wife—her great looks, her charm, I think I even heard the words "oven mitts"— but I couldn't stay focused. It was too painful. Too much like listening to my own mother, who could not stop jawing about my dad: how tremendous he'd been, how compassionate and brilliant. (Mythology made all the creepier, for me, by the niggling fact that, while he was alive, she never stopped sniping at him. She *hated* that he worked for the poor. "You're not kind," she used to sneer at him, "you're *weak*.") More than once I saw the mailman cringe when he spotted Mom on the patio and knew he had to suffer another round of Dad-rap. I could see him wishing the post office would arm him with Chat Repellent.

Little by little, my mother's life mutated into a nonstop testimonial. I could see the same thing happening with Mr. Schmidlap. Even though his wife wasn't dead, she was becoming *something* she had never been, and it wasn't good. He needed to keep that *before* part of her alive. He needed it badly enough to talk her up to me, a punk who'd just made carnival with his daughter on the rec room carpet.

I held my breath and Mr. Schmidlap parted the sliding doors.

"*Honey?*" he called softly. "*Honey, you awake?*"

There was no answer. He waved his stump and I followed him over the threshold.

"This is her, son. Take a look."

While I tiptoed to the bed, Mr. Schmidlap stepped aside and shoved his fist in his mouth. He bit down and broke into high-pitched keening, a drawn-out, spoon-in-the-garbage-disposal sound he tried to muffle by sinking his teeth in his knuckles. "*Eeeeennnnnggghhh . . .*"

In the half-light, Mrs. Schmidlap's face seemed to form grad-ually, like the image on a Polaroid. I didn't think anything at first but "big." Big fingers. Big hands on the bedspread. Big head wrapped in a black satin blindfold. If I hadn't glimpsed the *before*, maybe *after* wouldn't have been so grievous.

Not until I thought of that snapshot, of that happy lady with the Betty Grable do, did the impact of the sleeping monster before me sink in. Her pushed-out forehead, her prognathous jaw, slab-of-meat lips, and gnarled, rootlike fingers grabbed at my insides and squeezed the air out. That perky flip, the same style that made her such a doll in her husband's wallet, rode her head grotesquely. I thought, and hated myself for it, of Golden Book illustrations of the Big Bad Wolf, sprawled under Grandma's blankets with outsized chops and a lacy nightcap.

"It's not . . . I mean, it's okay," I heard myself say, but my host didn't bother to answer. He didn't want placating; he wanted a witness. I wondered how long he was going to hover over his wife's bed. He breathed hoarsely, in irregular gasps, and I was afraid he might burst out crying. There was another sound, which I finally made out as Frank Sinatra, belting out "High Hopes" from a transistor turned down low on the nightstand.

While I was standing there, gulping in the sickroom smell— a turned, citrusy scent I took to be part Lemon Pledge, part death—I felt something else. Something pressed against me from behind, warm on the bottom but wet on top. The warm part was Sharon's flannel bathrobe. The wet was her face, streaked with tears, where she laid it on my shoulder.

"Daddy's so sad," she whispered. "Daddy's so scary-sad."

This wasn't the vixen Tennie'd told me to buttwhack on the rec room floor. This wasn't the saucy towny who sneered and

perv—a love story

called me "big boy." The girl behind me now was angelic. She'd scrubbed her face and put her hair in pink rubber curlers. Her bathrobe had a flags-of-all-nations pattern. I had pajamas of the same material when I was nine. "I'm sorry I was so low-down," she spoke into my ear. "I just was."

The sleeping figure on the bed smacked her lips. She might have been dreaming of a lamb chop she'd once enjoyed. Mr. Schmidlap leaned over and ran a finger down her cheek. "I still love you," he cooed, before turning in my direction. "I still love her."

If the man of the house saw Sharon, he gave no sign. He stayed hunkered over her mother, executing a series of fussing, affectionate maneuvers. First he fluffed her pillow. Then he whisked a strand of hair off her swollen forehead. Finally he made sure the blankets were tucked just so under her fistlike chin, and planted a kiss on her mouth. I don't know what he did after that because I couldn't watch. I only know that this was love.

When I was in first grade and my lifelong, unrequited crush on a redhead in my class named Michelle Burnelka had just started, I used to fantasize that she'd catch leprosy, and no one in the world would help her but me. I'd risk losing my own hands and fingers if only to touch Michelle's once or twice before they fell off. "I love you," I'd say to her, "even without a nose."

I'd lost track of Michelle in high school, but never stopped obsessing about her. Now here was Mr. Schmidlap, living out my boyhood fantasy with his own misshapen love.

When Mr. Schmidlap started speaking again, his voice was singsongy. He'd picked up one of his wife's hands. It was as beefy and big around as both of his, with nails like hardened cheese. "See my life?" he said. "See it?"

I opened my mouth to speak but nothing came out.

Mr. Schmidlap turned and waved the hand gently in my direction, as if pretending the sleeping woman were saying hello. I was just about to wave back when he explained, his eyes glistening with tears, that she needed constant massaging or her joints would calcify.

"Y'see, what the acromegaly does is make her grow. On account of the tumor's plunked square on her pituitary, it's always pumping out them growth hormones. You don't keep her good and rubbed, Mom won't just jumbo up, she'll go concrete. First her mitts'll turn to stone, then the rest of her. Sharon, bed," he said, without changing his tone.

"*Dad*-dy," Sharon whined, stomping her foot and pouting. She sounded so much like a cranky four-year-old, I wondered who she really was. "Dad-dy, not fair!"

"Go on, sweetiepie, I'm not mad. Mad comes later," he added, I guess for my benefit.

Sharon slipped her arms from around my waist and padded toward the stairs. *"Tomorrow at nine,"* she mouthed over her shoulder, batting her lashes so boldly I was afraid her father would notice. If he did, he didn't show it. He continued smoothing and patting Mrs. Schmidlap, then straightened up, squared his shoulders, and marched toward me with a grin creasing his lips in a way I hadn't seen in the course of the evening. He killed the bedside light and slid the doors shut behind us.

"Well, that's that," he said. Keeping his face in that strange new grin, he palmed my head and pointed his fin at me. He was so close, the puckered tip touched my nose. "You did something for me. Now yours truly's gonna do something for you."

"That's okay," I said. "I should probably go."

perv—a love story

"You'll go when I say you go," he said, still grinning.

On our way through the living room, he caught me checking out Sharon's First Communion picture. He stopped and made a show of putting it facedown. Then he chuckled.

"Knew a pussyhound in the Army once. Guy by the name of Flatley. Used to call him Flatress the Mattress. Ended up with a steak knife so deep in his neck his Adam's apple came out diced."

The chuckle turned to a cough and his words scragged out between hacks.

"That's—HUACCH—that's not the worst part."

"It's not?"

"Not even—HUUUUAACCHHH—not even close."

By now we were shambling down the basement steps. The shadow of his skull on the paneling loomed huge as a beachball. His cough passed into a series of rumbling throat-clearings, followed by a minute-long belch. "Swamp gas." He smiled, going serious as soon as I smiled back.

"Ol' Flatley ended up with his dong chopped off and shoved in his kisser. You shoulda seen it. They left just the tip stickin' out, so's it looked like he was chompin' a Vienna sausage. My grandpa used to eat 'em right out of the jar."

"Holy heck!" was all I could think to say, and I could hardly say that. We were back in the basement rec room. Just the sight of the crumpled shag where I'd straddled Sharon made me want to gargle Lysol. Worse, I spotted the condom. The thing peeped out like a slug from just under that ratty plaid sofa. If I had one wish in the universe, it was that my host didn't step on it. He was still barefoot.

*   *   *

Mr. S. swayed beside me in silence, his face raised and his nostrils flaring like a hound. I could only imagine what he must have been thinking, let alone what he was sniffing for. He aimed another weird grin my way and tapped his pockets. He extracted a pack of Swisher Sweets and held it out.

"Can't beat a Sweet. You ought to try one."

"No thank you, sir."

I didn't tell him I never puffed anything but grass. I'd tried tobacco—my mother'd been leaving her Kents around the house since I was in utero—but I never saw the point. If it didn't get you high, why bother?

"Don't smoke," I told him.

"Until now," he said, and thrust the pack in my face. That smile never left his lips, though his eyes didn't look too happy. They seemed to be going rapidly red and yellow. I took a tiny cigar and he used his teeth to pluck one out for himself.

"That's better. Match me, Kitty-Cat."

"What?"

"Light the fucking things."

I fumbled in my pants for matches. My hands shook so badly, it took three tries to light us up.

"That's better," he said, "now fasten your ass to the couch while I get my kit. It's been a while since I inked anyone, but it's not something you forget. Kinda like humpin', right, Romeo?"

"I guess," I said, watching him turn and fumble in a metal cabinet I hadn't noticed before. I didn't know what "inked" meant and didn't want to ask. I kicked the rubber as far as I could under the couch.

His back to me, Mr. Schmidlap mumbled to himself, and I considered making a run for it. For all I knew he was fishing for

perv—a love story

a hatchet. I kept obsessing on that Army story: Flatress the Mattress with his dickhead peeking out of his mouth. I caught myself
thinking, absurdly, *Never liked sausage . . . more of a bacon man.* My
brain seemed in the grip of peculiar spasms. I licked my lips,
which had dried to tinder, and felt my entire body break out in
acrid sweat. *If I wait here I'm fucked,* said the top of my brain. *Try
and escape, you're gonna be more fucked,* said the bottom. Toad and
Farwell made it out and up the steps in seconds. But they hadn't
been hitting the Rheingolds. And they hadn't heard about Flatress the Mattress.

I was still waffling when my new best friend turned back
around. Wedged under his arm was a battered leather box.
A frayed black cord trailed out of the lid, ending in a three-
pronged plug that dangled at his knees. He plopped down on
the couch and set the thing on his lap. Then he cursed and got
up again and plugged it into a socket next to the fridge. When
he sat back down, he worked open the lid—away from me, so I
couldn't see inside—and started messing with some kind of
gadgetry.

He worked without looking up. And I noticed, when he
moved his whole arm, that his tiny, Tyrannosaurus one flapped
up and down like it wanted attention. Like it was trying to say,
"Hey, don't forget about the little guy! I'm important, too!" He glanced
up suddenly and saw me staring, but didn't mention it. Instead,
he went somewhere else entirely.

"You Jews got that Bar Mixer thing, right?"

"You mean Bar Mitzvah?" I didn't know how he knew I was
Jewish, and for the zillionth time in my life worried that it was
obvious.

"Excuse me for not speaking kosher." He sneered. "I'm makin' a point here. That whole shindig's about becoming a man, am I right or am I right?"

"You're right," I said.

"Well fuck that, matzohball."

With this, Mr. Schmidlap produced what looked like a cross between a fat black pen and a dentist's drill. He raised it to the light, giving me a view.

"Tonight big Schmiddy's going to make you a man. What do you think about that?"

"I don't know."

"Well you're gonna know. You can take that to the Bank of Haifa."

He fished out a smaller plastic box and unsnapped the top. Humming "Taps," he picked up a vicious-looking point and worked it into the contraption on his lap.

"Twenty years from now, when I'm dead and pushin' up lop-sided daisies, you're gonna look back and remember this night. You're gonna remember the time you and your snot-fuck prep school pals thought you were gonna cop some nook from a townie and you were the one got his piss-stick caught in the wringer. Trust me, you'll thank me later."

He hit a switch and the thing buzzed like a wasp in a jar. It even sounded painful. I only wished I had state secrets so I could spill them and go home to bed. Mr. Schmidlap plainly savored my discomfort.

"Just think, you'll be sitting there with that big creamy bitch you get to marry you, and you'll be telling her all about your crazy Mr. Schmidlap adventure. 'He was a hairy one-armed bastard,' you'll say, 'but by God he taught me a thing or two about life on this Planet of Crap.' You may mention Sharon, or you may not, depending on the broad. Now get over here before I change my mind and cut your shlong off."

He stuck his hand back in the leather case and came out again holding a plastic jar. Something brownish had leaked over the sides and dried.

"Is . . . Is that blood?" I asked.

"Yeah. Wanna drink?"

He got a good laugh from my expression, and squeezed the lid off. "It's Betadine, you buttinski. I gotta swab you down. God knows what you could catch in this house, huh? Last time I used this gun was on a thief wanted MOMMYLOVE across his ass-cheeks. He was goin' up to Attica for a deuce. The poor shnook figured if he had some Moms down there maybe the turd-burglars would spare his keester. I don't know if it worked. Got one postcard and he signed it 'Lulabelle.' Whaddya think?"

By now the pot and alcohol had faded, replaced by a fatigue so deep I would have done anything if he'd just let me keel over. Between the watery light and the smoke from those Swisher Sweets—the fear I might die and the fear I might not—I entered a room in my head I never knew was there.

"The light here's for shit, kid. Sit close so I don't fuck up."

He laid out another jar and some ointments on the arm of the sofa. But what got me was the gauze. I could have handled any-thing, I think, but the sight of that gauze. The field hospital feel of it, like maybe he was going to pluck my tonsils out, maybe remove my spleen in his moldy basement, curled my toes right into the carpet.

"You're not going to . . . I mean, there's no way you're—"

"No way what?" he spit back at me. "I'm gonna give you a goddamn tattoo, that's what I'm gonna do. Now there's two ways

you can play it. This can be painful, or this can be *real* painful.
I was you, I'd lie back and enjoy it, sweetheart."

"But wait," I blurted, unsure what I was going to say, but desperate to say *something*. "Mr. Schmidlap, please, I don't want a
tattoo. I don't want . . . I don't want anything."

Of course, I was squeaking again. I hated sounding like Jiminy
Cricket, but couldn't help it. I fought back sobs, along with a
pathetic urge to drop onto the ratty shag and hug his knees. One
wrong move and I'd be reeling like the hard-boiled killer who
cracks on the way to the chair, the blubbering tough in old-time
gangster movies who pleads for mercy while the chaplain pats
his head and the warden turns away disgusted.

"I am touched. Really," said Mr. Schmidlap. Dousing a plum-
sized wad of gauze in the rust-colored disinfectant, he crooked
his finger for me to move closer. "Consider this a gift. Believe it
or not, fellas used to pay me big to tat them up."

He swiped the Betadine across my left nipple, then circled and
recircled the left side of my chest until it looked like a sloppy
bull's-eye. I kept expecting it to burn but it didn't. It was only wet.

"Nice, huh?" Mr. Schmidlap surveyed his work. "Had a Mor-
mon in Korea slip me fifteen hunnert to do the Angel Moroni
on his back. Mind you, I don't know Angel Moroni from Rice-
a-Roni, but he told me God would guide me so I figured, 'Okay,
it's his skin.' Didn't use no stencil or nothin'. Went in freehand,
Michelangelo-style. It came out like Elmer Fudd, but what the
hell . . . I stuck a halo on it and he went home happy."

He swabbed the Betadine with another blob of gauze, until it
smeared to a pinkish film, then dropped the blob in his kit box
and rooted around till he came out with an old-fashioned straight
razor. It was pearl-handled and rusted shut.

perv—a love story

"Musta put her away damp," he said, sounding none too concerned once he'd pried the thing open. "Bit o' rust ain't gonna hurt a big boy like you. Besides which, you probably already had your booster shots. Hell, yeah! Anyway, you prep-wipes got your own sick bay, right? You start feelin' lockjaw comin' on just tell the doc and he'll getcha a tetanus."

He made a show of wiping the open blade on his pant leg, holding it up to the pallid light, then wiping it a little more. "Just don't wait till you foam up, that's my advice. Once you start sudsin' at the chops, you're in deep shit. Knew a guy once at Pendleton, lied about his shots? Next thing you know he cuts his thumb on a can of beans and ends up drinkin' out of the toilet. Man, was he Mr. Foamy!" He ran his thumb along the blade and looked straight at me, pleased with himself. "You heard the expression 'all lathered up'? Well, guess where it comes from."

"But," I pleaded one more time, "I don't *want* a tattoo!"

Mr. Schmidlap feigned shock. "You nuts? You're gettin' quality work for nothin'. I was you I'd stop sniveling and pull up my argyles. Know what'd be nice?" he asked suddenly, as if we were a couple of chums planning a picnic. "What'd be nice is a little inkin' music. Hop over to the machine there and pick out somethin' you like. Anything would be swell, s'long as it's Perry Como."

I was surprised, when I stood up, to find my knees were weak. I'd heard the expression "weak in the knees" but never experienced it. When I was three or four and my parents would shout at each other, so that the whole house felt like it was going to fly off its foundations, just implode from tension, I used to repeat a little mantra, *"Pretty soon now will be then."* I'd press my hands over my ears, go fetal under my bed, and keep repeating it. *"Now will be then. . . . Now will be then. . . ."* But when I tried that, in my mind, across from Mr. Schmidlap, it didn't work. His tone of voice was so friendly, so Regular Joe, it was hard to reconcile with the panic slamming around in my stomach. I wobbled over to the record player, a brown plastic portable propped on a footlocker, and plucked an LP from the stack. *Perry Sings for Lovers.*

Mindlessly, I set the needle down on the first groove and shuffled back to the couch. At the first strains of "Some Enchanted Evening," Mr. Schmidlap closed his eyes. He waved his thick, red-knuckled fingers in front of his face, swaying like some kind of hairy sea plant in time to the strings.

"Now *that's* beautiful music," he declared, as happy as I'd seen him all night. Somewhere between the time I got up to play Perry and plopped back down again, he'd dug up a pint bottle of peach brandy. Old Mr. Boston smiled off the weathered label, and young Mr. Schmidlap raised the bottle in a jolly toast. "Sit right down, Little Jew, and let the master do his stuff."

My host jammed the bottle under his stump and pulled me close.

"Now stay there," he said, getting down to business. "Unfortunately I don't have any shaving cream, so we're gonna go in dry." He enjoyed my panicky look. "Don't worry so much. I had to shave a balloon in barber school. I was the only guy whose didn't pop. Not right off, anyway."

He reared up and swished my chest with a dramatic flourish, then zeroed in for a couple of back-and-forth strokes before sitting back, satisfied.

"Perfecto! What'd I tell you? I mean, confidentially, you're not exactly what I'd call manly. Still, even girl babies got fuzz, and just a couple hairs can fuck up a masterpiece."

I ran my hand along my left pectoral, now smooth as an egg, and had to admit he'd done a hell of a job. I didn't know how tight I'd been squeezing my sphincter until he stopped, at which point the relief almost killed me. "It's . . . it's pretty good," I sputtered. I considered saying something about that "Little Jew," but decided against it.

"Pretty good?" He took a long pull off the brandy, gagging most of it back out in a minor coughing fit. "Pretty good?" he gasped, once he caught his breath. "Why, my tonsorial prowess is unmatched in this backwater province!"

I wasn't thrilled to see how drunk he was. He sounded like Foghorn Leghorn, but what could I do? I was stuck. What was obvious was how much Mr. Schmidlap enjoyed my jitters.

"Okay, I admit it, I was gonna kill you. Guilty as charged," he barked, putting up hand and fin. "But now I think I'll just experiment." He saw the look on my face and let out a giant guffaw. "Do I look like Joe Mengele? Can't you tell when Ol' Schmiddy's kiddin'? What I'm feelin' is inspired, buddy boy. I got an idea you're gonna love my work. Now sit still. I can't hit a moving target."

For the next few minutes, I tried not to breathe. Mr. Schmidlap, panting heavily, pressed a stencil to my chest and inked in an outline. He was so close I had to inhale his hair, which reeked of Vitalis. I didn't try to see what he was doing. Part of me wanted to peek, but part of me didn't. What struck me, in the midst of this nightmare, was that if I ever got famous, biographers would divide my story into what happened before this momentous evening and whatever happened after. Pre-ink and

Post. Breaking through this delirium, my skin began to itch where Mr. Schmidlap had shaved it. Like the poison oak I didn't catch from my dead dad's hands.

I didn't look when he switched on the tattoo gun and lurched forward to start. I resigned myself to tragic results. I was frightened. In fact, I was *beyond* frightened. I'd graduated to paralyzed, then nauseous, my fear finally mounting until it hit a numb spot in my brain and just lodged there. For the rest of my life, there would always be this *one thing*—whatever it ended up being—that I'd know was there even if nobody else did. I imagined the worst: scrotums, clown feet, swastikas. . . . Or maybe it would just be words, secret insults like *FAIRY, I DRINK PEE,* or *LITTLE JEW* emblazoned across my chest, condemning me to shower solo and avoid the beach, to clutch anonymous women in total darkness till the day I dropped.

"Don't look so glum," Mr. Schmidlap teased. "It only stings for a second, then you start to like it."

I needed to speak up, to make my case. But how? I thought about offering money—not that I had any, but I could offer—and if that didn't work, just grabbing a Rheingold and smashing his face. I'd never actually hit anyone, but I'd seen the bottle move plenty on television. With any luck I could fly off the couch and out the door before he'd picked the glass out of his eye . . . *But it was too late.* The needle was on me, and moving seemed more dangerous than sitting still. The first prick was startling. It didn't just sting, it burned. In spite of myself, I peeked down when the first red droplets started to show.

Mr. Schmidlap stopped and put the gun in his teeth, then plucked a rag he'd been holding under the armpit of his flipper—his flipperpit?—and dabbed the blood away.

perv—a love story

"I'm bleeding," I said stupidly, and Mr. Schmidlap gave me a look. He took the gun out of his mouth and spit on the carpet. "*Of course* you're bleeding. It's your attitude. You're fighting it. You're tightening up. You tighten up, it dilates the capillaries, squeezes all the blood to the surface. Relax your asshole and life's a rosy hue. That's a good rule of thumb in any circumstance."

The last thing I wanted was to get him mad, but what he was doing hurt, plus I had to piss like a racehorse and was too scared to mention it. Sitting quietly made the wasp sting on my chest even worse. I had to *talk*, just to distract myself. I was blacking out.

"So hey," I piped up, "if you don't mind my asking, how'd you lose your arm?" I heard my voice go Jiminy but kept blabbing. "I mean, was it a war thing? Did you get run over when you were a kid? My dad had a friend, a guy in his office, who had a wooden leg. Every time it rained he knew ahead of time, 'cause his shin itched. That's what he said anyway. I mean, he didn't really have a shin but—"

"*Shaddup, damnit!*"

"I'm sorry. . . ."

"Forget it."

Mr. Schmidlap appeared to freeze. He held the gun where it was, in midair, but didn't raise his face. For a long time there was nothing but the buzzing needle, the sawing rasp of his breathing. When he spoke again, he enunciated every word, clearly trying to keep the lid on.

"First off, I did not *lose* my arm. Okay? I know exactly where it is. As a matter of fact, it's buried outside, in a hatbox. It lost a fight with a Chevy Impala, if you wanna know. I even gave it a funeral after it passed away."

He took a big puff off his Swisher Sweet and blew the smoke in ragged circles.

"Sharon invited the whole neighborhood. She was five and a half. She wore a party dress. If you'd like to dig it up, see if I'm full of shit, be my guest. Secondly, I don't buy that crap about phantom itches. When it's gone, it's gone. Nobody's ever gonna make me believe they still get athlete's foot when they don't got any goddamn feet. That's pansie bullshit. I don't know who the fuck your father's friend was, but I'll bet you dollars to doughnuts he wasn't packin' wood. They haven't used wood since the forties. After WW Two the government got into prosthetics in a big way. I'm talking plastic, I'm talking polyurethane. I got a fucking plastic arm. Problem is it's got metal clamps on the end. They call it a gripper claw. Like that's gonna help me. They want me to drag ass to physical therapy for ten months so I can use a fork? Thanks but no thanks. I don't think so. Bad enough my kids grow up thinkin' Daddy's a friggin' gimp, I gotta be a pirate, too? I'm a *barber*, for Christ's sake! You think anybody's gonna want a trim from Captain Hook? Not fucking likely."

He went back to work and I tried to be quiet. Tried, but couldn't. Every second of silence filled me with dread. The last thing I wanted was to get him more excited, work him up to the point where he lost it entirely and tattooed my forehead. But I couldn't stop myself. My heart was beating so fast I was probably gushing red corpuscles, but I could not bear to look any more than I could bear to shut up.

"Sorry about the acromegaly," I yelped, closing my eyes to keep from seeing his reaction. "My mother's kind of sick, too.

perv—a love story

We used to think she took a lot of vacations, but after my dad died we found out they weren't vacations. She wasn't visiting her sister in Cleveland, she was in Western Psychiatric, right there in Pittsburgh, getting electroshock. She always came back happy. But after a while, it's like her battery would drain. She'd head south again, until she stopped getting out of bed to eat or wash. Soon as she started trying to pick the roses off the wall-paper, Dad would call the doctor, pack her up, and shoot her off to get recharged. She looked okay, except for a little sideways around the eyes. Once the depression hit, forget it. My sister and I used to call it 'the hates.' Like, *'Watch out, Mommy's got the hates again. . . .'*

"No matter what you said—'Good morning!' or 'How's your toast?'—she'd glare at you like she couldn't believe what just came out of your mouth. I mean, *outraged!* That's how she'd look at you. Believe me, after a lifetime of that, *you* go crazy, too. You start to think, 'Well, jeez, maybe I *did* just tell her to go shit in her Cheerios, I don't know. . . .'

"It was nuts," I babbled. "You knew she was cracked, that there was no reason for her to be looking at you the way she was looking, but *you still felt bad*. Know what I mean? You still felt guilty. My big sister Bernice went bald when she was fourteen, from picking at herself. It's like she wanted to give Mom a *reason* to look so disgusted. But Bernice left home early and my parents hardly mentioned her. For a while, I still got letters. Envelopes, minus a return address, from towns in Canada with names like Fresalia or Ripewater. I pictured windmills, though I don't even know if they *had* those in Canada. Bernice hooked up with a draft dodger, is what happened. But I had no idea what her life became after that. 'They're all *homosexual*,' Mom said whenever I mentioned Bernice and her draft dodger. And then, 'I do not want to discuss a child I no longer have.'

"It's so fucked-up! The last card I got—this was two years ago, when Dad was still pre-streetcar—Bernice said some feds were after her boyfriend, and she was tired. That was it. I still missed her, though. I even checked the mailbox every day when I lived at home. It's different to miss somebody when they're still alive. When they die it's like, 'Okay, I'm sad.' You're *supposed* to be sad. When they just go away, when they disappear, that's a different thing.

"Sometimes," I told him, "when I look at the moon, I think maybe my sister is looking at it, too. Then I feel okay for a minute. I look up at the moon and wave. But back home, I went a different route from Bernice. I didn't need to go bald to feel disgusting. I felt that way anyway."

My mouth was dry as a dead camel, but the idea of silence scared me more than sounding like an asshole.

"It's weird. From diapers on, I felt like there was something *not* good about me, but it was invisible to everybody but my mother. And whenever she looked at me, she had to let me know that she knew. That was her mission in life. Does that make sense? She knew the secret of my creepiness. *But she would never tell me what it was.* Which made it twice as creepy. It's like, I knew I was disgusting, but I didn't know *why*. So I spent my whole life worrying that one day the secret would get out. Everybody would see. That sickening thing inside me would show up, like a horn on my forehead. Then the whole world would turn into Mom. *A Universe of Moms.* They'd see what she saw and they'd all give me the *look*. I'd be fucked for life. Which is exactly how I feel anyway. Which is . . . Jesus, that thing stings!"

"Chatterbox," he mumbled, and stopped to reswab with a square of gauze dipped in disinfectant.

If I had control of what I was saying, I didn't know about it. Mr. Schmidlap seemed to sense this. He mellowed out. Or almost. It was the pain that made me talk. Maybe pain always did that. In which case Mr. Schmidlap had probably heard every disturbo confession there is to hear. After he swabbed me, he fired up a Swisher Sweet from the butt of the one he was still smoking. Then he plucked that one out and, making sure I was watching, stubbed it out on the tip of his flipper. I could smell the flesh where it burned through.

"Dead nerves," he explained, offering up a grin. He flicked the butt behind the couch. "Met a paraplegic in physical therapy used to roll into bars and bet five people he could put their cigs out on his legs and not scream. He'd get fifty clams from each one, then lift up his blanket and show 'em his thighs. He done it so many times, they looked lunar, if y'know what I mean. All pits and divots and the color of mozzarella. For an extra fifty he'd let 'em put the things out themselves, just reach down and grind out their Luckies. You wanna know the funny thing?"

"Definitely," I said. Anything to keep from thinking about what was being burned into *my* flesh (which, for all I knew, I could spend the rest of *my* life charging strangers fifty bucks a peek).

"Okay," said Mr. Schmidlap, bending to resume his work west of my solar plexus. "Okay, but it isn't pretty."

"What is?" I said, with no idea whatsoever what I meant. I was trying so hard not to pass out or cry, the only thing between me and crap-in-my-pants collapse was the sound of talking. It didn't matter who was talking, just that somebody was; that I wasn't forced to lump out and listen to my own thoughts, the ones banging their cages in my head, the ones shouting, *When he's through with you, you're gonna be as big a freak as he is.* At which point, thank you and good night, my mother's lifelong hints will have come to pass: I would finally be monstrous to the naked eye. Just like my half-bald, pacifist-loving sister. If I did hook up with Bernice, we could join a sideshow.

"Well, sir," Mr. Schmidlap resumed, his head lodged under my chin, the tang of his Vitalis burning my nostrils. "This one night, it was right around Christmas, my buddy was working his cigarette con. And there's this one joker wants to impress his date. You know where I'm goin' here?"

He peered up at me and flicked more ash on the shag.

"Not really," I admitted.

"Where I'm goin'," he said, "is straight to Uglyville. 'Cause this one time, like I say, some joker wants to play big shot. So he asks Budzo, that was my buddy's name, he asks Budzo could he put a lit cigarette out on his dick. Thighs aren't enough for this fuckwad, he's gotta go dick. It's rough, I know, but there you have it. You wanna see humanity at it's worst, you don't gotta go to no Khe Sanh. You don't gotta go to no Korea or the Battle of the Goddamn Bulge. I mean—*sit still, for Christ's sake!*—here's some shitbird who thinks it'd be cute if his girlfriend put her Salem out on my friend's manhood. And by God, when Budzo hears the guy, he says he'll do it. This paralytic sonuvabitch says, 'Okay, Ace, you show me the long green, I'll show you my sleeping beauty.' I know this 'cause I seen it, Mighty Mouse. *I was there.* And believe me, I wish I'd been in Reno instead."

perv—a love story

He lifted his gun hand and sneezed. I had the sinking feeling he could just as easily have lost control and buzzed my nipple off. It hit me that what Mr. Schmidlap was after was revenge. But revenge for what? I hadn't figured that part out before he chugged the last gulp of brandy. He tossed Mr. Boston over his shoulder and leapt back to the story. Miraculously, the bottle bounced off the wall and landed in the shag intact.

"Naturally," he rushed on, getting more and more into it, "the jerk askin' is a big fat guy, one of those rump roasts who don't know how fat he is and squeezes into a suit so tight you think his ass is gonna bust out and sing 'God Bless America.' This Santa Claus says to Budzo, 'Any clown can put a butt out on his shanks; what I wanna know, can you stub out a ciggy on your peter?' So Budzo says, 'Put up or shut up, Fats.' The porker flinches, but don't want to look bad in front of his girl. Little Miss Beehive's kind of embarrassed but kinda glassy-eyed, too, like she's goin' wetpants in spite of herself.

"They're a couple of pervaloids, the pair of 'em. But after a second Fatso says, 'Five hundred,' and Budzo says, 'Done.' Just like that. Next thing you know, my man's reaching under his blanket, pulling down his zipper and rootin' around for his johnson. The whole bar's crowded around. But Budzo doesn't give a fuck. He may be paralyzed but he's hung like an umbrella stand. Finally he whips out Mr. Footlong and says, 'You do it!' Just like that. The fat guy looks like he's been sucker-punched, but he can't back down. Budzo hands him his own cigarette—the sick fuck smoked Winstons with the filters ripped off—and Fatpants just kinda stands there, gettin' all pink and blotchy.

" 'What's it gonna be?' Budzo says, all teasing-like, but Mr. Five-by-Five can't make a move. He's seized up, so Budzo looks up at me, and he winks. Then he hands his cigarette to Porky's squeeze. 'How 'bout you, honey? For you I'll make it $485.' Well, that's it. I thought that lard-ass was gonna blow a gasket. But then, hold your fuckin' horses, the girlfriend kinda licks her lips, gets all sweaty-panty like, and kneels down right in front of Budzo. She puts her face so close it's like she's gonna blow him, right there in front of everybody, but what she's doing, it turns out, what she's doing is scopin' him out, lookin' for the right target. And then—BOOM!—before you can say Smokey the Bear she jabs his tip with the cigarette, I mean right on the hole, and Budzo just sits there, grippin' the sides of his wheelchair and bitin' through his bottom lip with this sorta groan that comes up from his toes.

"That boy was *excruciated*, but he held his mud. Do you understand what I'm sayin' here? He never took the grin off his mug. He took it like a man, and damned if that sadistic bitch didn't make her fat daddy peel five C-notes off his wad right then and there.

"Tell you the kicker," he said, stopping to gauze me off. He tamped down daintily, squinting at his handiwork through first one eye and then the other. "About an hour later, we're back at Budzo's pad. We're finishing a fifth of Jack, and I say to him, 'Budzy-boy, I never thought I'd say it, but it's a lucky thing your dick's dead. You keep this up you can make enough to buy a new one by Easter.' But then—"

Mr. Schmidlap stopped to re-light his Swisher and take an excited draw.

"But then, fuck me up the ass and kiss me, my pal just looks up and smiles. 'It's my legs are dead, pard. My dingus feels the same as yours.' "

perv—a love story

Mr. Schmidlap stopped and shook his head, waiting for the impact of the saga to sink in. I had no idea what to say, so I gasped and said, "Wow!"

" '*My dingus feels the same as yours!* '" he repeated. "Do you believe that? Here's a man who'd suffer the worst pain on the *friggin'* planet, just to see some porkchop squirm. Now that," he said, waving the buzzing gun so close to my nose I could see the needle, a blood-kissed dot of ink at the very tip. "Now *that* is a hero. *That* is Hall of Fame balls. And *that's* what you need if you want to get ahead in this dickless universe. You understand me? I'm done."

"You're done?" It had happened too fast. I wasn't ready for whatever came next.

He yanked the plug out of the socket and swung it in the air like Mick Jagger twirling the mike during "Little Red Rooster." "That's right. Done. You can boogie as soon as I get a bandage on. Just don't shower for twenty-four hours. And stay out of the sun."

"But . . . I mean . . . Isn't there—"

"Can it," he said, but not in a mean way; more like *indulgent* . . . *affectionate*, as if we'd been through something together and, even though he had his doubts at the outset, I'd won him over. "You trespassed and you paid the price. This is my house and I get to be the monster. Do you want a look?"

He wrapped the insulated cord around his instrument, plopped it in the leather box, and pulled out a sliver of mirror. "Here you go," he said. "Look now or wait a day. Just don't take the bandage off early. And don't scratch it or you'll fuck it up. Be like takin' a Brillo to the Sistine Chapel. You with me?"

I nodded and held my breath. The air around me seemed to quiver. My tongue felt like a wad of bloody gauze. What I wanted to say was "I can't." What I wanted to say was *"Please."* But please what? It was too late for mercy. I shook my head and Mr. Schmidlap said, "Okay, suit yourself," and handed me my shirt. Neither of us spoke. I buttoned up, put on my socks, and pulled my boots on. They were biker boots, and when Mr. Schmidlap saw them, he hooted. "You didn't tell me you were in the Angels. Or are you just trying to scare me?"

He snapped his kit box shut and shoved it back in the metal cabinet. After he put it away, he just stood there, the hand of his good arm tucked under the pit of the missing one. He regarded me with an expression I couldn't fathom. I had no reason, really, to still be hanging around, but the world had changed so much since I walked in I was afraid to walk back out.

At last Mr. Schmidlap nodded and grabbed my chin. "There's two kinds of people, kid: the kind who pretend they are, and the kind who pretend they aren't. Take my advice and don't be neither. You know where the door is."

With this he lumbered toward the stairs, and I had no choice but to head for the outside steps that led to the backyard. I was halfway out the storm door when I heard him calling. " 'What is it?" I called back. The night sky was already fading to gray.

His voice came back threatening and friendly at the same time. "You wanna see my little girl, you ask her on a date. Otherwise you're Alpo. I'll see to that personal."

"Yes, sir."

I was kneeling in their tomato garden, adjusting my boot, when I heard him again. This time he leaned out an upstairs window. I thought I saw another figure, a smaller one, silhouetted behind him. "Just for the record," he shouted, "you don't have to water it."

perv—a love story

I hollered back, "Water what?"

There were houses jammed right and left of the Schmidlaps, and I didn't want to wake anyone. All I needed was to get caught trespassing, or disturbing the peace, and I'd be packed off to my mother before lunch.

"No need to water it," he cried again. This time I heard hacking laughter, which was quickly muffled when he closed the window, and stopped altogether when the lights went off.

I made it all the way back to my dorm before I gave in. Crouching on a toilet in the hall bathroom—there were no doors on the stalls, to foil self-abuse—I gently peeled back the bandage and, heart ricocheting off my lungs, stole my first look at what, I fearfully believed, would define my entire future.

Under the bandage, in juicy-looking black and red, a silver-dollar-sized rose bloomed over my left nipple. I stared at it for a long time, horrified that it was so beautiful. Frozen under the fluorescent lights, I knew that I'd have to wear it, like an exposed kiss, from that moment on. There was no way around it. I couldn't tell my shame from my excitement.

perv

I was hard to picture my mother dating. But, since my father died, she'd apparently "gone out" with a few men. And once I'd been thrown out of school and shipped back to Pittsburgh, she arranged for me to meet one or two of them. The hope, of course, was that some sage fellow would speak the magic words, bless her son the fuckup with some much needed paternal wisdom, and steer him back on the right track.

Well, why not? The reason I got tossed out was Tennie Toad. He snitched. The Toad had been nabbed tramping back on campus after fleeing the Schmidlaps. Farwell made it back unscathed. But Tennie, feeling snacky after ditching me in the Schmidlap rec room, opted to stop at an all-night diner called the Toaster for an egg sandwich.

As luck would have it, the wrestling coach, Dick Ponish, had gulped too much java after a match in Scranton, and popped into the Toaster at three A.M. He thought a cruller would help him sleep. It was there, at the Toaster's takeout counter, that the coach spotted Toad. He grabbed Tennie in a full nelson and dragged him all the way back to campus. Next morning Headmaster Bunton called him in. They—the headmaster and the coach—gave Tennie an ultimatum: Tell on his confederates or bear the brunt of the punishment. Rat or scat.

Tennie was my best friend. But Tennie being Tennie, he said the whole thing was my idea. Although a senior, and a year older, he insisted I'd cajoled him into sneaking out and meeting a "townie." Since my father had died, he explained, he felt that I needed some counseling, some *camaraderie*. To this end, against his better judgment, he went along on our doomed and sinful mission. Doggone it, he just wanted to help.

Headmaster Bunton, who told me all this, ushered me into his office that morning without meeting my eyes. He'd plucked me out of an algebra test, so I knew things were serious. The headmaster was a sallow man with gummy eyelids and liver spots. Despite his pallid, gray-white hair, his brows were so lush and chocolatey they looked pasted on. The rumor was, his first wife had run off with the drummer from Three Dog Night—"*Jeremiah was a bullfrog. Was a good friend of mine"*—and no one knew for sure. His current wife looked like Shelley Winters and limped. In any event, he began by informing me that I did not possess the Hale School spirit. And more damning than that, my attitude was "shabby."

"Halies do not mingle," he said, with a significant raising and lowering of those cocoa brows. "Halies do *not* run roughshod over rules of good citizenship. Halies do not, I repeat, do not lure their companions into situations that could compromise their future scholastic careers. Your friend Talbot"—that was Tennessee Toad—"went with you because he was *loyal.* He was wrong to accompany you off campus, but he was *right* to think you needed standing by. *That* is the kind of principle a Halie understands."

While the headmaster paced, I sat in a tan leather chair that made me feel tiny, like a puppet backstage between shows. The headmaster's office was papered with hunting scenes, though Bunton did not look like a man who rode tall in the saddle. He looked more suited to cribbage. I wondered how long he'd last in a fight with Mr. Schmidlap, missing arm and all.

Still doing that up-and-down thing with his eyebrows—up for surprise, down for disapproval—he gazed past me out the office window. I got the feeling that just the sight of me was too much for him. He cleared his throat and continued uneasily. "Are you aware of the gravity of your transgression?"

"I think so, sir."

I was so sleepy from the night before, the experience seemed to be taking place underwater. My chest still stung where I'd been tattooed, but I didn't dare go near the area, for fear my inquisitor would suspect something and tear open my shirt. On

perv—a love story

top of that, I still hadn't showered. I stank, as my mother loved to say, "like something a dog wouldn't lick on a holiday."

Headmaster Bunton crossed his hands behind his back. He grimaced as he walked to the picture window that faced the quad. I could see past him to the boys in ties and blazers going from class to class. I never liked wearing blazers. I didn't like ties, either. It felt like dress-up: like everybody was pretending to be their own father. Though this was 1970 the Age of Aquarius had not exactly taken root at Hale. Most everybody still seemed to want to be grown up. They *liked* wearing blazers and school ties. Still, I'd have strapped myself in chaps and straitjacket if it meant not having to go back to Pittsburgh. To Mom.

"As you know," the headmaster said—he sighed, sniffing the air and wincing—"Talbot has attended our school for five years."

His tone was sour. It gave me the same feeling I used to get listening to my mother, the way she had of letting you know you were revolting without ever saying so. It was clear from the headmaster's expression that he believed he was being fair. Just as concerned and benevolent as my mother when she made me squirm. I was the guilty one. That was my job: being guilty. Which wasn't all bad. It was sort of like having a dead father—no matter what you did, you always had a built-in excuse for doing it.

"Talbot," my big-browed inquisitor droned on, "comes from a long line of distinguished Hale men. His father, his grandfather, and his great-grandfather all attended this institution."

By contrast, was the clear but unstated implication, I was but a lowly scholarship recipient—not to mention lowly *Jew*. On campus scarcely more than a semester. Roughly equal in status to Jo-Jo, the retarded giant who mowed the lawns, or Hanke, the Polish night watchman, who talked to himself and reeked of rancid ham when you got within ten feet of him.

There was not much more to discuss.

Two hours after my chat with the headmaster, having skulked back to my dorm and packed what little I had to pack, I was dispatched by train from Slotzville to Philadelphia to catch a six P.M. Allegheny Airlines flight back to Pittsburgh. My mother hated to drive, especially at night, and the first thing she said when she met me at the gate was Standard Mom. "I hope you're happy, because I can't see a thing! I nearly clipped a tractor-trailer on the parkway, and now *this!*"

"Now *what?*" I asked, mortified, as I'd been my entire life, at just being seen with my mother in public. For the occasion, she'd worn a shiny pink dress that would have been the toast of the Mocambo when Sinatra was starting out. Women in movies from Hollywood's golden era dressed the way my mother did now. My entire childhood, she'd show up at PTA meetings in bust-hugging sequins, the sight of which gave my father complicated facial twitches. She was flamboyant, really, in no other way. There was nothing Auntie Mame about her. Unless Auntie Mame had a penchant for public collapse, and I'd missed that part when I saw the movie. (In some odd gush of patriotism, my mother had once vomited on the Liberty Bell, the Statue of Liberty, and a bust of Benjamin Franklin in a single summer, aborting our vacation and causing my father to swear off historical sites till the day he died. Mom didn't projectile vomit much at home, but put her in line with a batch of seniors from Valhalla, PA, to tour the White House, and she'd be on her knees bringing up

perv—a love story

chicken salad or fainting until the guards came and ushered her out.)

Another boy my age, whom I'd watched combing his long hair in a pocket mirror the entire flight, was met on the runway by a Twiggy lookalike in army jacket and leather sandals. The girl planted a kiss on his mouth that lasted more than a minute. My mom gave me a peck on the cheek, then stepped back a foot and a half and wrinkled her nose. "Well," she said, taking in my stained duffel bag and unraveling corduroys, "nobody could accuse you of hygiene. Your father would *die*."

"He's already *dead*," I reminded her, playing out the exchange we'd been enacting since the day they closed the lid on Dad.

My mother stopped where she was, stalling a line of deplaning Pittsburghers to give me "the look."

"Don't start with me," she hissed.

Unfortunately, I'd smoked a joint in the airplane toilet. As had been happening since my father's streetcar move, pot packed the opposite effect of the one intended. Instead of giggles, bliss, or any relief whatsoever, the drug sent me straight to paranoia. This didn't stop me from smoking it, but, in those first loaded moments with Mom, left me frantically, *monstrously* conscious of my fate: fifteen, forced to live at home, possessed of a throbbing rose over my nipple and a crippling fear that one wrong move and I'd be stuck forever.

I'd seen it happen. Right on the street where I grew up, there was a guy named Herbert Pazahowski. Herb was a stoop-shouldered thirty-two or so. Absolutely ancient. He lived with his mother, Mrs. Pazahowski, a five-foot, evil dumpling of a woman with whom Herbert walked past our house, up the hill to the A&P, every day for lunchmeat. Some things you can't forget. A cashew-sized mole on Mrs. P.'s throat sprouted jet-black stubble. Another one, on her chin, was shaped like a squid and sprouted white. Much as I loved horror movies, the prospect of mutating into Herbert, of clutching my mother's hand as we shuffled to the store for our daily liverwurst, was more horror than I could stand without hyperventilating. It blew *Return of the Mummy* and *Mothra* right out of the water.

"The worst part," Mom used to say when we spotted the Pazahowskis on their daily lunchmeat trek, "Herbert's not retarded. *He's just a good boy . . .*"

Out of nowhere, as I marched through the airport by my mother's side, this remark began to resonate in my head. What if, I began to worry, *I* turned into a "good boy"? What if, after prolonged exposure to Mom-rays, *that's just what happened?* What if—the prospect made me squirm—what if I found out *I secretly loved living with Mom,* that I—be still my heart—just adored that daily round of errands and sandwiches, TV and snacks? Next thing I knew *I'd* be twenty-three, forty-nine, sixty-eight . . . Just another Herb Pazahowski humping up the hill for chipped ham with Mommy. "Get a load of that," Mom cracked, breaking my waking nightmare with an elbow to the ribs.

"Of what?"

We were riding the escalator down to ground level, and all I saw was the same boy I'd seen on the plane. Now he was making out with Twiggy in front of the exit doors. I tried to superimpose Sharon's features on the willowy blonde, but it didn't take. Sharon's face, I hated to say it, was more on the moonish side. Her toast-colored ponytail was nothing like this girl's stylish cut. For no more than the sixteenth time since deplaning, I asked myself why every thought in my head ended up depressing. And

perv—a love story

Jerry Stahl

made a silent pledge to flush the Baggie of grass down the toilet. (Tennie'd slipped the stuff in my suitcase before I left, with an unsigned note that said, "Good luck." I knew it was his because the paper had a grease stain on the corner. Everything Tennie touched bore some kind of stain.)

"Would you look at them?" my Mom piped up again, this time clicking her tongue to convey her disgust. When I finally peeled my eyes from the pretty blonde I'd never get to touch, I spotted the objects of her scorn. There were three of them, on the sidewalk beside the Yellow Cab stand, a trio of saffron-robed Hare Krishnas doing a twirly dance to the accompaniment of clapping, tambourine, and an unpleasant-sounding Hindi chant. All three sported the trademark shaved head and single pigtail. It took me an extra second to see that one of them, the tambourine player, was actually a girl. Weirder still, that I *recognized* her. Her name was Michelle Burnelka. She'd been in my class from kindergarten till the tenth grade, my last year in public school before I got sent away. And I'd pretty much loved her the whole time.

Unbelievable! The first time I masturbated, I was daydreaming about saving Michelle from a fire. In my pump-scenario, I'm walking by her house and notice smoke coming from the window, maybe hear a few screams. And then, defying danger, with no concern whatsoever for my own safety, I dash into the burning house, fling my redheaded dream-date over my shoulder, clamber out her bedroom window, and carry her down the ladder. (Don't ask where the ladder came from; it's *my* fantasy.) Flames lick the air around us; ash blackens our faces. And when we reach the ground, Michelle throws her shivering arms around my neck. She pulls me close for a French kiss before tugging my face down to her budding breasts (no more than nipples, really, in sixth grade, which is when I started popping my load in earnest). In some versions, she let me suck them and whispered my name. In some she dropped to her knees and blew me through her sobs. Other nights she hiked up her petticoat and wailed, *"Take me! Take me now!"* I don't know what got me harder, the chance to play Junior Superman or the nasty thank-yous. Either way, I'd squirt on my hand and wash off, waiting for spit curls to sprout from my palm.

Back in real time, my mother stopped right in front of the Hare Krishnas. Nudging my ribs again, she began talking about them. In Mom-logic, because they wore funny robes and looked weird, she did not have to worry about whether the people she was ragging could hear her. They were too peculiar to matter. They weren't quite human. She was the same way with foreigners.

"I bet their parents are *thrilled,*" Mom announced, thoroughly enjoying herself. Then she indicated Michelle with a giddy nod. "I bet this one's father and mother are just *kvelling.* I bet they just leap out of bed in the morning and say 'Thank you, Lord, there's nothing I wanted more for my little girl than to grow up, stick her *pupich* in a nightie, and parade around the airport like somebody put LST in her cereal!' "

"Mom," I muttered, "it's LSD."

"I don't care if it's LSMFT," she crowed. "I bet they're *delighted* that their little cutie pie is out here banging her tambourine. I bet her folks are glad they lived long enough to see *this.*"

I didn't tell her I actually knew Michelle—let alone that I'd had a crush on her since before time. What was the point? In my experience, you didn't talk to my mother. You just reacted.

Once safely ensconced in Mom's car—a two-year-old metal-flake beige Barracuda, one of those fast-back bubbletops Detroit put out after *The Jetsons*—my spirits plunged. Somehow, in my brief stint as preppie, I'd managed to forget the conditions of life at home: the very things that made me so glad to get away in the first place. The main one, at this moment, being my mother's driving. Despite the racing-ready look of her current ride (acquired, she claimed, from the bereaved parents of a boy who'd gulped "some of that mescatrine" and stared at the sun till his "pupils ruptured"), the woman who raised me continued her life-long habit of motoring a solid twenty miles per hour under the speed limit.

Beyond safety concerns, there was the disgrace involved. And who cared about safety? I would have gladly splattered like a gnat, provided death was instantaneous and I did not have to live on as Mommy's little shotgun. Moving this slowly provoked hate from everyone else on the road. But I had vowed, promised, *pleaded* with myself not to raise the subject of her tortoise-like driving habits. To no avail. When the hair-comber and his Twiggyesque flame passed on the right in a stylish Bonneville, I felt such mockery in their smirking glances I couldn't control myself. There was not enough room in Mom's sporty compact to slink out of sight.

"Mom," I heard myself whimper, hating my tone but powerless to stop, "you're no safer driving this slow. It's actually riskier, 'cause people behind us get all bunched up, and the people behind *them* have to slam on the brakes. It's a chain reaction thing."

My mother only sniffed. "Very nice! Mr. Doesn't-Even-Have-His-License wants to give me driving tips. Mr. Thrown-Out-of-the-Third-Best-Prep-School-in-the-Country wants to tell me how to handle a car."

"All right," I surrendered. "All right!"

I had not, needless to say, given full vent to my discomfort. The truth is, I was racked with embarrassment at merely *sitting* in a car with this shiny-dressed, crazed-looking woman hunched over the wheel. Creeping along at twenty when the entire known universe was doing a cool forty-five. Nor was it just her dress or her speed that tortured me. I haven't mentioned Mom's hair, which she wore in a sort of wings-at-the-side, frizzed-in-the-middle red flip. A modified Lucille Ball. Hairwise, the Lucy resemblance was huge. My earliest sentient moments were spent plunked before the Motorola in baffled wonder at how Mom could be puffing a Kent and yakking on the kitchen Princess, but *still be in front of me*, on the little screen, doing the cha-cha with Ricky.

Not that my mother, from the hair down, truly *looked* like Lucy. If anything, she worked the bulk and demeanor of a young Ethel. But that hairdo, at such a tender age, threw me for a loop. A dozen years later, this angst was amplified by the grim fact that, while all over America "young people" frolicked in communes, shunned barbers, gulped acid, and made love under Che Guevara posters, here I was trapped in my Lucy-Mom's Barracuda, nary a follicle over my ears, with no more to live for than canned spaghetti and the odd snuck joint in Mom's condo. Compared to me, Herb Pazahowski was Abbie Hoffman.

Buck up! I told myself, struggling to summon up movies where guys survived stints in the Foreign Legion or spaceships stranded on Venus. I racked my brain for a silver lining, but all I could come up with was "clean sheets."

We were passing Jones and Laughlin. The steel mill's stacks blasted acrid smoke, and Mom slowed to a crawl and rolled down her window. She inhaled deeply, smacking her lips, and made a show of savoring the sulfurous fumes. "You can't get *that* in your fancy-shmancy cities. *That* is the scent of your hometown."

I nodded in the mocking way I'd recently perfected. "Proud as they are, Mom, Parisians would kill for a good whiff of Pittsburgh."

"That's right, be sarcastic," she snapped, shifting her gaze from the bus ahead to my own sneering visage. "To some people, a steel mill smells better than a meadow."

Whatever else she was, Mom was a civic booster. She'd grown up in a town called Blawnox, on the Ohio River, where her father and uncles owned a defunct Buick dealership. To her, Pittsburgh was a shining city souls strived half their lives to someday inhabit. Or so she claimed. I'd never met a single person who was glad to be there.

"My son, the prep school fugitive," she went on as we passed the mill. "What do you plan to do, anyway? You know the schools are on strike, so you can't even go back to Lincoln. This year's kaput."

John J. Lincoln, my ex-high school, was named for a local man who'd swum out of a flooded shoe store with a nun under his arm. This happened in the forties, and the deed was sufficiently impressive to earn him his own high school. Not that Mr. Lincoln himself cared one way or the other. He'd drowned when his cuff snagged a parking meter. But Sister Rowena, the bride of Christ he'd salvaged, was still with us, and each year occupied lead wheelchair in the Golden Pittsburgher parade.

"What am I supposed to do," I countered, "get a job?"

"There's a thought." Mom bent to push in the lighter, then swerved to miss a mail truck when she drifted out of her lane.

"Jesus, watch it!" I cried.

"You watch it! You're the one with no future. I already had a life. You don't even have one, and you've already thrown it away. What were you *doing* with that girl anyway? They told me you made some boys go visit a, what was it, a butcher's daughter?"

"Barber, Mom. Her father was a barber."

"I *beg* your pardon! Barber is so much more prestigious. So much more *je ne sais pas what*! Make sure you mention *that* on your application to Yale." She slapped a fresh pack of Kents on the dash. "For the rest of your life, when people ask why a boy with such a prominent father, *with every advantage on the globe*, is sweeping streets for a living, make sure and explain that, genius that you are, you decided to visit a *BARBER'S DAUGHTER*. Because that is as good as it's going to get," she said bitterly. "You keep it up, that's going to be the high point of your little career. Now what do you want to eat? I've got veal chops at home, but I wasn't expecting you till June."

Mom turned back to the highway, her face stamped with a grin of martyred resignation. But I was too woozy to do more than grunt. Except for that brief steel mill interlude, she'd made a point of keeping the windows up. My mother harbored a fear of flying objects, having read about a woman from Muncie, Indiana, who'd careened off Route 80 when a juvenile delinquent shot her in the cheek with a paper clip. "Why leave yourself open," she liked to say, "when you can put up a wall of glass?"

By her seventh Kent, the haze inside the car made the sulfur gushing from J&L seem dewy fresh. I knew there was no point complaining, so I went the other way. I breathed in the billowing smoke until I achieved a half-conscious, headachy stupor. We

perv—a love story

drove on like that, for a few more miles, and then the keening began.

"Walter," I heard my mother chant through my Kent-induced coma. "Walter Walter Walter, Walter Walter Walterwalter-walter."

I pried my eyelids apart in time to see her lighting a fresh Kent with her left hand, dabbing her eyes with her right, and steering with her knees. Walter, of course, was my father. Since that magic moment at his funeral, when she'd dropped in the dirt and begged God to swoop down and take *her*, too, she'd invoked the name of Walter like Allah or Yahweh in times of high crisis.

"Walter, I love the boy, but I can't take it!" she wailed to my departed father.

Judging from the angle of her upraised eyes, he appeared to be lodged somewhere between the Barracuda's sun visor and the rearview mirror.

"I love him," she went on, her voice no more than a tobacco rasp, "but he is driving me insane. Walter, do you hear me! I am not supposed to have any stress. I am supposed to *stay calm!* Walter, the medicine is not working and I can't go back for more ECT until August. Walter, *make him good.*"

As suddenly as she'd begun communing with the spirit world, she stopped. She abruptly straightened and drove normally—or normally for Mom—letting cars whoosh past while crawling forward in the center lane. Then her beseeching resumed at even greater volume.

"Walter, do you remember, when he was little, we used to play mousy-mousy-mousy? I'd rub his belly. Like cream from an eclair, his little belly was so sweet, so white. Now look at him!

He's trying to *kill* me with the smirking, the attitude . . . the *barber's daughter*. Oh, Walter!" Her voice sank to a whisper, as if, incredibly, I was not supposed to hear. "Walter, listen to me, I'm taking him home. But what happens then? *What happens then?*"

Through slits I made of my eyelids, I switched my gaze sideways and held it there. I saw Mom glare at me, as if I were some evil djinn who'd popped out of her glove compartment. I flashed on what it must be like for her, what I must look like: the shabbed-out, army-navy clothes and muddy work boots (though I'd never done a muddy day's work in my life), my weird wannabe Jew-fro (function of Hale rules requiring "academic grooming," and my own dabbling in Negro hair-care products), not to mention the odd swath of connect-the-dots pimples sprouting like tiny toadstools from my chin, cheeks, and forehead. I didn't even look at myself in the mirror when I brushed my teeth.

When Mom had been silent a few more minutes, I ventured a yawn, pretending to wake from mobile slumber. I did my best to smile. Gripped by a sudden bout of empathy, I felt crushing pain for my mother, for myself, for the ludicrous forced march our lives seemed to have warped themselves into. But try as I might, there seemed no way to convey my feeling. The smile wouldn't hold. And grinding my brain for something positive to say, the words wouldn't show up, either. Whatever part of my brain-box controlled Mom interaction—actual conversation with this slightly deranged, grimly determined woman eating Kents and squeezing the steering wheel—the gears had jammed. I could no more turn her way and mouth, "I love you" or "Glad I'm home," than break into Chinese opera. But I tried. . . .

"So, Mom," I began, my voice sounding strained, if not, thank God, completely Cricket-like. "So, Mom, listen," I started off,

perv—a love story

willing myself to speech when I saw that we'd made our way to Superior Boulevard, the cobblestone street that fed the cul-de-sac where she'd relocated after Dad died. Once I was gone, she sold the old house and moved to her condo within a month.

We crawled past the Superior Market, the combination news-stand, grocery store, and doughnut shop that faced her condo-minium, the box-like Superior Towers.

"So, Mom," I began for the third time, "does Mrs. Fisk still work at the market?" I furrowed my brow, really *interested*, as though the comings and goings of local shopkeepers were the meat of my existence, the stuff I could not get enough of. "By golly," I actually said, "I'll never forget the first time I met her. She had a piece of ham sandwich hanging off her lip. Remember? It was the doggonedest thing. Here she was, making change and pouring coffee, and she's got this little ham-flag dangling from her mouth. That was the same day she scratched her back with the French bread. Remember that? She didn't think anyone was looking, just reached right around, slipped the loaf right under her blouse. 'Member? You wondered if we could get excema from eating the crust."

"Bobby!" My mother cut mightily to negotiate her condo driveway. "Why do you have to attack everyone? That poor woman never did a thing to you."

"But, *Mom* . . ."

We headed underground now, to her parking spot, and in an absolute first, she floored it and sailed down the ramp to Level One at breakneck speed. She whipped the 'Cuda into its slot, flipped off the ignition, and tore out the key like some meno-pausal A. J. Foyt.

"But, Mom, listen—"

"No, you listen for once! Even when you were little, you made fun. There was a boy in your school with a harelip. Arthur Noz- lillo. Ring a bell? This poor boy, who couldn't help the way he was, had to show up in class every day and listen to you imitate him, listen to you pretend *you* had a harelip."

"Mom, he used to spit on my Fig Newtons!"

"Can you blame him? Do you know your teacher finally called me up? So did Arthur's mother. They both wanted to know what was wrong with *me*, how I could let my child be so cruel. Where did you get that, Bobby? I know I'm not the sharpest knife in the drawer, but I'm not mean, am I?"

"Mom, come on . . . !" I was stunned, but what could I say? That Arthur Nozlillo was the first boy in class to get hair? That he was *shaving in fourth grade?* Did I go into how he liked to show off his pu- bes and armpits? Arthur the Lip's was the first hairy penis I ever saw that wasn't my father's. And I didn't especially want to see it. Dad's I took in every time we went swimming. A plump veiny red thing that reminded me of my Aunt Dot's brisket. She always un- dercooked. But I couldn't go into that. . . . Mom would say I was making fun again. But who was I making fun of?

"Let's just go," Mom said, shoving her door open and grabbing her cigarettes. "Let's just go inside and be a goddamn family."

In the elevator I experienced Mom's perfume—the White Shoulders she'd been spritzing since I was small enough to crawl around on top of her. I thought about that: how when you're a baby you're just *all theirs*. Your parents' plaything. For a while, they pretty much own you. Until, the older you get—and the

perv—a love story

more you know—the more you want out. Unless you were Herbert Pazahowski. If you were Herb, you were happy to stick around. The last thing you wanted was to say good-bye to Mommy.

That's it! Maybe the reason you can never go home again is that, once you're back, *you can never leave*. . . . The thought hit me like a blast of cold air. This was a train of thought I did not want to ride too far.

Breathing my mother, I couldn't tell if I was feeling high or feeling weird. Maybe I was high on weirdness. The elevator bulletin board had a sign for Potluck Thursdays and a mimeo sign-up sheet for Canasta Night. The Canasta sheet featured playing cards with tiny arms and legs, like they were doing the frug.

"Plenty to do here in Condo-land," I said. "It must be a regular social whirl."

I was trying to be pleasant, but Mom shot me one of her looks. Whatever I said, I got the *look*. Mom lived in 709. Five down from 714, the number they stamped on Quaaludes. The last time I did one of those I tried to eat a pancake with my feet. I was with Tennessee Toad at the Toaster. Who knew, a few weeks after those very Quaaludes, Coach Ponish would spot Tennie copping a post-Sharon snack and drag him panting into the night?

I'd been gone three hours, and already Hale seemed like a dream. Not even a dream. More like TV. Like it was some TV show I'd stumbled into by cosmic fluke, then stumbled out of to end up back here, on my mother's elevator. Not even, I kept thinking, back in my own home. I didn't *have* a home anymore. *My* home, *my* room, was gone. Mom sold the house to a family of Germans named Heikenberner. Skeetsy Heikenberner was in my year in grade school, until they held him back and stuck me in "gifted" classes. After that I only saw him in gym. Timmy was one of those soft kids with moist lips and an expression of permanent, drooly confusion. His mouth never closed all the way. If you stood behind him in the lunch-line, you could see green chunks in his ears. Spring potatoes.

Now he was sleeping in *my* room. Staring at the swirls in *my* ceiling. I had nothing against Timmy, but still . . . I wondered if he'd see the same faces I saw. I'd lay in bed gazing up at George Washington in a bath towel or Marilyn Monroe with a tail. I spent hours like that. And that was before acid.

On the fourth floor the elevator stopped. An old couple in matching blueberry shirt-jacs stepped in and said hello. They each nestled a chihuahua in their arms. I could tell my mother was revolted.

"Why ha-loo, Mrs. Stark," the man boomed. "And howdy to you, young man."

"You must be the *boy*!" added Lady Chihuahua, holding up the hairless, nervous-looking animal at her breast. One of its bug eyes oozed something viscous. "This is Lester!" she said, and then her husband raised the rat-sized creature he was cuddling. "And this is little Anne-Marie!"

"Would you believe it's their birthday?" they said in unison. My mother looked like she was going to vomit. Daddy Chihuahua continued, "Would you believe these little rascals are seventeen years young!"

I reached out and took Anne-Marie's paw and gave it a shake. "Congratulations, girl." I tried to pet her brother, but he growled. Pint-sized as he was, the growl sounded serious. Lester bared his

perv—a love story

teeth, revealing blue-black gums and a pair of incisors that looked like they could rip through tin.

"Tiny but tough," I said.

The man seemed delighted with the remark. "Egg-zackly! Did you hear that, Mabel? 'Tiny but tough!' "

"Oh that is a-*dor*-able. That is *per*-fect," Mabel cooed.

They were so friendly, I kept going. "So, did you throw these kids a party? Did they blow out all their candles?"

I knew Mom was dying, but couldn't stop. "We'll have to get you a nice soup bone," I said to Anne-Marie, patting her distended stomach. Her skin felt like a hot car-seat. "And you," I said, putting my face a few inches from Lester's, "we'll have to get you a dinosaur bone."

The elevator stopped with a shudder on seven and the doors hissed apart. "We get off here," my mother announced, squeezing out another smile for Mr. and Mrs. Mexican Hairless. "G'night," they said, waving their chihuahuas' paws in perfect sync. "Well, happy birthday," I said, and added, before the door hissed shut again, "I'm going to be here for a while; maybe I could visit." "Oh *do*," cried the woman, bending sideways so she could peek between the closing doors. "Nine-nineteen," the man shouted, and the rest I heard from the shaft as the car started up. "We're always home!"

Out in the hall, a wave of happiness, as unaccountable as it was unexpected, washed right over me. "They were nice," I said, hoisting my duffel on my shoulder and following Mom to her apartment. Even the fleur-de-lis wallpaper, a truly peculiar purple on green, struck me as the perfect pattern. I'd only been to the condo once before, on Thanksgiving break. Now I liked it. Maybe there was hope!

After my happy outburst, Mom stopped where she was and faced me. She was so angry she clenched her teeth while she spoke. "If this is what I can expect from you, young man, I can tell you *right* now we are going to have some trouble."

"But, Mom," I replied, sincerely baffled. "I *liked* those people. They seem like a nice couple."

"Nice," she said, turning away and storming on down the hall.

"Well, yeah," I called after her, scooting to catch up. "I thought you'd be happy I talked to your neighbors. You usually tell me I'm sullen. Now you're mad 'cause I'm not."

"For your information," she said, fishing in her suede pocketbook for her keys, "those two are not a couple. They happen to be brother and sister. Do I have to say anything else? Well, do I?"

"I guess not," I said, though I still didn't see the problem. I would have liked to raise mutant dogs with *my* sister, but she was off with her draft dodger and who knew if I'd ever see her again? For all I knew, they didn't even have chihuahuas in Canada. Not the hairless kind, anyway. When I was little Bernice used to step up to Mom when she'd begin to scream at me. "He's just a kid," my sister would plead, tugging at my mother's sleeve while she ranted on about crumbs on the carpet, skid marks, the ring from a grape juice glass on the coffee table, the expression on my face, or whatever bit of heinousness I'd happened to commit that day. Once, when my mother called me home from a Wiffle ball game in the street to scream herself veiny because I lost a sock, Bernice actually picked up a glass ashtray, a souvenir from Valley Forge shaped like Washington's hat, and smashed it off the kitchen wall to get her to stop. For about a second, the silence was staggering; then my mother turned to Bernice and

perv—a love story

said, in a voice you'd use to discuss the price of turnips, "If you think I'm marching back to Valley Forge to replace this, you're crazy. Now get your gluepot and get busy, sister!"

For years, after the ashtray incident, whenever Mom started wailing on one of us, the other would sidle over and intone, *"Get your gluepot and get busy, sister!"* Or sometimes just *"Gluepot!"* It drove Mom off the wall.

Stepping off the elevator with my mother in Rage Mode, I'd have given my left ventricle to see Bernice vault from behind a plant and give me the gluepot routine. But it wasn't going to happen. That's the thing about people you loved. They disappeared on you. I didn't know much, at the ripe old age of fifteen and a half. But, for better or worse, I knew that.

Turning the lock, Mom faced me a second time. She took a deep breath through her nose. Something else was eating her but I wasn't sure what. "What you can do for me right now is wipe the snide off your face. There's somebody I want you to meet and I don't want any problems."

Before I could even reply, the door swung open by itself and Mom jumped half a foot. "Ned, my God, you scared me!"

I stepped around her to see a largish, red-faced man with hair brushed back in a fluffy white pompadour. He owned enormous hands, one of which he thrust in my direction.

"Ned Friendly," he bellowed, doing a funny tongue thing with his lips. He ran the thick pink organ around his mouth, sticking it out and curling it upward before tucking it away again. "Heard so much aboutcha I'm already sick o' ya," he chuckled, giving Mom a wave. "Just funnin' ya, Bobby. You'll find out Ned Friendly does a lot of funnin'."

"Why don't we come in?" Mom said. Her voice had grown

smaller, as if she'd forgotten this was her home, not his. Her personality seemed dwarfed in the presence of his fleshy bluster.

We followed Ned inside and I noticed how broad his backside was in his lime-green golf pants. He wore a matching lime-green sweater and a polo shirt of lighter hue. The first thing I thought was, *His real name can't be Friendly.* And then, *It probably is.*

"Travelin' light, Ned likes that," Ned said, grabbing my duffel like it was a bag of pretzels and dropping it beside the couch.

I didn't say anything, and Mom wiped her hands on her shiny dress. "I . . . I invited Mr. Friendly over to talk with you."

She sounded tenuous. Her eyes flickered on and off. I don't know how long it had been since her last electroshock, but she had that startled look. Like she could use a jolt. Oddly enough, the Edison medicine calmed her down.

Ned boomed, "Tell you who I am; tell you what I am!" He did his tongue trick and settled his hearty buttocks on the velour La-Z-Boy. This was the one item she'd transported from our old house. The rest of the furniture I imagined, with some resentment, assorted Heikenberners were now lolling around on.

The La-Z-Boy I associated with my father. I'm sure Mom felt the same. He'd read his law books in that chair after supper, often as not ending up snoring, head thrown back and a fat brown municipal code open on his lap. Watching the white pompadoured, fullback-gone-to-fat Ned Friendly splonk into the recliner, I had the uneasy sensation he was sitting on top of my father. Blotting him out. Re-killing him by squashing him with that suitcase-sized behind.

"I'm going to scare us up a little something," Mom said. She fixed me in one of her shocked glances before rushing in to the kitchenette. What I wanted to do was duck into the den. See if

perv—a love story

I could crank open a window and sneak a joint. But now I was Ned Friendly's captive. I could feel him eyeing me, sizing me up with a constant nodding motion of his outsized head. When I looked at him, the word "florid" popped into my brain. It was one of those words I'd read before but never applied to anyone in real life. Until now.

I'd been staring at Ned for a while before I noticed the lump. Because it was the same burst-capillary scarlet as the rest of him, I hadn't seen it at first. But there it was: an elevated knob, as big around as a quarter, jutting out just under his hairline in the dead center of his forehead. Once I spotted the thing I could not stop staring at it. I'd hoped he would think I was just looking at him, in a normal way. Paying attention.

But Ned was too sharp for me. His eyes went dark. Gone was his hail-fellow-well-met manner. He glowered. "Don't stare at my wen, son, stare at me."

"Will do," I said, but Ned wasn't convinced.

"A wen's just a growth. You've got to consider the man, not the mutation."

"I . . . I do, I am," I lied. "Really. I didn't see anything 'til you said."

What he said made me think about Mr. Schmidlap. How after we started talking I forgot about his flipper. He was who he was, one arm or three. Unlike Ned Friendly, who, I already suspected, would always be the red-faced crank with the giant behind and the lump on his forehead.

"Call me a softy, I'm gonna believe you," he declared, then glared at me an extra second, as if considering whether to change his mind and poke my eyes out. I wasn't expecting what came next.

"It's our mother," he said, moving beyond my wen-fixation. "It so happens our mother's very worried about you. She thinks you're becoming a slack-off. A shirker. A young man who throws his pearls before swine. Gunks up his potential going after momentary pleasures. You with me, son, or is Ned pitching over your head?"

"What? No, you're with me, Ned. I mean, I'm with you," I said, willing my eyes away from his knob. I could hear my mother opening and closing the freezer and wished she'd come back in the living room. Ned Friendly eyed me soberly.

Despite my own phony-hobo clothes—the baggy corduroys, ragged denim shirt, and work boots—it was hard to dignify a man in pants the color of key lime pie. I had never seen clothes that zingy until I went to prep school and lived among the rich boys in Jell-O-colored country club duds.

Ned Friendly leaned forward in my father's chair. He folded his hands and plopped them on his ample midsection. He extended his forefingers, making a steeple and pointing it in a way that seemed vaguely Masonic, though I knew nothing about the Masons. (My first roommate at Hale, a Vermonter named Lloyd Huff, had been in the Order of DeMolay; he tried to enlist me until he found out I was Jewish, at which point he hung a bead curtain across his side of the room and stopped speaking to me.)

I fixed my attention on Ned's twin pointing-fingers while he began to talk. "Young man, the question I am about to ask may be the most important of your life. It's a question that has, within it, the power to change your life. The power to alter the course of your future. What do you say to that?"

"Don't know. What's the question?" I'd given up on resisting

perv—a love story

and flat-out stared at his knob. Maybe it was the airplane pot, but I thought I could see it swelling. I had a vision of that lump sprouting a face of its own, a wizened homunculus (another word I'd read but never used) that mimicked, in its nubby way, every gesture and expression of its beefy host.

"Direct and to the point." He nodded. "Ned likes."

"Glad to hear it," I said. I was getting tired of him, but if he picked up on my attitude he let it slide.

"Young man," he set off again, clearing his throat and aiming those matched fingers like little rockets about to launch at my forehead, no doubt to give me my own carbuncle. "Young man, have you ever considered scouting?"

"Excuse me?"

"Scouting. As in Boy Scouts. As in Cubs. As in Eagles."

Ned sat back in his chair, no doubt to let the impact of his query sink in. I had nothing to say and didn't try to fake it.

"I know, I know," he laughed. "You're thinking, 'This fellow Friendly looks a might bit old to be a boy scout, a tad thick in the breadbasket.' Well, I've got news for *you*! You're never too old. Matter of fact, not to boast, it so happens you're talking to the National Vice President. A National Vice President, I should say, since in all honesty the BS of A has a few of 'em. Fourteen to be exact. Don't want to give the impression I'm as important as Spiro Agnew. Ho no! Although our Vice President *is* a valued acquaintance of mine, and is, himself, an Honorary Eagle."

Ned kept the smile fixed on his face. He licked his sausagey lips again but retracted his erect forefingers as if they'd done their job, fired their secret finger rays, and could be safely retired for another day. When I didn't say anything, he spoke through his smile.

"Here's the caper. Ned happens to like our mother very much. And Ned would hate, repeat, *hate* to think of her having to worry about a son who did not want to be the kind of boy a woman like her deserves in her life. A boy who was afraid to say 'YES!' to scouting. A boy who did not want to adhere to the kind of values that the Boy Scouts of America represent."

"Gee, Ned, do I get to wear the uniform?"

"Beg pardon?"

Bad enough I'd had to wear a Hale blazer and tie. The notion of skulking around in sash and badges was enough to make my testicles ascend to my lungs. Next to me in a Boy Scout uniform, Herb Pazahowski would look like Jimi Hendrix.

"Does Ned Friendly hear mockery?" he asked.

"Does Bobby Stark care?" I asked back. "Ned Friendly sounds like a used car salesman."

Ned reextended his plump tongue and curled it upward. His capillaries flushed. "I can think of five scouts who would know how to deal with the likes of you."

My mother chose this moment to return with a tray of re-heated meatloaf and instant potatoes. Ned's pique switched quickly to polite delight.

Mom seemed to look between us. "Why don't you two men come into the dining room?"

"Time to strap on the old feedbag," Ned chuckled. "Howza-bout it, Bobby?"

"Not hungry," I said. "Bobby thinks Bobby wants to go to bed."

Mom froze, holding her platter of meat loaf. Ned shook his melon-sized head in an indignant I've-seen-boys-like-you-before kind of way. It was an odd moment. Not scary so much as . . . *disturbed*. There was so much I was feeling that I couldn't even

perv—a love story

name. Weirdness on all kinds of levels. First was that panicky, empty sensation of not having a home—of sliming back to this condo where, I realized when I thought about lying down, I did not even have a room. I'd have to crash on the velour sofa, which folded out. If nothing else, I was glad Ned had sunk his flanks in Dad's La-Z-Boy. If he and his Milwaukee goiter had flattened the couch, cakes to cushion. . . . Well, think about it.

The prospect of resting my head anywhere near Ned's lime-green behemoth of a keester, of taking a single breath where his buttocks had touched, filled me with such nausea I might as well have gulped bus fumes. But beyond being homeless and repulsed, there was the whole here's-this-guy-where-my-Dad-used-to-be issue. The sight of Ned hopping up to take Mom's waist, squiring her the nine steps to the dining room table, creeped me down to my toes. It's not like my father had died the day before, but so what? I could not tear my eyes from Ned's gargantuan fingers on my mother's body.

I'd rarely seen my parents hug, let alone kiss or hold hands. Only once, when I was about six, did I spot something that resembled affection. What happened is, I walked into their bedroom on a Sunday afternoon. I'd just barged into the house after playing football. My plan was to catch some upstairs TV. TV was better in their room. You could pile up pillows and stretch out on the bed to watch. Anyway, when I opened the door I saw them—you can't even say *hugging*—pressed face-to-face on Mom's bed (they had twins), absolutely still, squeezing each other so tightly I thought they might be dead. Fresh-frozen for eternity, like human relics from Pompeii.

Dad's eyes were cinched closed. And, more alarming, he'd taken his glasses off. He didn't even do that to shower. Beneath him, my mother's mouth hung open, like she'd had a stroke. They were both naked, tangled on top of the gardenia-print bedspread. The bed was still made. Mind-blowing . . .

What I couldn't get over, what kept me up that night clutching the sheets, was the way Mom's fingers dug into Dad's back. There were dots of blood where her nails had broken the flesh. Five in a row, like musical notes.

Imagine! My father was a squat, dark, powerfully built man who looked like a distinguished version of Moe Howard, the famous Stooge. To see him like that—asprawl and glasses-less and bleeding from the back atop my stricken mother—was almost more than I could take. I backed out quietly, then flew downstairs and ate nine bowls of Sugar Pops. The whole box.

So here I was, a decade later, house gone, Dad dead, me whatever the fuck I was, hunkered in Mom's condo wondering if she was going Pompeii with Ned Friendly.

"You don't wanna stay a scrawny dog, do ya?" Ned guffawed. "A scout eats three squares. Has to. Think you can survive in the wild without your essential nutrients? Don't think so. Not for long. No sirree Bob. First thing I teach my boys, consume your food groups. Consume your proteins! Consume your fats! Be surprised what a difference in attitude a wad of carbos in your gas tank can make. You don't believe me, go without."

"Without what?" I said, though I could tell Mom was getting upset. She set the plates down and stood cradling her head. Always a bad sign.

"Ned's sniffing some insolence," Ned said. "Ned's getting a

definite whiff you're a lad who thinks the scouts are for, what do you kids call them these days, *squares? Straights? No-goodniks?* Well lemme tell you, our boys are dying in that Vietnam. Our boys are laying down their lives so your friends can grow fleas! So your hippies can fornicate at will. You heard me! So your long-haired stumblebums can listen to that hootchy-cootchy music. Need I say more? Need I?"

"Not on my account," I shrugged. It was here, I believe, that Mom slammed down the potato plate and declared, in one of her patented contained screams—quiet as normal speech, but normal speech with the lid screwed on—"I made food and we are going to eat it."

She pulled out a Kent and Ned produced a lighter shaped like a little six-shooter.

"Mom," I said to her, "scouts probably don't approve of smoking."

Of course, she didn't respond. She simply marched back to the kitchenette to slam more plates. Ned Friendly hoisted his bulk out of the chair and started toward me. For one, cartoonish second I thought he was going to get physical. Instead, he sidled up next to me, so close I could see gin blossoms exploding on his nose and cheeks, flaming starbursts that branded his flesh with the same fiery patterns I'd see behind my eyes when I smoked too much Lebanese blonde.

"Fella, I got a sense about you," he whispered harshly. Outside it had begun to rain, and the first fat drops splashed Mom's picture window. "I got a sense you're some kinda sissy-boy, aren'tcha? You're one of them sit-down-to-pee'ers, am I right? A little light in the loafers. Oh sure, Ned can spot 'em. Ned can always pick up a hint of mint, if you know what I mean. Ned knows all about you fancy prep-school jokers."

"I didn't go for very long."

"Don't take long." Ned nodded. He pushed out his tongue like he wanted to lick the ceiling. "Oh hey," he added, resting a meaty paw on my shoulder. "Nobody's blaming you, son. How'd it happen? Strange town, all your friends someplace else? Ned knows. A lad gets lonely. Sure he does. A lad gets scared. And what happens? Here comes some slicked up slacks-and-ascot type takes you under his wing. Shows you around. *Introduces* you. Next thing you know he's telling you he likes your hair. Wants to feed you chocolates, teach you Greek. Oh sure, Ned knows. Ned knows all about it."

To my horror, he bent down closer. His boil glowed at eye level. His breath reeked of martinis and peanuts. Mom always put Planters peanuts out for company. My father used to crunch them by the fistful, despite a bleeding ulcer and the fact that they made him so sick he'd weep on the toilet for a week and a half.

"Ned can help you out," Ned whispered, his voice hoarse as he gave my shoulder an unsavory squeeze. "We don't need to tell our mother," he continued, nodding toward the kitchenette where my mother, I knew from experience, was banging around plates for the sake of banging around plates. (Bernice, who liked to name things, used to call it "rage music.") "Our mother does not have to know."

I blinked at him for a second, and then I hollered, "Mom! *Hey, Mom!*" I belted it out, as much to banish the creepy sheen in Ned's parboiled eyes as anything else. "Mom, I'm gonna go for a walk. I think I'm jet-lagged."

perv—a love story

My mother stepped out of the kitchenette holding a striped dishtowel around a bowl, this one filled with her famous candied carrots. Her manner was distracted. "But honey, we're ready to eat."

"I'll be back," I said, doing my best to arrange a smile both pleasant and mischievous. "Besides, you two kids probably want to be alone."

Mom looked close to the edge. Ned just kept nodding in that rancid, knowing way. I skipped to the door without the least idea in my head where I might be going.

"Ned Friendly understands," Ned called as I stepped into the hall. "Ned Friendly knows!"

I wanted to yell back that he should hang around bus stations, he'd have better luck, but didn't want to hurt my mother. Besides which, I only thought of busses because my father and I had to take one from Philly to Slotzville the first time we went to Hale, and in the men's room of the Philly station we saw a she-male.

There was a shitty cafeteria in the station, and with an hour to kill, my father thought we should wash our hands and grab a sandwich. In the men's room, we saw him—or her—and I could not stop staring. There were only three sinks. Three mirrors. At the middle one stood this dainty black person with a complicated soufflé of processed hair and the longest lashes I'd ever seen.

He/she wore a satin muscle tee—the type we used to call wifebeaters, though the owner of those lashes didn't look like he'd be beating any wife. He'd tied the T-shirt into a knot above a tawny belly and a snug pair of silver hot-pants. Most remarkable were his legs, which were muscular and wrapped in black seamed stockings that disappeared into stained white go-go boots.

The man dressed like a woman was glued to the mirror, applying mascara and repeating private slogans out loud. "Pretty *IS* as pretty *DOES* . . . Um-hmmm. I am beau-tee-ful *IN*; I am beau-tee-ful *OUT*. . . ."

That sort of thing. When he/she saw me, he grinned and threw up his arms like a singer thanking his adoring audience. There was some kind of white dust caked under his armpits, which were shaved to a patchy stubble. When I caught a waft, I realized it was baby powder. "I am *NOT* Little Richard," he sang, as though Dad and I had been poring over the question and he felt compelled to clear it up. "Little Richard be *ME*!"

My father and I dried our hands and got out of the men's room without further incident. I had the feeling he was more embarrassed than I was. I wasn't embarrassed at all. I was fascinated. I could have watched the dynamic Negro preen for hours.

Having just glimpsed a whole other brand of homo—if that's what he was—in the form of Ned Friendly, national vice president of Boy Scouts of America and friend of Spiro Agnew, I only wished that the two of them, Bus Station Preener and Boy Scout Veep, could meet and share some quality men's room time. Maybe Ned could have made a scout out of him.

Once outside Mom's condo, I spazzed and walked to the wrong end of the hall. I had to walk back past her door, and stopped to eavesdrop. "A boy his age," I heard Ned honking, "a boy his age has got to be around other boys! He can't be coddled. He needs to have it rough!" After that I got moving. I scrammed down the hall and pounded the elevator button before Ned called in the troops.

When the elevator opened, I flew in and hit B. Why not? The basement was as good as anyplace else. I closed my eyes and mashed myself to the back wall. While the car whooshed south, I thought about my father. Remembering. He hardly ever talked about himself, but one Sunday, when we were driving to pick up corned beef, he came out with an amazing story about riding an elevator in Germany. It was, he explained, a few months after the Nazis lost. He was a clerk in the Army, stuck in some crumbling office building in Berlin. Because chunks of the ceiling kept falling, people were always changing offices, and his job was to lug files from one office to the other, usually on different floors.

This particular afternoon, Dad steps into the tiny elevator with a stack of files higher than his head. But before he manages to press the button, the power goes out. Everything goes black. He's stuck. "Happened all the time," he told me, so involved in the story he didn't see the red light change to green. "I realized after a couple of minutes that I might be stuck awhile, so I put the boxes on the floor. While I'm bending down, I bump into something. I touch it, and it's big and furry. This startles me, but I figure it's some old dog. There were lots of dogs running around Berlin, and a lot of them had lost their bark. Something to do with all the bombing. They were traumatized. Couldn't bark anymore. Doggy shell shock. They'd stand there and stare, waiting for you to kick them. It was sad. But I was glad there was a dog in there. I sat on the floor scratching its back, just petting away. After a while I started talking to it. I told it about your mother, how much I missed her, how her hair shined in the moonlight. It was nice. I told the dog what I was gonna do when I got back to the States, how I was gonna go to law school and help people, all kinds of stuff, until suddenly the lights crank back on and I look over and it's not a dog at all, it's somebody in a fur coat crouched on the floor! Can you imagine? I'd been patting some lady's back the whole time. Except when she jumped up, I saw that was wrong, too. *It wasn't a lady.* It was some scrawny bald guy who'd just stolen the coat and was trying to sneak out of the building. I guess when the power went out, he figured he'd hide in a corner, and when I started stroking him, well, God knows *what* he thought . . ."

The recollection tickled him.

"Man oh man," Dad said, moving the car forward at last. By then the light had changed three times. "I was so surprised I let the thief run off with the coat. Didn't even report him. There was so much crazy stuff like that going on it hardly mattered. . . ."

I have to admit, I wasn't close to my old man when he was alive. He was hardly ever home. But now that he was gone, and I was back in Pittsburgh, I thought about him all the time. I felt closer to the guy since he'd been buried than I ever did when he was walking around aboveground. I realized how much I loved him.

When the elevator hit the basement, the doors creaked open and I stepped out into a blast of light, what turned out to be the condo laundry room. One washer was chugging away and two more had cardboard OUT OF ORDER signs Scotch-taped across their lids. The dryers were all dead. But it was cool. I loved Laundromats. When I used to sneak out of Hale and hitch to Philly, I'd always end up at the Soak 'n' Spin, a twenty-four-hour Laundromat five blocks from Penn Station. The night manager was a Puerto Rican named Felix who played harmonica with

perv—a love story

his nose. For the price of five dryer tokens you could stay all night, nursing vending machine coffee and listening to nasal renditions of Motown classics. At the time, I thought Felix had a perfect life.

By condo tradition, I suppose, people ditched their old magazines in the laundry room. I noticed a batch of them on a plastic chair. *Reader's Digest, Time, Sports Illustrated.* Nothing good. So I just hung. Breathing in and out. Fighting the shine from the fluorescent lights and the screaming yellow cinderblocks. More and more, I'd been having this feeling of zeroness. Of *HERE-I-AM-AND-IT-JUST-DOESN'T-MATTER.* I wondered how long I could stay upright, thinking and doing nothing. Willing myself into some kind of two-legged furniture. This was my classified truth: I wasn't sad after my father kissed the streetcar. If anything, it was a relief. Much as I missed him, his dying gave me an excuse to feel the way I already felt. Which was the way I felt right now, under the laundry room fluorescents: hollow, pissed off, wanting to be wherever I wasn't. Until I got there. Then I wanted to be somewhere else.

I don't know how long I'd been standing, trying to induce some kind of acid flashback—the papers were full of flashback stories, but I never knew anybody who actually had one; it would have been great—when I spotted the basket on the chair in front of me. A plastic basket, the same scald-your-eyes yellow as the walls. It had been there all along, but I was so busy trying to get inanimate I didn't see it.

While the one good washing machine whooshed and rattled, I stepped forward to investigate the pile of clothes. Amazingly, there seemed to be nothing but panties. A panty Himalaya, with a handful of bras thrown in. Could women, I wondered, wear bras over and over, but panties only once? Was that the rule? Without thinking about it, I hunched over the silky mass and began sifting. I plucked out a white-with-tiny-pink-roses and held it to the light. Sharon Schmidlap's undies, wadded at her ankle, seemed to be the same plain cotton as my BVDs. A sad and worn-out yellow-white. This lady, whoever she was, had more elevated tastes.

Still grasping those pink roses, rubbing the silky bottom between my thumb and forefinger, I lifted them to the light and saw the faintest shadow: two fingers' width of dark between the front and back, what Tennie used to call the 'taint. (As in " 'taint their ass and 'taint their pussy," your classic Tennie-ism.) That's when I noticed the swath, a plump strip of padding that reminded me of Dr. Scholl's corn pads, but made of regular material instead of moleskin.

This could not, I imagined, be the same thing as a corn pad: It wasn't like the flesh of a woman's sex was bunionlike, and needed the smooth relief of moleskin. Or *did* it? Did that happen when they got older? Cunt-bunions? I couldn't believe that. To check it out, I grabbed the panties with both hands. Like a surgeon doffing his mask, I closed my eyes and plunged the bottom half of my face into the padded fabric.

I sniffed, caught the scent of something so private it scared me, then went whole-hog and inhaled till my lungs nearly burst with the vanilla-gone-bad waft of whatever had caked the patch at my nostrils. I pulled off the panties to check again, flashing back to my own underwear trauma: my mother's threats to take Polaroids of my underpants, then send them to the *Post-Gazette*— *"so everybody in Pittsburgh would see!"*—if I so much as grazed an-

perv—a love story

other pair. Whole chunks of my childhood were spent chafing my sphincter, trying to extricate every molecule of stain-producing excrement. *And it still wasn't enough . . . .*

To block out the memory, I quickly went back to snuffling. After a minute or two, I even got a rush. Some groovy blue light went off in my forehead. It might have been fumes, or I might have been hyperventilating. I didn't care. I just wanted more.

Dizzy with rapture, I soaked myself in the intimate stink of whatever lovely had sullied that slightly stiff, lightly caked patch of silk clamped to my lips and nose. I rubbed it on my mouth and breathed still deeper. It turned me on, and then some. I gulped as if this sex-soaked elixir could not just get me hard, but transport me, *get me out of there,* somehow lift me up in a whirl-wind of female perfume and whisk me off, up out of the laun-dry room, away from the Superior Condo, far from Pittsburgh and the gaggle of grown-ups like Ned Friendly and the Hale headmaster and my well-meaning but badly electroshocked mother. . . . A whole population who seemed to exist for no rea-son other than to render my existence a battery of constant, gnawing dread.

"Oh please," I mumbled, spinning around and groaning under the laundry room fluorescents without even knowing it. "Oh please, baby, please . . . just open it . . . just show it to me, show it to me . . . open it up and—"

"A-*hem.*"

"*EE—YAAAHH!*"

I screamed and dropped the panties, careening off the plastic chair and knocking the clothes basket to the floor. When my eyes refocused, I saw a short, barrel-shaped woman with blue hair and enormous glasses that magnified her eyes so much she appeared to be peering at me through a double microscope. She had to be seventy if she was a month.

"I . . . I . . . I . . ."

"You what? You like my underthings?" she asked, more or less unfazed. Unless I'd completely lost it, she appeared as full of honest curiosity as any kind of disgust. She daintily adjusted those microscope glasses and then stepped closer. The way she looked at me, I felt like a specimen. I might have been a caveman, glacially preserved in the Pleistocene and thawed back to life in the laundry room of her condominium.

"You . . . like old ladies underthings? They . . . how do you young people say it? They 'light your fire'?"

"Well, not exactly," I stammered. My tongue had gone linty. "I mean, they don't *not* turn me on. I mean, well, kind of. . . ."

The old lady made a scraping "hmmmph" noise and stepped forward to pick up the clothes I'd spilled. I was beyond mortified, but still had my manners. I stooped to help gather her unmentionables.

"You know," she sighed, after everything was just about back in the basket. "I should be shocked, but, accch . . . you kids today! I see you there, sniffing my underpants, and I think to myself, 'Dolores, you're sixty-eight years old, what do you know? Is it a drug thing? Is it some kind of free love? Are you from one of those cults?' "

"Panty worship," I said, handing her the last of her undergarments, a solid lacy number minus that perplexing swath of padding. "That would probably get me going back to temple. If they passed out panties instead of prayer books, I'd be there. I'd probably become a rabbi."

"Oh, a comedian." Her gigantic, jellyfish eyes swallowed me

perv—a love story

up. "All you kids are comedians now. Well I got news for you, Mr. Jackie Mason, my granddaughter is in a cult, and it's no joke. It's no joke at all. Help me unload." She raised her gnarled hands. "Arthritis."

"I'm sorry."

"Sorry he says. Just pray to God you don't get this pain when you get old. Pray to God you don't get old, *period*."

I don't know what I expected her to do—call the police, spray me with bleach, run off into the basement—but after our chat the old lady simply went about her business. I could tell it hurt just bending her fingers. The knuckles of each hand were the size of jawbreakers. We tugged out her sopping laundry, shoved it in a dryer; then she held open the washing machine lid while I dropped in her dirty underthings—including the pink-rose print I'd worn like a Muslim girl in purdah—and she added a cupful of Tide. That done, we backed up and checked each other. A batch of fuzzballs dotted the yellow mohair she wore over her slacks, and I picked them off. For the first time Dolores smiled.

"You're actually a good boy, aren't you? Just a bit of a perv."

"Perv?" I wadded the fuzz and tossed it behind the dryer.

"You're a pervert. Like my husband, Albert. May he rest in peace. One day I come home from the School for the Blind—I did volunteer work, after Madge and Marty were grown—and there's Albert, sitting on our Barcalounger watching *The Dick Van Dyke Show*."

"What's so perverted about that?"

"If you'd let me finish, Walter Cronkite, you'd find out. He's wearing what he always wore, his gabardine suit pants and a white shirt buttoned to the top. *Except.* Except the pants are open. They're pushed down under his tush. And his member—my God

I have never told this, not even to Albert's sister, though believe me, there have been plenty of times I wanted to tell that b-rhymes-with-ditch what her brother the saint was really like. But never mind. Back to Albert. His member, pardon my *française*, is completely erect. And he's got it covered in one of his socks. An argyle, if you please, navy blue with tiny yellow clocks. 'Albert,' I say to him, 'what in God's name are you doing? It's three o'clock in the afternoon.' What the time has to do with the price of tea in China, I don't know. I was upset, that's all. I was beside myself. Albert's sitting there, like a *blintz*, with his thing wrapped in a sock, and—*acch!*—his mouth hanging open, *mit* the jowls. . . ."

She raised her eyes suddenly, as if dazed by her own confession, and put her hand on my shoulder.

"Albert was a handsome man, but after fifty"—she shrugged—"he got the jowls. . . . But that's not the point. The point is, right there, right on the TV, Rose Marie was sitting in Rob's office, sipping coffee with Rob and Buddy, and Albert is, what's the word?"

She snapped her fingers with surprising volume and I waited, hands still wet from her wash.

"Albert is *transfixed*. Yes! 'Dolly,' he says to me, and God strike me dead, there are tears in his eyes. He's tugging on his *thing* like some shmuck in a raincoat, but there are tears. 'Dolly, I love you more than any man could love his wife, but this Rose Marie, she . . . is . . . a . . . *FIRECRACKER!*'"

I was so startled by her intensity, I stepped back and knocked over her basket again. Dolores didn't notice.

"Who knew?" she wondered aloud. "My girlfriends and I spend hours playing bridge and clucking our tongue about free love,

perv—a love story

about the hippies, about the whole can of knishes, and meanwhile my Albert is sitting in our apartment pulling his Poughkeepsie in an argyle sock."

She scoffed and plucked a linen hanky from her right sleeve.

"So I'm going to criticize you for taking a sniff of my unmentionables? Hah! Be my guest. Maybe it'll keep you off the hard stuff. Maybe you'll stop *mit* the panties and never do those drugs. I don't know. Maybe they should pass my underwear, God help me, to kids in high school, to keep them from trying the marijuana, the LSD. If I have time this afternoon, I'll write to President Nixon, see what he thinks."

She blew her nose daintily, then opened the hanky and examined its contents with a quiet sigh. She might have been reading tea leaves.

"Okay," she said, "so I'm a little bit *fertitzed*. Who the heck knows what's right and wrong anymore? I am a grandmother twice and I couldn't tell you. Thirty-three years you live with someone, and you find out you don't know the first thing about them. Of course you're too young to understand. But listen to an old lady anyway: it's not what people do, it's what they *don't* tell you they do. *That's* what hurts. *That's* what you think about when the television signs off and you're still bright-eyed and bushy-tailed. I even went to a psychiatrist, thank you very much, a very nice man. My daughter made all the arrangements."

"She sounds nice," I said, just to say something. I was so grateful to get her off the subject of my behavior I wanted her to keep going on hers. But I didn't have to say anything. She'd forgotten I was there.

"Who's nice?" she asked, as perplexed as if I'd woken her from a coma.

"Your daughter," I said. "I was just saying, she sounds nice."

"My daughter?" Her giant eyes grew wide. She reached into her laundry basket and fished around with her hand before realizing we'd already emptied it. "My daughter is not nice. Not even close. What was I saying?"

"Your psychiatrist," I coached her. "You were going to your psychiatrist."

"Right. Well," she resumed, fidgeting with her hanky. "I get there, it's a very nice office in the mall, and he says to me, 'Mrs. Fish, how do you feel about your husband's behavior?' How do I *feel*? For this he wants forty dollars? I told him the same as I'm telling you. I was shocked. Not because of the sock-thing—though that didn't thrill me, I can tell you that, that was disgusting, is what that was—no, I was shocked because of the secret. Because my husband, after all these years, had a secret. From me." She pounded her bosom. "From his *WIFE!*"

"So then," I asked, "what got you upset is not so much what he did, it's that you caught him doing it? Is that it? What he did, the sock stuff, you think it's okay?"

"It's okay? *What's* okay? What are you saying?" The old lady looked baffled again. Now, I thought, maybe she *is* going to panic. Maybe I've made her senile, if *that* can happen. I should have just shut up, but it was too late now.

"You know," I went on, speaking like you would to a child, "what your husband was doing. And what"—I faltered, but I had to know—"what you saw when you walked in. When you walked in here . . ."

"When I walked in here? What I saw in here, your little panty routine? Please!"

I should have stopped. But I was worried. I needed an opinion.

Beyond getting caught doing what I was doing, deep down I wondered if there was something wrong with me for doing it. Dolores gave a shrug and pulled her glasses off. Her eyes, without the industrial-strength lenses, were quite tiny and rimmed in red. She pinched the bridge of her nose and fluffed her hair, touching the aqua-blue permanent wave as if to make sure it was still there.

"Let me tell you something, mister. If I had walked in on your little performance two years ago, before I waltzed in on my husband watching Rose Marie with a sock over his thing, I'd have probably plotzed. No probably about it, I *would* have plotzed. Now?" She gave a weary shrug and threw up her knotted hands. An overhead fluorescent flickered as the washer shifted cycles. "Now I don't know anymore."

"Look," I said, "I apologize." And I meant it.

I wanted to explain about my mother, about Ned, but she interrupted me, smiling sadly. "It's not you. The whole world's meshugah. My granddaughter, who used to be a cheerleader, who dated the captain of her high school football team, who liked to do *needlepoint*, if you please, now stands around in airports in an orange nightie. A bald head and a pigtail she's got. This beautiful girl who used to have tresses that would have made Rapunzel jealous. Every night, till she was thirteen, my daughter used to brush her hair. Now—*what hair?* She's got this little pigtail from the top of her head. 'Grandma,' she says to me when she visits, 'it's so Krishna can pull me up into heaven.' 'If he's really God,' I told her, 'he'll send you a helicopter. He'll call a cab. He'll do something, but no God would make a child chop her tresses and wear her hair like some kind of coolie. No way, Jose. If he's God, he'll get you an appointment with a hairdresser.'"

Dolores had worked herself up. She'd begun weaving on her feet. I snatched a plastic chair and slid it behind her. She plopped down heavily, shaking her head. From above, I could see her pale scalp, the color of wet paper towels, visible through her wispy blue tufts.

"I'm sorry," she said, then caught herself. "A panty-sniffer I'm talking to, and I'm saying 'I'm sorry.'" She threw up her hands and glared at the ceiling. "This is what I'm talking. *This* is the cockamamie, upside-down world we live in. I sometimes think Albert, strike me dead, was lucky to have the heart attack. You children . . . you have everything. But what does it matter? Here you are, a nice young man, and I walk in and see you doing this dirty thing, this . . . dirty, dirty *thing*. And my granddaughter! Now my sweet little granddaughter is traipsing around the airport selling that Baghdad Jeepers or whatever it's called. She tried to tell me, but who could understand such hinky-chinky?"

Dolores sat back with a heavy sigh and the color washed out of her. She aimed those egg-sized eyes at me, deflated, then came back to life at the memory of what had set her off in the first place. "Maybe I'm just an old lady, but anyone who walked in and saw you doing what you were doing, they'd call the police. They'd call the Vice Squad. Maybe I *should* make a call!"

Normally, in a situation like this—not that I'd ever been in a situation like this, but if, say, I got caught shoplifting—I would march out my dead father, explain that my mother had emotional problems. The old one-two. I'd let them see that I wasn't bad, I was *troubled*. The Troubled Teen. (Poor kids were "juvenile delinquents"; the rest of us were "troubled.") It always worked. This was, I sometimes thought, the last gift my father gave me. And

perv—a love story

the best: His death stood out as the supreme-o excuse for fucking up, for being a successful fuck-up.

I was all set to lay this on Dolores. I knew the drill. To keep her from telling on me, I'd lower my gaze, slump my shoulders, sniffle a little like I was trying to "be brave." Since she was a mom herself, I'd kick off with how sick my mother was. Play the "mental illness" card. Honk on how sad she'd been since Dad, well . . . *I don't usually tell this to people, but since Dad committed suicide, etc. . . . etc. . . . .*

For dessert, if necessary, I'd throw in how a father's dying, for all intents and purposes, leaves a boy on his own. I was going to plunge right in—I probably should have—but, to my own surprise, I put on the brakes. I couldn't go on. How could I, after she'd mentioned that her granddaughter was a Hare Krishna? That changed everything. My heart throbbed with this intense, stranger-than-fiction feeling—that Dolores was talking about the girl I'd seen at the airport. The girl dancing with her pigtail whirling over her scalp like a broken propeller. The all-but-bald girl of my dreams. Michelle Burnelka.

How many daughters of Pittsburgh, after all, could have grown up and gone the shaved-head-and-saffron route?

After her Vice Squad outburst, neither of us spoke for a while. The only sound was the chug-a-chug of the washing machine and the panty-filled dryer. When I gave in and popped the question, I tried to sound matter-of-fact.

"Call me crazy," I piped up, circling like a bird over a landfill, "I *like* the sound of washing machines."

Dolores simply grunted. "That's not why I'd call you crazy."

She stirred on her plastic chair and shot me a sidelong glance. "When I think of your face in those panties . . . *Ecch!*"

I forced a grin, as if "ecch" were some kind of bon mot. That done, I squinched up my face and smacked my forehead. "Wait a sec!"—like, hey, the thought just came to me, out of the blue— "your granddaughter, the one hawking the Bhagavad-Gitas, her name wouldn't be Michelle, would it? Michelle Burnelka?"

Dolores jumped straight out of her chair. If fondling her skimpies was offensive, the idea of the fondler knowing her beloved granddaughter was a complete travesty. Terror stamped her features. She lifted her magnified eyes to mine. "You're one of them, aren't you? You're in that cult! *Mein Gott,* how did you know when I did my laundry? What is happening to this country?"

I knelt beside her, right there on the concrete floor. "I'm not one of them, okay? We went to school together, that's all. I saw her at the airport this afternoon."

But Dolores didn't hear. She continued gaping, rearing back as if trapped in a cage with some foul beast. A bad man from the Panty Gestapo. "Is . . . is that part of it?" she asked, her voice grown small as a child's, compelled to know more though the knowing was killing her. "Does Krishna make you . . . *smell things?*"

Now I was the horrified one. Besides everything else, I liked Dolores. The idea of her not liking me, after all that had happened, was more defeat than I could handle in one day. I did not even know I was grabbing her hand until she tried to free it. I wouldn't let go, which freaked her out more. This was not what I'd planned at all. My words squeaked to life cracked and high. Jiminy Cricket redux.

"I am not in a cult, okay? My father died a little while ago and my mom lives on the seventh floor. Maybe you know her. Mrs. Stark? Shrieks a lot? Wears sequins? It doesn't matter. I got thrown out of prep school and I just got home today. Except it's not really my home. I've never lived here. Mom sold the house after Dad died and I went away. So now, I don't even *have* a home. But that doesn't matter either. What I mean is, my name's Bobby. I've known Michelle since kindergarten. I saw her today at the airport. And when you mentioned about your granddaughter, I just, you know, took a guess."

"You know her? You know my darling Michelle?" She'd heard nothing else.

"That's what I've been trying to say. I know her. I *knew* her. But not in a Hare Krishna way. In a grade school way. Junior high, too, until I got sent away."

Dolores stared past me, at the fire extinguisher mounted over the bank of dryers. She spoke as though each word hurt. "She doesn't even call herself Michelle anymore. Now she's Lala, or Leeeway, or some such nonsense." Her voice trailed off. "I don't even know what language. . . ."

"Maybe I could call her," I said, adding quickly, "I could tell her that you're worried. That you still love her."

"What? What do you know?" Dolores swiped the air in front of her and flung open the washer, though the load was still bouncing inside. "She doesn't care if I love her. You don't know anything. God damn it, Albert, *what were you doing?*"

I left her there, pulling soapy panties out of the machine and muttering to her dead, Dick Van Dyke–obsessed husband. "Rose Marie!" I could hear her cry as I headed out the metal door to the underground parking. *"ROSE MARIE!"*

* * *

Now what? I wanted to hot-wire a car and drive to San Francisco. I wanted to drop acid. I wanted to break into a pharmacy and steal a *Playboy* and a bottle of cough medicine. I wanted to do *something*, and tripped on all the different things I could be doing—but wasn't—as I trudged on the elevator and rode glumly back upstairs to Mom.

I didn't have a key, and had to knock for five minutes before Mom arrived. When the door opened, Ned Friendly was nowhere to be seen, and Mom's lipstick was smushed. She was poured into her favorite nightie, a lox-colored, nearly see-through floral print she wore whenever she "laid in"—Mom's term for staying in bed when I was a little boy. For a solid year or two—if you combined all those three- and four-week stretches—Mom stayed in bed, in her floral print lox, and called downstairs for different items as the cravings struck her. *"Bobby, get me a peach . . ." "Bobby, grab me a liverwurst sandwich . . ."* And the worst, for a lot of reasons: *"Bobby, I want something and I don't know what it is . . ."*

This last meant at least six trips up and down the steps. Bringing her ginger ale, bringing her white meat turkey, bringing her "Velvet Mussies" (Velveeta and yellow mustard on saltines). When Mom had the "Indefinables," as Dad and I called them, it meant things were getting grim. Mostly it happened when he was out of town, which was often, sometimes three weeks out of a month. Mom didn't shower then. She didn't cook. She didn't do anything. She kept a soup pot beside the bed so she wouldn't even need to walk to the bathroom. (Guess what my job was.) "It's all so depressing," she'd say, but blithely, not sounding depressed at all when she called out requests from her dark bedroom, with the curtains drawn and no light but the constant, quavering blue of the muted TV.

perv—a love story

The worst thing about the "Indefinables" was not actually the trips up and down the stairs. It wasn't even the endless slouching in front of the open fridge, thinking *chocolate pudding*, thinking *leftover creamed corn*, thinking *maybe eggs*. No, the worst part was how, when I managed to come up with what she wanted—the desire she knew was there but could not, somehow, give a name to—Mom would give a grateful yip and fling back the covers, releasing a hot, eye-watering gust, like a blast from some churning furnace of Momness.

The rush of Mom-aroma would make me gag, but I couldn't show it. I couldn't show it when she pulled me close, when she mashed my head in her exposed bosom, which was always moist, bidding me breathe in the fetid, unwelcome waft of her. It was something pungent, something I shouldn't have known about it. "Let's cuddle," she'd murmur, and then I'd blank everything out: the flesh and weirdness, the suffocating blankets of shame.

Seeing that faded nightgown, it all came back. Standing wracked and irritated in Mom's doorway, the very last psychic terrain I wanted to revisit was packed into that nightie, and the smeared-up lipstick that went with it. The phrase "wanna cuddle" clanged off the walls of my skull. I was sweating all over.

Mom had already set out sheets on the Castro convertible, and there was a plate with three Oreos and a napkin. My own little picnic.

"Milk's in the fridge," she said, before drifting down the hall to her bedroom and closing the door.

I fell asleep with a cookie in my hand, pressed under my nose so I could smell the cream.

love-in

The next week, Mom lined up another fellow for me to "talk to." Mr. Weiner (pronounced, she kept reminding me, "*WHY*-ner") was a friend of my father's from the public defender's office. I'd seen him a lot as a child. He even attended my bar mitzvah. But it had been years, and he sounded different. When he called, Mom and I were watching the news. Walter Cronkite said President Nixon had sent troops to Cambodia, "to destroy North Vietnamese sanctuaries." They showed Nixon making a speech at a VFW lodge, where all the men had fat necks and party hats.

"You ask me, he looks like he could use a good BM," Mom said, heading to the kitchenette to refill the potato chip bowl and snag some more of her special dip. (A bag of Knorr dehydrated French onion soup dumped in sour cream—you could burp just looking at it.)

"Cronkite or Nixon?" I asked.

"Well, both," she explained, "but mostly Nixon. You'd think, for all the money we're spending in Vietnam, they could afford to buy the President laxatives."

I was still chewing on this when the phone rang. On TV, a hollow-eyed GI crouched on his helmet. Usually I let Mom get it, but since she was on dip patrol, I answered myself. We watched the war every night, snacking our way through the dead and wounded. I'd heard the grass was pretty strong over there, and hadn't decided whether or not to burn my draft card when I got one. Luckily, I still had a few years.

"Stark residence."

"B-B-Bobby? It's M-M-Mr. Weiner!"

"Oh, um, hello. . . ."

I'd forgotten he was going to call. Mom had been telling me all day, but Tennie's pot—which I'd started to flush, then plucked out of the toilet and dried in Mom's toaster-oven when she was out playing bridge—worked a number on my short-term memory. I could tell you who I sat behind in second grade (Michelle, of course), but space on what I'd read in *Newsweek* five minutes ago.

"I'm d-d-down in the lobby," he stuttered. "Th-thought we'd gr-gr-grab a bite."

"Now?"

"Who is it?" Mom called from the kitchen. "Ed McMahon? Did we win the sweepstakes?"

"It's Mr. Weiner," I called back. Palming the receiver, I added, "He says he's down in the lobby."

Mom swayed in with a tray of fresh dip and chips. Today was a sherry-and-Seconal day. "Of course he is, hon. He's picking you up at seven."

When she saw the look on my face, she frowned. "I told you, Bobby. I asked him to talk to you. He's had . . . experience."

"What do you mean experience?"

Instead of answering, she snatched the phone from my hand and sang into it. "Keep the motor running. He'll be down as soon as he brushes his teeth. Onions," she added, with lowered voice, lest a man I hadn't seen twice in half a decade wondered how my breath smelled.

"Jesus," I said when she hung up, "you didn't tell me it was tonight."

"If you'd clean the wax beans out of your ears, you'd know I told you twice. Now scoot."

My memory of Mr. Weiner was of a trim, feisty man with a crew cut who made funny noises. The kind of guy who broke into woofs, pulled quarters out of your ear, or stole your nose. Unless I'd been so young that he just seemed bigger, the fellow sitting in the Rambler Ambassador out front had experienced some shrinkage. But he himself didn't seem to notice. That was the odd part. Before I even stepped in his squatty car, I could see he was still wearing the same clothes he must have owned when he was normal.

perv—a love story

"D-D-Door's a little m-m-moody," he cried, leaning across the seat to bang the handle. Sprawled sideways like that, his head poked out of his collar like a Tootsie Pop on a stick. His shirt puffed out emptily over his pants. Even his wingtips, when I caught a glance, looked like Daddy shoes. His seersucker suit might have belonged to a giant.

"Wh-Why, you've grown up," he said, offering a clammy hand to shake when I got in. I don't know what I answered. I was too busy trying to wipe my palm on my pants without his noticing. There was something else about him. He'd become hard to look at. His forehead was quite broad, with matching divots the size of poker chips on either side. I wondered if this is what they meant by "Forceps Baby." Or if Mr. Weiner was a Forceps Adult. For once, I was glad I hadn't snuck a joint before sneaking out.

"S-S-So," he continued, slapping both hands on the wheel, "what'll it be? You h-h-hungry? F-F-feel like drivin'?"

"Really? It's okay?"

By way of reply, he tossed me the keys.

I liked him better already, though he was so nervous it made me nervous. "Mr. Weiner wants to talk to you," Mom had said, sending me out the door with a five-dollar bill. She didn't say what he wanted to talk about. She didn't have to. After your father dies, a certain breed of grown-up feels a need to sit you down for "meaningful talks." *Now you're the man of the family. . . . Life's not always easy. . . . Your daddy's gone home to God. . . .* That kind of stuff. It made them feel better.

Once I slid behind the wheel, and Mr. Weiner'd jogged around to the passenger side, I realized I was in for something different. (I didn't mention that I had no license; he seemed uptight enough already.)

We jerked forward, until I released the emergency brake, and Mr. Weiner mashed his face in his hand.

"Are you okay?" I asked him. He nodded, and I got the car moving more or less normally. I pulled onto Superior Boulevard without incident. But Mr. Weiner had cracked a sheen. I'd only been driving for about thirty seconds, so it couldn't have been that. "Are you sick?" I said to him.

"That's r-r-right," he replied, almost shouting. Forcing a smile. "That's r-r-right, I have a *d-d-disease!*"

Both his hands were braced on the dashboard. He was breathing fast. I was afraid if I stopped suddenly he'd break his nose. I didn't know what to say. His skin stretched taut across his face, as if his cheekbones might rip through at any moment. "I'm really sorry," I said. "Can you take anything?"

"T-T-Take anything?" He grabbed my wrist, nearly sending us over the curb. "I t-t-took everything!" He smiled again, in that painful way, as if the rest of his face wanted to burst out crying, but he wouldn't let it. "My b-b-best fr-friends were J-J-Jackson Daniels and J-J-Jonathan Walker. Ring a b-b-bell?"

I didn't answer. Didn't know how to answer. Mr. Weiner twisted sideways to face me. "I kn-kn-know what you're thinking, B-B-B-Bobby. Oh, here's another b-b-boring grown-up to talk about D-D-Demon Rum."

"Demon rum?"

"It's a h-h-heavy subject, for sure," he said. So h-h-heavy, apparently, that merely addressing it sent him into stuttering fits. I didn't remember the stutter from before. Either he wasn't nervous then, or he was too busy making cuff links disappear and plucking dimes out of my nostrils to do much chatting.

"I'm n-n-not talking to you like a g-g-grown-up, Bobby. I'm

perv—a love story

over thirty, but you can t-t-trust me." He cracked another on-the-rack smile. "I've *b-b-been* there, okay?" His grin died when he saw the mystified look on my face.

A Chevy full of freaks tooled by and I could imagine what was being passed around inside. That was the car to be in. Instead, here I was, heading nowhere with the most un-laid-back human being I'd ever seen. Driving wasn't even fun. We made it onto the Fort Pitt Bridge, and I was afraid if he grabbed my wrist again we'd end up in the Allegheny. I did not want the last face I saw alive to be Mr. Weiner's.

I focused on the rear end of the bus in front of us and tried to concentrate. But Mr. Weiner still had things to say. He'd peeled his hands off the dashboard, and now sat erect. With a long sigh, he pulled a grayish hanky out of his pocket and wiped his forehead. "Alcohol was my *b-b-bag*," he announced, almost proudly, like he'd read the expression in a guidebook and wanted to work it in.

When I didn't say anything, he touched my arm again. Fortunately, we were over the bridge. The water plunge wasn't a worry. The worst we could do was pancake a pedestrian. But now *I* was jumpy. I hadn't been downtown in a while, and the place seemed mobbed. I didn't think I could handle it. People seemed to stream into the street without looking.

"B-B-Bobby," Mr. Weiner went on. "Your m-m-mother told me you had a problem."

"What?"

All I wanted to do now was park. Just stop driving. There were crowds everywhere. Unless I was hallucinating, they were all hippies. At a red light on Forbes Avenue, a parade of girls in flower-patch bell-bottoms and guys with bushy beards passed in front of the car. I wondered. I'd never been to a demonstration. The only love-ins I'd seen were in *Life* magazine. But I had a feeling. . . .

Four longhairs—I couldn't tell if they were boys or girls— skipped across the street with their arms over each other's shoulders. The one on the end—definitely, when I squinted, a girl— stared right at me. I wanted to die. I saw what *she* saw: a kid with hair that didn't come over his ears driving a suit with a crew cut. I knew what I'd think if I saw us: narcs.

Mr. Weiner slapped the dashboard. "B-B-Bobby, I *know*," he said. "Your mother told me. She said she f-f-found something. In your boot."

"Oh that." I tried to think fast. "When I left school, I mean, when I got thrown out, somebody must've put some stuff in my suitcase. Some pot. Some pills and stuff. I don't know what it is. Anyway, when I found it I didn't know what to do with it, so I stuck it in my shoe. That's what Mom found."

"L-L-Let's be honest," he said. "Do you use d-d-drugs?"

"Well," I said, knowing he had me. "I'm not gonna lie, I've done some experimenting. But I didn't like it! Y'know, not that much. . . ."

"Do you d-d-drink?"

"Drink? Never," I said. Which was not completely true, but almost. "Drinking's cornball. Only young Republicans and old people drink. I mean drink-drink, like martinis and stuff."

For some reason, this hit Mr. Weiner hard. He sagged forward in his seat, gasping "Oh my God!" Then he touched a hand to his scrawny throat. "B-b-but I'm an *alcoholic!*"

perv—a love story

He jerked back again and clamped his palms on his knees. Color flushed his waxen skin, tinting it pink. "You see, I thought. . . . I m-m-mean, when your mother . . . Oh God, I'm sorry, I've . . . I've been t-t-talking too much." He pounded both fists on his thighs. "I t-t-talk too much, that's all. Oh G-G-God. I am so sorry."

"It's okay," I said. "Really. It's okay."

I felt so bad for the man, I wanted to reassure him. Maybe get drunk so he could help me home to bed. He seemed inconsolable. I couldn't steer and deal with this weirdness at the same time.

When I spotted a fire hydrant, I pulled over. With all his other troubles, I didn't figure a parking ticket would make much difference. "Maybe we could walk," I said. "I don't think I want to drive anymore."

If Mr. Weiner heard me, he didn't show it. He was still trying to explain himself. "Bobby, I th-th-thought. . . . You see . . . In other words, I-I-I-I-I-I-I—"

He clamped a hand over his mouth to stop. With his other hand he clenched his head, right where the divots were. I couldn't help wonder if that's how he got them: talking too much, then getting mad at himself and squeezing his temples. Doing his own forceps work. It was awful and amazing to watch.

"Oh God, this is the disease!" he cried. Tears dotted his eyes. "What you're s-s-seeing right now, that's what it is. Do you understand? What I'm s-s-s-saying," he stammered, "what I'm s-s-s-saying is, I'm an alcoholic. *I lost everything.*"

Out came the hanky again, polishing his forehead.

"It's okay," I said, "really. I think it's . . . I mean . . . why don't we get out and walk around a little?"

I didn't want to sit in the car and watch him weep.

As it happened, we were catty-cornered to the Point. Point State Park. Where the Allegheny, the Monongahela, and the Ohio meet. When I was in third grade, I won an essay contest, sponsored by the Daughters of the American Revolution, on Why I Love My Country. (*"I love my country because in Russia, you can't watch what you want on TV!"*) The prize was, I got let out of school and driven by the vice principal, Miss Negretti, to read my winning entry at a ceremony at the Blockhouse. This was a shack with a plaque on it from 17-something, what was left of an old fort built where the Point was now. "William Pitt took a dump here," is what the runner-up, Billy O'Connor, whispered right before I had to get up with my essay.

I felt weird *then*—itching in the gray flannel suit my mother made me wear and forced to read to a bunch of old ladies with hair the color of blueberry popsicles. And I felt weird now—stepping out of the Rambler with Mr. Weiner, a man with a crew cut who seemed three seconds away from bawling. I thought about making a run for it, but that would have been mean. I didn't dislike Mr. Weiner, I just didn't like being seen with him. Besides, he seemed so close to the edge, I imagined him cowered on the curb, crying into his hands while longhairs threw things at him.

I forgot about everything when I heard the man on the PA. Out of nowhere, the raspy voice began to boom. "THIS WAR IS ILLEGAL! THIS WAR IS OBSCENE!" he was shouting, in a voice like the guy on the Woodstock album who said *"Okay people, everybody stay cool!"* (I wanted to go to Woodstock, but I was taking typing in summer school.) I would have liked to get closer, find out what was going on, when I noticed Mr. Weiner fishing in the glove compartment.

"L-L-Little B-B-Bobby," he sighed over his shoulder. "Walter's l-l-little Bobby. Do you remember my wife, Bobby? Do you r-r-remember Uta?"

I said I did, because he looked like he was going to pieces. Outside of a funeral or car accident, I'd never seen an adult so upset in real life. But what I really wondered about, when I saw it, was the little animal in his hands. Whatever he'd pulled out of the glove compartment, unless I was seeing things, had at one time either eaten out of a bowl or answered to "Kitty."

"Of course you remember," he said before I could get a better look. "Uta l-l-l-liked you. Uta was so b-b-beautiful. She l-l-loved *me*, but *I couldn't stop.* Do you know where I'm c-c-coming from? Are you l-l-listening here?"

"I'm listening," I said. "Really."

He might have been standing on the ledge of a building, on the fifty-eighth floor with a policeman leaning out the window trying to talk him down. I'd seen a movie like that, with William Bendix. But Mr. Weiner was in a movie of his own, and he'd brought his own costume. That's what I realized. He was holding a wig. A long-haired wig. A head of Jim Morrison hair, with some kind of white netting inside which he proceeded to lick.

"B-B-Bobby"—I watched his tongue glide over the wig's interior—"B-B-Bobby, listen to me."

Mr. Weiner's voice cracked and he held the furry thing to his chest. He spoke in a buzzy, robotic whisper, like a tracheotomy victim. For the briefest second, his stuttering stopped. "In the beginning, I t-t-took a drink," he buzzed. "And then the drink t-t-took me. Do you understand?"

I couldn't take my eyes off that hairpiece, but couldn't interrupt him, either. His divots throbbed in and out, like tiny bullfrog throats. The sound of him, and the sight of those puffing divots, made replying impossible. After a few deep breaths, Mr. Weiner got going again. Now the buzzing was gone but the stuttering came back worse than ever.

"I c-c-c-couldn't even g-g-get to your f-f-f-f-father's funeral, and your father m-m-meant so much to me. Do you understand? When I joined the Public Defender's office, everybody looked at your d-d-dad like he was, I don't know, M-M-Martin Luther King or something. A white Martin Luther King. Not that he l-l-led m-m-marches or anything. But he had this h-h-holiness about him. Like he didn't care what h-h-happened to him. He didn't even care what he w-wore. It used to d-d-drive your p-p-poor m-m-mother crazy, I know."

As he talked about my father, his stutter faded. An odd light came into his eyes.

"All your father cared about was that every mother whose little k-kid got run over by a city bus, every Negro who got thrown in jail for assaulting an officer when you knew the cop was two hundred pounds and the Negro was some scared twenty-three-year-old who looked like he couldn't s-s-lap his own shadow . . . every underdog who was out there feeling lost and hopeless with the Big Guns of the world lined up against them, your father wanted all of them to know *they weren't alone*. He believed everyone deserved a voice."

Mr. Weiner stopped and licked his lips. He wiped his soaking

perv—a love story

forehead with the back of a seersucker sleeve. He saw me staring at him, the hairpiece dangling from his hand like a little dead thing, and the stuttering started up again.

"Do you understand what I'm saying, Bobby? He l-l-loved the law. Your father used to say, and I'll never forget this, he used to say the l-l-law was a blanket designed to provide warmth for everybody. N-N-Not just rich people, or c-c-corporations, or the g-g-government. But the th-th-thing is"—this troubled laugh burst out of him, and he grabbed my collar, holding on, so that his waxen face hovered no more than an inch or two away from me, and I could see the water welling in the corner of his eyes— "the th-thing is, your father gave warmth to me. I mean . . . he made me feel w-w-welcome. See, I didn't st-st-stutter so much then, except when I had to speak in court. That's the f-f-funny thing. And everybody else in the office, these supposed l-l-liberals, they *l-l-laughed* at me. Which was okay. I was u-u-used to it. But they wouldn't eat lunch with me. They wouldn't invite me to their h-h-homes. Except for your dad. He made me his sp-sp-special project. He t-t-taught me things."

Here he smiled, through his tears, revealing a set of teeth so perfect it made his stutter that much more peculiar.

"L-l-like, 'when a client walks into your office,' he told me once, 'don't see them as a problem you have to solve. That's what most lawyers do, you know.' He said, 'Always view them as a whole or-or-organism, as unique, as a h-h-human being. Most important, d-d-don't ever talk about their situation right away. No m-m-matter how urgent it is. Ask about their dr-dreams,' he said. 'Ask what they l-l-like to do with their kids. R-r-respect the *person.* . . . Because th-th-these people have been f-f-fucked by the system their whole lives.' "

Mr. Weiner smiled again and let go of my collar. He looked into my eyes, to make sure I'd heard him. I wondered when he was finally going to slap on the toupee.

"It was the only time I ever heard your d-d-dad say 'fuck,' and it was so f-f-funny coming from him. But it was the only t-t-time he had to say it, you know?"

I said I knew, and at the same time liked my father in a whole new way. Liked him not for being such a good guy—I *knew* he was a *good guy*, that was one of the most oppressive facts of my existence, that I'd never be as *good* as he was—but because he was a good guy who said "fuck" when he had to. I loved him for that, and had a sense, when I heard Mr. Weiner's story, that maybe he'd love me, too. Even now. Even in the middle of the not so good, not so lovable version of myself I seemed to be occupying these days. He wouldn't see me as a *problem*, the way Mom did. He'd see me as a human being, a young human being with hopes and dreams and all the rest of that greeting card cat-puke you kind of want to believe in but can't because it's been so lame-ified by school assemblies and bullshit political speeches that just hearing those kinds of words makes you want to smack whoever's using them.

Watching Mr. Weiner, I figured if my father could take this divot-skulled stuttering wreck and treat him special, treat him with love, then he'd be able to take me, his fucked-up, panty-sniffing, prep-school-reject son and love me, too. Maybe love me even more.

"He did so much for th-th-this young attorney," Mr. Weiner continued, almost wailing, "and now your mother tells me y-y-you're as messed up as I am!"

He shook his head, then leaned in and jerked the rearview

perv—a love story

mirror in his direction. After that, incredibly, he gently placed the long-hair wig on top of his crew cut, sniffling as he adjusted it just so.

"THIS WAR IS NO LONGER JUST ABOUT *VIETNAM*," the voice from the PA was blaring, "THIS WAR IS ABOUT *KENT STATE*. THIS WAR IS ABOUT *ATTICA*. THIS WAR IS ABOUT EVERY ONE OF US TRYING TO *LIVE FREE OF FAS-CIST OPPRESSION!!*"

I turned back to Mr. Weiner. He was still sitting there talking. "I'm not b-b-blaming you," he said, apparently satisfied that he looked enough unlike himself to leave the car. "We all need some kind of r-r-r-relief."

Now I was half in, half out of the Rambler. But the urgency in his eyes made me nervous. I flashed on Coach Ponish, whose favorite saying was, *There's no deodorant for desperation.* Something desperate was definitely steaming off of Mr. Weiner when he finally stepped out and locked his door.

"R-R-Ready to go? Looks like a d-d-demonstration."

"You're wearing that?" I had to say something. I couldn't help myself. A boy in a Nixon mask jostled me, then flashed a peace sign. Mr. Weiner flashed one back.

"See," he said, "it works. S-s-so many of my clients are N-N-N-N-Negroes or l-l-longhairs, I've learned that this makes it eas-ier. They tr-tr-trust me."

In spite of myself, I was fascinated. "What about when you go to court?"

"M-M-Most just plead out. They n-n-n-never get to court."

"But what about the ones that do? What happens when you have to, like, see a judge?"

He shrugged. "I t-t-take it off."

"Well, what about your clients?"

"They're s-s-surprised," he said. And then: "I'm tr-tr-trying to change the system from within."

Five minutes later, we were strolling among Real Hippies. Ahead of us loomed a makeshift platform, no more than a pile of crates and boards, which someone had set up in front of the Blockhouse. There were some policemen around the edge of the crowd. Two cops, slapping their batons off their palms, stood on either side of the little stage. They both eyed a guy in a cowboy hat who was up there clapping and making out with a pair of girls in granny skirts. Behind him, a short Negro with the biggest Afro I'd ever seen blew into a flute.

I guessed it was the longhaired cowboy who'd been shouting about Kent State and Attica. He whipped off his hat and slapped it on one of the granny girls. Then he shook out his hair, which came down his back, and pointed at the cops with the batons. "We're not here to fight, Mr. Pork-man. We're here to love!" The girls ate this up, and started kissing him all over again.

I wondered what it would be like to be him, to be King of the Hippies, just for a night, instead of living with my mother and hanging out with Mr. Weiner. One problem was my hair. My hair wouldn't grow long. It just got fat. Just frizzed out, fatter and thicker, sticking out sideways and never reaching my shoulders. Until my head was shaped like the Ace of Spades.

I had a feeling, if I didn't get a haircut for a year, I wouldn't be able to fit through doors.

One of the girls shouted, "Right on!" into the mike, and sounded like she was about nine. Everywhere I looked kids not much older than me were lying on the grass, passing joints, playing folk guitars or just moving their heads back and forth, like something was going on inside them they didn't need to talk about, because everybody else knew what it was and felt it, too.

Not far from us, a circle of maybe a dozen people sat with their arms over each others' shoulders. Somebody passed around a bottle. A redhead with a daisy chain in her hair took quick, rabbity puffs from a roach clip.

I'd noticed, by now, that Mr. Weiner's seersucker suit was getting stares. But I couldn't tell if people thought it was cool or not. He kept flashing the peace sign to everybody. To my surprise, people flashed it back. I kept expecting somebody to run up and shout, *"Are you kidding, that's a wig! You're a lawyer with a crew cut!"* But no one did.

Mostly, looking at the circle, what I felt was kind of sad. I couldn't help thinking, *How do you get to be part of that?* Did they know each other before? Did they live in the same crash pad? Way inside my chest, I felt a giant sadness. I wasn't sure I could really ever be a good hippie. I was too shy.

"B-b-back to what I was saying," Mr. Weiner said, stepping around a throbbing lump I realized was a boy and girl in a sleeping bag. His hair fell over *hers*—or vice versa—creating a seething, wavy mass at one end of the army green canvas.

"There's n-n-nothing to be ashamed of," Mr. Weiner continued, when he was directly above the writhing couple.

For a second I thought he was talking to them. As though, on top of everything else, the wig had turned him into some kind of free love advocate. "A real *svinger*," as Mom would say. That scared me more than anything. I was relieved when, settling beside a concrete bench a few yards farther on, he turned back to me and finished his thought. "With what you've been through, you need relief, t-t-too. There's n-n-nothing to be ashamed of. Men are al-lowed to f-f-feel sad. It's ok-k-k-*kay*." He started sniffling, as if to prove the point, and I was instantly embarrassed for him.

Two girls in floppy hats and a third with amazing blond hair and a guitar were wandering toward us. I wondered what they'd think of a weeping older guy in wig and seersucker. And if Mr. Weiner would understand when I claimed I'd never seen him before in my life.

While I pondered, he forgot about his handkerchief and ran his wrist under his nose. "Your father, my G-G-God! Such a tragic loss!" He shook his head, careful to hold on to his Jim Morrison hair. *"And a st-st-st-streetcar!"*

This seemed to hurt him most of all. The streetcar factor. I had a feeling, if Dad had just jumped off a bridge, or stuck his head in an oven, Mr. Weiner might have been able to shrug it off. But he couldn't. That streetcar got to him. The park lights came on, brightening the dusk, and I watched Mr. Weiner sigh and fade from pink to yellow. I'd read somewhere that squids showed emotion by changing color. What if Mr. Weiner was part squid, part human? In *Squid-Man*, the movie, I'd be the Eager Young Biology Student. He'd be the Top-Secret Government Project Gone Horribly Awry. Only Bobby Stark could foil his plan to transform Western Pennsylvania into a giant aquarium, run by Evil Squid People.

His stuttering pitch aborted these thoughts before I got to the climactic battle scene. *All Stark had was a broken speargun, and plenty of guts!*

"F-F-Few things I'd like to d-d-discuss, B-B-Bob."

"Fire away," I said.

Then I zoned again.

                              *   *   *

Whatever the original point of the demonstration, it had broken into scattered pockets of hippies, each hunched in its own
little circle. What was it about hippies and circles? The girls with
the folk guitar and floppy hats lolled on the grass a few feet
away. The blonde was picking out "Hey Jude." I saw another
group step giggling over the humping sleeping bag couple, and
tried to imagine feeling so casual about sex. Was it because they
were used to people just up and balling wherever they felt like
it? Or was it because they had so much sex themselves it was no
big deal? I could only dream about a life like that.

   Mr. Weiner was still talking about something, and I let it drift
until I heard him, his hands cupped around his mouth, calling to
the three girls to "boogie over and join us."

   I couldn't believe it. I didn't know whether to be mortified or
thrilled. The "Hey Jude" girl, whose tresses fell to her waist like
the nude prepube on the cover of that Blind Faith album, before
it was banned, actually raised her eyes and smiled. So did her
two friends, both of whom had been staring at the sky since they
hit the lawn.

   I didn't get how people could be so friendly. The blond guitar
girl yelled over at us, "Moonlight and Tammy are tripping. They
can't talk."

   "B-B-Bummer!" Mr. Weiner called back. "H-H-Happened to
me on blotter at Woodstock. Br-bring 'em over anyway and we'll
groove!"

   I couldn't believe what I'd just heard. More remarkable, Guitar
Girl stood up immediately, her two out-of-it friends following
wobbly, and hurried over to join us. No sooner had her friends
sort of tumbled onto the grass, and she'd sat down with her

guitar—cross-legged, in a single movement, like a genie return-
ing to the lamp—than Mr. Weiner started up again.

"I was t-t-telling Bobby," he said, clapping me on the back.
"We don't n-n-need to get relief through dr-dr-drugs. That's what
they *w-w-want* us to do."

The guitar-blonde shifted her glance back and forth between
Mr. Weiner and me. I spotted the Zig Zag Man tattooed on her
arm, and wanted to show her my rose. I wanted to explain that
I hardly knew this crazy seersucker guy, that I was really like *her*,
but Mr. Weiner just plowed right on. Working himself up further
with every word.

"We're n-n-not really *escaping* with our m-m-marijuana, with
our uppers and d-d-downers, with our ha-ha-hallucinators."

"Hallucinators. Far *out!*" The blonde pulled out a pack of Zig
Zags, then plastered a paper on her tongue while she went in
another pocket and scooped out a bud the size of a walnut. Then
she massaged the bud between her fingers, crumbling a fat cat-
erpillar of grass onto the paper and rolling it up.

Impressed as I was—she could have given lessons—I confess
I was afraid Mr. Weiner would make some kind of citizen's arrest.
Drive her to jail so he could switch into his Public Defender
mode and get her out again. Instead, he just drank her in with
his mouth hanging open.

"These are f-f-fake salvations!" he blurted. He grabbed my
hand, and it was like touching melting candles. Moonlight and
Tammy had begun to giggle quietly.

I was dying. The one time in my life I managed to get next
to some hippie girls, and I was trapped with a stuttering old guy.
I couldn't bear to speculate what they thought about me. Somewhere across the park, people had picked up a chant. It sounded

perv—a love story

like *"HELL-O WE WANT MOE!"* But why that? Was it some Flower Power code? By the time my heebie-jeebied brain caught on it was *"HELL NO, WE WON'T GO!"* it died out again, and Mr. Weiner had started up.

"Don't light that!" he said to the girl with the grass. She had the joint in her mouth, and the lighter halfway there. I realized Mr. Weiner was still holding my hand, and quickly broke free.

Forcing his drum-tight skin into a grin, he flapped at his jacket until he found what he wanted. It was a light blue pamphlet. The cover featured a health-book-style drawing of a man in a suit and tie hunched over a desk with his head in his hands. A woman who looked like Beaver Cleaver's mom stood next to him, her hand on his shoulder. A boy and girl who might have been Dick and Jane hovered on either side of their unhappy Dad, Junior's arm slung across Sis's shoulder.

Mr. Weiner waved the pamphlet in front of us, and the two tripping girls began to laugh. For a second, it was laughter-laughter; then it mounted to great, howling gasps that had them clutching each other and rolling on the grass like lady wrestlers. When the blond girl with the joint picked up her folk guitar, I knew it was over.

"W-W-Wait!" Mr. Weiner pleaded. "Please. Th-Th-These are 'The Twenty Questions.' "

"The what?" said the guitar girl, wiping her eyes. She'd lit up the joint anyway, and I felt myself salivate watching her inhale with a deep, arching toke that left her chin pointing at the sky and the joint just burning in her hand, available, like it didn't care if I grabbed it or not.

" 'Twenty Questions,' " Mr. Weiner repeated. "It's a quiz. If you answer any of them yes, there's a good chance you're one of us."

The blonde flipped her hair over her shoulders, then turned to blow the longest stream of smoke I'd ever seen directly at me. "I am definitely not one of *you*," she sneered. Then, handing the joint to one of the tripping girls and taking the other by the arm, she uncrossed her legs and stood up with her guitar. "Come on," she said, "let's find those Penn State guys with the hash oil."

I watched the three of them leave like a man seeing the last ship he'll ever see sail off from a desert island. I wondered what it was that kept me from running after them. Mr. Weiner must have read my thoughts. "You're d-d-doing the right thing," he said, and for the first time I wanted to cry as much as he did.

"Go ahead, let it out," he said, right before I reached up and snatched his wig.

"Why even wear it," I cried, "if you're going to act so retarded?"

"Th-Th-at's okay," he said. "Go with the r-r-rage. G-G-Get it out. We f-f-feel too much. That's the problem with us. We f-f-feel more than other people."

"Who's *us*?" I hissed. "There is no *us*. All I feel is pissed off." The more time I spent with him, the more the extent of my father's kindness impressed me. The guy really shrunk on you.

Mr. Weiner sputtered something, but it went right by me.

I must have snagged a semi-buzz from that smoke in my face, and started freaking in my head about Michelle's robes. I was suddenly obsessed with the idea of sticking my head underneath them. I wondered if Krishnas wore special underwear, like Mormons. Then wondered, with a panicked flutter, if I was becoming some kind of underwear freak. The wig felt damp, which freaked me even more, and I dropped it back on the ground. It wouldn't have surprised me if it scampered off.

I caught a glance of Mr. Weiner, moving his lips in a kind of giggly weep. *Paranoia.* I began obsessing harder on Michelle. I wanted to believe it was a sign, running into her at the airport. I needed to feel there were cosmic forces at work to reunite us. (Despite, I had to admit, never having been united in the first place. But still . . .)

I'd found four Burnelkas in the phone book that afternoon, and picked up the phone a dozen times. But I never called. Fear had me by the throat. I stared hard at the face of the non-wigged lawyer in front of me. The man was a girl repellent. But it wasn't just that . . . *What if,* I thought, as he muttered something about "letting go and letting God," *what if Mr. Weiner hailed from some secret outreach wing of the Hare Krishnas?* Maybe they had plainclothes Hindus, decked out to lull you into a false sense of security. *But why?* It made no sense whatsoever. Now I desperately regretted not taking a hit off the blond girl's pot. If just a whiff had got me this wrecked and paranoid, imagine what an actual puff would have done. . . .

A waft of sweet hash drifted by, and I wanted to float after it like Wimpy levitating at the scent of a hamburger. There was a bright light jerking around by the Blockhouse, but other than that the park had emptied. Just a few clumps of hippies smoking or laughing in their private circles.

"Okay," Mr. Weiner was saying when I tuned back in, "l-l-let's get back to those questions."

"What?"

"The Twenty Questions. R-R-Remember? They're put out by AA."

"The Auto Club?"

"That's Triple A. This is Alcoholics Anonymous."

The strain of being enthusiastic stretched his skin even tighter over his skull.

"Okey-d-d-doke, Bobby. 'Question number one. Do you ever drink by yourself?'" Oddly, he didn't stutter when he read. "G-G-Go 'head and change d-d-drink to 'use drugs,' 'smoke marijuana,' or whatever f-f-feels comfortable. It's a b-b-big tent."

"Okay," I replied. "No."

Mr. Weiner shot me a doubtful look, then read the next question from his little blue pamphlet. Despite his general nervousness, his voice took on a forced, professional quality, like the man who narrated those "Your Friend, the Policeman" films they made us sit through in social studies.

"F-F-Fine," he said. "'Question Two. Do you ever drink,' I mean use d-d-drugs, 'to get rid of unpleasant feelings?'"

"Never," I said, without thinking about it. That whiff of supergrass was wearing off, and I was getting grumpy.

"All right. 'Question Three. Do you think about drinking'— i.e., using d-d-drugs—'on the job?'"

"Nope." I answered, fixing my eyes directly on Mr. Weiner's. This might have been fun if it weren't such a nightmare. Grunts and squeals reached us through the darkness. I made out the sleeping bag couple still at it on the park lawn. Some people!

With much sighing, my inquisitor folded his pamphlet and slid it back in his jacket. "B-B-Bobby," he said sadly, dramatically, "we're only as s-s-sick as our secrets. How can God remove our d-d-d-defects if we d-d-don't admit what they are?"

"How should I know?" I shrugged. "I guess if he's God he can read minds. I mean, he's God, right?" This was something I'd actually thought about. "Of course if *I* knew what *you* were think-

perv—a love story

ing, and you knew what *I* was thinking, we'd probably have heart attacks. It's like X-Ray Vision. You think it'd be far out seeing through women's dresses, but who knows? It might drive you nuts. Superman blew his brains out, right?"

"Oh, B-B-Bobby," was all Mr. Weiner said. Then he staggered to his feet and announced he had to "urinate."

I waited on the lawn, listening to the puckered sounds of the couple making love fifty feet away, the laughter and strummed guitars from across the park. I would have probably stayed like that—flat on my back, stargazing, swiping at bugs—except for the sudden gagging sounds behind my back. I wasn't sure where Mr. Weiner had gone, but followed the sound till I came to a fat pillar propping up a bust of William Pitt. I stepped behind it, and I saw him. Mr. Weiner, head thrown back, one hand propped on Pitt's three-cornered hat and one tipping a pint of Four Roses down his throat.

"Bobby," he cried, before I could sneak away. "Bobby, wait!" He shook the last drops out of the bottle and staggered toward me. "You understand, don't you? You have a problem. *I* have a problem."

Part of me wanted to run away. To just leave him there. But the man was so earnest, so *pathetic*, another part of me wanted to pat him on the head. Tell him it was all right. That his secret, if that's what it was, was safe with me. What did I care if the man drank? He looked like he *needed* a drink.

Before I could get anything out, Mr. Weiner grabbed my shoulders. His breath could have removed stains. His eyes and nose were both watering. "Don't you see," he sobbed, "it's okay! We're not bad people trying to get good. We're sick people trying to get well." He squeezed me harder. "Don't judge by *me*, Bobby. The program works. Really!"

I pushed him a little, to get him out of my face, and he fell backward against the Pitt statue. His eyes were wild now. I reached down to help him up, and he clutched my hand with both of his. I wanted to tell him I was sorry. I didn't mean to knock him down. I didn't mean anything. But the way he squeezed my fingers, on his knees in front of me, I couldn't open my mouth.

"Did you notice?" he laughed, his chuckles escaping between ragged sobs. "Did you notice? I'm not stuttering." He let go of me to throw out his arms, like Al Jolson doing "My Mammy." "I'm normal now! When I drink, *I'm normal!*"

"That's great. So why don't you just drink?" I asked him.

"Because," he said, backhanding the spittle from his lips, "once I start, I don't stop. And then I can't talk at all."

"Tough choice," I said, somewhat stupidly. That's when I noticed the strange quiver affecting his lips, the way his cheeks had begun to puff and vibrate. "Hey—"

Luckily, I juked out of the way before he vomited. Some of it splashed my shoes, and I used his wig to get it off. I figured he could get it dry-cleaned.

"Now do you understand?" he pleaded, his voice a kind of rasping whisper as he palmed the last strands of gruel from his gums. "Now do you see why I miss your father so much?"

I said, "Yeah," though in fact I didn't really see what my father or anybody else could do for him. Unless Dad was that rare breed of human who didn't mind being puked on or watching a man turn himself to shit. Even then, I didn't see what he could

perv—a love story

offer a guy like Mr. Weiner beyond simple kindness. But maybe that was enough.

"Were you always—" I began, but he cut me off.

"No, I wasn't. Before, it was *ma-na-gea-ble*," he pronounced carefully, getting the word out with some difficulty, "but after your dad passed away . . ."

Instead of finishing the sentence, he reached over with both hands and pinched my cheeks. The stink on his fingers was blinding. "Oh God, Bobby, seeing you! Seeing *you*," he blubbered, and broke into a sniffly laugh. "Now I guess you know my little secret. I pretended to your mom that I could help her little boy, but what I really wanted, what I really *hoped*, was that you might be able to help me. But you can't. Can you, Bobby?"

He looked at me so sadly, a part of me wanted to answer yes. But I didn't want to lie. For once in my life that seemed worse than telling the truth. "If there's anything . . ." I said. "I mean, what could *I* do?"

Mr. Weiner threw his head back, giggled at the stars, and brought his wet-eyed gaze back to me with a lip-chewing leer. "Just m-m-make me go away," he said. "That's all I want, to make *me* go away."

The scary part is, I knew what he meant. And I knew what it felt like to feel that way. I felt the same way the majority of time I was awake to think about it.

"That's kind of tricky," I told him, catching him as he pitched forward. (My reflexes, for no known reason, remained lightning fast.) "But if I can't do that, you know, I can at least talk to you when you need to."

"That's okay," he sighed, with what sounded like sudden clarity, but turned out to be the last words out of him before he collapsed entirely. "By the time I need to, I can't talk anyway."

It took some doing lugging Mr. Weiner across the park, and after I'd managed to persuade the second concerned policeman that I had not, in fact, mugged him, I finally dumped his seersuckered bulk in the backseat of the Rambler and listened to him retch all the way back to my mother's condo. I turned the FM station up pretty loud, but not even Cream could drown out a man who can't talk when he's expressing himself.

I drove Mr. Weiner's car back over the bridge and left it in the Superior Market parking lot. It was a short walk down the hill to the condo. Mom was still awake when I got home. I didn't say anything. She seemed to know what happened anyway.

"Okay, I'm sorry," she said. She bit her knuckles, then tore her hand out of her mouth to press my cheek. "He was a good friend of your father's, but he's different now. I thought he was more stable." Her tone grew defensive, then worked its way to indignant. "I only dated him once, all right?" She paused to rub teeth marks from the skin of her hand. "He was a mess, but he wasn't so tense. AA really helped him. I guess the bottom fell out when the city fired him."

"Wait a second," I said. "You *dated* him?"

"That's right. He called me up. Is there something wrong with that?"

"Well, no. I just . . . No, it's fine. It's great. He's better than Ned Friendly, anyway." It was all so sad . . . "I didn't know he'd been fired. He didn't say."

perv—a love story

I don't know why all this bothered me. It just did. If there was any sentence you didn't want to hear from your mother, "I dated him" had to top the list.

Mom smiled and brushed something from the shoulders of my denim workshirt. "He took me to the Ice Capades. They were doing *Peter Pan.* He cried whenever Tinker Bell showed up. I should have known."

"Jesus."

"Don't Jesus *me,* mister." Her smile dropped. She spun around to slam the brass chain-lock on the door and spun back again. "I'm not the one who got tossed out of prep school."

"Oh, here we go."

Listening to her, my tattoo began to throb. This had started happening when certain subjects were broached: prep school, the future, the entire idea of Mom dating. *Especially* the idea of Mom dating. I pictured her—the thought wouldn't go away—eyes glazed, Kent dangling from her lips, shiny dress hiked up and her thighs wishboned around Ned Friendly's giant red face while Mr. Weiner stammered, *"T-T-Take it, b-bitch!"* and ground his waxy yellow organ into her from behind. (Maybe the two men would kiss—I'd seen that in a *Swedish Love* magazine Tennie snuck back from Manhattan.) For some reason, in my itching tattoo vision, they were tangling in Mom's car, steaming the bubbled-up back window of her Barracuda. This made it even worse. I had to dig my nails in my thumbs to keep from scratching my rose. I could hardly breathe. If I didn't know anything else, I knew I couldn't sit through another round of advice from another man who was not my father. After Ned Friendly and Mr. Weiner, I could only imagine what the next guy would be like, and the one after that. If Dolores's hubby, the Rose Marie freak, was still alive, she'd probably have dragged him in, too. The whole idea was curling my toes.

"What is wrong with you?" Mom shouted, snapping her fingers in front of my eyes. "You act like you've got a salamander in your shirt. Are you drinking cough syrup again?"

"I am *not* drinking cough syrup."

She was referring to the time, in ninth grade, I'd been sent home bleeding from the face and tearing at myself. That morning, I'd downed a bottle of Tussirex that Stuart Cornfeld, the sloe-eyed kid with the locker next to mine, had stolen from his grandfather, a retired coal miner who Stuart said was a "lunger." We mixed it with ginger ale and spent the next three hours curled in the metal shop closet, scratching and cackling until our cheeks hurt. I didn't realize how much I'd scratched until the cackling stopped and I saw that I'd tiger-striped my yellow oxford cloth in blood.

Mom licked a napkin and dabbed it off the edge of my mouth, catching a crumb. She'd been doing this since I was two, and it drove me just as insane now as it did then.

"Stop it," I cried, and slapped her hand away. "I'm not a child, all right?"

"You're not?" Mom clapped a hand over her mouth. She opened her eyes wide in mock surprise. "Oh, that's *right*. You're a man of the world now. My son the Latin lover. You're a regular Cesar Romero."

With this, she swooped up the clamshell ashtray and stomped down the hall to her bedroom, stopping at her door to take another shot.

"Did I mention that we won't be getting a refund from Hale? Why no, thanks to your little barber's daughter, we'll be paying

perv—a love story

for some other lucky boy. Isn't that nice? I'm living on your father's pension now, and I get to pay for some other boy's education."

"Jeez," was all I could think to say. But it wasn't enough. Mom had a way of pumping herself up once she got started. It didn't matter if you said anything or not. If you tried to argue, that got her mad. If your kept your mouth shut, that got her madder.

"You want to be a man, why don't you wash a goddamn dish? Would that kill you? Or maybe, just for the novelty, you could take the garbage out once in a while. You'll like the incinerator, it'll take that stink of marijuana off your clothes. Is there some law I don't know about that says you have to wear the same shirt every goddamn day? The same work shirt, no less? Not that anyone could accuse you of working."

"Mom, listen . . ."

"No, *I'm* talking now. *You* listen. This can *not* go on, do you understand me? This can NOT go on!"

I saw what was coming, but once it started there was no way to slow it down. All you could do was watch. Mom dropped the ashtray she was carrying—she'd pace like that, for hours, relighting Kents and flicking the ashes with her right hand into the clamshell ashtray she carried in her left—and began pulling her hair. She worked both hands around a hank of perm fluffed over her forehead, yanking her face up toward the ceiling, then switched to a clump in back and tugged forward, driving her chin into her chest.

"Walter he hates me! Walter he hates me! Walter he hates me," she ranted, exactly as she had at my father's funeral. In public it was gruesome, but alone with her, like this, it was awful in a different

way, in a *no-one-out-there-knows-what-goes-on-in-here* kind of way. Her hysterics were our little secret.

I kept thinking how, up and down her condo hall, people were watching TV, people were sleeping, chatting, making snacks. . . . None of them knew, none of them *could* know that fifty, sixty feet away, their neighbor Mrs. Stark stood vibrating with foam on her lips and her fingers dug in her own scalp: a not-quite-normal woman twisting her features because she could barely speak, she was so crazed, so sick with grief that it just leaked out, drop by drop, all day and all night. Until, once in a while, the leak swelled to a torrent and the torrent gushed out of her and all over me.

"You'll never be a man," she croaked, like one of the three witches in the movie version of *Macbeth* they showed at school. "Do you hear me? You will never ever ever be the man your father was— *and he was not even a man.* That's the God's honest truth. He was weak. Like you. That's where you get it. *Pro bono* this, *pro bono* that . . . Leave your wife at home; eat steak once a month because some *Negro* boy who sticks a kitchen knife in his sister can't afford a real lawyer and *you care.* . . . He cared and cared. He cared so much he cared himself to death. But you don't, do you? You don't care at all. About anything. Not even yourself. You don't even do that, do you, Misery-guts? That's what you are. My son the Misery-guts. You think it's easy for me? *DO YOU?* Do you think a woman my age even has a chance? You are on the brink of your entire life and you won't be happy until you throw it away. Until you smash it right into the garbage can, just to get back at me. Well, I don't care anymore. Do you hear me? I do not care. I have cried and slaved and cleaned up after you for

perv—a love story

the last time. Can you understand that? I ... *DON'T* ... *CARE* ..."

When she'd run out of words, or the energy to spew them, she fell against the wall for a second and stayed there, breathing heavily but not sobbing, until she slid down and began plucking spilled cigarette butts off the carpet and dropping them, one by one, back into the tarnished silver clam.

"I'm going to bed," she said wearily, when she'd dragged herself up again. "Don't fall asleep with the light on, your brain'll think it's daytime."

Five hours later, I crashed out on the Castro Convertible—as I'd been doing since sliming back to Pittsburgh—without even bothering to open it up. I don't know what Mom used on her sheets, but they always itched. When I'd try to show her the map of rashes on my thighs and stomach, she'd say, "Try a shower," and leave it at that. So I stayed on the velour. Mostly I watched TV and jerked off. Or tried to. It was tough sledding trying to work up a boner for Greer Garson or Bette Davis, who seemed to be in every movie that came on after two. Throw in the constant threat of a Mom-event, and you're not exactly in one-hand heaven. More than once, she'd trundle past at 3:43 or 4:15 to reload her cheese 'n' cracker plate, and I had to be vigilant.

When I *could* jerk off, I made sure to do it in my sock, like Dolores's husband, the Rose Marie fan. I'd shove myself in a sweat-crusted all-cotton up to the toe, squirting inside so I could toss it right in the laundry. As long as I didn't forget and trot to our shared toilet with footwear dangling from my penis—a mistake I made one pot-muddled midnight, when Mom, thankfully, was too phenobarbitaled to notice—it was an effective technique.

Only once, on the Chronic Masturbation Front, did the secret deed land me in some scalding water. That was years earlier, at the DOP—The Dawn of Puberty. I was twelve and three quarters. New to the practice, but already dedicated, I'd begun to experience shooting pains in my penis. It felt like I was trying to pass wet Brillo pads. This got so excruciating I told my parents, who promptly made an appointment with a urologist.

I can still remember the man's name—Dr. Mushnik—along with the curious slant of his smile when we met. It was as if he wanted to smirk but held back, out of deference to my parents, both of whom accompanied me to his office. Doctor M. worked out of a modern, three-story medical building full of nothing but urologists and dermatologists. (I prayed I'd never need both at once.)

On the elevator, I found myself gazing at the other riders, trying to guess their disease. If they didn't have flagrant eczema or elephant hide, I assumed they suffered some below-the-belt leakage. (I'd spotted "adult diapers" in the drugstore while shoplifting No Doz, and always wondered if they came with "adult playpens." Now I got it.)

In the waiting room, the peppy oldster in the chair next to mine nudged me and pointed to an ad for "bladder pads" in a medical journal. "There's yer happy tomorrow. There's yer Swingin' Sixties." He tittered and wagged a finger in my face. "You take my advice, you'll keep an eye on yer teeth and yer plumbin'." He unbuttoned his carcoat and tapped a bulge just under his concave chest. "Yessir, stuck me in a bag, that's what they did. Ileostomy," he exclaimed, like it was the Congressional Medal of Honor. "I don't even know when I'm peein'. How ya like them apples?"

Before I could think of a reply—or flee to a corner of the waiting room, in case he splashed—an unbelievably pretty nurse stuck her head out and called my name. She looked like Joni Mitchell. It was demoralizing having my parents there, but since they weren't speaking to each other it was not as bad as it could have been. They'd fought in the car over what they always fought about: My mother nagged my father about being the only non-rich lawyer in the world. And my father, gentle as he was, could not keep from asking why my mother had to wear a sequined dress to a urologist's office.

"Not that you don't look great," he said, in that sad way he had, not wanting to hurt anybody, ever, if he could help it. "As a matter of fact, darling, you look *too* good! You'd be the prettiest girl at the ball. Except we're not going to a ball. We're taking our son to a urologist." His face broke into a wistful smile, and he suspended the diplomacy for one rare moment. "It's . . . *peculiar*, honey."

My mother was not as gentle as my father. She wasn't gentle at all. *"Peculiar?"* she lashed back at him, scowling from behind the wheel. (No matter what, my mother drove; she thought my father swerved.) "What's peculiar, *honey*, is that I helped put you through law school, and now we're living on hot dogs and beans."

Such was the ho-hum scenario all the way to Dr. Mushnik's.

So, once we reached the urology office, I was not exactly unhappy my parents had reached the nonspeaking stage. A half-dozen patients—including my friend the bag man—crowded the off-white canvas chairs. I was grateful that, on top of everything else, I did not have to hang there and feel my cheeks burn while my mother and father bickered in front of them. I'd already spent an enormous chunk of my life playing deaf in public, staring hard at menus or pretending to study the swirls on my fingertips while Mom shouted and Dad smiled his wan smile, practicing his own brand of passive Zen. I was thrilled to just sit in peace, more or less.

But what happened is, the doctor, a lanky, handsome, and deeply tanned fellow with nostrils the size of quarters, invited us all into the examining room. (I wondered, in a cringing way, if those nostrils had anything to do with sniffing out "plumbing problems," and tried to eighty-six the thought from my brain.) He asked me a few general questions, then politely requested that my parents wait outside. Though they still weren't speaking, they went out of their way to appear "happy" in front of strangers. Almost in tandem, they said it would be *fine*, they didn't mind *at all* if he talked to me alone. Mom bent and planted a smooch on my forehead. Dad gave my shoulder a "manly" squeeze. They may even have held hands on the way out. The title of this play was "Happy Family Goes to the Doctor's Office."

Once they'd left, the handsome, wide-nostriled urologist had me mount the exam table and pull down my pants. He made his face into that semi-smirk again and said "Undies, too, boss."

I was, like I say, around thirteen, and already terrified that my practice of early and insistent masturbation had somehow stunted the growth of my dick, the way smoking cigarettes was said to stunt the rest of you. To make matters worse, I could not tear my eyes from the colorful, cutaway penis poster on the wall. Up there, the thing looked like an elongated layer cake, complete with urethra, sperm sac, and glans—a batch of words that all but made me gag. I did not even like knowing I *had* this stuff, let alone that things could go horribly wrong with it. Plus which, the organ in the cake drawing loomed proportionately larger than my own. By comparison, I was a ladyfinger.

The disgrace literally had me shaking. Burning shame over the

perv—a love story

girth of my newly furred member was matched by a terrible urge to ask an expert, straight out, if I'd ruined myself forever by chronic self-abuse. In his casual manner, Dr. Mushnik asked if I'd mind removing my hands from in front of my genitals. It wasn't even their modest size that had me cupping myself. By now I was a veteran of shrinkage. It was their condition. I had, to my bottomless horror, been unable to resist playing with myself that very morning. And that extra-long tug—it was hard to concentrate, knowing I'd be showing myself ninety minutes later to an expert who would no doubt know—had left the underside of my organ puffed and swollen, like the bags under Mom's eyes when she hit the Blue Nun and Miltown extra hard.

Dr. Mushnik touched the tender flesh, nodding as he bunched it between his remarkably well-scrubbed fingers. I could soak them in lye, and still never get my own fingernails that clean. But it wasn't my fingernails that worried me.

The doctor let go of my organ, giving it a sort of good-bye pat as he let it flop against the examination table. He regarded me for a few minutes. Then he tossed out two words to see how I'd react. "Heavy petting?"

"Heavy petting?" I echoed. I remembered the phrase from a brief dip into *Pat Boone's Tips for Teens*, one of the laugh riots in the Hygiene Section of the local library. I used to read it periodically, reciting "Dating Do's and Don'ts" out loud and annoying other readers.

Mistaking my confusion for shyness, Dr. Mushnik gave me a punch on the shoulder and rephrased his query. "You're lucky. In my day, none of the gals put out. It was 'N-O spells No!' until you pinned them or gave 'em a ring. The little monkeys! There was none of this free love business, I can tell you that."

He grinned, to let me know he was a regular guy, then squared his shoulders and got down to cases. "What I'm saying, Bobby, is that if you've been doing some heavy petting, that would explain the pain and swelling."

Stupidly, I did not take the doctor's cue. Instead of confessing to the lesser charge, heavy petting, I admitted that I had not been doing any petting at all. At which point the doctor's friendly, huge-nostriled expression shifted instantly. Gone was the buddy-buddy approach, replaced by naked disgust. (Could he, I wondered, have noticed a wanton sock-thread?) The doctor quickly caught himself and recovered his casual manner, but it was too late.

"Perhaps," he mumbled, stepping over to the office sink to wash his hands—a bit, I thought, too thoroughly, as if even that were some sort of comment on my general and now-unveiled unsavoriness—"perhaps I ought to have a chat with your parents. What say you get dressed and wait outside?"

I was now beyond mortified. I tiptoed back into the waiting room as my mother and father headed past me in the other direction. The man knew my secret: the contemptible thing I did, and how much I did it. *And he was going to tell my parents.* As usual, Mom charged ahead, rushing past me with one of her "looks," while Dad, slightly sheepish, trailed behind and stopped beside me long enough to offer a wan, not very reassuring smile.

The entire ride home, my parents kept sneaking glances at the rearview. I could feel them regretting me. No longer their son, I'd devolved to some untamed, embarrassing beast with which their lives had been saddled. So shaken were the pair of them, they didn't bother to bicker. For the first time in memory, my father sat behind the wheel.

In spite of everything, I was happy about that.

But that was then, and this wasn't.

Hours later, I was still propped on the couch, scoping Bette Davis in *Jezebel* and trying to muster an erection. I'd found a chunk of hash in the cuff of my purple corduroys and huffed it by the incinerator. I floated back to the TV awash in jagged memories. It was impossible to stroke myself without the ghost of Dr. Mushnik showing up on the condo ceiling, side by side with my father. The two of them peered down at me, Dad shaking his head, the swarthy urologist no longer hiding his smirk. Behind them, plump tongue licking his parted lips, loomed the monstro visage of Ned Friendly.

At last, relinquishing all hope of lust—something in Bette's shaved eyebrows set my teeth on edge; instead of sexy she was scarifying—I stumbled off the moist velour and over to the picture window. For maybe a minute, maybe an hour, I stared out at the streetlights and the odd twinkling windows in the homes beyond. I pictured somebody in one of those still-lit rooms gazing up at the condo. Imagined that, if the two of us could somehow make contact, we'd understand each other. Talk ourselves to sleep . . .

I wasn't exactly bored. And I wasn't just lonely. It was more like I was holding out for the right emotion to come along so I could grab it and claim it as my own: There, *that's* the one I need!

Once I knew what I was supposed to feel, I figured I could get on with life.

After *Jezebel* departed, Randolph Scott rolled onto the tube in

Virginia City. I hit the kitchenette for my fifth fistful of Oreos, this batch with marshmallow "creme" on the side. While rooting through Mom's fridge, I got the idea. Call Mr. Schmidlap. I could rap to him. I could *relate*. Were we not, in a funny kind of way, friends?

I slunk down the hall to make sure Mom was asleep—she whistled when she snored, like Popeye—then crept back to the kitchenette. Wedging her avocado Princess to my ear, I dialed Slotzville information.

It sounded like I woke up the information lady, which was oddly exciting. I pictured a row of operators on cots, leaping to their feet like firemen when they heard a ring. Miss Information had a gravelly voice, like Ray Charles but female. She reminded me of our old cleaning lady, Thornetta. One of my biggest jerk-off fantasies was getting Thornetta to bend over the toilet and scrub while I looked up her dress. She always wore the same kind of hose: these heavy nylons with black seams that rolled into doughnuts way up at the tops of her thighs. In my fantasy she'd turn around and beg me to put it in. That's how she'd say it, "*Come on, Bobby boy, put it in!*" She'd called me Bobby boy since I was five, when she replaced Lorraine, an older lady who spent most of the time sitting on a kitchen chair by the radiator, rubbing her knees with horse liniment.

"*Come on, Bobby boy, put it in! Put it in!*"

Thornetta was huge. Her thighs, the few times I'd gotten a glimpse above the doughnut line, were the size of fallen tree trunks. But when you stood beside her, she gave off this spicy smell, like clove chewing gum mixed with french fries. Around the house as a boy, I had to fight the urge to dunk my head under her tent-like, faded peach dress and breathe her in. One

perv—a love story

morning—a banner day in my development—I accidentally walked in on her while she straddled our basement toilet, her mountainous brown thighs spread far apart and her enormous bush just *there*, like some kind of small farm animal taking a nap. A day later, I could barely walk. I broke my own personal record of six squirts in a single twenty-four-hour period.

I can still hear Thornetta, barely raising her voice from the toilet. She was hunkered with a wad of pink toilet paper trailing from one hand. The other rested atop a slab of jumbo cocoa-colored thigh: "You best put them eyes back in your head, junior, somebody liable to pick 'em up and eat 'em." This was the only time she'd ever called me junior. And, despite the weeks of masturbatory fodder the spectacle provided, it served to further my private sense that, way down, in the most secret part of me, there was something deeply "junior" about me that I would never outgrow. I would never transcend that "junior" status, never become the kind of manly man who could step up and satisfy a sequoia-thighed goddess like Thornetta.

I asked Miss Information if she had her shoes off, if they let her snack and watch TV. All that hash had left me chatty and paranoid at the same time. But she wouldn't answer. Whoever she was, she just clicked off the numbers, in that husky voice, and that was that. There were three Schmidlaps. The first, an Orville, lived on Binnie Avenue. This sounded familiar, and I went with it. The problem was, we always snuck to Sharon's house in the dark, through the patchy woods behind the Hale soccer fields. I didn't know Mr. Schmidlap's first name. But I had a vague sense about a street called Binnie, so I took a shot and dialed.

The glow-in-the-dark clock on Mom's stove showed 3:40 A.M. While the phone rang, I wondered why you'd need a glow-in-the-dark clock on an oven. It's not like people cooked with the lights out. But what did I know? There was just so much shit I had no idea about. The entire fucking world. . . .

While the telephone rang, my thoughts just drifted. I didn't know who, if anybody, Mom had cleaning her condo, and wondered if Thornetta's number might be in some old address book. I'd seen her at my father's funeral, looking ample as ever, if a little gray. But I'd gulped so many of Mom's Seconals that sneaking a sympathy-peek of the maid's little porcupine was out of the question. I spent most of the day nodding at strangers, absorbing Mom's abuse, and trying not to drool on my suit.

The phone rang eleven times before someone picked up. There was a pause, during which they swallowed and mumbled something like "Shit-steak" before breaking into an extended cough. Just hearing that cough again made me happy. *"HUACCHHH-HUACCHHH."* And then: "This better be good, or I'm coming after you."

That voice packed all the death I remembered. "Mr. Schmidlap!"

"Who's this?"

"It's Bobby. Bobby Stark."

"Who? Oh Christ-on-a-keychain—*HUUACCCHHH*—what do you want?"

"Huh?"

In my eagerness to reach him, I never stopped to think what I wanted to say.

"I said what do you want? If it's Sharon, forget it. Sent her to a convent. Those nuns'll keep her panties up if they have to staple 'em. So don't even think about it. Don't tell me she called you, either, or I'll personally rip the Mother Superior a new cake hole."

perv—a love story

There was another pause, another long gulp followed by that extended "*Ahhh. . . .*" He broke into a brief coughing fit—it sounded like rattling chains in a well—and started up again. "You still didn't say why the fuck you're calling."

"Well . . ." I cleared my throat and cast my eyes wildly around Mom's kitchenette. An enormous potato sat on the counter. The way its eyes bugged out, it might have been staring at me. Thinking, in its potato way, *This boy is not groovy.* Still, the way those eyes protruded . . . "It's your wife," I blurted.

"What?" Mr. Schmidlap's voice grew low. A pit bull growl. "What do you want with my wife?"

"I just . . . I just wanted to know how she was."

I scooped up the giant potato. It was distended on one side, with mottled spots. What did it want from me? "I've been thinking about her," I said. The mutant spud knew everything. "I met somebody who has the same thing she has and—"

"*Had,*" he barged in. "Mary Anne was buried last Friday."

"Mr. Schmidlap, this is gonna sound strange," I confided, opening the knife drawer and throwing in the potato. "But I had a feeling. You know what I mean? It's like, my tattoo, it started to glow. I swear." At that moment, I so wanted him to like me, to *talk* to me, I would have told him her face showed up on a salami sandwich if he'd only chat for a while. "I got this feeling around the same time you're talking about and—"

"And *shit.* You're full of *shit,*" he interrupted again, not sounding particularly mad about it. "But thanks anyway. I was thinking about you, too. Woke up screaming. How'd the tat come out?"

"The what?"

"The tattoo. Are you deaf *and* stupid?" (He pronounced it *deef.*) "You didn't scratch, did you?"

"No," I lied. "I mean, a little, but it came out okay."

He smacked his lips and let out another beer commercial *"ahhh"* so I knew he was swigging something. I could picture him down in the rec room, eyeballing his one-armed trophy and guzzling his thirty-seventh Rheingold.

"You know, you could have called Sharon," he snarled. I twisted the phone cord around my wrist and bit it. "It wouldn't have killed you, would it? You could've at least written. I thought you behaved like a pig, but she liked you. Thought you were different from the other boys." He belched and added, as an afterthought, "Do you know it's nearly four in the fucking morning?"

"I know," I said. "I apologize. But I didn't think you'd want me to talk to her. After what I, y'know . . . after what happened. Maybe you didn't know, but they threw me out next day. Now I'm back in Pittsburgh with my mother. She's not too, I mean it's . . . Well, I'm sorry," I said again, realizing I'd turned into a chatterbox. Why he'd want to hear my troubles, after all the trouble I'd caused him, was beyond me. Now that we were actually speaking I couldn't believe I'd had the gall to call. Sometimes what I did five minutes ago scared the fuck out of me five minutes later. This was one of those times.

"HUACCCHHH."

Another cough rocked through the receiver, which I fumbled to cover and muffle. Like I was going to catch something over the phone. Like whatever was killing Mr. Schmidlap you could get from germs. *Like it mattered.*

"Fuck you very much," he spat, breaking into a few after-hacks and settling down. "That's what my CO used to say in Korea. Man, I can't sleep for shit. Alone too much. Tonight is the worst." He took a difficult breath and sighed. "You know I slapped the

perv—a love story

priest at Mary Anne's funeral? Silly four-eyed prick called her Miriam. So I slapped him. Simple as that. They're all fags anyway. But you shoulda seen the in-laws. Real crap sandwiches. Her brother's an accountant. Clancy. Handles all the books for Mrs. Smith's pies, so he thinks he's a big shot. He saw me whack that sky pilot and just about hoiked up on his rosary. . . . *HUACCHH*. The fuck do I care? They all thought she married below her station. That's the phrase she used, my mother-in-law the saint. 'Below her station.' Like she's royalty 'cause her baby boy counts meringue tubs for a living. Shit! Every Sunday her son Clancy"—here he stopped, gulped, and belched wetly into the receiver—"what kind of name is that, anyway? What's wrong with Bob or Tom? Fuckin' Tarzan's better than *Clancy*.

"Where was I? Oh yeah, every Sunday Clancy'd march over with a stack of store-bought—pies, turnovers, crumb cakes—like he was some kind of *made* guy for bringing day-old dessert. Some made bakery guy. Christ, we ain't talking Sam Giancana here. The little jag-off worked for Mrs. Smith's."

I picked my toenails and watched the oven-clock's second hand. "You keep saying Mrs. Smith, I thought she made fish sticks."

"That's Mrs. Paul's, you mango. Mrs. Paul's is fish sticks, Mrs. Smith is *pies*. That's the trouble with you young fucks. Ignorance! All that long hair keeps air from getting to your brains. Man, what was I talking about? Do *you* know what I was talking about?"

"Yeah," I answered, though in truth I'd begun to drift. I couldn't concentrate. God knows why, but I was absolutely dying to ask him, *"What do you miss more, your arm or your wife?"* The answer, I was irrationally convinced, would reveal much of what I needed to know to survive in the universe. It was *urgent*. That happened on hash: Out of nowhere, a solution to some significant life-mystery would show up in your brain, like a Jehovah's Witness knocking on the door. The trick was catching the thing before it split and hit the next house. Somehow you never could. Enlightenment had a three-minute fuse.

I was going to grab some milk out of the fridge, then pop the arm-versus-spouse question, when Mr. Schmidlap tore back into his mother-in-law.

"She blamed me," he barked between mini-coughs. "Can you believe that shit? Her mother thought, since I'm only workin' one arm, Mary Anne caught something from me and got deformed. Like I sneezed and she got a brain tumor. Fuckin' trailer trash. They're all pea-brains."

I didn't tell him I'd had a similar thought, minutes ago, when he'd scream-coughed into the receiver.

Mr. Schmidlap swallowed, burped, and gagged so hard the phone nearly flew out of my hand. "Get this shit," he howled. "I find out the old whorebreath's been spouting this stuff to Sharon. Behind my back, I find out at the funeral, Grandma Hag has been telling my own daughter that *I* gave her mom the acro. Like I need this shit after my wife dies? You son of a *cunt!*" he shouted abruptly. "You *fuckwad!* You had your hands all over her. You and your prep-ass friends!"

He'd switched gears so quickly, I didn't know if he meant his wife—whom I'd never touched, let alone seen more than once, when she was lobstered-up and unconscious—or his daughter, whom I'd seen and handled. I only knew he was ranting, which was okay. It was still better than silence. Than being alone all night with Bette Davis and Randolph Scott. . . .

That afternoon I called a kid I knew from public school. He yapped about his girlfriend, the colleges he applied to, his sum-

perv—a love story

mer job as a veterinary assistant. Normal stuff. But I didn't have normal stuff. I was a sixteen-year-old holed up with his mother. Without a bed. I hadn't even talked about colleges with Mom. She was too preoccupied. Her life stopped the day my father stepped in front of the Dormont Local. Though I had the feeling, fucked up as it sounded, that maybe now she had the life she wanted. She was in permanent mourning. She got to do absolutely nothing. Snack and whine. For all I knew I was jealous.

Denny Marchetti, the kid I called, was my best friend growing up. But he sounded scared when I said it was me. That's how it was: Bobby Stark, the kid with the crazy mom. My father dying was bad enough—people disapproved of death, even if they didn't come out and say it—but what happened after was worse. Mom taking the twenty-nine tranquilizers, me calling the police, two white-smocked giants hustling her to the ambulance strapped to a stretcher and screaming in front of the neighbors—that's what really did it. Dad was Mr. Streetcar. Mom was Mrs. Pills-and-Stomach-Pump. So what did that make me? Sicko Boy? Did I get my picture in the yearbook under "Most Likely to Commit Suicide"? I didn't blame people for wondering. I wondered myself.

The night Mom ate the twenty-nine tranqs, I had a big decision. Did I phone for help or didn't I? To call or not to call, that was the question. When she first screeched down from her bedroom, I thought she just wanted another peach, or a grilled cheese and sardines. Maybe more Melba toast.

I didn't know she'd already washed down a batch of Miltowns with flat ginger ale. That she was calling me up so she could die in front of me. *"I want you to watch, Bobby. I took every pill I had, twenty-nine of them, and I want you to sit here and watch. I know you*

*wished it was me instead of Daddy. Now you get your wish. I want to do
something to make you happy."*

My deepest secret, outside of the jerking-off stuff (which, call
me a hair-splitter, occupies a different category), is that *I didn't
make a move.* I didn't rush out and call people. Not at first, anyway.

What I did, when Mom lolled her head sideways on the pillow
and mumbled, through lips already gone slack, *"I want you to sit
here and watch"*—what I did was . . . think about it. And what I
thought was, *Why not?* I kicked it around. *Once she's gone, I'll have
every excuse . . .* The world would give me a pass. *People will expect
me to be fucked up. "First his father, and now his mother . . ."* I could
already hear them, could feel their repulsion and concern like
warm sun on my face.

I pictured—no, I fantasized about—Mom's funeral. I antici-
pated the pills and sympathy, then flashed forward to a lifetime
of cashing checks, getting high, and watching game shows with
naked girls on my lap till my brain melted into my bell-bottoms.
When Dad died, the government started sending me social security money, Monthly "Survivor Benefits"—$225 a pop.
Unfortunately, Mom kept them. . . . With her tranquilized into
an early grave, I'd get everything there was to get: insurance,
social security, my dad's Army and Public Defender pensions. It
seemed like a better plan than college. I could read on my own,
plus there was no PE requirement.

But it wasn't the money that slowed me down. It was the way
she said the words *"Watch me die."* That smirky tone. Daring me
to call her bluff, to hang around on Dad's twin bed and kill her,
more or less, by not picking up the phone. Like that scene in
every Grade Z western, the one where the Bad Guy stares down

the barrel of the good guy's gun and says, "*Go ahead, pull the trigger! I don't think you got the guts . . .*"

Which in the case of my mother and me, was true. I didn't. Which made the sneer on her face that much worse. For five minutes I tried to do nothing. I even got up and turned on the TV. I stared at *The Price Is Right* with host Bill Cullen. Bill grew up in Pittsburgh. He went to the same high school as Denny's mom, who said he had polio and did the whole show drunk on his ass in a wheelchair.

During the first commercial—I even remembered *that:* Speedy Alka-Seltzer, who looked like my cousin Marvin, but smarter— it hit me what I was doing and I freaked out. Mom's face had darkened to a splotchy gray, except for her lips. Her lips were blue and quivery, but still—this *really* got to me—formed in a sneer. She'd soaked through her nightie. Peed herself and puked up a little. Her speech was slurred, but her speech was always slurred when she took tranquilizers. I'd seen all of it before. How did I know this wasn't a test?

"You're not a man," she kept muttering, foaming up on the side of her mouth that mushed the sheets. Mom never slept on a pillow. She slid the pillow between her knees. She slept flat on the mattress, one arm slung dramatically over her eyes, the gesture suggesting, even in sleep, it was all too much for her. . . .

"*You're not a man,*" she repeated, in that croaking whisper. "*You're not a man. You'renotaman. You'renotamanyou'renotamanyou'renot amanyou'renotamanyou'reNOT . . .*"

By the time I called the ambulance I was crying. But I wasn't sure why.

Anyway, after the twenty-nine-tranq episode, talk of which soon made its way to school, Denny and I stopped being friends.

He said his parents didn't want him coming to our house. He didn't have to explain. Not long after, I got sent away. We didn't speak again until this afternoon, when I felt like I had to talk to somebody or scream.

As it turned out, I'd have been better off screaming. I figured Denny would *have* to be friendly. I knew the one thing about him nobody else did: He was a rubberbones. He could suck his own penis. I'd seen him do it. The summer we were nine we'd gotten into a show 'n' tell thing. A competition. I could wiggle one ear, but Denny could blow himself. Needless to say, he won. Neither of us could say exactly why being able to lollipop your own cock would be so handy. But even without practical application, it was impressive.

I didn't mention Denny's self-lapping capacities when I called. Instead, I listened to him chat. I heard about his job with the pet doctor, his girlfriend-who-worked-in-special-ed, his college backups, the brother of a guy we knew who died in Vietnam. . . . Nothing that mattered. It was easier talking to Mr. Schmidlap, since I didn't have to feign interest. I got the feeling Mr. Schmidlap was already talking before the phone rang. That he'd be still talking after it was hung up again.

The barber bounced back from a coughing fit and spoke in tortured cadence. "I'm not mad at you, damnit, I'm . . . My wife is . . . dead. My little girl, well . . . thanks to you, she's not a little girl anymore."

With this, he let out a wary growl, like a dog deciding whether to attack or crawl off on its belly.

"Aw hell, that's not true either. You weren't the first little jim-jim to come sniffin' around Sharon. You were just a higher class of shit. But shit's shit. It looked like you guys were pullin' a train,

perv—a love story

but what could I do? What could I do? Sharon told me later she invited you all over." He made his voice go girlish. " '*It's just friendly-like, Pop. None of them boys even has a Daddy. I wanted to help!*' An' you wonder why I drink my breakfast? This kinda shit could make a man guzzle *sprat-water.* . . ."

"We had a club," I offered, as though that would make him feel better. "The Dead Fathers Club. We did things together."

"Did things?" he yelled, his voice going strangled and wild. "DID things? You mean like catch a ball game? Toss a Frisbee? *Gang-bang my daughter?* Oh Jesus! Of all the sorry-ass fuckmeat son-of-a-cunt *BULLSHIT!*"

Suddenly there was a loud knocking on the line. I checked the wire. I couldn't figure out what it was, until I realized, with the fifth or sixth clunk, that it was Mr. Schmidlap. Banging the receiver off his head. Each knock was followed by a muffled "*Ouch!*" When that stopped there was a moment of raspy panting; then he started up again. " 'Sharon, for Christ's sake,' I says to her, 'Florence Nightingale wasn't some hoo-er. She didn't show puss to them poor soldiers. She wrapped their *bandages.* She held their *hands.* She made them fucking cocoa.' Am I right or am I right? 'Baby, for God's sake,' I said to her, 'make 'em a cup of friggin' Ovaltine! You don't have to fuck 'em to cheer 'em up! Play some goddamn *Parcheesi!*"

I thought back to that night and, in all honesty, agreed with him. Considering what happened, I'd have been just as happy if we'd slurped Ovaltine and listened to Perry Como records. I never liked Perry Como, but it would have been fun anyway. Just to get high and laugh at him. Say what you will about a

Como festival, chances are it would not have ended with me on a plane back to Pittsburgh, crashing on scratchy velour, trapped in the Condo of No Return with my well-meaning, pill-popping mom. God bless her.

"You know what I been doing?" he shrieked, knocking me out of my Perry Como mode.

His voice sounded different now, like a wire stretched as taut as it could get, then twanged with a hammer. "I'll tell you, you little phony, I been sittin' here, that's what. I been sittin' down here in the dark for three days, talkin' to myself and drinkin' straight whiskey. I can't even get any beer. Goddamn distributor won't deliver. His boy says I shot at him. Fuckin' pansy. Had the cops out here, too. You believe that? And me a goddamn veteran! Like that matters more'n a pile o'turds on an anthill."

"It probably matters to the ants," I said, sounding so fakey-earnest I felt even phonier than he thought I was. I meant to say that I wouldn't have lasted the bus ride to boot camp. I'd have started crying when they shaved my head and made me run three miles in army boots. Forget about actually going to war. . . . What I meant to say was that I admired him. But Mr. Schmidlap was in no mood.

"Shut up," he bellowed, followed by a glug-glug-glug and yet another lip-smacking *"ahhh."* "Let me tell you somethin' else. I'm holdin' a gun, right now. A thirty-eight. Blue steel and oiled like a whore's behind. Got the safety off that motherfucker, too."

"What are you gonna do with the gun?"

"What do you *think* I'm gonna do, Jew-boy? Shoot pigeons? Make myself a little squab soufflé? I don't think so. I gotta little itch on the roof of my mouth, and I'm gonna scratch it."

perv—a love story

His voice shifted again, going into his own version of Jiminy Cricket. Jiminy Cricket cranked up on booze and bitterness and bent enough to blow his own antennae off.

"You mean"—this was probably the dumbest thing I've ever said, but I said it anyway—"you're gonna scratch the roof of your mouth, with your gun?"

"Christ, you're swift," he cackled. "That's exactly what I'm gonna do. I'm gonna scratch that itch. If you want, you can listen. You wanna, huh, you wanna listen to me scratch it? What the hell, could be good for your education."

"Hey, c'mon," I said, "you don't have to . . . I mean, seriously, don't put the gun in your mouth . . ."

Wondering what to do, I ran a finger over my tattoo. It was still tender. I tried to think of something to make Mr. Schmidlap slow down. Make him feel better. I kicked around *"When you have your health, you have everything . . ."* But the amputee deal made health a gray area. Could you call a flipper guy healthy, even if he lived to be 103? I wasn't sure, and waited out another blast of monstrous coughing. At least the head-pounding had stopped. I pictured him hunched up on that plaid couch, his gun nestled in his pecs like a shiny baby. I'd just decided to say something nice about Sharon: how much she looked like him, how much she loved him, how she'd told me a couple of times how much she really, really dug her dad when I heard a howl. It was the kind they called "bloodcurdling" in movies.

"Mr. Schmidlap?" I cried. I was breathing hard, trying to keep my own voice calm. A light in the condo across the street flashed on, then off again, like some kind of signal. "Mr. Schmidlap, are you okay?"

"Am I okay? *Am I okay?* I just found your wet scumbag under my couch, that's how okay I am. What do you think of that?" he croaked. "I can't even have a drink in my own home without you showing up, even if you are out there in Plattsburgh fartin' in silk."

"Pittsburgh," I corrected him.

"Who gives a fuck, you little cunt-bug? I drop a bottle on the goddamn rug, and when I'm flat on my face trying to pluck it up I stick my nose in a soakin' Trojan. What is THAT?" he bellowed, tears stabbing his voice. "You shove the rubber under the goddamn sofa, like I'm not gonna find it? Like the father of the girl you turned out is not gonna stumble on your stink sooner or later, and when he finds it, he's not gonna want to *KILL*?"

I thought about explaining what happened, how the thing got stuck in Sharon's hole, how we tried to find it and it kind of scooched out on its own the second he burst into the rec room and scared the shit out of Tennie and Farwell. But was that a good idea? I couldn't imagine working his daughter's vagina into the conversation. Not now. Not when he was drunk, enraged, and holding a loaded thirty-eight to the roof of his mouth. God, did I feel *fucked*. I'd figured the worst fallout from that long-lost condom had already fallen out: me getting kicked out of prep school and Sharon probably getting whupped within an inch of her life. Now it looked like it might kill a man, too. *Jesus!*

"Aw hell," he sighed, as if the air just went right out of him. "You don't even care, do you?"

"Hey, come on," I said. "That's not—"

"Just shut up," he said, but not unkindly. More like he was just too tired to have to converse anymore.

"Howzabout we kiss and make up?" he said, with a harsh, coughing laugh. "Whaddya say?"

perv—a love story

I had to think about that. Was it some kind of test to see if I was a homo? Was it a joke?

Before I could ask, he gave me the answer anyway. An enormous bang, like a metal garbage can dropped from a roof onto a concrete slab. Bang, then nothing. An explosion followed by a loud, dull thud.

Then the line went dead.

I held on, clicking for a dial tone. Babbling *"Hello? Hello?"* like the jilted boyfriend in some *Million Dollar Movie.* I kept clicking and babbling long after it was obvious he wasn't going to answer. That there wasn't going to be an answer.

What I did—after it hit, in a dreamlike way, that I'd heard a man die—was call the Slotzville operator. I gave her Mr. Schmidlap's phone number. His name and address. Told her to call an ambulance.

Then I hung up, and the silence roared around me. Everything shimmered. For a while I stared at my hands. I could not wrap my mind around what had just happened. But I couldn't unwrap it, either. The person I'd been talking to on the phone had fired a gun. Had shot himself. First my father, I thought. Then Mr. Schmidlap. I felt like a black widow—if black widows could be sixteen-year-old boys with bad skin and sex problems. . . . I was suddenly hungry, and wondered if that was normal. Who knows? Regret was ten flights up from whatever I was feeling.

I kept hearing that BANG. That THUD. And then the silence. That endless, echoing . . . *NOTHING.*

And that was it.

tv in heaven

Every year or two, you heard on the news about an exploding furnace. About a family of nine in Butte who blew up in their sleep. That type of thing, often on holidays. (If it wasn't the furnace, it was a Christmas tree: bad wiring, dry needles, the dog. Same deal....)

I wanted to believe that what I'd experienced, long-distance, was that kind of situation. A rogue toaster. Imploded

boiler. *Anything* but Mr. Schmidlap, distraught over his dead deformed wife, over the behavior—I swallowed hard—of his slutty
daughters, over the hopeless, gone-to-hell, all-around degenerate
state of his life, blowing his brains out. Even if it wasn't a holiday.

But the after-effect: that skull-thumping *BOOM*, the silence
after, was too much. There was not even a dial tone. As though
he'd flown backward on impact and ripped the plug out of the
wall. Or maybe the bullet to his temple took out the telephone,
too. Or maybe *this* . . . Maybe *that* . . . I could not stop hallucinating bad scenes. It was like being on ratty acid.

The notion that I'd just talked to a dead man, that maybe I'd
even killed him; that somehow, if I'd only scoped out my Trojan,
he'd still be alive—pissed, but breathing—lurked too far off the
Guilt Map of the Known Universe. There was no absorbing it.

I kept on trying Mr. Schmidlap's number. Then trying again.
Nothing. I gave up and redialed the Slotzville operator, who got
me the police. I put down the phone after babbling to some kind
of dispatcher—*accident, Schmidlap, Binnie Avenue*—and the living
room walls began to pulse. The velour on the couch glowed like
radium. The cushions were whispering, *Killer! Killer!* I glanced at
the window, where a clan of tiny faces stared back from the glass.
Little Tennies. *We know what you did!* they chittered, just below
sound.

Walking underwater, I moved to the kitchenette. Opened the
refrigerator and forgot what I wanted. Turned around and
kneeled on the linoleum. For a long time I gazed at my reflection
in the oven door. Cloudy glass. *This is my face*, I explained to
myself. *This is the face of Bobby Stark, who just talked to a man who
blew his head off.* My own eyes looked through me. I'd been chat-

ting with a dead man. Who'd been talking to himself. Now who was I talking to?

I felt . . . not *numb* exactly. More like overloaded. Vibrating. Like my heart had blown a fuse. I didn't know I was crying until Mom shuffled in. Ragged slippers. Salmon nightie. Lit Kent dangling from her lip. She didn't mention the kneeling. She only asked what I was doing with the fridge door open. "Damnit, I've told you, *that eats electricity*. Do you want to cause a power failure. Is that it? *Do you want to drive me crazy?*"

When she saw that I was fighting back tears, my mother clutched her throat. The wee hours were not her best. "Oh God," she moaned, "now what?" As if I made a habit of weeping. "What *is* it? Are you on *drugs* again?"

I wanted to reply, but what could I tell her? That I'd just orphaned Sharon Schmidlap? That I'd dropped a condom and killed a man? My mother and I never even discussed sex, let alone sex and murder.

When I didn't answer, she seemed relieved. "Excuse me, I need my pills," she muttered, and elbowed me out of the way so she could get to her prescription bottles. Some pills Mom kept in the medicine cabinet, some—the exact same kind, Miltowns and phenos—she stored in the kitchen drawer. I never figured out the system. My guess was that she needed the security of knowing, wherever she was, she was never more than a short stagger from relief. It was an MO I could appreciate.

Placing the pill between her teeth—she claimed they worked faster if you *crunched* them—Mom stopped and rested her shaking hands on my shoulders. I aimed my face at the floor. Tried not to inhale. Even without breathing, there was no escaping the heat that escaped that salmon nightie. That maternal blast furnace. The gust that soiled my boyhood sails.

"Now dell your mozzer," she implored, shaping her words around a speckled tranquilizer. "Izzit Daddy?" She bit down on the pill and winced. With visible effort, she swallowed the dry crumbs, gulping loudly two or three times before she could speak. "You never cried for Daddy. Is that why you're crying now?"

"Mom," I began, but where could I go? The way she gaped at me, with that *"Please don't!"* look, that troubled-mammal panic in her eyes—there, at this stage of her existence, more or less permanently—I knew I had to reassure her. "It's not Dad, it's not anything," I lied. "It's my stomach. Too many domino bars."

"Oh, *honey!*" Her relief was palpable. "You always did love your mother's domino bars, didn't you?"

She plunged a hand in her mouth and I turned away. Now that she'd munched her medicine, she could take her teeth back out. An exercise I had no desire to witness. I studied the black and pink tiles and counted to twenty. When I looked up again, she was grinning around her gums. (At night she dropped her teeth in an old herring jar, and that view of her: lips fallen in on her gums, hair shmushed and her bald spots showing, almost *did* give me a stomach ache. It made me think back to Mr. Schmidlap, who'd told me how, in barber college, the worst thing they made you do was shave skid row rummies. Fucking alkies never had teeth, so you had to stick your finger in their mouths. Pop their cheeks out to get some traction for the straight razor. "Your finger," he said, "would stink 'til next week's dinner.")

Still . . . I would have hugged my mother if we were the kind of family who hugged. If touching her weren't impossible. If her sub-nightie waft was not so utterly, fatally repulsive.

That's how much I loved her.

"I'll bake tomorrow," Mom continued absently, gumming the words around a toothless smile. "You know how much I love to bake. Your mozzer can do a few things right, despite what some people around here might think."

"Hey, come on," I managed, by way of jolly reply, "you're a legend."

"Aren't you a doll?" she said dreamily, the pills already doing their job.

Since the death of my father, Mom had baked domino bars, and nothing but domino bars (her name for butterscotch-fudge brownies) on an almost continual basis. She foisted them on friends, left them at neighbors' doors, shipped them by the dozen to far-off second and third cousins. The tragic part: Her baking had grown defective. *Dangerous*. At Hale, I would routinely receive cookie tins packed with luscious-looking two-tone brownies, only to bite into one and discover, one more time, that she'd used paprika instead of cinnamon. Garlic salt instead of sugar. Not that our family were strangers to culinary trauma. My mother, back in those heady, pre-streetcar days when Dad was alive, when my sister hadn't yet dashed off with her draft dodger (once, in a letter to me, she let slip his name was "Raoul," and his parents lived in Altoona), and I was a young moron in grade school, my mother used to like to throw dinner parties. These were lively events, attended by a half-dozen couples or so, in which my sister and I were enlisted as de facto greeters, plate-clearers, all-around ambassadors of cute, and apologists for

perv—a love story

Mom's behavior. Which, in the matter of dinner parties, began and ended with her cooking.

"I made everybody's favorite, candied beets," she'd inevitably announce at the outset of the actual meal. Hearing this, smiles would freeze on veterans of the Hilda Stark dining experience, while newcomers would rub their hands in happy anticipation of the treats to come.

My father, at such times, adapted—or lapsed into—a Zenlike stoicism that enabled him to dispense head-of-the-table pleasantries while simultaneously, to the practiced eye, withdrawing into that private void he visited when he had to be present in body but absent every other way. Ever eloquent, my sister called this state the "goingaways." As in "look at Daddy, he's got the goingaways already, and we haven't even gotten to the chicken breasts."

The goingaways were characterized by a trance-like equanimity in my father's manners. It was almost alarming. You could tell him anything—"Dad, I stuck a fork in my spleen and blood's dripping down to my underpants!" "Dad, I heard they found Pat Nixon dangling upside down from the Washington Monument in nothing but hairnet and baseball cleats!"—and he would smile, chuck you under the chin, and say "That's the way the cookie crumbles."

Dad wasn't cold when he was like this. What people always said about my father (it must have been mentioned ten times in the memorial service they held in the Public Defender's office) was that he was "a good listener." People confided in him. He didn't judge. He didn't say much but when he did, etc. . . . etc. . . .

What I suspect is that he was looking his confessors right in the eye, smiling in his concerned way, and floating so far out of his body they could have poked him with cocktail toothpicks and the smile would have stayed on his face. If people noticed any of this, they didn't seem to mind. My father was a pretty well-loved and respected guy. But I don't know. The more I look back on things, the more I wonder if maybe he wasn't as far away as he seemed.

Maybe, after being raised in an orphanage, shunted to a coal mine at twelve, and never sampling anything resembling a family until he started one himself, he found a way to survive and just stuck with it. Maybe he figured a smile and silence was as good a response as any to whatever torments people confided, or he happened to be enduring himself.

The nice part was, the couples that came to these soirees, as Mom was fond of calling them, actually seemed to enjoy themselves. It was pretty much the same people over and over. Staff from the PD's office—including Mr. Weiner, before his wife, a statuesque Swede named Uta, skipped out on him—a few people from the law school, and one black couple, the Deardens, both attorneys, who my mother would make a point of seating right next to the head of the table. ("I want them to know we think they're just as good as us," she never tired of explaining to me. "I don't even mind if they use our towels." I was never completely sure what made towel-sharing so momentous, but, for Mom, it pretty much signified the height of civil rights in action.)

Until dinner was served, folks would chat, drink, and listen to my sister play the piano. Naturally, Bernice hated the piano, and had only bothered to learn two pieces: "Summertime" and "La Cucaracha." But my mother would nag, cajole, and basically shame her into an "impromptu" performance before people sat down to dinner. The only time she said no—about a year before she disappeared with Altoona Raoul—was a night the dinner ended abruptly when one of the guests, the aforementioned Mrs. Dearden, bit into a fish canapé that had a sardine key in it. Somehow, the little metal prong had gotten wedged in with the minced onions, capers, and mashed-up sardines. This happened right in the middle of a civil rights discussion. Civil Rights was a favorite dinner party topic, with my mother loudly espousing that white people should all adopt black babies to help things along. Others insisted, as gently as possible, that that might be as much an insult to "the Negro race" as keeping them out of lunchrooms.

My sister, who was, at the time, dating her debate partner, a bespectacled Negro fellow named Darnell, was the most vocal proponent of the latter view. "How'd you like to be raised by Eskimos?" she kept shouting at my mother, who shouted right back, "I'd love it. Then I wouldn't have to hide my blubber!"

In the middle of one such discussion, as Mom and I were bringing out the chicken (she only made chicken, along with those candied beets, a dish she called "curly apple sour," and creamed corn), Mrs. Dearden leaped from the table, spat a tooth in her napkin and said, almost weeping, "Hilda, you're a very nice lady, but Congress should pass a law to keep you out of the kitchen."

For a moment or two, nobody said anything. The lady lawyer, as a rule, was the most demure woman in the world. But she was beautiful, too, in an almost intimidating way. She must have been five feet five, but looked well over six on account of her turbulent Afro. Mom never tired of telling her she looked like

Eartha Kitt. This, despite the fact that even a nine-year-old like me could see that Mrs. Dearden did not exactly take this as a compliment. She was, like I say, demure. Until the moment she bit down on that sardine key, at which point she thrust her tooth in front of her, like some bloody heart out of Edgar Allan Poe, and blurted her critique of Mom's cooking. Right then it was clear that her demureness, if that's even a word, was just the mask on top of something every bit as no-nonsense and forbidding as that militant dandelion of Angela Davis–like hair sprouting out her skull.

As the silence after the outburst lengthened horribly, I noticed my father smiling mildly into his salad. My mother seemed less concerned with Mrs. Dearden's tooth than the slur on her culinary prowess, and responded with a comment that brought cringes all around. "But I thought," she declared, with a meekness that bordered on disbelief, *"I thought you people liked seafood in cans!"*

This stunned Bernice, who jumped out of her chair and did something I've never seen anybody do except in movies about Greek peasants. She snatched a plate off the table and hurled it to the ground. Unfortunately, our carpets were too thick and it didn't break. Most of the food just splattered on the dining room wallpaper. This frosted Bernice even more and she began to yell. She called Mom "bourgeois"; then my mother called her "plump"; then Bernice threw another plate, lodging the half-cooked chicken on a curtain rod like some kind of wet pink trophy.

Before I realized what was happening, the guests all seemed to be jangling their car keys and heading for the door.

Through all of this, Dad maintained his pleasant equanimity, shaking hands and offering a reassuring word to one and all as

perv—a love story

they made their exit. When the last diner disappeared, he turned back to us with nothing more than a battery of rippling eyebrow twitches to show that he'd even been affected by the catastrophe.

With the house empty again, things went back to normal: Mom slammed her silverware tray and screamed, "I don't know why you invite these people; they can't get you anywhere!" Dad slumped in his favorite chair—the one Ned Friendly subsequently distended—and allowed himself a sigh. "I'm not saying you're a bad cook, honey. I'm just saying you have to be a little more careful."

They were so busy bickering, and I was so busy finishing off the leftover drinks—three gulps of Cutty Sark, and I could convince myself it was all a bad TV show: *Donna Reed* with Jews and screaming—that none of us noticed, until it was time for bed, that Bernice was missing. She was sixteen, six years older than me, and not in the habit of going out nights unannounced.

My mother, who could work up a crisis if the mail was late, began to howl even louder over her missing daughter. And my father's wan smile gave way to lip-chewing and mumbling as he dragged himself from closet to closet, checking to see if Bernice was pulling one of her suffocation acts. From the time she was five or so, my sister expressed her disapproval with the world in general, and my mother in particular, by locking herself in tiny places. Her true preference was under the sink. When she grew too big for that, she hit the closets.

I sat on the couch, tipped sideways from imbibing so much grown-up refreshment, and let the action kind of float around me. I thought strange thoughts under the influence. Obvious notions rang with new profundity. Things like: *This is my family. . . . I live here. . . . If I die, they have to bury me. . . .* Booze has a different effect when you're, like, ten. It doesn't round out the edges so much as wash you right out of the picture, so that you can wallow in whatever nightmare's playing out around you but not react.

In this state, observing my high-volume mother and quietly seething dad, I drifted into my room and lay down for what seemed like hours, but turned out to be five minutes before the knowledge came to me, literally, like an announcement from a tiny radio playing inside my head. *"She's in the trunk."*

Without thinking about it, I slipped out of bed. I was still in shoes and socks, though for some reason I'd taken my chinos off, folded them, and tucked them in a drawer. Such behavior would not have occurred to me sober. I padded my way down to the garage, fished for the magnetized hide-a-key Mom stashed under the back bumper, and unlocked the trunk.

Sure enough, there was Bernice, curled in a fetal position, nibbling from a snack-sized bag of Wise potato chips and reading *Steal This Book* by flashlight. She looked so content I was jealous.

"Poor Daddy," she said, pushing me away when I tried to crawl in with her, but offering me some chips. "He shouldn't let Mommy make things. Her cooking is like some family poison. We can handle it. We're *immune*, like those cowboys who take tiny sips of rattlesnake venom their whole lives, until they can gulp down a glass and still go to a square dance. But people outside the family haven't been exposed. It's not safe."

She clambered out of the trunk and dusted herself off, then reached in for her book and flashlight. "The funny thing is, she's not a bad cook. She just can't concentrate."

With this Bernice slammed the trunk shut and we both snuck back up to the kitchen and picked through leftovers. Bad as it

perv—a love story

Jerry Stahl

tasted, nobody in our house could find the nerve to toss Mom's cooking in the garbage. We'd all just keep searching until we found something halfway edible—in this case, her candied beets, which were so soaked in Karo syrup they tasted like some weird dessert Bulgarians would eat at Christmas. The whole time, we'd be telling ourselves, "Maybe this stuff's actually okay. . . . Maybe she knows what she's doing. . . ."

The same thing happened, a zillion years later, when I'd get Mom's paprika-laced domino bars up at Hale. I could never bring myself to throw those away either. I stashed a tower of domino bar–stuffed cookie tins in my closet, a trove of taste-mutated baked goods that Tennie and I would raid on only the most extreme-o, three A.M. narcotized food jags. Wrecked on pot and Darvons or crashing off acid, we'd pry open the obligatory Currier-and-Ives-printed lid and shove an entire bar into our mouths. Convinced, in the grips of red-eyed, sweating sugar-need, that they weren't that bad. That the pepper thing was okay. Later, we'd either puke them up or sneak into town and shoplift Pepto-Bismol.

Before my mother made the return trip to her bedroom, where the TV and Kent smoke cast everything a death-ray blue, she offered to whip up some eggs. "Hot buttery scrambleds," she gummed, but I declined. She had a tendency to get shell in the bowl. Mom sniffed her disgust, as if egg-refusal were yet another sign of moral decay, and scratched at a spot between her sagging breasts. "Your *father*," she let fly as she reeled back down the hall.

"My father what?"

"Your father loved his hot buttery scrambleds." Her voice slid south as the tranqs kicked in. "Used to smother 'em in ketchup.

He couldn't help himself," she said in her crumbling whisper. "That man would put ketchup on spaghetti sauce."

I had to smile. Mom's buzz showed up faster than state police after a three-car accident. She felt her way along the wall to her bedroom, and lumbered into it.

"Mom," I called into the dark behind her. "Mom, I, um, love you, okay?"

Of course, she was too loaded to hear. Which was probably why I let myself say it.

Mysteriously, after saying sweet good-night to Mom, I had an urge to sift through the breakfront drawer where she kept my father's photos and mementoes, remnants of the Walter Stark shrine she'd set up on our old TV, a stove-sized Motorola, the day after his funeral. Whenever I thought of our ex-house, what came to mind was the Dead Dad Altar, up there where most people kept *TV Guides* and after-dinner mints. Mr. Schmidlap, of course, had the same idea.

Mom hadn't bothered to resurrect her Walter shrine in the condominium. But the bulk of it, for better or worse, could be found in the same drawer as her discarded needlepoint and un-used wall calendars. (She always saved blank calendars, as if planning to block out alternatives to the life that had actually passed: to go back and mark things that should have happened, instead of the things that she wished never had.)

I plucked a photo at random, a faded newspaper picture of my father posing beside a stunned-looking, emaciated black woman on the steps of the county courthouse. The caption read: "Walter Stark Counsels Mother of Meat Market Victim."

I was only three when the picture was taken, but I remembered

perv—a love story

Jerry Stahl

the story. The woman, whose name was Donita Griffin, had come home from work as a night nurse to find her nineteen-year-old son, Ray Lee, sprawled on the carpet with his skull split open. Before Ray Lee lapsed into a coma, he told his mother a policeman had clubbed him when he was trying to buy some ground round for supper. Only a sentence or so of the story was left below the photo, which had been ripped out of the *Pittsburgh Post-Gazette*. " 'Ray Lee, he loved to make me burgers,' said a tearful Mrs. Griffin, interviewed at her modest home in the city's Hill District. 'He was a real good boy who would never—' " It ended there.

I tried hard to see into my father's eyes. Since his death, whenever I looked at his pictures I always searched for clues. For something that might explain him to me. With every passing month he became vaguer, a little more like a character in some show I used to watch all the time before it was canceled. Even when he was alive, he wasn't home. He left the house before I woke up and got in after I went to bed. And he visited the office on weekends.

I held the picture close. I squinted at it. Touched my finger to his face, careful not to damage the already flaking newsprint. Doing this—no matter what—I felt self-conscious. Like I was forcing an emotion when the truth was I didn't know *what* emotion I felt, if I even felt one. The dark, round face, the deep-set eyes, and strange streak of silver on the right side of his wavy black hair. . . . *Who was that masked man?*

I was ashamed at the hard life my father had—losing his natural parents somewhere in Russia, raised on gruel and wormy mattresses in that county orphanage, jobbed out to local coal mines till he was old enough to join the Army, then get out and snag a job and work his way through college in the J&L steel mill. I was ashamed because my life was so much easier than his, *yet I was still unhappy.*

Not until he died, and my life was rendered instantly "tragic," did I finally feel close to him. Now we could relate: We were united by the taste of tragedy. Two boys with bad daddy-luck. His death, finally, let me feel like his son.

"I'm sorry," I said, aiming my gaze into his. "I'm sorry for all of it. The drugs, the sex stuff with Sharon, getting thrown out of school, and now this thing with her father, who I think, unless I'm crazy"—the import hit me all over again when I said it out loud—"who I think I drove to suicide. . . . I'm sorry."

I focused on his right eye while I confessed. It was smaller than his left, which was large and intimidating. The left eye said, "Life is serious business." But that right one—slightly hooded, conspiratorial—that right one said, "None of this crap matters anyway, does it?"

I brought the paper closer. The breeze from my words fluttered his face.

"Daddy, what do *you* think?" I tried to make out an answer in the troubling glare off his glasses, the slight twist of his lips. "Should I get the fuck out of here? The schools are on strike, anyway. I'm just sitting around. But where should I go? I'm stuck. I'm scared. I think maybe I'm brain-damaged. And poor Mom—" But here I stopped myself. I stopped myself, feeling, rightly or wrongly, *the man's got enough trouble.* I didn't need to lay that on him. He might get depressed, and then what? If he was already dead, he couldn't kill himself. Even if there *were* streetcars beyond the grave. . . . I was tired of making everybody who knew me miserable. Making them die. Or worse, making them want to.

perv—a love story

Jerry Stahl

I raised my eyes from the photo. Looked back out the picture window. There wasn't a light to be seen, not one friendly square. No one awake in the visible world but me. The silence hummed. I kissed the photograph, careful not to damage it. A sob stabbed at my chest and my face squinched up the way it did when I cried. (The second time I took acid, I watched myself in the mirror for nine hours. What I realized, when I stared, was that my face looked exactly the same when I cried as when I laughed. After a while I couldn't tell which I was doing. Relief was just pain inside out. Tears and snot, snot and tears. It was disturbing, and then not.)

My father's image curled forward in my fingers. *If he can see me,* I thought, *he's probably disappointed. Maybe heartbroken.* But what could I do? I thought of all the things he might have seen since he passed away, and hoped he'd been watching something else. Maybe that was the difference between heaven and hell: In hell you had to watch the living, in heaven you could pull the plug. If I was on TV in heaven, he could always turn me off. Make eternity a little easier.

I put him back in the drawer.

It was before six when I jerked awake on the sofa. I'd passed out with my arm behind my back. It hung from the socket like a dead thing. Not even tingly. Dough-flesh. As though Mr. Schmidlap's missing slab had been grafted onto my shoulder, penance for my murderous phone call. No doubt he wanted me to know what death was. What he was now: dead-weight, heavy sausage, gravity fodder.

I believed, as I did about so many things—sudden lightning, strange commercials, overheard nuns in busses or scraps of

Newsweek blown under my boot—that my meat-arm was a sign. Such occurrences were my father's way of speaking to me. Of communing. And now, apparently, they'd become Mr. Schmidlap's.

Dad's biggest message, of course, was dying in the first place. That was the clearest statement of all. *NO MATTER WHAT*, his death said to me, *THIS IS WHAT HAPPENS*. . . . They found his legs a quarter of a block from his torso. That's how long it took for the streetcar's brakes to work. I flashed on Mr. Schmidlap and my father hanging out in some post-dead rec room, talking absentee femurs and elbows, swapping stories of phantom itch. Perhaps they could pal around in the afterlife. . . . A silver lining!

I said, *"Thank you,"* like I always did, for this latest message: that the rest of me was going to be as dead as my arm if I didn't move fast. My arm was like a sneak preview. It crystallized a sense I'd had for a while—that I'd misplaced my life and was not likely to find it lounging around Mom's condo catching all-night movies, let alone sneaking laundry-room joints or sniffing old ladies' panty-pads. I knew today was the day. I just didn't know what day that was. . . .

With effort, I swung my sleeping arm up off the velour. If I cut it off now, it wouldn't even hurt. I could pack it in ice and track down Sharon. Make amends. I'd knock on her convent door and hand it over in a long flower box tied with pink ribbon in a bow. I had my speech all ready. *"I know I helped kill your daddy, but look! Now I'm a uniarm, too! Now I've repented and come back to be with you, to make love in the rumpus room and polish your dad's amputee bowling trophies. . . . Do you understand me?* NOW I'M JUST LIKE HIM!"

Something like that, but with more finesse.

perv—a love story

* * *

There were mornings I thought drugs made me insane and mornings I thought they kept me from going that way. I wasn't sure which this morning was going to be. All I knew was that after seven, the laundry room would start filling up with early sudsers. Insane or not, if I wanted to make the day endurable I had to head down there as soon as possible. Since my embarrassing fling with Michelle's grandmother, Dolores, I'd taken to lugging around my own meager laundry. Just in case. Once I'd snuck a few puffs, I could space out and stare at the faces in the dryer window. A rich, full life. I must have washed the same five sweat socks and tie-dyed T-shirts eleven times. Now everything was approaching peach.

On the elevator down, before the car jogged to a stop in the basement, I had my vision: Michelle Burnelka, in her orangeade robes, whooshing over the condo like Sally Fields in *The Flying Nun*. Only Michelle was *The Flying Krishna*, and she was saying something that got lost in the wind. Something I needed to hear.

I had to call her. That's all there was to it. Lately I couldn't breathe from being so lonely. I clung to the mortifying hope that, if she were really holy, Michelle would have to be nice to me. Have to at least hang out. Maybe I'd say I wanted a Bhagavad-Gita.

All I could focus on, by the time I pushed through the laundry room door, was what, if anything, Michelle wore under her robes. I was back to that. Where did Krishna stand on underwear? Was it something followers had to give up, like veal chops and hair? Or were there special saffron skimpies? Sanctioned Krishna-panties? Somehow I doubted the existence of Hare-lingerie. No, when the gods pulled girl-Krishnas up to heaven, I imagined, the rest of us would stand on the ground, faces raised, gazing upward between their legs. We'd see everything. And if, on some day of reckoning, all the Krishna-ettes hit the sky at once, forget it! From Teaneck to Beirut, legions of unholy men would strain their necks to catch a peek of Hindu beaver.

The more I smoked, the more convinced I became I had to call her. But call her *where?* And how? If I bugged Grandma Dolores for her number, the old lady might flip out and call the Vice Squad after all. Or she might want to rap some more about her husband, Albert, the late Rose Marie freak. Not that I *minded* listening. I enjoyed it. I just didn't have time. This was urgent. I foresaw the rest of my life as a bad movie I'd be forced to sit through until the credits if I didn't make a move soon.

A *Life* tossed on the top-loader lay open to a color photo of Haight-Ashbury. Two waifs in a room full of paisley pillows painted flowers on each other's foreheads. Two other girls in headbands danced dreamily behind them, blowing cantaloupe-sized bubbles at a shirtless, long-haired boy with daisies behind his ears. The boy might have been my age. All four girls wore granny skirts. You didn't need X-Ray Specs to notice there wasn't any bra action underneath.

I studied the hippies in the magazine. And then, figuratively speaking, I studied myself. The question was obvious. There was a world out there full of face-painting, bubble-blowing, bra-free girls. Boys with flowers in their hair. *So what was I doing in a laundry room in Pittsburgh?* For better or worse, I knew the answer. I still thought like a good boy. The embarrassing truth. Even though I got in a lot of trouble, I still thought like a boy who came home and helped with the dishes. I never stopped worrying. My guess was, it was probably genetic. I had anxious DNA.

perv—a love story

Still, if my sister Bernice could run away, why couldn't I? Maybe that was in the gene pool, too.

As usual, I popped my clothes straight in the dryer without washing them. An economy measure. A dime bought twenty minutes. By the time I finished my pin-sized joint the machine's whirring had metamorphoed to windy voices—the Oracle of Maytag—telling of Significant Portents. Communicating Dad-clues. I closed my eyes, the better to hear. He was saying one word over and over. One word: *worry. Worry worry worry worry.*

Well, yeah! What was the main thing about the San Francisco picture? More than that airy, sunlit parlor. More than the daisy-faced girls. More than the paisley ceiling, the painted footprints up and down the walls. . . . More than anything, what I now noticed was what was, amazingly, absent. What my father was on about: worry. There was no worry in that room. *That's* what I couldn't comprehend. Even stoned, or taking a bath, or jerking off, even when I was *sleeping*, I was still worried. I couldn't not be. If nothing bad was happening, I worried *something would*. If something bad was happening, I worried it was going to get worse. Yin, yang, over and out.

I'd have traded a kidney to be able to live like those *Life*-hippies: wrapped in buttercups, playing with bubbles and throw pillows, days drifting by like happy kisses blown from flower children named Sunfeather and Gear. But how could I? Happiness, to me, was no different than Mom's paprika-laced domino bars: something that looked sweet until you took a bite, and then made you want to vomit.

You couldn't be happy if you were always ashamed. There was no way around it. Unless—and this is where my Michelle Bur-nelka vision, the image of my soaring classmate, bestowed the tiniest hope, offered at least a hint of future relief—unless *this* is what happened when you went the Krishna route: You stopped worrying. . . . Permanently. About anything.

Maybe *that* was it! If you could hang around airports smiling like a pinhead in a muumuu and not give a hoot, what could possibly bother you? Someone laughs in your face? Spits on you? Calls you a heathen freakazoid? So *fucking what*! You were on board with the other muumuu people! Better still, after a hard day hustling Bhagavad-Gitas and banging tambourines, you'd all pack into the van back to the ashram. And chant the whole way! In other words, *you'd have each other*. That was the cool thing. That was the ultimate!

I was getting so crazy from being alone, I'd have shaved my head and done the hula in clownfeet to have someone to talk to. Just to have that.

What was life, *really, but everything you couldn't see?*

Vegging out in front of the dryer, I tended to get philosophical. I remembered how, when I was nine, I was sent to the doctor after Mom found a lump on the back of my head. Turns out it was something called my occiput. Dr. Minger, the starchy neighborhood M.D., told me it was an important thing to have. Without one, he explained, the bones in my skull would collapse and my brain would fall out. *"Wouldn't want that, would we?"*

My mother was always sending me to Minger to have things "looked at." He was always nice about it. But this visit, as it happened, was during the five minutes I thought I wanted to be a doctor. And there was one doctor-question that had been eating me since I'd made the decision to become Albert Schweitzer.

I hemmed and hawed, and finally spit it out when he started

perv—a love story

drumming the tongue depressor on his prescription pad. "Doctor, what about, like, fat old ladies? I mean, you know, touching them . . . ? Having to touch them? *How do you do it?*" It was a crude question, and I felt crude asking it. But still. . . .

And Dr. Minger, who had a broad pasty face and thinning hair, whom you saw once and just thought *bland,* Dr. Minger slapped down his depressor and regarded me with a very serious, very different kind of look. It was as if he were asking himself, *Do I tell him or don't I? Can I trust him or not?* Until finally, crooking his finger, so that I had to slide a little closer on the examining table, he lowered his voice and told me something that changed the world as I knew it from that moment on.

"*Sometimes,*" he whispered, as though afraid his secretary, an ancient, dumpling-faced Slavic lady named Mabel Binek, might be listening at the door, "sometimes I get these really fat ladies, these *really fat,* smelly ladies, and I have to examine them, inside, and it's not fun, you know? It's so disgusting I have to hold my breath. But I can't let them know. So I hum. Years ago I found a way to hum and hold my breath at the same time, so they don't see me go green around the gills. That's the trick, see? If they hear me humming 'Que Sèra, Sèra' or 'Bridge over the River Kwai,' they think I'm *happy* to be spreading their big, fat old-lady behinds. They think everything's hunky-dory."

After he told me, the doctor gripped my shoulders. He looked hard into both my eyes—left first, then right—then let go and shook my hand. He nodded gravely. *Now you know what I know. Betray me on pain of death!*

With that handshake, a curtain was drawn aside. I'd witnessed the Secret Room. People *pretended* to be nice, but behind the nice was something else: the truth. *Everything you couldn't see.* . . . And even Dr. Minger, maybe the nicest, blandest man in the entire city, even Dr. Minger had a secret room. From inside of which he peered out and made pleasant faces at the baffled and unhappy patients who paraded through his office. He hummed away the sight of all that pimpled, sagging humanity. The pleasant doctor "Que Sèra, Sèra' "d the desperate souls who soured his world with halitosis, smelly assholes, and naked fear. And that was life.

That was life.

I pondered these things all the way back up the elevator from the laundry room. In the kitchenette, I spotted the note Mom taped to the fridge:

Bobby,
Gone to beauty saloon. Dominoes in oven!

Your Mother
ps How 'bout those poor astronauts?!?!

Reading her note, I had to smile. NASA's third moon-shot had just fucked up. And Mom, God love her, was concerned. She never missed a launch if she was home. In honor of my mother, I tried to give the event some consideration. To forget about Minger and the Secret Room and feel something. Which, in my own way, I managed to do.

I really *grokked* the Apollo 13 guys. I imagined bobbing around in the ocean and wondering, not just if you were going to be rescued, but whether, if they *did* get you pried out of the can, you'd be laughed at. Whether you'd be branded some lifetime loser for having to be saved in the first place. My life—and this

perv—a love story

hit so hard I nearly toppled over—my *life* was Apollo 13! Launched with high expectations and pathetically crashed. Instead of stranded in the Pacific, I was flopped in Mom's condo, writhing on velour and beating off in sweat socks. *Houston, we have a problem. . . .*

The obvious question: Was it better to die now or go on living ashamed of the fact that you were still alive? Why wasn't that on the SATs? *Compare and contrast.* Instead of landing on the moon, the astronauts belly-flopped. Instead of heading to college, I languished in Pittsburgh, inhaling my mother. No matter where I went when I made it out of here—if I ever did—the secret weirdness of what I'd escaped would trail me. Probably the only way to get Mom's nightie-smell out of my nostrils was to chop my nose off. But then I'd be an outer mutant *and* an inner one. If I hacked it off, and *still* smelled her Momness, if her scent was actually in my brain, soaking it like cat spray on a couch. . . . *Well, then what?*

I realized I'd left my clothes spinning in the dryer, but it didn't matter. Where I was going, maybe I wouldn't need clothes. Michelle would tell me. I'd decided that. She was the key.

I'd cooked up a plan by the time I unearthed the phone book from under the sink and looked up *Burnelka.* There were two of them: a Dolly and a Carlton. The first turned out to be her grandmother, which I would have known if I'd bothered to look at the address beside the number. (Who knew Dolly was short for Dolores? Not me.) The address was the same as my mother's, just a different apartment. When I heard that quavering voice, I said, "Sorry, thought you were Sears and Roebuck," and hung up. I considered making up a name, saying I was president of the Rose Marie fan club, but decided that was cruel. Out of curiosity, I looked up Dolores Fish right after, and found Michelle's grandma listed that way, too. Either she couldn't make up her mind, or she was leading a double life. My guess was that she buried Mr. Burnelka before she buried Mr. *Fish*, then stayed in the phone book twice so as not to offend either. That was something I could understand. You didn't want to offend the dead. You didn't know how they'd react. . . .

I tried the Carlton number right after Laundry Room Dolly's. Let it ring nine times. I nearly dropped the receiver when I heard the voice. *Her* voice. Even in kindergarten, I'd been struck by how deep her voice was. How throaty, as if she'd been smoking Camel straights and guzzling whiskey straight for years before making it out of nursery school. *"I've seen things,"* that voice announced, *"you better believe it."* I don't know why, but I fell in love with the sound of her first. Just hearing Michelle say, "Present," when the teacher called roll made me woogly in the knees.

Michelle whispered, "Hello?" like it was a scary question. It gave me shivers. Then I realized, just because *I'd* been beating off picturing her holy-robed vagina, imagining even *that* was hairless—Tennie used to call it "shaved clam," and claimed he watched his mother "de-pube" before big dates, when she'd let him rinse the razor—that hardly guaranteed *she* was thinking about *me*. Why would it?

For all I knew, Michelle didn't even *have* thoughts anymore. Maybe all that chanting wafted thought right out of your brain. I'd seen an ad in *Popular Mechanics* for a machine that drove fleas off dogs by making high-frequency sound waves. Humans couldn't hear it, but the noise sent fleas packing. Maybe the whole *Hare-Hare* thing was like that. You just kept chanting until

perv—a love story

your thoughts vacated your brain like high-frequencied fleas. And you did it in airports.

The whole process sounded relaxing. But Michelle didn't sound relaxed. She sounded freaked-out.

"Hello?" she whispered again. "Who is this? Shiva, is that you?"

"Michelle? Uh, no . . . This isn't Shiva. It's—"

"It *is* you, Shiva. Don't lie! I *told* you! I'm going. You fucker, I'm going as far away from you as I can get."

This tripped me up, but I couldn't stop now. "Michelle, please, don't hang up!" I pleaded. "It's not what you think. I'm—"

"Shiva, you *prick*! Don't pretend it isn't you? Do you know what you did? Do you even *know* what you did to me?"

"Well . . ."

She had such a distinctive voice: permanently surprised, but sad, too. Like Judy Garland in *The Wizard of Oz*. But deeper. A voice that left you feeling, at any second, she might break into complete hysteria. Not that I was any judge, but it didn't seem like she'd attained eternal peace since the last time I'd seen her.

I took a breath and started over. "Michelle, it's me. . . . I mean, it's Bobby. Bobby Stark? We were . . . I mean, you remember, don't you? We went to school together. I mean—"

"Bobby Stark?" I could hear her surprise. "Bobby Stark? *From grade school?* Did Shiva tell you to call. 'Cause if he did—"

"Not just grade school," I babbled. "We were in high school, too, for a couple of years. Then I got shipped away. Anyhow, I don't know any Shiva." I was so nervous I kept chattering, like I always did, even though I wanted to stop. Plus I was getting Jiminy Cricket-y. "The only Shiva I know about is Ye-shiva. Have *they* been calling? Are you being hassled by *Hebrew teachers*?" I heard my own lame jokes and thought, *MORON!*

But Michelle was too paranoid to take in any of it. My lame-o jokes went right by her. The fact that I'd called at all weirded her right out the window. "Bobby Stark?" she kept saying. "Bobby *Stark?*" The way she repeated it, my own name sounded ominous. One of the Seven Signs of the Apocalypse. "Bobby Stark? How'd you know I'd be here?"

"I didn't, Michelle. I just tried your number. I've been sort of stuck in Pittsburgh for a while. But when I flew in, at the airport, I saw you, y'know, in your, um . . . uniform. Doing your thing. I didn't really think you'd be living at home. . . ."

"I don't live at home," she replied, very quickly. "I don't live anywhere. I was staying at the ashram, in Shadyside, until— Are you sure you don't know Shiva? Because . . . well, just because."

"I'm telling you, I don't know anybody."

Despite the chilly response, I felt giddy talking to her. I was doing a jig around the kitchen, making faces in the stainless steel toaster, when I heard the key turning in the lock. Mom, naturally, at the worst time in the world.

"Michelle, listen," I blurted, cupping a hand over the receiver. "Oh shit. . . . Hang on."

"Hellooo!" my mother called, the way she did whenever she guzzled sherry on top of her medication. She liked "a little drop" at lunch, but sherry-and-pheno always got her floaty. She'd pad around like the Queen of Happy till she passed out with her sequins on. "Hellooo, anybody to home!"

"Michelle?" I whispered, barely audible, like somebody with burglars in the house talking to 911. "Could I call you back?" I hoped I didn't come off too *pleady*. It sounded like she'd had enough trouble from Shiva, whoever he was.

"This is far out," Michelle giggled, getting chatty at the exact

perv—a love story

moment I had to hang up. "Why I thought you knew Shiva's 'cause nobody else would know I was back at my house. I don't even live here anymore. I haven't been in a year. I only snuck back to get some stuff. Clothes and money, if I can find any. Do you have any money? 'Cause I have to get out of here. I can't even talk now. I have to go. I just walked in, then you called. I don't even know why I picked up the phone."

"Michelle, look," I said, glad my mother owned kidneys the size of Chiclets. She zipped to the bathroom the second she reeled in. "Michelle—"

The toilet seat slammed with a muffled bang. "*Bob*-by!" Mom sang. The seat had a furry blue cover, but still, when she washed down those tranqs with a glass or three, it rattled the windows. "Darlin'," Mom warbled, "I'm just a-lovin' you all *over* the place!"

"That's nice!" I hollered back, smashing my hand over the phone. I would have died if Michelle heard. Once in a while, Mom went country-western on pills-and-alcohol. Out of no-where, she'd start tossing off "darlin's" and "honey-chiles" like Patsy Cline's neurotic cousin. Patsy Clinestein. Worse, she loved to chat from the bathroom. If I had friends over, and Mom was bombed, I'd have to remind her to shut the door. Otherwise she'd invite us in for a sing-along.

"Is someone there?" Michelle asked, sounding panicked again.

"Yes . . . no," I said. "I mean, not right here. Anyway, where are you going?"

"I don't know," she answered. I could hear drawers crashing, things being thrown around. *Banging.* It conjured up Mr. Schmid-lap. I nearly had a white-out just thinking about it. But Michelle brought me back. "I don't know where I'm going," she said, breathing hard, "I just know I'm going."

"Well. . . ."

I could hear my mother flushing. (She always flushed twice, to prevent "return engagements.") Then she started singing and washing her hands. She belted out "Home on the Range," one of her faves, though the words were slightly altered. In her condition, it sounded like "Homo Deranged." But I couldn't worry about it. I kept my palm over the receiver, leaving a tiny space to speak through. Michelle-wise, it was now or never.

"Well. . . . Can we meet? Somewhere? Anywhere?"

"I don't know. Did you say you had money?"

"Some," I lied.

"Okay. How about the mall? In fifteen. In front of the petting zoo. But I won't wait. I can't."

She hung up before I did. No good-bye. I got the receiver down a second before Mom bubbled into the kitchen.

"Oh, Bobby," she giggled, primping her hair, fluffing her *I Love Lucy* do and waiting for compliments. "Were you talking to someone?"

"Oh, uh. . . . just the library. I was calling the library. Looking for a job."

"The library. Terrif! Do you like it?"

"The library?"

"My hair, cleverboots. I had Ricardo add some henna. A mother has to look pretty for her baby boy. *Me* don't have to go *gway* if me don't *wanna*. . . ."

"Of course you don't." I was creeped out by the baby talk, but glad she hadn't started smooching. After County-Western, as a rule, came Baby-Talk, and after Baby-Talk came the Smooches. That was Mom's routine on booze. She'd end up begging for kisses, and begging to give them. It wasn't pretty. If I could duck out now, I'd avoid the smooch-fest. In the meantime, I wanted to make nice. Who knew when I'd see her again?

"What are they gonna do," I teased, "put you in hairdo jail? Of course you can add some henna. But you don't have to, Mom. You look fantastic, I swear. How is Ricardo, anyway?"

"Oh, you know Ricardo," she tittered.

Actually, I did know Ricardo. I knew him when he was still Dick Purdewski, big brother of Jinxy Purdewski, a kid on our old street I used to play with. The Purdewskis were the first kids I knew whose father died. Pop Purdewski was a meat packer. He died the day before Thanksgiving. When a pulley snapped, he got crushed under a ton of frozen turkeys. After Dick opened Beauty By Ricardo at Miracle Mile—the same mall where Michelle was probably already waiting—my mother started going there for her weekly Lucy-do. Since then, Dick's background as Jinxy's brother was somehow forgotten. Mom came to believe he'd "trained on the continent," and there was no point telling her "Ricardo" had never been farther afield than the Cleveland Academy of Beauty.

"That Ricardo is *amazing*," she chirped. "You know he's up on all the latest styles. And he always asks about you."

"That's great," I said, not even sure if I was being sarcastic. Sometimes when I tried to be sincere, Mom got on me for "being snippy." When I was actually *being* snippy, she thought I was "a perfect little man."

Right now, whatever I was, I wanted out of the condo. This was my chance. I felt it down to my corpuscles. I had about twelve minutes left to get to the mall. It was a ten-minute walk, if you ran. And I hadn't even made it out of my mother's living room.

*   *   *

I didn't know what to grab before I split, so I went for the drugs. I kept some pot in a Sucrets box stuffed in the pocket of a rolled-up work shirt, and a knuckle of hash in tinfoil shoved inside a pair of my father's old brogans. (Mom saved all his clothes, in case he came back from the dead and dressed for dinner.) That stuff I stashed in my boots. The other items—two hits of orange acid Tennie swore was Sunshine, but I suspected was baby aspirin, and a fistful of pilfered Reds—I slipped into the lining of my windbreaker.

"Going somewhere, doll-puss?"

"Huh?"

I was banking on Mom napping after her lunch and Lucy-perm. But she was on the prowl. Worse, she was brewing coffee. A bad break! Instead of her usual MO: heading into Baby Talk and Smooches, then collapsing altogether, now she'd perk up and launch into the C and C. The College-and-Cancer Report. I knew this from long experience. Whenever she met with her friends, at some point afterward I'd have to hear about their kids, who were all doing fabulous—*"Kevin's Pre-law, Kathy's engaged to an orthodontist!"*—and then their husbands, who either had pros-tates *"the size of beach balls"* or had just sprouted some kind of "thing." As in *"Poor Tessie, the doctor's just found a 'thing' under Harv's arm. . . . He's going in Tuesday."*

Much as I hated to cop to it, on some level I could not get enough of this. Especially the Tumor News. Something *hap-pened* when my father died. I've tried to explain this, but I don't know. . . . Suddenly, I had a license to fuck up. When Dad was alive, knowing how bad he'd had it growing up, I felt obligated to at least try to appreciate all I'd been blessed with: warm house,

perv—a love story

food on the table, my own clothes. Dad never talked much about the orphanage, but I know from my mother that it was like something out of *Oliver Twist*, without the cute hats and Cockney they stuck in the movie version. Much as I loved my dad, I felt sorry for him, too. I didn't want to make the miserable life he'd endured any worse by being a problem, myself. But all that changed when he died. More than my sanctioned failure (what else was the son of a suicide supposed to do, if not fuck himself up?), I had a new attitude. A new way of thinking—call it Negative Serenity—that sprang from the certain knowledge that everything ran to shit in the end. Mr. Schmidlap knew all about this. Meeting him was like meeting Moses. He brought the bad news down from the mountaintop, and he stayed drunk for the whole fucking trip.

My credo boiled down to a slogan I'd inked on the arm of the mayonnaise-colored vinyl chair in my room at Hale. It was just two words: *Death Anyway*. These came to me one Sunday, when I was curled under a blanket doing mescaline in my closet. My eyes were closed, and the words flashed like neon against a black sky.

Death Anyway meant "Look at my father, he worked himself sick, and ended up waltzing in front of a yellow streetcar. . . ."

Death Anyway meant "What the hell, even Hemingway sucked on a shotgun. . . ."

Death Anyway meant "Why not stay wasted, since life was a knife-up-the-crack, crawl-across-broken-glass bummer anyway . . . ?"

Death Anyway, when you came down to it, meant why in God's name would you want to be Pre-Law, Pre-Med, or Pre-Anything, when any microbe could see that just being alive was no more than *Pre-Death*.

As far as I could tell, life was nothing but a forced march down a mined highway. Even if you did everything you were supposed to do, sooner or later it was your turn to step on a claymore.

Watching the war on TV, what always got me were the Bouncing Betty guys. GIs who'd had their bottom halves blown off *just walking through the jungle.* You'd see them being rushed through some rice paddy onto a helicopter. There'd be a medic holding an IV bag on one side of the stretcher, some shuffling grunt on the other with his head half-blown off. The walking wounded's eyes would be wrapped in blood-soaked gauze, and he'd be puffing a Camel for his Walter Cronkite moment. In every clip it looked like the same cigarette—ash an inch long and holding—and the same damaged soldier waiting to be tossed on the chopper alongside his laid-out pal.

That was the world, to me. If you showed up—if you did what they told you to do—you'd *still* end up with your skull in bloody gauze or your balls hanging from a branch. So why bother? Nothing mattered. *Death anyway....*

The reason I'd stayed at Hale, instead of rolling onto the turnpike and sticking my thumb out, was that there were so many decent drugs, and it was easier to just hang around with Tennie and do them. That, and the embarrassing fact that I was too scared to do anything else. But now all that had changed. They'd thrown my ass out. I was rotting in condoville and my brain felt like it had gangrene....

I zoned back to reality just as Mom was hitting her stride.

"Would you believe, Bitsy Simon's boy Donald got into Cornell? Hotel management!" She skipped into the living room with her compact open and her mouth mushed out so she could check

perv—a love story

her lipstick. She favored the same screaming magenta she'd worn since I was in the crib, staring up at her and thinking, in babified panic, *"Mommy grape juice!"*

That was a family joke: how my first words weren't Mama or Dada, but "grape juice." Because that's what she seemed to have smeared on her puss.

"It's such a *riot,*" Mom went on. She smacked her lips and checked to make sure none of the magenta stuck to her teeth. "When Donald was just a little pisher, he liked to play house. Can you imagine?" She looked right and left, as if we weren't alone in her living room, but camped in a den thick with spies. "You know," she said, nodding significantly, "I always thought he went to the bathroom *sitting down.*"

This was Mom's biggest fear, and her fave piece of info about friends' sons. On Sunday nights, when the family was plunked in front of Ed Sullivan and some cheesy dance number came on—Diana Dors, say, doing splits and riding the shoulders of smiley men in leotards—Mom would ogle the male dancers, then glare at me.

"Bobby, I don't care what you do, but don't you *dare* grow up and become a dancing boy!"

"Why not?"

"Because," she'd shriek, already suspicious that I had to ask, *"they go to the bathroom sitting down . . . !"*

All sins were preferable to failure to urinate on two legs. . . .

I loved how Mom could "adore" her friends, listing their children's mammoth accomplishments—all, by implication, damning her own offspring for their utter lack of anything resembling a triumph (I won a spelling bee in seventh grade, and it was downhill from there)—while at the same time unveiling their most heinous personal failings. There was Darren, who (what else?) "peed sitting down." Or Mrs. Nussbaum, "with her little kleptomania problem." Not to mention her "great friend" Emily Tierney, and her colossal crying jags. *"Nobody knows why she cries, she just does."*

Secretly delicious as I found these midday dish sessions— Mom drunk and tranquilized, me high on pot, the two of us in some private buzzy bathysphere where, for once, it wasn't only *my* failures being savored—I was also hugely paranoid. I lived in throbbing fear that if I didn't hurry up and tear myself from this condo-womb, I'd lurk here forever. I would wake up and be Herb Pazahowski: a stoop-shouldered retard with his pants pulled up to his sagging paps. . . . Today I could not give in. Today I *had* to head out. I had to meet Michelle.

"That poor Mrs. Frankel," Mom sighed, arranging herself on the velour couch and patting the seat for me to join her. "Her husband had dandruff that turned out to be cancer. Can you imagine? And she's such a sweet woman."

"Mom," I said, dying to hear more, but dying just as much to wriggle out of there. "Mom, I really do have to go. The library, you know, they gave me an interview. . . . I really don't want to be late. . . ."

"Oh right, the library." I could tell she was disappointed. But since she'd been hassling me to get a job, she couldn't say anything. "Grab my purse and take a couple of dollars. I'm so proud of you! Get yourself something nice for lunch." Her head lolled sideways and she went baby again. "Bwing Mama home some turtles and we'll celebwate. I wuv woo, Bobby. . . ."

"Uh, me too, Mom."

This was bad. Turtles were the chocolate-covered peanut and

perv—a love story

caramel clusters my father brought home on special occasions. Every anniversary he'd slog into the house, hang down his head, and pretend he'd forgotten what day it was. And every year, the little playlet wound up with Dad reaching in his fat leather brief-case, shoving aside some "Innocent Negro" files, and pulling out a gift-wrapped box of Fannie Farmer milk chocolate turtles. Just hearing Mom mention them, wanting me to go buy some—to pretty much take over for Dad—pumped me full of rank happiness and bottomless dread.

I really did have to get the fuck out.

Mom made her pouty "little girl" face and aimed it in my direction. "Nobody bwings your mommy anything since your daddy died. . . ."

That she never failed to chide him for not getting the double box, that when he did get the double-decker box, she nagged because it was stale, were items she'd seemed to forget altogether.

In any event, I knew what was coming. She'd get weepy. Ask for a snuggle. One wrong move and I'd be on the couch getting nuzzled, inhaling chemical fumes from her fresh permanent. The scent already burned my pupils from across the room. I didn't know if Ricardo/Dick dipped her curls in formaldehyde, but that's what it smelled like. Biology lab. Mom's hair could have preserved a frog.

"So, where *is* your purse?" I asked, trying to head off the Cuddles. "If I'm going to grab some turtles, I guess I will need a little green."

I wasn't consciously planning to steal. But when something drops in your lap, what can you do?

"It's been so long," Mom sniffled. "I don't know what good candy costs. Where *is* my baby monkey purse?"

I rubbed my chin. Acting. "Let's see, didn't you go to the bathroom when you came home?"

"Oh, you're so smart! You really are. Check *la salle de bain.*"

"*D'accord,*" I hollered, shooting down the hall to the toilet. French was another liquid lunch-and-pill thing. Between us we knew about nine words, though I'd taken French 1 three times. Soon enough, however, everything would wear off. Mom would sink back into depression and back to bed. Until the inevitable, it was nice to see her feeling chipper.

I was poking around the hamper when Mom called from the living room. "Eurekavitch! It was behind the TV. Oh wait!"

I dashed back to the living room. At this point, I'd have to break the land speed record to meet Michelle. Mom tossed the baby monkey purse on the carpet and threw up her hands.

"*Crimenetly,* my wallet's not in here! I swear, I'd lose my boobies if they weren't screwed on."

I didn't love this kind of talk, but there was no point saying. After Mom trundled off to the kitchenette, I spotted a lump under the *Newsweek* on the couch. I waited until I heard pans crashing before I checked it out. The lump was her wallet, stuffed like a Dagwood with dollar bills. I liberated the whole wad, along with a credit card, before sliding the thing deep under a cushion a second before she blustered back in.

I'd nipped a few bucks here and there—what red-blooded kid hadn't?—but never thought to pocket a credit card, let alone take every cent my mother had. Before this, I thought I was probably coming back. Now, whatever happened, I wouldn't be able to. When she found the wallet, she'd know. I just hoped there were some twenties shoved in with those ones.

The second Mom breezed back in, I slapped myself on the

perv—a love story

forehead. "Jeezy peezy, look at the time. . . . I told the library lady I'd be there ten minutes ago. Gotta scoot!"

I felt so sincere I almost believed myself.

"Wish me luck, okay? Maybe I can bring you some best-sellers, new Micheners and stuff, before anybody else gets a crack at 'em!"

Caught up in the charade, I leapt forward and sploshed a kiss on Mom's cheek. This was so unprecedented, she stepped back to double-check—or so it struck me at the time—that I wasn't high again.

"Well," she panted, placing a hand palm down on her mammoth bosom, "you go out and knock 'em dead, Mr. Dewey Decimal. Tonight Mommy's making your favorite. Baked chicken and candied beets! Nothing's too good for my little man!"

And that was that. I hated myself, but what else was new? I waved good-bye. Squinching my toes in my boots to feel the hash, I tapped the wad in my back pocket and skipped out the door like the wholesomest sixteen-year-old on Planet Earth. It felt so good, going off to do the right thing, that for one, teetering second, I thought, *Maybe I will go to the library. . . .* I let my brain fly with it: I'd get a job, buy Mom those chocolate turtles, slide home, and squidge the card back in her wallet before she realized it was missing. After that, who knew? Get back in school. Apply to Pitt. Check out the whole Pre-Dental thing. . . .

In my mini-fantasy, I heard Mom bragging to her friends about her boychick, little Joe College. *"And all this time, I thought maybe he was one of those chorus boys. . . ."*

I was so moved by my amazing comeback, only the memory of Michelle's neck brought me to my senses. I stepped out of the elevator as a cream-colored Continental glided by the lobby entrance, and an image seized me: the downy flesh beneath her hair, the pale skin exposed when she swung her auburn mane in triumph after giving the right answer in Geography. *The capital of Peru is Lima! The main export of Saudi Arabia is petroleum!* I'd been gazing at the back of her neck in awe for as long as I could remember.

By the time I careened out the door, I was nearly drooling. Seized by the thrilling notion that, thanks to the peculiar hair beliefs of the Hare Krishnas, that gorgeous neck, which for almost a decade of scholastic boredom I'd sat behind and studied, admired, breathed heavy over . . . would now be liberated. Naked unto the world. Not only that, but this lovely sub-hair area, the same creamy-smooth shade as the suave Continental, might now be available to me. With any luck, I could touch it that very afternoon!

The possibility brought me trembling to a crossroads in my mind. Did I do the good thing: sign up at the library and make Mom happy? Or did I do the thing that felt good: run my ass off to the mall and meet Michelle?

The haggard face of Mr. Schmidlap floated above me, followed by the dark, disapproving globe of my father's. I leaned against a condo pillar and shut my eyes on both of them. All month the FM station had played this one Blind Faith song over and over. The lyrics were simple: *"Do what you want. . . . Do what you want you want. . . ."* I never caught the name of the tune. Just the chorus, going on forever. *"Do what you want. . . ."* But could you? Could life actually not be hell?

I watched the creamy Continental swing out of the condo driveway into Superior Boulevard. The first drops of drizzle tickled my Jew-fro, though it was still sunny. A bus roared by in a

perv—a love story

blast of exhaust. The day itself felt confused, like it couldn't make up its mind what to be. I had, in some crippling flash, one of a series of revelations that were to plague me in the hours to come. It arrived, as if from on high, in my father's voice. "Whatever you do," he said, somewhat wearily, in a tone that seemed to imply, *I'm not really thrilled to be talking to you, but somebody's got to fill you in,* "whatever you do, you're going to regret it, so just go ahead and do *SOMETHING. . . .*"

I wondered, yet again, if the streetcar conductor had rung his little bell, and if my father closed his eyes before he hit the tracks.

Eight minutes later I burst panting through the Miracle Mile doors. Halfway there, jogging down Superior, the drizzle switched to a downpour. I arrived at the mall so soaked that the hash in my boots squished like melting chocolate.

I stared in panic down the row of stores to the petting zoo. I scoured the shoppers for saffron. Not a lot of folks wore orange of any shade, as far as I could tell, although plenty of boys wore madras shirts. Some even marched around in madras pants, and a surly gaggle of madras guys clustered by the revolving doors. They pretended to punch each other, waiting for the rain to stop so their threads wouldn't bleed.

My whole life I'd felt nervous around big groups of kids. I always assumed they were planning to gang up on me. (More than once, a total stranger had stepped up and informed me I had the kind of face he'd "like to smack." And in grade school, often enough, I'd been knocked around, on general principle, for the simple fact that "the fuckin' Jews killed Jesus.") Just by wearing my tie-dyed T-shirt and corduroys, my work boots and puffy hair, I announced that I was on a different team. The whole world now broke down to Heads and Straights, Freaks and Squares. Tie-Dye versus Madras. And I was definitely not in Tie-Dye Country.

Still, it wasn't the likelihood of a pounding that got me up-tight. It was the chance that some Johnny Madras might take off with Michelle.

Suddenly every boy I saw was a threat. I knew this was cracked. I hadn't seen Michelle—or said more than a hundred words to her—since eighth or ninth grade. But my lungs filled up with broken glass at the thought of anybody else going near her.

If I closed my eyes, I could almost count those soft hairs on the back of her neck. One day I'd even leaned forward, pretending to drop my pencil, and inhaled her until the top of my head started to steam. A scent of butterscotch wafted off of her, and it was all I could do not to plunge my face in her shag and let them take me to jail. I seriously considered it: On the one hand I'd go to prison; on the other, I'd have that butterscotch waft in my nostrils as I languished in solitary. . . . It was romantic or demented, depending on what mood I was in when I thought about it.

I made my way past Village Cobbler and Ye Olde Sterling Shoppe to Modern Miss, where a dozen miniskirt-clad manne-quins stood frozen in mid-frug. One statue, whose platinum fall shone only slightly less white than her snug mini-and-go-go boot ensemble, would not stop staring at me. When I stared back, her eyes glittered with desire. Her lips parted. Her mom could have been the White Owl cigar lady. One hip thrust forward, she held her hands at her waist, arms akimbo, in a defiant what-are-

perv—a love story

you-gonna-do-about-it-big-boy? pose. It was as if, not only could she see me, she really thought I was groovy.

I stared at her and pondered. If she were real, I'd have to decide: Michelle or White Owl Cigar Girl? Or maybe I could have both. Just loll around with a beauty in each arm, like Hugh Hefner. Maybe I could stretch out in a revolving bed, on satin sheets, with one of those stereos that shot out of the cabinet when you pressed a button. Press another one and the black lights would go up, setting LUV! or WAR IS UNHEALTHY FOR CHILDREN AND OTHER LIVING THINGS aglow over the headboard. Maybe I'd even meet Peter Max.

I was still ogling Modern Miss, daydreaming about me and Hef double-dating, when I saw another face beside mine in the window. This one small as a fist between a low-brimmed Beatle cap and the turned-up collar of a navy pea coat.

"Mini skirts suck," said the tiny face. "They show right into your booty and every creep with a peter looks at you like you're a cream sandwich."

My daydream shattered, I turned around and stared.

"Michelle?"

bummed-out hindu

I'd expected robes, an ethereal smile, divine peace—not to mention that shaved skull. (I'd already fantasized about rubbing it, then covering it with kisses, before deciding that licking was the way to go. I only had to think the word "stubble" and I overheated.)

Instead of Little Miss Krishna, though, instead of angelic, Michelle looked like one of those tough runaways who hung around in front of the bus station. Any hour of the day you'd spot gangs of them, some no older than sixth-graders, hunched together under the Greyhound sign, lounging on their backpacks with Marlboros dangling out of their mouths. I used to see them on Sundays, when Dad and I drove through downtown on the way to Squirrel Hill for lox and bagels. I'd always slink down in my seat if we got a red light in front of the station. I was ashamed to be seen sitting in a car with my father, going for bagels, when these kids were years younger and already out panhandling on their own.

"Something happen to your spine?" my father asked one Sunday, when a pack of preteen smokers crossed the street in front of our Valiant. I was already in full cringe-mode, waiting for some twelve-year-old to peek in and call me a candy-ass. I told Dad I had a cramp. . . .

Not that I was disappointed in Michelle. In her pea coat and Beatle cap, her cherry granny glasses and lemon-colored bell-bottoms, she looked every bit the little hippie girl. Except that you couldn't tell she was a girl. Her pea coat was so big on her, there could have been anything at all under there.

"I thought . . ." I started to say, then caught myself and started over. "I mean, I didn't know Hare Krishna let you wear regular clothes."

"They don't."

"Well, okay," I said, for lack of anything better. I wished I could make out her eyes, but didn't say anything. Her skin, what I could see of it, was still as soft as I remembered. What the commercials called Ivory smooth.

"Look," she said, sounding annoyed, "I'm getting the hell out of the Krishnas. I thought you knew."

"I figured something like that."

Michelle slid her shades off and squinted. Her eyes were red and runny. She'd either been crying or smoking grass, or both. Even so, they glowed the same spectacular green I dreamed about. She grabbed me by my shoulders and pulled me close. For one heart-pounding moment I thought, *She's going to French me.* Then she opened up.

"Listen, man, I risked my ass getting out of the ashram, okay? Shiva's gonna flip out. He's got airport duty till midnight and I wanna be far away by then. Why didn't you meet me at the petting zoo, anyway? That's what we said, right? The petting zoo? I've been standing there smelling goat poop for twenty minutes. Plus I got bit by a lamb. That's so typical. In all these nursery stories, lambs are like, all fluffy and cuddly. Meanwhile, you try and pet one, they take a chunk outa you." She raised her thumb to show me the scratch. When she licked it, I almost fainted. "You think lambs got rabies?"

I admitted I wasn't up on sheep diseases, but that you could usually tell a dog was rabid if it foamed at the mouth. "Lambchop looked pretty clean," I said, but the joke went right past her.

"Well what do *you* know? If you hadn't stood here staring at her"—she jerked her head at the hip-slung mannequin—"none of this would have happened. I do not have time to get a bunch of rabies shots." She looked at the miniskirt in the window and back at me, slitting her eyes. "You're not some perv, are you?"

Man! That was twice in one week. I wasn't certain how to answer—"No, I'm *NOT* a perv!" just didn't sound right—so I tried another approach. "Look, I'm sorry," I said, adding weakly, "I thought I was early."

Michelle wrinkled her nose. "Are you sure you don't know Shiva? He didn't send you here to stall me?"

perv—a love story

"We've been through this, okay? I already told you." Right then I caught myself thinking about Mom back in the condo, waiting for turtles. She'd just be tuning into the *Million Dollar Movie*. "I don't know anything about any Shiva."

Michelle seemed cooled out and gave me a nod. "All right, but you better not be cornholing me! I've been cornholed a lot lately. I've been cornholed enough to last a lifetime."

She hadn't smiled once, and I wondered what had happened to her. (I didn't even want to think about what cornholing meant. I had a pretty decent idea.) This wasn't the girl with auburn tresses I remembered from Geography. It was hard to believe she was the same creature who'd swung her hair with such glee at guessing the population of Guadeloupe.

The second she grabbed my hand and bolted, everything changed. I had to trot to keep up, and the feel of her flesh on mine made my brain steam. She shouted as she ran for the exit.

"If we leave now, we might make it to Chicago before tomorrow."

"Why Chicago?"

She didn't answer. Then she stopped in the middle of the parking lot and turned on me. In the station wagon beside us, a pair of twins in Pirate hats tried to poke each other in the eye. It was half raining and half not.

"God, Bobby, you used to be smart. Why do you think? 'Cause it's on the way to San Francisco."

I used to be smart? I wasn't even sure she knew I was alive. Now I find out she thought I had brains. That was something, anyway. I wanted to ask if she ever thought about me the way I thought about her. If she missed me, even. But this didn't seem like the time. Cool as she tried to come off, Michelle was in some kind of panic situation. In a no-fucking-around head. Whatever happened between the last time I'd glimpsed her in high school and this throbbing minute, it had not exactly left her carefree. If anything, she seemed angry. She seemed in a hurry. She didn't seem like she wanted to reminisce.

We moved down a few rows, making for the street on the other side, when she stopped again. "You have bread, right?"

"Some."

"How much is some?"

"I don't know." I tried to sound casual, though the truth was I was as scared that I'd ripped off a thousand dollars as that I'd stolen a fistful of singles. I knew Mom had cash in the bank, but that's all I knew. . . . It started to pour again, but we ignored it. I fished in my rain-soaked pants for the wad, and as soon as I plucked it out Michelle snatched it.

"What'd you do, rob a candy store?"

"Maybe."

For the first time since we'd re-met, Michelle smiled. She started to count the money, slowly transferring the bills from one hand to the other. I'd just seen *Bonnie and Clyde* and got sort of excited. *Bonnie and Clyde. Bobby and Michelle.* It had a ring, that was undeniable. Michelle talked as she counted, keeping her eyes on the money.

She obviously had zero interest in me, or what had been going on in Bobby-land. But that was all right. It gave me the chance to be as tough as she was. So I shut up and listened. I let her words wash over me, feeling a little like my father must have felt, listening to somebody's problems. I reveled in the fact that, at that moment, I was the only person in the world hearing her voice.

perv—a love story

"Listen," Michelle insisted, "I wasn't, like, into the Hindu bag, okay? I just joined the ashram 'cause of my dad . . . Well, actually my stepdad, Maurice. He moved in after my real dad moved out, and then it started."

Michelle stopped talking then. She even stopped counting. For a second or two we both stood there, saying nothing while the rain spit down and people on either side of us ran frantically to their cars. Michelle blinked and licked her lips. Her jaw clenched tight and she tipped her chin up defiantly, as if daring me to say the wrong thing.

"Michelle," I said, as carefully as I could, "is everything cool?"

She raised her shining eyes and wiped them. This accidentally tipped the Beatle cap back on her head, revealing the naked scalp underneath. The sight was weirdly heartbreaking. With all that skin over her forehead, her features seemed lost and small: eyes, nose, and mouth crowded together like tiny buildings all alone in a giant field, little places you'd see from an airplane and wonder about. At that moment my heart literally began to ache. I was so in love it hurt. I thought, without really thinking it, *This is what they mean by "smitten."* I would have done anything to brighten those delicate features, to make those tiny places less lonely.

"He had hands like helicopters," she went on, her voice sounding so much younger, the way I remembered it from grade school. Throaty, but somehow innocent, too, like everything still surprised her. She stared down as she talked, keeping her gaze aimed at the cracked asphalt of the parking lot, folding and re-folding Mom's money. "That's what my little sister and me used to call them. Maurice would get drunk on Southern Comfort and Iron City and call me into the TV Room when Mom was working graveyard at J and L. She's the assistant mill-nurse, which means she gets the melted guys. Lots of times the molten steel splashes out of the bucket, and when it hits your skin it burns right through. What I wished was I had a bucket of steel to pour on Maurice, all over his shiny pig-face, just to watch him scream. Every time, right before I went in, Jennie'd grab my hand and squeeze. 'Watch out for the helicopters, Mi-Mi.' That's what she calls me. 'Watch out for the helicopters!' I always went in, though. I had to, 'cause if I didn't he'd come after Jennie, and she's only nine. I could handle it. Until I couldn't, and I ran away and went to the ashram. That's where I met Shiva."

"The guy you keep talking about, right? He sounds intense."

"He's not intense. He's a mystic," she said. "That's more intense than intense. It's intense *and* holy. That's what I used to think anyway."

"I'll bet," I said, for lack of anything else.

I tried to keep my voice neutral. The Maurice thing was terrible. Worse than terrible. No wonder she didn't ask me anything about myself. Her own problems pretty much swallowed everything else. What her stepdad had done, as far as I could figure, took up all the space in her brain. There just wasn't room to squeeze a whole lot about Bobby Stark in there. Even so, she seemed to want to tell me things—to see if I'd be shocked—like it was some kind of test. If it was, I thought the best way to pass was to say nothing. The truth was, I could have told *her* things, too. Stuff about me and Mom, but that would not have made what happened to her any better. I wasn't as brave as Michelle. What went on between me and Mom—the salmon nightie, the cuddles, her damp hot fish-skin—was something I wasn't ready to march out in the parking lot of the mall. So I just listened. I

perv—a love story

didn't ask about the helicopters. I didn't say a word about her stepdaddy's hands. I only nodded. Tried to focus on Shiva (I pictured a cross between Mick Jagger and Gunga Din) and didn't let myself think about Maurice. What Maurice did, what it must have made Michelle feel inside—and what she had to wake up, walk around, and go to bed with because of how that feeling never went away—I thought I could best address by being kind. Being easy. By not saying a word, one way or another, besides "I'm sorry."

Michelle let out the longest sigh in the world and walked on. I saw her shove the money in the pocket of her lemon bell-bottoms. But I didn't say anything about that, either.

"I do *NOT* want to get into Shiva," she said, staying a few steps ahead of me. "Not now. We've got ninety-three dollars and I've got to pee. Come on."

Lightning cracked overhead. Without the least hesitation, Michelle jumped back and clutched my arm, shrieking, "I'm scared! I hate this shit!" It was the highest I'd ever heard her voice.

When the thunder hit, seconds later, she burrowed her face in my shoulder. I wanted to hold her, to put my arm around her like Cary Grant, but I wasn't sure how. I racked my brains, trying to remember some movie with a couple-caught-in-the-rain scene. Did you go over the shoulder, and pull close? Or did you slide in under the arm, grip under the tit? I could feel her shaking. Her body vibrated under the heavy wool. Finally she grabbed my arm and flung it around her shoulders, behind her neck. "I never liked thunder," she hollered, her whole body quivering against me, so that I felt almost noble—or what it would be *like* to be noble. "Never ever fucking ever!"

I thought we should move but we didn't. We stayed there, frozen in the middle of aisle C of the mall parking lot while pissed-off drivers honked and swerved around us. I can't say I didn't notice the weather—the raindrops had graduated to hail and stung when they slapped into your skin—it's just that the other sensations, the ones I got from Michelle holding me so close, from a girl (this was totally new) from a girl *needing* me, filled me with a tingling warmth I never even knew about. I felt excited but stupid. The way you do when you choke up at a TV commercial. But maybe it was okay. I had no idea. . . .

Something nubbed me from behind, and I swung around to see an old man behind the wheel of a green Buick waving his hands. He'd been leaning on his horn but I didn't notice. The old guy was so furious he'd hit me with his bumper. "Okay!" I shouted at him. "Okay!"

I clasped Michelle tighter and tried to steer her away. "We should move," I said, pressing my lips to her ear, letting myself nuzzle up to make sure the words got in. But she wouldn't move. She looked fresh-frozen, her eyes so wide the whites showed all around them.

"It's the lightning," she whispered, her voice quavery and small. She might have been six again. "It's the sky. It's happening."

"What's happening? What?" I tried pulling, but she dug in. I could see the raging fart behind us panting to run us down. "Come on!"

A line of cars stretched behind us, all honking, the drivers hanging their faces out in the downpour and screaming. "Move your ass!" *"Fucking hippies!"* "MOVE IT!"

Michelle seemed so tiny, I couldn't believe how hard it was

perv—a love story

to uproot her. Hail cracked in my eyes. A pellet of ice lodged in my ear. The car horns sounded like wild animals. I tried to get her in a bear hug, struggling to lift her off the ground and just lug her out of harm's way. That's when she grabbed me back. Pressed her face close to mine. She'd gone pale as skim milk. "It's Shiva. Don't you understand? He said this would happen. If I left. . . . He said he'd make it happen. The sky," she whimpered, "look at the sky. . . ."

At this point I seriously worried we'd cause a riot. The old man, a yellow mackintosh tugged over his head, was dragging his skinny carcass out of his Buick. His hatchet face contorted sideways, like it was pressed into glass. Other car doors opened and slammed.

"Michelle," I cried, ignoring the impending mob. "It's not Shiva. It's the weather."

In movies, the hero smacks the hysterical girl. He says *"Snap out of it!"* and bitch-slaps her. I raised my hand, but I couldn't do it. The only girl I'd ever slapped was Sharon Schmidlap, across the ass, and that was only because she wanted it. I wasn't a hero. I put my hand back down and tried talking some more.

"Michelle, I swear, I watched the news last night. They said it was going to storm. They predicted it. That weather lady with the bouffant and the wand. Come on . . ."

The old Buick guy had got hold of a tire iron. Behind him two other guys, a father and son in matching Steelers ponchos, stomped out of their pickup and left their doors open.

Somehow I managed to lift Michelle off the concrete and, puffing into the hail, half carried, half dragged her between a dented canary Impala and the same creamy Lincoln I'd seen when I stepped out of the condo. Just to be safe, I took a breath—all that pot and hash had messed up my wind—and wheezed through the line of cars in the next aisle to an empty space. Still yelling, the hatchet-faced man and the father and son Steelers fans climbed back in their vehicles.

I stopped to catch my breath and Michelle began to slide down my body. Her face dropped from up around my chest, down past my stomach. Lower than that. She ended up on her knees, her mouth mashed into my pants. In spite of everything—her screaming, those hailstones, the old maniac with the tire iron—the *feel* of her, even the idea of her down there was getting me hard.

"Michelle. . . . Hey, Michelle . . ."

"Cool it, Bobby. I'm not Michelle anymore. I'm Lela. That's what's happening. Shiva's mad 'cause I went back to Michelle. He said I could run away outside, but I couldn't run away in."

"Okay," I said, trying to keep my voice steady. "You were Lela for a while. Now you're Michelle again. What's the difference?"

The hail and rain stopped as suddenly as they'd begun, and Michelle—she was still Michelle as far as I was concerned—started up again. Her mood changed back to where it had started, before the thunder. She was pissed off all over again.

"Fucking show-off," she sneered. "It's just a trick." She pulled her hat off and ran a hand over her hairless dome, front to back, squeezing the water out of her pigtail.

"What's a trick?"

Michelle stared up at me, still kneeling, then pushed away and stood up by herself. "All this bullshit," she said. "The storm, the hail. All that lightning. He knows I'm scared of that shit."

"He meaning Shiva?" Without discussing it, we were walking again. Heading toward the highway. I had no idea what came next. "Shiva's heavy, huh? He controls the weather."

"You know him? If you knew him, you'd know I'm serious. You'd know he has powers."

She stopped again, halfway over the curb that separated the Miracle Mile parking lot from the sidewalk. A man driving a Roto-Rooter truck whooshed by and made a face. Michelle checked behind her. I thought she might run away, and my heart jumped in my chest. I did something I'd never done in my life. I reached for her shoulder. When she juked, like maybe I was going to hit her, I pulled her to me and grazed my hand across her cheek. Just brushed the backs of my fingers over her rain-soaked cheek, down over her wet lips and along her throat.

"Michelle"—I wanted her to know I was serious—"Michelle, I don't care if he can walk on water and talk like *The Mod Squad*, I told you, I don't know the guy. You can believe that or not, but it's true."

She tugged her hat low on her forehead and squinted up at me, peered through the slits of her lids like she was searching for some secret printed on my eyeballs. She roamed my face, and I thought of those Find-the-Pictures they had in *The Weekly Reader*. Find the ice cream cone in the tree, the panda in the bushes.

"Well, I still have to pee," she said, as if daring me to do something about it. When I didn't say anything, she hopped back over the curb, checked right and left, and squatted down between a pair of station wagons.

"Hey, come on," I said. This was a whole new situation.

But her pants were already down. Where her coat fell open I could see the pale flush of her pussy. *No underwear.* I thought my eyes were going to melt in their sockets and run down my cheeks, Nagasaki-style.

"Don't look at me, watch the lot," she snapped, tugging her yellow bells to her ankles. I could barely breathe. People were everywhere. Cars zoomed past. Doors opened, trunks banged shut. And here was this amazing, beautiful, split peach right in front of me. The lips were smaller than Sharon's. Daintier. A delicate smile instead of a guffaw. *And no one knew this was happening but me.*

I didn't officially see her go. I made myself look away, pretending to watch for pedestrians. But I heard her, the first quick whisssh, then the sputtering gush. I saw the pee run and puddle the damp cement. A frothy stream ran under my work boots but I didn't move. It wasn't piss. It was *her* piss.

I couldn't believe it. After my whole life, Michelle's pussy was right there . . . *and I stared somewhere else.* When the puddling stopped, she tugged my pant leg. She raised her face and gave me a funny smile. "You want to?" Her voice was sweet and girlish again.

"Want to what?"

"You know. . . ." Shy and defiant at the same time. "Wipe me. Girls have to wipe when they pee, you know. My daddy always wiped me."

"Your daddy?"

Maybe I could tell her about Mom's cuddle-flesh.

My mouth went so dry I could have spit wood-chips. The sun peeped out of the clouds and everything looked superclear. More real than real. The wet crease between her legs was the color of champagne. My parents served it every New Year. I never liked the taste, but now, sneaking a peek—because it was too much, because I would die or go blind—now I guessed I'd love it.

perv—a love story

"I . . . I don't have any tissue," I sputtered, but Michelle only shrugged.

"So?"

That's how it happened: in the middle of the Miracle Mile parking lot, I not only got to feel like I loved a girl, I got to feel what you feel when you touch one—down there—and love her at the same time. I trailed my finger so lightly on her slit, I hardly touched her at all. I'd have strangled puppies to do more, but there were all those people, those cars. All that light and traffic. The air felt like cold tinfoil.

I thought, idiotically, *What would Bob Dylan do?* Then I freaked. I imagined a station wagon owner footsteps away, ready to catch me. But catch me what? All I was doing—and I couldn't believe I was doing it—was brushing my hand along Michelle's cleft, feeling the hot wet of her. The warm droplets in her champagne slit mingled with the chilly rain still on my fingers.

"Lick it," she said. Just like that. Matter-of-fact. "Lick it."

And, still standing over her, sort of leaning in, I slowly brought my hand up to my mouth. Yes! All the traffic noise seemed to fade away. The volume of the world had been turned down, leaving nothing but the roar of blood rushing from my balls to my ears. I let her see what I was doing. My tongue sponged along my knuckles, over the backs of my hands. I tasted the briny flavor of what I guessed was pee. I made a show of it, darting my tongue between my fingers, wiggling it, like a goldfish plucked out of its bowl. Then she spoke up again.

"I didn't mean that, Bobby. I meant this."

I stopped my knuckle lapping, looked down again, to where her finger was describing little circles. Her wrist blocked all but the purple-pink clit. "You know," she said huskily, "the little man in the boat."

"You mean . . . right here?"

My face got hot. I imagined police. Choppers swooping out of the sky, fixing us in telephoto lens, filming everything and presenting the evidence to a horrified jury. I could see the witnesses: Dolores Fish and Dr. Mushnik, Ned Friendly, Mr. Weiner, Tennie Toad and Farwell and Headmaster Bunton. All of them dying to testify, itching to send me to Perv Jail.

My head wouldn't stop. I saw my mother, pill-drunk and burbling baby country-and-western, hike up her salmon nightie and tell the judge, *"He wuvs to cuddle . . ."* They'd drag her from the courtroom facedown in a box of turtles, yelping for electroshock. Somewhere in sweaty heaven, watching all of it, Mr. Schmidlap would crack a Rheingold with his flipper while Dad banged his head off the nearest wall.

"BOBBY!" Michelle's harsh whisper brought me blinking back. "Bobby, *GO AHEAD.* Bobby, I *WANT* you to. . . ."

She touched herself and I shivered.

"But there's . . . I mean . . . There's all these people."

"I know," she said, but huskily, edging her back against the tire well of the VW bus. She parted her naked thighs slightly further. "I know."

The way she studied me, it's like she was measuring something, seeing how far I'd go. Or else—and this really made my stomach sink—how much I loved her. I was so hard I thought my dick would crack off. But all those *people!* Those *cars!* The *weather. . . .*

You didn't think of sex and weather in the same breath. You

didn't have to. Not normally. Not ever. Except for here, in the Miracle Mile parking lot, where Lela the Hare Krishna, who used to be Michelle Burnelka, was on the run from Shiva—whoever Shiva was—and on her haunches for me. Whoever I was. That's what I wrestled with. Not *Can I do this?* But what the fuck was it I thought I was doing? And who the fuck was doing it?

Even the raindrops seemed to mock me.

"Michelle," I stammered. I was ready. But then . . . A Negro lady gawked at me from a Dodge Dart and it seized me up. I had to pluck the words out like olives caught in my throat. "Michelle, I can't. . . . *I can't do it.*"

I heard myself and I died. It killed me to find out this was me. I had everything I ever wanted. *AND LOOK WHAT CAME OUT OF MY MOUTH!*

It wasn't like I was being a "good boy." It was like, I don't know, like I was *scared*. Or not even scared, just . . . guilty. That was it. My psyche sputtered like defective neon. One thought wrenched my brain: Mom's seen a husband stroll under a street-car. She's seen a daughter disappear to Canada, her son fucked-up and flown home, kicked out of a pricey prep school. If that weren't enough, picture her expression when I got arrested for public pee-tasting, or whatever the legal term happened to be. How could I face her if I got popped for a sex crime? For the ten zillionth time I wished I was an orphan, like my long-gone father, so I could just relax.

Just to make things perfect, my voice squeeched into Jiminy Cricket. "Michelle, I really like you. . . . I mean, I've always, like, loved you, it's just that . . ."

"Forget it," she said, her face hardening. She pulled up her pants and launched herself off the station wagon in a single movement, as though she'd been bouncing off cars and asphalt her entire life. "Forget it, Bobby. It's nothing."

"Really?"

This was so hugely untrue, so clearly not nothing, I hated myself for needing to hear it.

I held my hand out to help, but Michelle ignored it and dusted herself off.

"You don't," she said, with a brittle laugh. "You don't think I was serious, do you? You don't think I'm some kind of *exhibitionist*."

"Gee, I don't know," I said. I just knew I wanted to rip my tongue out at the sound of "Gee." This was worse than Jiminy Cricket. My voice box had been hijacked by Wally Cleaver. Because I *never* said "Gee." Never before and never since. I was not a "gee" type person. But I couldn't tell Michelle that. What was the point?

To Michelle, from here on in, I'd be the geek who said "Gee" and didn't have the balls to lick her pussy in broad daylight. With one move—or lack of one—I'd killed something horribly important. Whatever else happened, I knew I'd spend whatever time I had left walking upright trying to redeem myself.

When Michelle slouched off toward the highway, I resolved two things: one, that I was sticking with her, no matter what. And two, I was going to be a badass. A rebel. A daredevil. Keith Richards with Jew-hair. Whatever it took to de-lame myself, that's what I'd do.

With no plan to speak of, I announced, "We need sleeping bags." To which Michelle replied, "Sleeping bags cost money."

Remembering that she had all the money, and knowing I'd

look like an even bigger lightweight if I asked for it back—suppose she said, "No!" Suppose she said, *"Fuck you!"* Then what?—I heard myself mumbling, Marlon Brando–style, "Don't worry about it. One thing I know how to do is steal."

And without another word, I headed back to the mall. Before I left, I thought I caught a flicker of respect in her eyes. It gave me hope. (And a partial erection.)

I was back in ten minutes with a pair of lightweight goose-downs, army green and waterproof.

When I handed hers over, I could tell she was impressed. With any luck, I wouldn't have to knock off a gas station to make her forget my cowardice. I could probably kill a man with my bare hands, and it wouldn't matter now. *Too-chicken-to-lick.* It might as well have been tattooed on my forehead. *What do you do when you're branded and you know you're a man?*

Michelle's eyes grew huge under her Beatle cap. At some point, she'd dumped the rose-petal grannies, and I didn't miss them. She squeezed the sleeping bag, then smiled. "You . . . you stole these?"

"No big thing." I shrugged, and pretty much stood still while she hugged me. I didn't want to look too eager. Didn't want her to know what I felt. Most of all, I didn't want her to accidentally touch my ass. The credit card was in my back pocket. The last thing I needed was her finding out I charged the bags to my mother.

I'd never hitchhiked with anybody else—let alone a girl—and the idea scared me. I kept thinking of those old movies, where the stranded ingenue flashes some calf by the side of the road. When the hayseed in the fruit truck slows down, her lunkhead boyfriend pops out from behind a billboard and the driver wags his fist and speeds off.

Not that Michelle and I were exactly girlfriend and boyfriend. But it looked that way . . . She'd peed in front of me, which must mean something. (Pat Boone didn't cover that in *Tips for Teens*.) Plus which I'd touched her. *Down there*. Even if it wasn't the way she wanted.

What truly spooked me was having to protect her. Even semi-hairless, soaking wet, stuffed in an oversized pea coat, Michelle, as Tennie Toad used to say, was a girl with the "fuck-mes." (*"Ah takes one look,"* he'd drawl, *"and ah wants her to fuck me."*) She tried to hide it with that Beatle cap and turned-up collar, but all you had to do was look close. Her dainty features, those darting green eyes and longish, curled-up lashes gave her a kind of Nasty Bambi look. A Bambi with breasts she didn't bother to lock in a bra. Even if nobody else knew she didn't wear underpants, *I* did. And that knowledge, as we stood beside the Miracle Parking Lot, adjacent to a Bob's Big Boy and a Johnny Rotator Tire Center, pumped me with scrote-tightening dread every time a man drove by and rubbernecked to check her out.

"Don't look so happy," Michelle teased once we settled in. "It's not like we have to run away together. I'm *fine* on my own. Animals can smell fear, you know."

"I don't have fear," I told her, trying to scoff and failing miserably. "I just want to be careful."

"Don't be so uptight," she cried, waggling her thumb at a VW bus stuffed, not with flower children, but, according to the sign on the side, THE CAN-DO RANCH CHRISTIAN CAVAL-CADE. The suit-and-tied teens inside stared out their windows,

perv—a love story

and Michelle waggled her tongue at them. "As Arjuna speaketh," she went on, " 'the material body of the indestructible, immeasurable, and eternal living entity is sure to come to an end.' Chew on that awhile and unsqueeze your butt."

"I feel better already," I said, as the young Christians sped away. "Who the fuck's Art Juno?"

"Arjuna, dummy. He was Krishna's nephew, once removed. And he knew his shit. You gotta get mellow, Bobby. Your brain's like a flower and being uptight'll turn it brown."

Before I could respond to that, and remind her of her own less-than-mellow vibe from the moment I'd got her on the phone, a curly-haired fat man in a gold Toronado slammed on the brakes and craned sideways to have a look. I'd had some experience with fat men, none of it good. One time outside of Allentown, after a Santana concert I'd snuck off from Hale to see by myself, a two-ton baldie in Coke-bottle glasses, stained undershirt, baggy madras shorts, and black shoes and socks picked me up in a dented Beetle. He smoked Camel straights and kept yammering about his Little League team: how he had an "eye for talent," how the trouble with this country was that young men didn't get enough "hands-on training in the basics."

I let him talk, as I'd learned to do from hitching around. But two exits before Slotzville, he cranked his thick lips into a smile and asked how old I was. I told him fifteen. He shook his head and stubbed out his Camel with a phlegmy laugh. I can still hear that laugh. It sounded the way laughs are spelled in comic books: *"Heh-heh-heh."* He went, *"Heh-heh-heh,"* and planted his meaty hand on my thigh. "Too bad you're not eighteen, skipper, or I could give you a juicy blow job. Whaddya think of that?"

"My loss," I said, dying to shove his albino bowling ball of a head through the windshield. "Guess I got something to look forward to when I'm eighteen besides being drafted."

"Right-o-rama," he said, and smacked my leg. Even after we pulled over he kept his grasp on my pants. "Hands-on training," he repeated, managing to speak and keep his sausage lips peeled back in a gluey smile at the same time. "Hands-on training. You may not dig it now, but you will. An opportunity like this doesn't come every day. Be my Tootsie Pop?"

By then I could spot the walnut-size bulge in his shorts. It kept shifting, like a little trapped mole. I tore out of the Beetle before Black Socks decided I shouldn't wait three years to get hands-on. In retrospect, it was like dress rehearsal for Ned Friendly. Ned in Bermudas and a Bug. I tried not to wonder why I was so popular. . . .

The Toronado speeded up again a minute after slowing down. I watched Michelle watch it go. She'd shed her pea coat when the sun came out. Of all things, she had on a Mr. Natural T-shirt, untucked over those lemon bells. Besides worrying about staving off rapists, I was itching to clear up the Shiva situation before we really got going. The problem was, I didn't how to bring it up. I could not exactly act casual—"*Say, what's up with this lug nut who's coming after you out of the sky, the one who can change weather?*"—but I couldn't wait till she informed me he could turn into a golden retriever, either. With my luck Old Yeller would hop in my lap the first time we got a ride. And then what?

I'd finally geared up to grill her, opting for a direct approach—"*So who the fuck is Shiva and what'd he do to you?*"—when a shiny brown El Dorado slowed down in front of us. The Caddy swerved within an inch of my boots and squeaked to a stop fifty feet later.

perv—a love story

A couple who looked remarkably like Dennis the Menace's neighbors, Mr. and Mrs. Wilson—if the Wilsons had been earth-tone Eldo types—leaned forward and waved as though they'd been hunting us for days.

We both started running, and Michelle said, "Bummer, we should've smoked a joint," right before we got to the car. I caught up with her and opened the door. As she was getting in, I made sure to whisper, "Don't mention any pot stuff. You never know."

She called me "paranoid" and shot a how-stupid-do-you-think-I-am? scowl over her shoulder. I waited for the Mr. Wilson guy to creep out of the front seat and open the trunk.

"Where you kids goin'?" he hollered. You'd have thought I was half a mile away and not on the other side of his fudge-colored Cadillac.

"San Francisco," I hollered back, liking the sound of it.

The old man seemed just as happy as I was to hear about it. He was taller than I'd expected, with sunken cheeks and a long flat nose that looked like someone had slammed a book on it. He unlocked the cavernous trunk and shouted my way. "Got a daughter out there. Darlene. She's living in that Haight-Ashbury. Leastwise I think so."

I tossed in our sleeping bags. "You're not sure?"

"Well sir, yes and no."

He unfurled a yellow hanky from his back pocket and wiped his forehead. Up close, the liver spots showed in the pockets of his cheekbones. His gaunt hand quivered up and down, as if constantly waving hello.

"Name's Howard, F.Y.I. Retail men's wear. Retired."

"I'm Bobby."

Howard nodded like he'd made a note of it. He picked up where he'd left off, at top volume.

"Spent my life in boxer shorts, that's the big gag in the menswear game. What was I sayin'? Darlene! Last letter we got, the postmark was from Frisco, but that had to be, oh Lordy, a good while ago, and Darlene was never one for keeping a regular phone number. So Henrietta—she's been my wife since '41, met her in the PX in Fort Lee, Virginia, buying Cornish hens—Henrietta and me decided we oughta drive out and take a look-see. See if maybe we can run her to ground."

Right away, I found myself rooting for old Howard. I wanted to tell him it would be all right, that he'd find Daughter Darlene and she'd leap in his palsied arms and call him Daddy. It was a blatant lie—she was probably tripped out in some crash pad, balling Crosby, Stills and Nash—but what the hell? I liked the way he didn't want me to see how bad he felt. It was clear that Darlene had torn a hole in his life, but he didn't broadcast it. Which still amazed me. In our house, the second you felt a shred of pain or annoyance, it was almost a duty to announce it. (With enough embellishment, if possible, to make everyone feel as terrible as you did.) That was your job.

In my family, misery didn't just love company, it wanted hostages. But here was this kindly scarecrow, doing his best to put a happy face on a doomed trip to the wilds of California to find his lost little girl.

I'd known Darlene's daddy all of ninety seconds, and I already felt guilty I couldn't do more for him. I tried to picture Howard, decked out in spanking new safari jacket and matching slacks, his wispy white hair parted down the middle, Mr. Wilson–style,

perv—a love story

poking shakily around those pot-soaked, braless streets. No doubt he'd pick his way through the speed freaks and panhandlers with his arm tight around his plump missus, the bun in her hair arranged just so, jumbo knitting needles sticking out of her purse like Martian toothpicks. . . .

The notion of these two tramping daintily through throngs of acid-crazed, barefoot freaks was enough to dent your heart. I could imagine the *Life* magazine photo: forty-seven cavorting hippies, with Mr. Wilson peering out of the background, looking confused and missing his wallet, but still smiling. Always smiling. . . .

After the old man closed the trunk—lovingly, I thought, as though not wanting to cause his Cadillac the least discomfort— he flicked a tuft of hair off his forehead and extended his hand.

"Where the heck are my manners? The name's Howard," Howard yelled, forgetting he'd just told me. "Howard Bill. My daddy gave me two first names and nothin' to last, but we all got our cross to bear, huh?"

"You're right about that," I answered.

Once more I caught myself meeting holler with holler. I didn't have the heart to tell him he'd already introduced himself. Maybe it was a technique to get people to remember your name. Maybe that was part of the Menswear Game. After Intro Number Two, my new pal crooked a finger for me to come closer. I stepped toward him and braced myself for a shout, but he held his voice to a moderate din. Tilting his head toward the front of the car, Howard clicked his tongue and boomed, "Say, that's one cute filly. You kids gettin' hitched?"

"Not today," I told him, hoping that was enough to keep us on board, should it turn out the Bills were churchgoing folk who frowned on premarital frolic.

But Howard surprised me. "Don't rush in," he said, only semi-shouting, which to his ears was probably a whisper. "You young-sters have the right idea. Take a test drive before you buy. Lease to own, if you can."

I asked him if he ever sold cars.

"No," he chuckled. "I'm strictly a suit and pants man. But I been saddled to Henny probably twice as long as you been alive and belchin'."

Before I had time to digest this, he clapped me on the shoulder and bellowed through a shaky grin, "Let's get these l'il dogies rollin'!" Then he tugged me close again and shouted directly in my ear. "Got a good one. Why did the man buy a dachs-hund?"

"I don't know, why?" I said.

"Because . . ." Howard Bill spat out a laugh. "Because his fa-vorite song was 'Get Along Little Dogie.' Get it? Get a *long* little doggie. Good one, huh? I got a skillion of 'em."

"That's a good one," I agreed, doing my best to cup a hand over my ear without seeming rude. "It really is."

Back in the Cadillac, so close their heads touched, Michelle and Henrietta huddled over the top of the front seat. Whatever they were whispering about, they stopped when Howard and I got in. They stared at me with an expression that left me flattered and embarrassed at the same time, as if they'd been discussing an adorable birth defect.

"Henrietta said their daughter Darlene's in San Francisco," Michelle announced. "Can you believe that?"

"That's true, retired five years," Howard called over his shoul-der. His wife waved and made a dramatic ear-tapping gesture, repeatedly patting the tip of her forefinger to her downy left lobe. She was also mouthing something, which it took me a while to decipher: "HARD OF HEARING."

Right around then, I realized what struck me when I'd peeked in the trunk: The Bills had no luggage. A spare tire in a fuzzy black doughnut, a shiny jack in its slot. That was it. For a cross-country trip. Not so much as a bowling bag.

"So," I asked, as Howard nosed off the shoulder back into the traffic of Superior Boulevard. "You're leaving now?"

When he didn't reply, I caught myself and repeated, shouting this time, "So you're on your way to *San Francisco*? Right now?"

"We're on our way to San Francisco," Howard bellowed back at me. "When Darlene headed off, she said 'Dadsy'—that's her pet name for yours truly, you'll find that out about kids when you have your own, they'll stick you with pet names, whether you want 'em or not—'Dadsy,' she says, 'I don't want to go to nursing school. I want to go to San Francisco and be free.' 'By golly you are free,' I says to her. 'This is America, isn't it? You're not some Red Chinee.' But she just packed up her backpack with all her woolies and off she went. Stubborn girl. Just like her mother."

Henrietta, who'd sat pretty much silently through all of this, tossed down her knitting and whipped around to Michelle and me. "She was twenty-two. That's plenty old enough for a girl to fly the nest."

Howard kept a jolly, out-of-it smile plastered on his face and gave me a wave in the rearview. "We're just gonna make sure she's fine," he thundered. "Then turn right around and head back to Monongahela. Simple as that."

Henrietta worked her jaw but didn't say anything. I got the

feeling they were continuing an argument they'd been having before we got in the car, an argument they'd keep on having after we got out again. Whatever thrilling notions I'd nursed about hitting the highway, *Bonnie and Clyde*–style, were more or less dispelled then and there. The prospect of a cross-country jaunt with bickering seniors was disheartening at best.

Michelle picked up on this, and chose that moment to give her opinion. "Personally," she declared, pulling her cap down low, "I think there's something freaky about staying home till you're old. I got out when I was sixteen. I'd have left earlier if I could've found somewhere to go. I joined an ashram, which was a big mistake, but at least I was out of there, if you know what I mean."

"Same as my sister, Bernice," I told her. "She split with a draft dodger her senior year. Now she's in Canada somewhere, hiding out."

Michelle looked at me darkly and concluded, "Some places are just better than being where you were, even if where you are isn't so great, either."

At this outburst, Henrietta adopted a vexed expression. Howard maintained his placid smile, though I suspected he hadn't heard a word. For my part, I just wished my traveling companion would slide closer. I tried, nonchalantly, to stretch my leg in her direction. Just as nonchalantly, Michelle rolled herself toward the door and pressed her face into the window. The Caddy backseat was just too huge. It was comfortable, but maddening.

The whole situation was getting me antsy. I leaned forward and yelled in Howard's furry ear. "So are you going to San Francisco or not?" I didn't mean to sound harsh, but I had to know.

" 'Course we are," Howard yelled back at me.

"Just not now," Henrietta added, her voice a good deal softer.

perv—a love story

It was like she didn't want him to know they weren't going at all.

Michelle and I swapped glances, and she hunched up her shoulders in a silent giggle. It was such a private thing—this shared, secret joke between the two of us—that the bruising sadness beginning to grab me loosened up and left me almost happy.

I'd ridden up and down Superior a thousand times. But spotting Mom's condo out the Caddy window, I might as well have been watching a newsreel of Hungary. I may have lived there, sort of, but it was like I'd never really seen it before.

I counted floors, from the lobby up, and tried to make out 709. Squinting hard, I visualized Mom on the far side of the window, sleeping off lunch and dreaming of caramel turtles. Then I looked back at Michelle and got the tingles. She'd pulled her pea coat back on over Mr. Natural. Between that extra-big coat and the Beatle cap still tugged over her troubled bunny eyes, she could have been eight or nine again. The pale-skinned angel I wanted to fondle in Social Studies.

My own luck scared me. For two seconds we stared at each other, my tattoo athrob. Then Howard banged his hand on the Cadillac dash and boomed, "Dag nab it, I like what's going on with you young people today! Where you kids going?"

Michelle rolled her eyes, and I bit my cheeks to keep from laughing. Henrietta caught us. "The Eskimos have a saying," she said shrilly, making sure to divide her dirty look—what Tennie used to call "stink-eye"—equally between us. " 'As I am now, you too shall be,' " she whispered, as though invoking a curse. "Can you two understand that?"

Michelle only rolled her eyes again and said, "Heavy."

She had this snotty side I didn't remember from school. Not even snotty, exactly. More like nervous, sort of hard, and cynical in one jumpy package. I had a feeling she wanted to believe everything, but that every time she'd believed anything she'd been burned. So now she was Miss Who-Gives-A-Fuck. Or trying to be.

Henrietta grew snippy. "Do you even know what I'm saying, young lady?"

Michelle shrugged and replied in a manner grown-ups would call talking back. "You're saying, even though I'm young and carefree, some day I'm gonna wake up and be a pissed-off old lady who knits. Well guess what, *Henny*, maybe it's not so hot bein' me right now either. Maybe as-you-are is out-of-sight compared to as-I-am-right-this-goddamn-minute. What do *you* know about it, anyway?"

The last thing I wanted was to referee, so I kept my mouth shut. While the females exchanged glares, I watched the deaf-but-happy Howard steer his land-yacht up Superior Boulevard. He'd long since forgotten that he'd asked a question, and contented himself singing as he drove. At first I couldn't make out the tune. But it sounded, oddly enough, like "Satisfaction." As in *"I can't get no . . ."*

In a high-pitched warble—he had his own Jiminy Cricket gene, except he sang with it—Howard squeaked out his version of the Stones' megahit. *"I can't get no satisfaction,"* he whinnied. *"I can't get no girly action . . ."*

He only knew the chorus, but the more he repeated it, the more involved he became. He slapped the wheel, bobbing his frail skull up and down until the veins began to stand out on his

perv—a love story

forehead. His tongue flopped out of his mouth and I thought he was going to drive us into a tractor-trailer.

Luckily, Henrietta knew when to intervene. Graceful as a bird, she swooped forward and gave her husband a loving pat, smoothing a cowlick that must have been there for sixty years, and the old guy returned to his jolly self.

Without missing a beat, Henrietta twisted back in her seat to face Michelle. "I am not saying you have it easy," she declared, with surprising ferocity. "I wouldn't want to be a young lady today for all the tea in Shanghai. All that freedom would scare me, thank you very much. No, dear, all I'm saying is, Howard has lived a long time and his mind is not as sharp as it used to be."

"I don't know," Michelle said, shrugging her shoulders and speaking deadpan. "He knows the words to 'Satisfaction.' " With this she began to sing, imitating the old man's Alfalfa-like screech. *"But I try, and I try, and I try, and I TRY—"*

"Stop that! That's not what I mean." Henrietta slapped at Michelle's hand. "I mean the poor man's going senile. And some day, if you live long enough, if any of us live long enough, that will happen to us, too."

"Live slow, die old," Michelle said, and that was it. I knew we were gone the second she said it.

"That's enough!" the old lady snarled. "Please get out. Get out now!"

It was strange to see somebody so gentle-looking turn so fierce. The temperature in the Caddy plunged.

Howard chose this moment to burst into chat again. "Should probably tell you kids, me and Henrietta are rollin' to San Francisco. Got a daughter there. Henny, show 'em a flyer."

Henrietta clenched her lightly pinked lips and breathed furiously through her nose. Squinching her eyes at us, Wicked Witch–style, she unsnapped the glove compartment and removed a neatly folded stack of mimeographed sheets. Fingers shaking, she handed one to Michelle without a word, then gave one to me.

Michelle raised the sheet to her nose and inhaled deeply, explaining that she loved the smell of ink. Mrs. Bill ignored her. She waited till we had a chance to survey the paper before speaking.

On the paper was a smudged photo of a smiling, round-faced girl in butterfly glasses and Penn State sweatshirt waving at the camera. It was hard to see much detail, beyond a ribbon in her flip and large rabbity teeth that peeked out between her lips. She looked happy enough. Of course you could be perfectly happy and still want to split nursing school, ditch your folks, and hitch to California. Under the photograph, in big, curling letters written with a heavy backhand, it said:

DARLENE BILL
IF YOU SEE HER, CALL 412-FIELDBROOK 1-9838

There was something else, though, something I couldn't pin down until Michelle mentioned it.

"She's pretty," Michelle said. (I was relieved she was being so nice, since her bad manners made me uncomfortable; I was the type of person who'd say anything to anyone, just to keep things pleasant.) "She's pretty, all right, but if she's twenty-two I'm a TV dinner. This chick's my age."

Howard caught sight of the mimeo in the rearview and let out a proud hoot. "Pretty as a picture, ain't she? And smart! That gal could spell the buns off a schoolteacher!"

perv—a love story

"Yes, dear," Henrietta shouted back at him. "Now you keep your eyes on the road."

This seemed to quiet him down and Mrs. Bill went back to her quiet mode. "Of course she's twenty-two," she said, "but in that picture she's fifteen. Howard came up with the idea of making these circulars, and I didn't have the heart to tell him the truth."

"So she didn't run away," I said. "She grew up and left."

"Years ago. But Howard's been like this for . . . for a while."

Michelle pouted. "And we're not going to any San Francisco, are we?"

"Did I hear someone say Frisco?" Howard bellowed. "By gum, that's where we're goin'! Did you tell 'em, Henny?" He slowed the Caddy to a full stop at a yellow light and swung around at the wheel. "We got a daughter out there! Darlene. You kids know her? What we aim to do is head out to that Haight-Ashbury and drop in on 'er. There's not a thing wrong with a surprise-and-howdy!"

"They know, honey."

Henrietta gave her husband another pat on the head—these seemed to be her main form of affection—and the frown on her face faded to simple resignation.

"Now why don't we drop these two off and get you home for your nap?"

"Then we go to San Francisco?"

"Then we go to *San Francisco*!" she bubbled, in a voice you'd use to promise a dying five-year-old a trip to Disneyland.

Howard swung the chocolate Cadillac to a stop in front of yet another Burger King—in the brief time I'd been away, they seem to have spawned and sprung up every four blocks—and danced out of the car like a stun-gunned Fred Astaire.

Temporarily blank, he stood holding the door for Michelle, then recovered and hollered at me. "Don't you worry 'bout boot camp, Private. The first two weeks are the hardest. After that it's a cakewalk. Semper fi!"

That stopped me for a sec, but Henrietta mouthed something like *"Just say okay!"* So that's what I did.

While Howard and I retrieved the sleeping bags, Michelle and Henrietta commiserated. You would have never known they'd tangled. Michelle leaned in the window, hugging the old lady. People driving by smiled to see such a sweet display. What with the Generation Gap, you didn't see young people dressed like Michelle hugging old people like Henrietta all that often.

As the Bills disappeared, Michelle jumped up and kissed me. I thought it was love until she reached in her pea coat. "Check it out. I ripped it off while she was giving me advice on premarital sex." She giggled and pulled out Mrs. Bill's purse, complete with yarn-and-knitting needles. When she waved it overhead, I instinctively pulled down her arm. What if a cop spotted her doing the Statue of Liberty and pulled over?

"So she told you sex was bad?" I asked, trying to take the crime in stride.

"Au contraire," said Michelle, smirking hugely. "Henrietta was a funky old lady. She told me, 'Get it while you can, 'cause there's gonna be a long time later when you just plain can't'." Michelle moved in close and imitated Henrietta's disapproving cluck: " 'It's *a fact of life, hon, men don't last as long as we do. . . .' "*

perv—a love story

"Good advice," I said, guiding her by the elbow as we stepped over a concrete embankment beside the Burger King to the on-ramp for Route 80. Michelle fished around in the bag and scooped out a tomato-shaped change purse and worn leather wallet. Before I could stop her, she threw the gutted accessory over her shoulder. The purse proper dropped into some shrubs. But Mrs. Bill's knitting, a swath of scarlet mohair that started life out as the front of a sweater, hung from the branch of a stunted elm like some bloody flag. A few drivers stared, but no one looked shocked enough to call the authorities.

"Now we can really get rollin'," Michelle sang, riffling through the cash in the wallet's bill slots. She held up a few greenbacks, a couple of credit cards, and a paper-clipped packet of what turned out to be coupons for Duncan Hines cake mix. "Guess ol' Howard likes his angel food, huh?"

Michelle tossed the neatly clipped items into the air, watching, wild-eyed, as they fluttered into the brush that dotted the shoulder and onto the highway. Again, I worried that some-body—a policeman, a concerned citizen, an anti-litter nut—might see her confetti act and come screeching over. But I could still hear Sharon Schmidlap calling me "nervous Nellie," so I stayed mum.

"All right! Time to boogie," my not-quite-girlfriend announced. The cash and cards were now stashed in her bell-bottom pockets, and the tomato emptied of change. "You ready, Bobby Stark?"

"Ready, Michelle Burnelka."

For the second time, I really did feel like *Bonnie and Clyde*. This time, though, I wasn't just excited about it. I was scared. I was also starving. I hadn't eaten since the night before. The two things, fear and hunger, combined like a fist lodged in my chest, squeezing my heart until I had to gasp. If we didn't get a ride before Mrs. Bill realized her purse was AWOL, I'd never get to be Clyde. I'd go straight to *Birdman of Alcatraz*. And I wouldn't even have a crime spree to kick around with the other inmates. (I didn't think purse-snatching bought me much.) One more time I shuddered to think about what the swells in Cell Block 8 would make of me: some Johnny Jew-fro who copped chump change from his own mother . . . a non-shaver (sometimes I lathered up and used Dad's old razor, but I didn't need to) who helped a lapsed Hare Krishna slit he was too scared to lick in public rip off retirees. Jesus! I knew I had to shove something in my stomach, just to shut my brain up.

"Since we're here anyway," I said, jerking my thumb at the Burger King, "why don't we grab a bite before we hit the highway?"

Michelle didn't say anything, and I felt a need to press my suggestion.

"I know it's not vegetarian," I blathered, eager to impress her, as if I were some kind of non-flesh eater, the kind of enlightened swell who only dined on lotus sprouts and kelp. "But we could still get milkshakes. I think they have strawberry."

More silence, then Michelle perked up. "It takes two hands to handle a Whopper," she sang, breaking into the Burger King jingle that was all over the radio. I didn't know they even let you listen to that stuff at an ashram. "Buy me some burgers and I'll eat something," she announced. "Just don't give me any of that vegetarian crap. Fucking Shiva was always going on about how he wouldn't eat anything that could smile. So I said, 'Oh, like when the fuck is the last time you saw a chicken smile?' And he said, 'Well, really, it's just the face. I don't eat anything with face.' Meanwhile, two nights later I catch him pigging out on pepperoni pizza, and he says to me, real cocky-like, 'It's okay. Pepperoni doesn't have a face, either.' Fucking asshole."

"Sure sounds like it," I said, trying to keep things light. I was just glad we were going to have lunch, and didn't want to spoil it with some kind of giant Shiva discussion. One wrong move and she'd tell me he controlled the french fry machine.

It turned out Burger King was mobbed, and the second I walked in I felt like a criminal. Like people were watching us. This was actually cool. Since being stuck with my "academically appropriate" Hale haircut, I dreamed of situations like this: rolling into a place and having respectable souls look askance—mothers pull their young ones a little closer, dads set their jaws in grim disapproval, daughters grow haughty and disturbed, secretly hot at the prospect of getting next to an anti-establishment, society-rejecting rebel type like me.

In reality, it was Michelle they were staring at. To my surprise, she'd stopped and produced a tube of white lipstick on the sidewalk up to the Burger King entrance. After applying that, she dipped back in her jacket and pulled out a kind of half-moon, rubber-tipped tweeter thing I'd never seen before. (Bernice, God love her, was not the sort of girl given to beauty products. She thought makeup was "a capitalist tool," probably because of my mother's constant harangue to "do something about the shine" on her nose. For her part, Mom was a fanatic for skin care products, especially cold cream, which she occasionally wore around the clock.)

Before my no doubt shameless gaze, Michelle proceeded to pull out both her eyelids and, planting the half-moon of orange rubber on each one, curl and fan her lashes with a tortuous, upward roll of her wrist. The end result, if such a thing were possible, lent her even greater Bambi-ness than she possessed already. The new Michelle—not the one I'd dreamed about, but the one ready to place an order and slide beside me in Burger King—had evolved into such a unique, petite, and astonishing beauty, every head in the place swiveled our way when she walked in.

For all her riveting prettiness, though, Michelle still looked pissed off. Especially when she turned up the collar of her pea coat and pushed her way to the front of the order line. She was the real thing: the kind of tough little hippie chick who drove straights crazy. Sometimes you don't really see a person until you see the effect they have on everybody else. And Michelle, it was clear from the eyes of the burger-eaters, Michelle looked like the kind of girl who left a Harley running and her old man picking his teeth with a bayonet he kept in his boot. She was that kind of intense. It was obvious people wondered what the hell she was doing with me.

"You know you can live off ketchup and water," Michelle said when I set our tray down on the table. "They call that hobo soup."

"Well, we don't have to do that," I said, eyeing the mushy red glup she'd stirred up in the paper cup in front of her. "We have real food." I don't know why this annoyed me.

"Real food," she giggled, like I'd said something genuinely witty. "You always had kind of a mouth on you, didn't you?"

She unwrapped her Whopper and began at once to pick the sesame seeds off the bun. I was so famished I didn't wait to get the wrapper off mine. I just tore into it. But her comment made me stop in mid-bite.

perv—a love story

"I used to love it when you made fun of the teachers. Like what you did to Miss Wentz in fourth grade. Remember? The mean lady with the fat arm?"

Miss Wentz, for the record, was the first person I ever knew who had cancer. Hers was breast. As a side effect, I guess, one of her arms swelled up thick as a boa constrictor. Now that I thought about it, I wondered what Mr. Schmidlap would have made of that. Maybe he'd have been jealous. They were a perfect match.

"Do you remember?" Michelle went on. "You used to pretend to sneeze. You'd go to the boys room and run water on your hand, then fake-sneeze and spritz Miss Wentz when she came down the aisle picking up test papers. God, one time she got so mad she called you a deviant. Remember that? A 'social deviant.' Nobody even knew what it meant."

I remembered. And, now that I thought about it, I had to ask myself if maybe she was right.

The good part, Michelle was actually laughing. All that hardness left her when she giggled, and I realized why I loved her all over again. There was a funny little girl inside the tough-as-nails chick she tried to foist on the world. I felt almost privileged she'd let me see it. I felt like she let me in.

"Fuck!" she howled. "I'll never forget that. You sprayed the back of her neck, and she just freaked out. Her whole face turned red. We thought she was gonna have a cancer attack or something."

"Wow," I said. "I completely forgot about that."

Which wasn't true, but I didn't want her to think I sat around mulling over this kind of stuff. Especially since I did. Constantly. Grade school was more real to me than yesterday afternoon. I recalled the faux-snot routine like it happened three minutes ago.

What blew me away was that Michelle remembered, too. That she remembered and thought it was cool.

I started to say, "I can't believe you noticed," but stopped when I realized how pathetic that sounded. Instead, emboldened by her new girlishness, I told her, in a teasing kind of way, "Maybe I wanted to impress you."

"Impress me?" Michelle dipped a fry in the puddle of ketchup she'd made on the table. She planted it between her lips like a greasy cigarette. "Really, Bobby, all the girls thought you were cute. I know I did. I felt like we were kind of alike, but only we knew it. You know what I mean? It's like we had this connection, but it was invisible. We were both aliens. We didn't have to say anything."

"I wish you would have," I said, sounding more plaintive than I intended.

Michelle looked out the windows. All those cars, full of regular people. "How could I? You were always clowning around. I figured it was 'cause your Mom was so crazy, the way she'd show up at school dressed like it was prom night at ten in the morning if you forgot your lunch or something."

"She's not crazy," I said, surprised to hear myself defending my mother. "She missed her own prom is all. See, *her* mom fell down the stairs that night and broke her neck. Then my mom had to stay home and take care of her. So her whole life she regretted she couldn't go. Since then, you know, she kind of always dressed for it. Just in case."

"Just in case, huh?" Michelle nibbled thoughtfully on her fry, then reached across the table and slowly ran the back of her hand over my cheek. I couldn't believe how that made me flush. She was sort of smiling, but sort of not. It was hard to tell. "You

perv—a love story

also lied a lot," she said, and stopped to take a gurgling suck off her strawberry shake.

"Well, I—"

"Hey, it's *okay*! The stuff I had going on at my house I had to lie, too. Believe me." She chewed on the straw, considering, then spoke up again. "I'll tell you a secret, something I never told anybody. The first time I had sex—the boy's name was Buzzy Dworkin, from Belthouver, I don't think you knew him—anyway, the first time I did it he asked how come I didn't bleed, like a virgin. So I told him this freaky story about how one day, when I cut class and stayed home, the mailman peeped me through the screen door and saw me doing my nails in my bra and panties. Before I knew what hit me, he burst in, whacked me over the head with his mailbag, then dragged me to the couch and stuck his thing in before I came to."

"Is that true?" I asked.

Hungry as I was, I forgot to chew, I forgot to swallow. I just let the food sit in my mouth while she told me all this.

"Is what true? The crazy-mailman story, or that I made it up and laid it on Scuzzy Buzzy, 'cause I didn't want him to know the real reason I was fifteen and didn't have my cherry."

"No, yeah. I mean that you really lied," I said. "That's what I'm asking."

What really bothered me was that I *did* remember Buzzy Dworkin. He was this loud, oversized blond guy who made farting noises in study hall and got thrown off the football team for flunking everything except metal shop. It was the kind of story that went around the school, the kind you heard about even if you didn't give a shit. What I wanted to say was "WHY HIM? *Why didn't you do it with me if you thought I was so fucking cool, if we had this connection?"* Buzzy was dumb as a can opener. I couldn't believe how jealous I felt.

A family of chickenheads—that's what they looked like, Mom, Dad, Sis, and Junior—began to stare at us from the opposite booth. Michelle turned on them with such fury it startled me. "What are you staring at?" she shouted. "You never seen a Whopper before?"

The poultry-faced family went meekly back to their hamburgers. Michelle turned back to me as if nothing happened.

"Of *course* I lied," she continued, lowering her voice and sliding closer in the booth. "You think I'm gonna tell some dodo the truth about my fucking stepfather? What *he* did?" She shrugged and put her hand on my leg. I watched it there, but didn't do anything. It felt more friendly than anything else. But more than friendly. It felt *intimate.* "Sometimes you have to lie," she went on. "You know that. You tell people the truth, they look at you funny. They freak. So you lie. Like you saying your mom didn't get to go to her prom, or me saying I was attacked by Charlie Mailman. It's not like I don't want to be normal. It's just I never had the chance. You know what that's like, right?"

I didn't answer. This whole conversation weirded me out. I couldn't tell if she was including me in some special club, or telling me we were both completely fucked-up. Maybe both. The thing I didn't get was whether this meant that maybe Michelle really liked me all these years—that I could have had her if I'd done something about it, if I hadn't been so shy—or if it meant that, yeah, she'd noticed and thought about me, but what she'd noticed and thought made me the last person on earth she'd want to be with. Even if we were both aliens.

It was all so confusing. Twenty minutes ago she'd asked me

to wipe her in the parking lot. To give her that little lick. But what did that mean? Pat Boone still didn't cover public cunt-licks in *Tips for Teens*, and there really wasn't anybody to ask.

I didn't realize how long I'd been sitting there, digesting all this, until Michelle threw herself back against the booth with a dramatic sigh. The moment had passed, but I think we both felt like we'd gone somewhere new. I did, anyway. The whole silent connection thing felt suddenly real.

"That was almost good," she said, dropping the husk of a sesame bun into her ketchup-lake with a dramatic plunk. (She'd given up plucking the seeds off, and just scooped the dough out of the middle.) "How come you didn't finish your food?"

I saw a third of a Whopper still plopped on my wrapper and shrugged. "I don't know, I guess I can't feel and eat at the same time. Did I tell you my father died?" I asked, without knowing I was going to. "He walked in front of a streetcar."

Michelle gave a little snort. "God, would that piss me off! What did you ever do to him?"

This was not the response I expected. It took me a couple of seconds to realize that she had a point. On top of everything else: the sadness, the shame, the night sweats . . . I was pissed at my father. He bailed on me.

"I figure he had his reasons," I said, but Michelle wouldn't let it go.

"There's always reasons. There just aren't enough streetcars."

The way she said that bummed me out and cheered me up at the same time.

"Sometimes I don't even know who I am," she confided, licking grease off her fingers. "I just know what *happened* to me. My mother wouldn't believe it when I told her about my stepdad.

It's like, she didn't believe I was me. Living in that house was like acting in a play. I hated every single line."

She didn't talk after that. She just looked at me, then scooched sideways and gave me a peck on the forehead. That's all you could call it, a peck. It wasn't even close to real kiss territory. But it was something.

"You're so . . . *you*," she said, and bolted off with her little twitch-butt, Krishna-walk to the Burger King doors. At the other side of the restaurant, she spun around and hollered. Like there was nobody in the place but us, and even if there was, she didn't give a fuck. "Bobby, we gotta get going. We don't get a ride soon, we're gonna grow old in this shithole!"

After she shouted, I slunk down in my seat. Hippies were always shouting to each other in crowded places, just to show how *free* they were. As if on cue, the entire population of Burger King glared at Michelle, then shifted to me when she flew out the door. But I didn't care. I was still wrapping my mind around everything she'd just said. Finding out that, all along, Michelle had actually dug me, had felt *connected*, was like being handed 3-D glasses to look back on the whole movie of my childhood. Every memory had new impact, had something in it I could see in a whole new way. I felt like I'd just had the last ten years of my life rearranged. It was amazing. Completely thrilling and insanely sad. *IF I'D ONLY KNOWN . . . BUT I DIDN'T . . . BUT I DO NOW. . . . CHRIST!*

The bun I'd just bit into went dry in my mouth as I trailed her out the door.

An hour later, watered and fed, we were still stuck on the on-ramp next to Burger King. A half hour after that, my thumb actually started to ache. I was getting worried, but Michelle didn't seem to mind.

"Relax," she kept saying, "the world is an illusion anyway. Nothing matters. It's all a big cartoon inside God's head."

We sat hunched on our sleeping bags, thumbs stuck toward the traffic, waiting for someone to come along and take us away. The whole situation was strange. We were only minutes from Mom's condo. I had a sinking feeling that if we didn't leave soon, I'd be sucked up like Judy Garland's bed in *The Wizard of Oz* and dropped in front of my mother's television. I could already taste the chips and onion dip.

Michelle picked up on my jitters and accused me of "dwelling in mind-stuff."

"What happened," I said, "they sprinkle Zen on the french fries?"

She ignored me and kept going. "Arjuna tells us, 'All is false-hood, but the one true godhead.' Your trouble is, you think everything is real. When you realize it isn't, you can relax."

This was getting to me. Without thinking about it, I reached over and pinched her nose, giving it more of a twist than I in-tended. Michelle screeched and slapped my hand. "Ouch! You asshole, what did you do that for?"

"Do what?" I pretended to watch a semi speed by, shielding my face from the rush of diesel fumes. "How could you feel something that wasn't even real?"

Michelle sulked for a minute, then rolled her eyes. "You sound just like Shiva now. That's the kind of crap he would lay on me after he. . . ." She stopped and chewed on a hangnail.

"After he what?"

"Never mind, okay? It's none of your beeswax."

"Okay, fine."

But I knew it wasn't. Whatever it was, I knew it was bad. Michelle, I was starting to see, was just the kind of person bad stuff happened to. It was becoming pretty clear that I was, too. I wondered if that's how it worked: Bad Stuff People somehow found other Bad Stuff People. Good Luckers stuck with other Good Luckers.

If this was true, it wasn't something I particularly wanted to know about.

"You feeling okay?" I asked, just to get my mind off this new, unwelcome insight. Unless two Bad Luckers could rub together and make good luck, like multiplying negative numbers to get a positive, I figured I was doomed.

"I'm feeling groovy," Michelle declared, and made a show of sticking her thumb out extra far at a Chevy full of men in American Legion hats. The way they leered, you'd have thought they wanted to stick us on a spit and roast us. One blobby-jowled lunk shoved himself belly-deep out the window. He raised his middle finger, pressed it to his mouth, and hocked a huge gob of phlegm over the top of it that landed by my boot. Proud of his performance, he ripped off his Legion hat and waved it at us, shouting, "Not today, girls!"

"Oh wow, that's nice," I said, glad to be thinking about something besides what was going on in my head. "Good thing it wasn't real. I guess if we're stuck out in the rain all night, that won't be real either. It'll be okay to stand here soaking and get pneumonia. It'll be fun! 'Cause it'll just be an illusion, right? We're all just little Porky Pigs in God's big Looney Tune."

Michelle ignored me. No doubt on the lookout for flaming chariots, she squinted at the sky, which was already smudging to

perv—a love story

dusk, then lifted her hat to give her pigtail a squeeze. The ritual tail-squeeze reassured her. But not me. I saw her scalp and I juked. It was like traveling with a pretty carnival act. How was it possible to be so turned on and so freaked out in the same breath?

When Michelle lowered her eyes, something had changed. It was spooky, since it came out of nowhere, but also nice, since what was different was her attitude toward me. Whatever she'd spotted in the clouds over the mall, the message seemed to be "Be nice to Bobby." I was nearly ready to let myself believe that the way we connected over burgers was the way we could be from now on.

Michelle took a step toward me and slipped both her hands around mine. A station wagon screeched to a halt twenty yards ahead, and a skinny girl threw a pair of Budweiser cans out the back window. But I was too engrossed with this new Michelle to do more than notice.

"Krishna says, 'Right on,'" she whispered. "He lives in my heart and tells me what I need to do."

It had begun drizzling again, so I wasn't sure, but her eyes glistened with what looked like tears.

"See, I didn't come to the ashram—I didn't come to *Him*—with love in my heart. I came 'cause my stepdad was diddling me up, down, and sideways and I had nowhere else to go. You're a boy, you don't know. But when a girl runs away, the whole world's like nothing but arms and fingers. Everywhere you go it's *"Get in the van!"* or old married guys with fake muttonchops talking about 'free love.' Shit like that. Shit you can't believe. I saw these kids in orange robes, and I found out they were Hare Krishnas and anybody could join, so I moved into the ashram. I figured it had to be better than home. But even there it was still *'Girls have to do this, boys get to do that.'* Like some kind of holy summer camp. Even the hair thing. Did you know girls are supposed to keep their hair? It's just the boys who shave their skulls. But I was so tired of all that. My stepfather made me tired of that. The creeps with fake muttonchops made me tired of that."

She gave my hands an extra squeeze and tilted her head to the left, then tilted right again.

"So one night I did it myself. I stood in front of the mirror and I said to my reflection, 'If Krishna loves me, he'll let me get to heaven, too. He'll pull me up just as fast as he pulls up any boy. If he doesn't, then fuck him, he's a fake, he's just my step-father with a throne in the sky and an eye on his forehead.' "

Now it was really raining, but the way she squeezed my hands made me so warm it was like the rain steamed right off. I loved that she was telling me things, even if I hated the things she was telling me. I loved the way her head tilted sideways, like the RCA dog. Mostly, I loved that even though she was so tough, she acted like she needed me. At least a little. I never had that feeling before: being needed by someone. I didn't even know I liked it until I felt it, though it made me just as sad as it made me happy.

Michelle nearly swooned as she described that night with the scissors.

"Oh, Bobby, it was so groovy. With each lock of hair that hit the sink I turned beautiful. I was never beautiful before."

"But Michelle," I said, "you were. You *were!*" By now the rain was pounding us. "You were always . . . I mean, in second grade I used to lie in bed and make up movies where I rescued you, saved you from burning buildings, from pirates, because you were so . . . even then . . . you were so . . . I don't know, so . . ."

I wanted to say *beautiful*. I wanted to say *perfect*. But before I

perv—a love story

could find a way to say anything, she pushed her hand over my mouth. This was so . . . personal. I wanted to taste her palm but I was afraid to breathe.

"You don't understand. I *couldn't* feel anything good," she said, her words coming out fast, as if she'd been waiting a long time to say what she had to say, and needed to say it before she changed her mind. "I didn't feel anything good about myself until I started chopping my hair that night, my second week in the ashram. Only Sri Shiva—he was like the swami in charge, this Elvissy guy whose real name was Marty Ciccone—Sri Shiva came in when I was finishing up and he swore at me, he actually swore, because the Vedic texts are real clear. Girls don't shave their heads. It's a guy-god thing. So what he did, Shiva dragged me by my hair out of the bathroom. And the whole time, he's screaming, right in my face, so close I could see the tiny veins in his eyeballs, 'You wanna be pulled to heaven? *I'll* pull you to heaven, you little she-bitch . . . !'

"But I didn't know, see? I didn't know he was just being a guy and not a Hindu. 'Cause I only went into the ashram to get away from my family, and all that, and then when I got there I, like, started to believe. I started to feel all this love energy. To feel holy. So when this cool, older boy who's supposed to be really wise, really cosmic, when he throws me down on his straw mat in his room, in front of his candles, in front of his Divine Grace Swami Prabhupada poster, I thought, *Well maybe, you know? Well maybe this is holy. Maybe this is what Lord Krishna wants.* Except that . . . except that—"

"Except that what?"

It was really pouring now, but I didn't feel it. I didn't feel anything, except my fingers, which Michelle squeezed in hers.

She'd taken her hand from my mouth and grabbed my fingers. Everything was right there. Where she touched me. Where the water soaked between her skin and mine and melted away.

"Except he hurt me," she said, her voice so small it was all but drowned out by the cars shushing by. "He . . . *did* things, you know? And when I screamed he put his prayer cloth in my mouth and said, 'This is how you learn. This is how you learn about illusion. . . .' When it was over, I went back to my little room. I don't even remember how I got there. But I shared the room with two other girls, and I didn't want to wake them. I still had his prayer cloth in my hand, so I used it to wipe myself. I couldn't even walk to the bathroom, because I was afraid I might see Shiva again, so I wiped myself, and he was so big, there was blood, both places, and I kept staring at the candle. We had to keep one burning on the altar all the time, night and day, and while I stared at it, I felt the hot between my thighs, the sticky wet where the blood's still trickling, and that's when I saw him, I saw Lord Krishna, I saw the Super-soul, the Everything, right there in the flames, I saw Him, and He smiled at me. He smiled right at me, through the fire, and all three of His eyes were open. And then, like magic, the middle eye turned bright blue, then bright green, like an emerald, then yellow, scarlet, purple, until it was just this swirling, diamond rainbow with the universe and space and every color you can imagine rushing into me, like an electric current from Krishna's third eye straight into mine, and I fell back and I knew, I knew, that was the sign. *That it was okay.* Do you believe me, Bobby? Do you believe me? Do you?"

I was scared but I said yes. She was so shaky, her little teeth were chattering. Her lips flushed blue. "I believe you," I said, though my mouth had gone dry and I had no idea what the truth was. "Of course I believe you."

Michelle let go of my hand and hugged herself. She wrapped herself in her own arms and began to rock back and forth. Rocking and talking in the rain in a voice that didn't seem to come from her. It was more like something was talking *through* her, and it was only her lips that shaped the words. She went from the end of the story, back to the middle, until I didn't know where I was, and just let the words wash over me like raindrops exploding my skull.

"When I got back to my bed—which wasn't even a bed, which was, like, an air mattress, like you'd take to the beach, with sheets thrown over the plastic, that's what they gave us—when I got back to bed, as soon as I laid down I had this vision, like you have on acid, but without the acid. . . . And it was my stepfather, only it wasn't my stepfather, it was Shiva, too, only it wasn't just Shiva, either, it was JFK but not just JFK, it was Jimi Hendrix and Mister Ed and J. Edgar Hoover, and . . ."

She went on like that, talking about the snakes in Hendrix's hair, the thousand-armed Richard Nixon, the painted elephants, the angels with weeping vaginas that sang Ave Maria and nipples that dripped blood into the mouths of baby deer. . . . All of it, she insisted, all of it in the candle, that night, in the vision that took the pain away.

Finally we heard a horn honk and somebody calling us, and it was like we both came out of a trance.

hippiesmack

O h, lovebirds! Over here!"

A grinning, longhaired guy with droopy handlebar mustache and wraparound sunglasses waved at us from a cream-colored Lincoln Continental. I thought it was the same one I'd seen before, but I wasn't sure. It was a '63, with suicide doors. The kind Kennedy got shot in. The driver, another hippie, said something that made the first longhair laugh. He coughed out a cloud of smoke and called us again.

"I'm talkin' to you, cutie pies. Get on in!"

This time he waggled what looked like a joint and the car jammed into reverse and swerved backward. The back tires spat muddy gravel and Droopy Mustache wriggled out of the passenger window. I could see he had on a leather fringed vest with no shirt underneath. A bunch of necklaces clanked against his chest, which was completely hairless and muscular as Tarzan's. Dangling among the crosses, beads, and turqoise was a long red feather. He flapped the feather at us, then dropped his voice to a kind of dirty whisper. "We have drugs! *Come on . . . !*"

Michelle picked up her bag and tore over, but I wasn't sure. This was one of those situations where you know you'll regret what you're about to do, but you know you're going to do it anyway. I had that feeling a lot. When I thought about it, I couldn't remember ever not having it.

"Oh good, she's *coming!*" Fringe-vest howled to the driver, whom I still couldn't see. Then he pursed his lips in a theatrical pout. "What about *you*, handsome? Not going to let your girlfriend get in with *strangers*, are you?"

Michelle stopped halfway to their car and turned around. "Come on, Bobby. Let's go!"

"Yeah, Bobby, *come on!*"

Everything out of Fringe-man's mouth seemed somehow mocking, but I couldn't say why. He leaned even farther out the window, until I could see the rippling muscles in his stomach— what Coach Ponish called "beer cans." That's when he blew me a kiss.

I froze, but he just reached back, opened the rear door from outside—you could do that with suicide doors, the rear handles were right next to the front ones—and flapped his feather some more.

"Going, going, gone," he sang, before breaking into giggles again.

"Bobby, get in!" Michelle yelled. "This is great!"

I was still waffling, but ran over anyway, so as not to look like a coward. Michelle tossed in her sleeping bag and got in, with me behind her. The pot fog blasted us both at the same time.

Michelle was thrilled. "Far out!"

"Yeah, really *groovy*, huh?" said the muscle-hippie. He swung around and I saw that he was older than I thought. Despite his long blond hair his shiny skin was shaved clean. Deep grooves ran beside his lips, and his cheeks bunched up when he smiled, like Howdy Doody's. He looked like Howdy Doody, but dangerous.

"Name's Varnish," he said. Laughing and coughing, he whacked the driver, who still hadn't turned around, across the back of his thick, bull neck. "And this here's Meat."

Meat's hair was even longer than Varnish's, dark brown and banded at the back in a fat ponytail that hung out of sight against the torn car seat. His face bloomed into a full, bushy beard and he wore silver reflector shades. Even when I caught him in the rearview, there was no way to actually make out any features.

"Come on, Meat," chuckled the one called Varnish, "play nice."

Meat lifted his hand slowly off the wheel, like an Indian saying *How*. "Everything is everything," he announced solemnly, in a voice so low he might have been speaking from the bottom of a well.

perv—a love story

"Meat's a man of few words," cackled Varnish, who seemed incapable of staying in one position for more than a second. Flecks of white dotted the corners of his mouth. Feathery spit. "Oh wait," he yelped, popping suddenly out of his seat. His head hit the ceiling but he didn't notice. "This is a *nice* person's car! I just know it! I love nice! Have a stick of dynamite, friends. Doobie-doobie-sock-it-to-me!"

The Lincoln ran so quietly, I didn't realize we were moving until Meat passed somebody fast and my bag flew off my lap. Everything was like TV. My senses were frazzled.

"Exciting, huh?" said Varnish. "Meat and me are going to California to get in the *film* business. We're *investors*, but we're artists, too. We have vision," he howled. "Like Fonda and Hopper in *Easy Rider*. You see *Easy Rider*? That's our bag, okay. That's our *thing*. Gotta do your own thing, you know? Doesn't matter how you make your bread, it's what you do with it that counts. All money is green energy. Green green green green *GREEN* green green green energy!"

"Right on," Meat added, so low you could hardly hear him.

"Right *right* on!" said Varnish, and they both cracked up, Varnish hysterically, Meat with a long, hissing laugh that reminded me of the exercises I did in grade school speech class, when I had to repeat *S-S-S* over and over to kill my lisp. That was how Meat laughed. *S-S-S*.

When Varnish recovered, he reached under his tongue and pulled out the fat joint he'd been jiggling out the window. He handed the wet cigarette to Michelle. She'd been watching him with her mouth open since settling in the car.

"Man, you are one fine *señorita*," Varnish said to her. Then he grinned over at me. " 'Course everybody's got their own *bag*, right, *Handsome?* I'm gonna call you Handsome 'cause you're so goddamn . . . *handsome!*"

Varnish made a face at Michelle and they laughed like they'd known each other forever. We'd been in the Lincoln two minutes and I already felt left out.

Varnish picked a mud-streaked cowboy hat off the car floor and slapped it on his head. "Maybe you wanna ride up here with us," he said to Michelle, cracking up again and lighting a match one-handed under her nose. Michelle leaned forward, until the flame touched the spit-soaked joint. She inhaled in an exaggerated way that made me feel mad on top of laughed at. Left out and lame-o. Our clothes were soaked, but Michelle seemed okay with it. She seemed fine.

"Crawl on up here," Varnish said. Then he reached back and tapped me softly on the side of my head. Softly, but like it meant something. "Handsome won't mind, will he?"

Michelle erupted in high-pitched squeals. It was a sound I'd never heard before. I didn't expect her to ask permission, but I thought she could at least have looked at me before clambering up front between the tough-looking hippies. Now I was alone in back. Still, I had that sopping joint, and made sure to take two or three giant hits, sucking in as much as I could before handing it to Michelle.

Varnish eyed me, and clicked his tongue like a prissy teacher. "Careful, Handsome, that's not just marahoochie you're snarfin'. Meat sprinkled on some of his special blend."

It was too late, though. Michelle took her hit and shot sideways across Varnish's lap to puke out the window. In another second my own head felt like one of those glass balls with the Eiffel Tower inside, the ones that snow when you flip them.

Instead of snowflakes, though, it felt like greasy rain, like my eyeballs were sweating and the inside of my head was drenched in dirty Vaseline.

"They die, you bury 'em," Meat said, in that rumbling voice of his. Though he might not have said that at all. It was all very far away. He might not have said anything. I couldn't tell. The hum of the Lincoln's engine swelled to a sonic roar, and I jammed my hands over my ears, afraid I might bleed. I could feel things happening below my scalp. Where my brain used to be.

"Oh God," I heard myself groan. My voice oozed out of a loudspeaker under my hair.

I just wanted Meat to drive straight, to drive without swerving a millimeter left or right. The smallest motion swooped through my stomach. I needed air. But I wasn't sure how to open the window and I couldn't ask. I couldn't move my lips. They'd gone numb. It took everything I had to concentrate on inhaling and exhaling, to keep from throwing up domino bars on the upholstery.

"I'm flashing on Suzy," Varnish hooted from the front seat. I could see Michelle's head in his hands, her lips mushed sideways, dripping blue. She looked wrong-eyed. "Suzy was not a bird," Varnish crooned. "Suzy was a lynx. Suzy was a righteous lynx. I am flashing on her, man. Can you dig that? I mean, *can you?*"

"Suzy. Suzy, yeah," Meat said, in that rumbly way, and twirled the wheel to pass a moving van. I read LONG DISTANCE HAULING in dripping letters. The swerve sent me sideways against the door. Then the colors flew out of Meat's face, melting and re-blending like the monsters in *Jason and the Argonauts*. Ray Harryhausen monsters.

I closed my eyes but the pictures were worse behind my eye-lids. Meat's beard exploded into hairy worms and the worms were screeching. *"Eee-eee-eee,"* I heard from somewhere. *"Eee-eee-eee."* Only it wasn't the worms. It was Michelle, screaming, *"Shee-ee-eeva!"* Screaming and pleading *"Shee-ee-ee-vah, I'm sorry, Shee-ee-vah, I didn't tell...."*

But underneath her screaming was that roar, and underneath that the blood sloshed through these sopping tunnels that hon-eycombed my skull. I was lost and marauding through wet-flesh tunnels. I was running, chased by Meat, but my feet were sponges. Everywhere I turned, Varnish popped out and licked me. He lapped with a tongue like a cat's, scratchy and foul, licking my tongue with his. I couldn't close my mouth. I couldn't move. "Hey Jude" blared from the radio, only it mutated to "Hey You," then "Hey Jew." Hate who?...HATE YOU! until the sound swallowed itself in the buzz of blood and the noxious throbbing of my heart.

When I opened my eyes, the hair-worms were gone but Var-nish was staring at me. Hard. Smiling his spit-flecked smile. We were parked somewhere, stopped on a dead stretch of road. I didn't see Michelle, didn't remember her until I struggled up from the mud, the viscous rut my mind had rolled into and stalled. I had to concentrate: *Car... hitchhike... Michelle.*

Varnish mouthed something I couldn't make out. Couldn't decipher until I caught myself reaching for the volume knob—*to turn it up*—and panicked at doing that, thinking, *What volume knob...? What is wrong with me...? AM I RETARDED NOW?"*

"Smack and DMT," was what Varnish was saying. He peered

perv—a love story

up from the joint he was rolling and I wondered, in a vague sort of way, why he was in the backseat. My neck hurt and I tasted blood where I'd I bit my tongue.

"Smack and DMT," Varnish repeated, running the plump joint in and out of his mouth with a funny smile. "They call it a slider. The smack straps you in and the D sends you over the moon. Hendrix wrote a song about it, but he forgot it. I mean DMT, man. Higher than Sunshine, faster than crank. Shit gets you there and back in under forty-five. The smack makes sure you land with a kiss. You don't crash, baby, you curl into a ball and drop . . . Like it?"

"*Mmmmeeeech . . .*" I said. My jaws felt welded on rusty hinges. The rest of me felt like poison Jell-O *"Mmmmi-chelle . . . Mmmichelle-yallright???"*

"Mee-chelle ma belle," Varnish sang, before Meat popped up in the front seat and Michelle climbed out from underneath him. Her face wore a bleary smile. Her eyes might as well have flashed little tombstones. "I love Meat," she mumbled, her lips gone puffy. "I really do."

"So you're okay?" I managed, before my heart dropped down a long, dark well.

"I . . . am . . . groovy," she sighed. Then Meat pulled her close and, making sure his shades were aimed right at me, plunged his tongue between her swollen lips.

I opened my own mouth to say something. But say what? To who? I closed it again and tried to just breathe. I was still high but it was steadier now. I was back, but different than when I left. Everything had trails if I moved too fast. But the scary, am-I-losing-my-mind part had passed and things were just sort of . . .

harsh. Painfully serene. Like they'd cheese-grated my eyeballs. Replaced my blood with marshmallow creme. I was weirdly content. Savaged, but blissed-out.

Until . . .

Varnish ran his hand through my hair and let it rest on the back of my neck. "How 'bout you, Handsome? How you feelin'?"

He squeezed, but not too much. More like he was letting me know he *could,* but that he wouldn't if he didn't have to. I started to move and he applied more pressure, his face frozen in a smile so wide it showed both rows of teeth. A gold one glittered in back, on the right. The rest were yellow and pointy as a German shepherd's.

"Oh, Bobby," Michelle giggled.

"Oh, Bobby, what?" It killed me to look at her, but I didn't want to act panicked. I wanted to act like it was okay, like I was used to having strange men fondle my head, having them hold me.

"Oh, Bobby, you're too much."

Varnish smiled at her dreamily, firing another joint with his free hand. "Don't listen to her, Handsome. Listen to me."

"I'm listening."

"Good." Varnish hurricaned smoke in my face and flip-flapped the joint like he wanted me to snap at it, to do some kind of doggy drug trick. "Good," he said again, " 'because I'm talking to you. I'm asking you something important. I'm asking, 'Do you think love is a good thing?' *I* think love's a good thing. All kinds of love. Love is where it's at. Love is the grooviest groove of all. Love is what *is,* brother. Am I right or am I right?"

"You're right," I said.

"Can't hear you."

"You're right, you're right!"

"Then if I'm right, and I am *RIGHT*, there is no wrong kind of love. Do you understand me? There is no such thing as what they call PRE-*VERSION*."

With serious effort, I shifted sideways, toward Meat, who nodded and scratched his beard when he turned around. "Everything is everything," he intoned, breaking into a purple-lipped smile. I saw myself reflected in his shades and was embarrassed more than scared. Varnish had me cradled. His right arm was slung over the back of my neck. His left rested along the seat, the hand dangling just over my middle, fingers fluttering, like a man with a candy box who can't decide if he wants caramels or jellies. A man delaying the decision, just to tease himself, to make it more fun.

"Suzy," Varnish piped up suddenly, and Meat laughed his hissing laugh again. "Oh yeah, we got us a primo Suzy."

"You guys!" Michelle giggled, right before Meat swung at her, fast, like he was going to hit her in the face, but clapping, instead, loud as a gunshot, a quarter-inch from her eyes.

"Oh wow," Michelle cried, panting hard. "Oh wow. That was . . . oh wow."

To my surprise she flung herself upward, pressing her mouth over Meat's.

"Couple of Suzies," Varnish said, taking a hit on the joint, then thrusting it in my lips and holding it there, mouthing *"Suck it, suck it"* until my throat started burning and I coughed out smoke. He ripped the thing out and made a show of licking the very tip, where it was wettest.

"I didn't used to know about love," announced Varnish, TV preacher–style. He cracked up, then stopped, going serious again.

"I used to think love was one thing. Can you dig that? Love was one thing. But love is *not* one thing. Is love one thing, Meat?"

"Nope."

Meat came up for air while Michelle's eyes rolled back, like a scared pony's, showing the whites before rolling forward again.

"Okay then," said Varnish. "Meat agrees. And Meat's a smart guy. Meat *knows* things." He bent back over me, his breath like burning rubber, and made his mouth into a perfect O. "One thing? Or a lot of things. Which is it, Handsome? Which is love?"

I thought about it, decided there was no right answer, and then answered anyway. "It's a lot of things."

I was hoping—and hated myself for it—I was hoping to say the right thing. Hoping to please him.

Varnish grinned. "That's right, Handsome. That's very right. See, I knew you were smart. You got that high forehead."

He was so near, his lips brushed mine when he talked. That's when I realized the music was off. I barely noticed the tape when it was playing—*Highway 61 Revisited*—and now "Desolation Row" echoed in my head. *"The beauty parlor's filled with sailors. The circus is in town."* So creepy, but so . . . I don't know. So *vivid*. At some point it had grown dark. I didn't even remember stopping. Outside the car, wherever we were, there were no stars at all. No streetlights. Just the glow of the joint, the shimmer of Meat's reflector shades, the wet shine around Michelle's eyeballs.

The pressure on my neck came and went. Varnish varied his grip—squeezing, then letting up—his fingers solid, not hurting exactly—squeezing, then letting up—*letting me know* . . .

"You're mine now, but you like it. You like it, don't you, Handsome? And that's okay. That's *beautiful*. Love's a lot of things. You

perv—a love story

know that. Your girlfriend knows, too, don't you Michelle? You know it's okay."

Michelle's eyes poured into mine, and in that moment she looked so kind, so *understanding* I wanted to rip my spleen out. Sometimes, it's like you know what people think: You know what they're thinking, and you know it's wrong. All you want to do is change their mind, but you can't. You can't. I knew Michelle was thinking, *"He likes it. Bobby likes what Varnish is doing . . ."*

I had the sense she was accepting me, only what she was accepting *was not what I was*. It was just what was happening: Varnish pressing his cheek into mine, like we were dancing, his waxy, clean-shaven cheek so close our lashes brushed when we blinked at the same time. His face glowed like quartz in a museum.

"You can love me," he murmured, with his burning breath, his hot mouth snail-crawling around my lips. "That's all right. Remember what I said. There's all kinds of love."

"Varnish, hey," I said, squirming futilely. "Varnish, man, c'mon . . ."

"S'okay," he cooed. "Don't worry. Like I say, ain't no such thing as pre-verts. As pre-version. Love is love is love. JFK, right?"

"JFK?"

I was trying to follow, but how? The smoke, his skin. Everything so fucking *wrong*.

"You know," Varnish pressed on, like he was reminding me of something, refreshing my memory. "JFK. And Mickey Mantle. JFK and the Mick had these parties. Real wild scenes." He whacked my head. "I ain't talkin' out the side of my neck, man. This is known. This is *fact*. These guys could get anything they wanted. Chicks, chicklets, you name it. Pigs ain't gonna bust *their* ass. Why? Because they are heroes. This is the President. This is the Mick. But their thing was plate jobs. Can you dig it? They had these special tables made, these glass tables, and they'd get all drunk and buzzed and crawl underneath. Kennedy had his doc bang 'em in the ass with B-twelve and crank. Get 'em all nuked-up. Soon as the missiles took off, man, they'd crawl underneath, so they could stare up. And the pussy, man. The most beautiful pussy in the world. They'd lay a thousand bucks on these chicks to climb onto those tables, open up their pretty cheeks and unload. I'm talkin' about hot lunch, man, right down over their faces. They used to feed the ladies pâté de foie fuckin' gras, to make it classy. Dig it! These are heroes. These are like kings, man. The President can fuck anybody. And Mantle? Come on! The guys beating 'em off with a bat. But what do they want? What they want is to lie on their backs and watch these beautiful girls pinch a loaf. Right on their faces, man. Now why did they want that, Handsome? I'll fucking tell you. *Because there was nothin' left they could feel.* Understand? There was nothin' left they hadn't done. But they still needed to take it to the limit. They wanted to cross the line, understand? Is that bad? Is that evil? I mean, they didn't want to hurt anybody. That wasn't their bag. They weren't violent. They only offed cats when they had to. JFK and Mantle, man. Do you hear me? They just wanted a plate job, that's all. Maybe it's not my thing. Maybe it's not yours. But this is America, man. It's not about somebody's a fucking pre-vert. It's about the fucking pursuit of happiness. And that's okay, right?"

I realized he wanted me to say something, so I said, "Yeah, I guess it's okay."

perv—a love story

I was trying to listen, but Varnish had worked himself up. He was talking fast, spitting little speed-feathers.

"No, it is not OKAY!" he screamed. Sweat was oozing out of his scalp. "It is not okay. I am talking *philosophy*, man. Philosophy says, 'Right on. There's nothing dirty here. Nothing bad.' But the USA. The US of fucking A says 'Ho no! Ho no, you stick to in-and-out.' The USA has this uptight, Ozzie-and-Harriet puritan bullshit, man. You have sex like fucking Lawrence Welk or you're evil. Everybody who don't make love like Uncle is some kind of pre-vert. So that's what happened, man. Jack Ruby."

He stopped and shook his head, panting. I wasn't sure I was hearing right.

"Jack Ruby?"

"Jack Ruby had *movies*, man. Jack Ruby had secret movies of JFK getting plated. He got a girl inside. Had her hide a camera in her snatch. That's why they had to snuff him."

"Kennedy?"

"No, *Ruby*." Varnish pounded his fist into the car seat. "Aren't you *listening*? I am *telling* you things here. Ruby killed Lee Harvey because Lee Harvey fucked up his plans. Ruby was gonna black-mail Kennedy. Sell the film back to him. Over and out, baby. Hush and flush. But after Big John bought the farm, Ruby couldn't do it. He was patriotic, you know. A patriotic Jew. Hebes can go that way. He didn't want to slander a dead President. But he was so pissed off at the bread Oswald lost him, he snuffed *him*. Jews, right? Then the CIA had to do him, 'cause by now word's out on the street he's got the movies of JFK under the table, getting plated. Mantle didn't care. He was a wild man. Drunk at noon. Fuckin' Mick would make popcorn and show the flicks on the Yankee bus. But Kennedy, man. *Kennedy*. Figure it out! You know what the Russians could have done with that? The fuckin' Red Chinese? Oh man, Handsome. It's just *sad*."

Varnish patted my face, then slapped it. "Do you see it now? There is nothing that's bad between two people. Do you see that? Love comes in all flavors. As many flavors as God. What I'm telling you is, I am not a pre-vert, man. JFK?" He clapped his hands. "You figure it out. What *I* do *I* do with *love*."

By now I was just as scared by what Varnish was saying—the impassioned insanity of it—as what he was doing. Worse, all that preaching had left him sweaty. And his face was still pressed close to mine. Awful.

I tried to twist away, peeking past Varnish's ear. But Meat's smile curdled in front of me. He wrapped Michelle's pigtail around his hand and tugged, whipping her head back. He thrust it down again, whistling, and twisted her face up to his own. Despite what was happening to me—Varnish pressing my windpipe, jabbering and squeezing—seeing Meat manhandle Michelle, *my* Michelle, was a million times worse. I kept thinking, *I knew her in kindergarten.* Her little girl face, when I stared at her, hovered above her sixteen-year-old one. Her powdered-sugar mouth, when she nibbled cookies at lunchtime . . . Her milky-smooth neck when she tossed her hair. I blinked up at twenty Michelles, all the Michelles I'd known, up until this one, until the *Wrong Michelle*, the one smiling up at the bearded freak who pulled her hair.

Jerking his tongue in my direction, Meat winked and parted his lips wide inside his facial bush. His mouth, from my cramped position, was a purple cave in the jungle. It opened impossibly, like the snakes you see on nature shows, the ones that dislocate their jaws to swallow piglets whole.

perv—a love story

"Hey, Meatpipe, stop slapping your swamp thing and put on some more tunes, man." Varnish hooted, in a whole new mood entirely, and gave me a lick on the forehead. "Get rid of Bobby D., brother-man. What we need's some egg-crackin' music."

Meat shoved something in the eight-track without looking. Junior Walker and the All-Stars. "*Shotgun . . . Shoot it while you run now!*"

"All right! Sock it to me one time!"

Varnish took a long hit on his joint and burst into high-pitched titters. Then he leaned his face over mine, rubbing noses. I thought, *Hippie Eskimo.* Do they have those? He snapped his fingers and slapped me, but softly again.

"Don't drift off, Handsome. We got a show going here. We got a happening. We got a *love-in.* Meat's showing off his stuff. Lemme just take off my beads and baubles and get down." He scooped up his leather necklaces and feathers and tugged them over his head. Tossed them on the car floor. "Hoo yeah, that's better. I got paisley-brain! I need room to move! I'm a love-love-*love*-LOVE-LOVE-monkey, motherfucker!"

"Fuck you," Meat hooted, laughing up snot. He tugged Michelle's head by her tail and twisted till our faces almost touched over the front seat. Michelle's eyes rolled back again. I thought she was gone. Thought whatever was happening, whatever chemical blast she'd ingested had sent her off. Socked her straight to Krishna-ville.

Varnish whispered in my ear, "Feel like a kiss?"

Out of nowhere, he switched his grip and, shifting fast, jumped behind me. He jammed my hands high up my back, pinning them and keeping his free fist gashed into my neck. Breathing hard, he pushed my face even closer to Michelle's.

"Love is beautiful. It's all you need," Varnish cackled, and broke into a coughing fit, wetting the back of my neck.

"You know what I say?" Meat hissed. "I say 'Fuck Junior Walker,' that's what I say. 'Fuck the nigger music.' "

Grabbing Michelle, he banged her head into the Lincoln stereo, crunching buttons till the tape stopped. Until there was nothing again. Crickets. Woods. He pinched Michelle's earlobe and whispered hoarsely, "Love me?"

"Yes," she whispered back. "Yes, really."

"Show me," Meat said, and when he let her go she sat up. She threw her arms around his shoulders. She kissed him, then pulled back, panting, and kissed him again. Watching her, my eyes went rotten in their sockets. Saran Wrap covered the world. Everyone shiny and together. *Preserved.* Everyone but me, feeling this, always this: *I am outside other people.* Mr. Schmidlap, seeing three boys on his daughter's sex—*like feasting maggots*—Mr. Schmidlap must have felt this way. The air scalded my pupils.

"I don't," I started to say, "I don't—"

And then Michelle did something. She reached over the car seat. Her hand floated toward me. Drifted by itself while her eyes stayed shut, while her mouth worked on Meat's. Her fingers, sweet and marijuana-stinky, found my lashes, my cheekbones, my quivering lips and chin.

Her eyes still closed, she edged her thumb along my gums, then onto Varnish. He let go of me long enough to grab her fingers and work them inside his mouth, soaking them. Strings of cottony saliva webbed the tips when he pulled them out, smiling, and shoved them down my throat.

"L'il taste of Mojo," he muttered, his eyes gone to glittery slits. "A l'il taste of Mojo for my man."

"You want the camera?" Meat hissed at him, his voice muffled, still French-kissing Michelle. "I got it in the trunk. We could do it, man. *Two-Lane Blacktop.*"

"Huh-uh. Fuck that." Varnish churned Michelle's hand in my mouth, choking me, jamming her knuckles off my back teeth, scraping the roof with her nails. "Two Lane Suzy? Fuck that shit. I'm in it now, man. I am *IN IT.*"

While they talked, Michelle opened her eyes. I stared into them. And staring back, she smiled so sweetly, so unlike the tough-ass street girl she'd been since we met in the mall and ended up on the highway before ending up here, in this Hell-mobile, that I wanted to claw something. She was sweet and she was kissing him. She was four years old and a man named Meat was stabbing his tongue in her face. She shivered but it wasn't pain. That much I knew. Pain was not what this was. Pain was only part of it. The little girl in kindergarten, sucking Meat.

"Michelle, are you . . . ?"

"I am beautiful, Bobby."

Meat leered at me. "Hear that? She's beautiful, *Bobby.*"

"Bobby? *Bobby!*"

Varnish growled at the car roof and punched it. His face twitched a cigarette's length above me. Still squeezing Michelle's fingers, he ripped them out of my mouth and poked them at me, just missing my eye. Her nails nicked my left ear. But I couldn't turn away.

"There is no *Bobby*," Varnish jabbered. "Suzies don't have names. Suzies are Suzies. Goddamnit, what is happening here? What is happening? The Greeper is coming down, man. Can't you feel it? I'm calling an air strike, man. I'm calling a No Bummer Zone. Right now. You hear me? This is not some bad scene. *This is NOT some bad scene!"* He poked Michelle's nails in my cheek. "Is this a bad scene, Handsome? Is this a bad scene?"

"I—"

"You what?" he screamed. "You what?"

Meat hissed, "Psychedelic." Just like that: *"Psychedelic,"* and Varnish stopped screaming. He seemed to freeze for an instant, then reanimated, laughing.

"Psychedelic," he repeated. "There it is. Psyche-fucking-delic."

Varnish swung back to me, like he'd forgotten he was squeezing my neck, jamming Michelle's acrid fingers against my nostrils, my chin. I thought, insanely, *His hands have no idea who he is.*

"Are we being mean?" Varnish asked his partner. "Are we? Ask the Suzy. See what the Suzy says."

Meat smiled and grabbed Michelle. Pulling her up by the ear, he murmured, in a reasonable voice, "Are we mean, little girl?"

"No, Meat, you're not mean. You're just . . . you're just Meat."

"And you love me?"

"I love you."

"And what else?"

"I . . . I don't know what else."

"And I'm your one true god. Say it."

"You're my one true god."

"And you love me more than Jesus' peter. More than Krishna's little pink dick. Now say that."

"I love you more than Jesus. I mean, more than, I forget, I'm sorry, more than—"

"That's good enough, baby. See that?" Meat nodded and stroked his loaf-of-bread-sized beard. "See that?"

"See it, be it, free it!" Varnish shouted. "Fuck Timothy Leary. I am going to California! I am making a *movie*. It's gonna be called

perv—a love story

See It, Be it, Free It! and then it's gonna be *ME,* man. It's gonna be me all the Suzies wanna go Suzy on."

"King of the Suzies," Meat said, and I saw myself smiling at him in his silver shades. Saw my face wanting to be whatever he wanted, to get out alive.

Varnish leaned back, taking a giant, complicated suck on the joint. Then he pried my mouth open and blew in smoke. He bent into the cloud and licked my face from my chin to the top of my nose. His voice went into my pores. "Do you wanna love her now? Do you wanna? You can do her," he whispered huskily, "that's cool. Do your thing. Mmmmm . . . Do you like this?"

Almost—there's no other word—almost tenderly, he hugged me. He eased me off the seat and held me, cupping my head on his shoulder. And suddenly, *I missed my father.* A wave of Dad-pain juddered through me. A shock of yearning so intense I could smell his cologne—Williams Lectric Shave—could fully recall the safe-in-his-big-arms sensation when he gave me a bear squeeze, could breathe in the Lucky-Strike-chest-hair-and-Yuban musk of him when I shoved my face in his jacket the second he came home from work. *Daddy . . .* The door opened and I launched myself off the living room carpet into his arms.

"There there," Varnish whispered. And horribly—because I knew this was Varnish, knew this was crazy and wrong—the relief nearly made me faint. Some things, I believe, you don't know you miss until, out of nowhere, you have them back, or have them back but back *all wrong . . .* The way, after a dream where you've kissed someone who, in real life, you'll never kiss again, maybe never kissed at all, you wake up and realize, in the throbbing pit of your stomach, *how impossible it is to live without kissing them again.* How the rest of your life will be a hollow trudge toward death until the dream-need passes, until you shake off the unconscious truth and go on about your shabby business . . .

Varnish hugged me tighter, and I opened my eyes to witness Michelle's head propped on top of the seat, her chin tilted upward and Meat mounted behind her, pinning her shoulders. One second, Meat was panting, a mass of hair mouthing trash, the next he jerked still, like he'd been struck by lightning. Seized up with his eyes fried open.

"Meat's got the falldowns," Varnish chuckled, rocking me slightly as he talked. "Man fix enough of that smack he'll stone up in the middle of a scoot." He angled his face so we could look in each other's eyes, and lowered his voice. "Don't mention this to anybody. Meat's got a problem."

"A problem?"

He'd been holding me for so long I sort of forgot about it. We were talking like it was normal—me being squished into him, him breathing on me, pushing once in a while so I had to feel him.

But, the weird thing—maybe it was that smack they dusted on the joints—the weird thing was I didn't *worry* about what was happening. It was like my worry gland had been defused. I knew I was scared, but the dope dulled it down, disconnected the wires.

Varnish zoned and came back again, pissed off. "Who's got a problem?" he snapped, after a kind of tape-delay.

Time itself seemed tainted. The space between things kept expanding and contracting. Had I ever not been trapped in this fucked-up Lincoln, smashed and cringing on a hippie's lap? Had I ever not breathed speed-sweat and rancid upholstery?

perv—a love story

"I don't got a problem," Varnish declared, "do you?"

"No," I said. I felt dead and lit-up at the same time. "I didn't . . . I mean . . . you're the one who—"

"Who what? Am I mean? I'm not mean." His eyes went fluorescent. "What's goin' on with you, Handsome? What are we doin' here? Huh?"

I felt Varnish's hand grope down along my belly, over my belt buckle, stopping between my legs. He found me and squeezed. Then something clicked off in my brain. Wrongness choked off my oxygen. The sound of his voice smelled bad.

"Love's a muscle, Good-lookin'. Love's the universe. Love's the flavor Buddha likes best."

I heard my mouth say "Daddy" and hated myself, then blurted out "Michelle, Michelle" and gulped back vomit. I was going in and out. My thoughts kept skidding sideways, so I'd think I was one place—in Dad's chair, in second grade homeroom—then blink twice and see Varnish leering over me, shiny and vibrating, or Meat passed out on Michelle's back, pinning her to the front seat.

The good thing, Varnish didn't hear me say "Daddy." He would have said something, I know, and I wondered if I had said it or thought it. I felt like a talking coma victim. I didn't know if they had those, or if I was the first. Maybe coma people could talk to each other, and I could call Mrs. Schmidlap on the phone. Except she was dead. I remembered that now. She was dead. Mr. Schmidlap was dead. My dead dad's hand waved from a bush behind my eyeballs. *"Hi, Bobby! Hi, Dancing Boy!"* His voice was alive, but the rest of him was as gone as I was. . . .

I thought, *I can see through my eyelids.* Through membrane. I saw Michelle's head loll sideways and Varnish tickle her chin. She drooled into Meat's hair and, eyes showing only white, grinned spacily between us.

"Guess baldy-girl ain't goin' nowhere," said Varnish, taunting but not. His fingers found my zipper and started to rub. "Personally, I like a creative hairstyle. Free your mind! Liberate your scalp! Right on!" He dropped his voice an octave and went FM, talking like a late-night DJ. "Now what I want you to do now is shush. Shush now, Handsome. Shush, shush, shush."

I freed one hand, then didn't know what to do with it, and Varnish, very gently, lifted it to Michelle. Her face edged forward into my cupped palm, a peach in a bowl.

"Mmm, that's nice," he droned. "Go ahead and touch her. Meat won't mind. Meat's dead meat."

"Say wh-what?" Meat raised his chin off Michelle's shoulder, then let it fall again, like his strings were clipped.

"See what I mean?" Varnish said.

"Please," I muttered.

"Please what? If you don't like it, make me stop."

"Okay, please stop."

"I said make me."

I tried to move and Varnish grabbed me harder, one finger curled in the flap of my BVDs, looped under my penis and wringing my testicles. It was the weirdest feeling. It hurt but it got me hard. I couldn't stay *not hard*, and Varnish kept pressing, like he'd found a button that made me stiff. Part of me wanted to ask him, *What are you doing?* in case I ever needed to press it myself, to make myself stand up. At the same I wondered—*worried*—am I sweating?

My dad, I suddenly remembered, used to powder his balls on hot days. On vacation once, in Wildwood, New Jersey, I saw

perv—a love story

him take off his shorts, place one foot on the toilet seat, then daintily pinch his scrotum, which glowed scarlet, and hoist it up over his thigh to douse Desenex underneath. "Dad," I said, kind of horrified, "isn't that foot powder? You afraid of getting athlete's balls?"

My father, as ever, just smiled his sad smile. "Well," he said, "you're old enough, so you might as well know."

I must have been seven or eight, and I was scared. I thought he was going *National Geographic* on me. I'd been freaked by an article on manhood rituals in Tanganyika. I had to stop reading at the phrase *"once the bark is inserted in the penile shaft."* That was enough.

Dad spoke with a gravity befitting the occasion. "There's things that go on under your gonads you don't even know about. You don't want to know! But you have to! You have to go right in there and take care of business! Baby powder will make you *feel* good," he explained, making no secret of the contempt he had for mere feel-good solutions. "Baby powder will cool you off. But your antifungals"—here he held up the yellow Desenex can, smiling at the product like a man in a TV commerical—"they can keep you cool *and* keep you defungied. The trick is, you gotta dust your undersack. A lot of men don't know that and still get the chafe. Do you know what I'm talking about?"

"Pretty much," I said, mostly because I wanted the conversation to be over. People were starting to stare. But Dad was nothing if not deliberate. I wondered if his scrote hurt from the squeeze he was putting on it, using it for demonstration purposes.

"I'm talking about jockrot," he went on patiently, dousing once under his right Roma tomato and twice under his left. "Lemme demonstrate." I dropped my pants and he inspected my still-hairless orbs with an approving nod. "They hang small but they itch big," he said, "don't let anybody tell you otherwise."

Here he handed me the can and, smiling proudly, bade me dust my own baby testicles. When I hesitated, Dad said, "That's okay, I'm your father," and deftly palmed my ball-sack, almost like he was weighing it, just long enough to sprinkle Desenex in the crevice beneath it. "Now give 'em a shake," he instructed, and when I did, doing a kind of gimpy shimmy to spread the dust around, he stifled a laugh and rubbed his hand on my head like I'd made him proud, like we'd just gone fishing and I'd caught the biggest trout in the pond.

Looking back, Dad and I never really did too many father-son-type things. Bonding-wise, this was pretty much it.

Varnish breathed into my ear, reeling me back from Dad-land. "You're not trying very hard to stop me. You're not trying at all, Handsome."

I blinked like a cartoon character who'd been dropped off a cliff, and Varnish broke into a dirty grin. "Know what heaven is, Handsome? Heaven's a long dick and an elephant's trunk. You see what I mean? That might feel damn good. Anything's cool as long as it's cool. Ain't no pre-vert in this car. Think about that, Handsome. It's one of them Zen koans. Give it a chew."

Michelle picked this moment to resurface. The look she gave me was everything. I never thought, from the moment I couldn't lick her slit in the parking lot, I never thought she really liked me, not the way I liked her. But somehow, seeing me now: zipper down, humiliated, propped on Varnish's arm like a ventriloquist's dummy with actual organs, her attitude changed.

"Oh, Bobby, baby. Bobby, you're so . . . you're so—"

perv—a love story

"Lucky stiff," Varnish snorted. "She got the shimmies for you, *amigo*. And here I am hogging the party."

"Hey listen," I pleaded. "This isn't cool. . . ."

"No, it is cool," said Varnish. "It *is* cool. Free love's what it's all about. We can have us a love-in. Right here. What do you think of that? You wanna do her? You wanna do her for *me*?"

The more he talked, the lower his voice got. Going FM again. Working himself up. He let go of me and slid his hand down into his own jeans. Moving slow, but moving.

"You . . . oh man. . . . You wanna kiss her? You wanna tongue her? For me? You want her puss-puss? Go 'head, Handsome, make Papa proud."

Michelle pulled her T-shirt down, crumpling Mr. Natural's head. One nipple peeped over the collar. Her tit seemed tiny. Childlike. *Tragic*. "Kiss on it," Varnish breathed, rubbing me, rubbing himself. "Kiss it all over. Do it!"

He let go of me long enough to slap me, backward and forward, across the top of my head, then grabbed me by the back of my neck and half lifted, half pushed me up and into her.

"Kiss," he ordered, and Michelle perked up and puckered her lips. Varnish scowled. "Not *smooch*, goddamn it, KISS!"

Varnish ripped his hot hand out of my pants and jammed it behind my head. Grasping Michelle with his other one, he pushed us toward each other, pushed us together. For one careening second, I tried to twist loose, and Varnish shoved me down. He ground my head in the seat, as if trying to push me through it.

"You like that?" he hissed. "You like that?"

My lips were too smushed to reply. Face mashed in that sticky upholstery, I made out an S-shaped red stain on the car rug, beneath a smattering of roaches. In front of that, jammed under the front seat, were an empty bottle of Boone's Farm and a black leather belt, looped all the way through its "pot leaf" buckle.

"Jeez, ease up!" I cried, once I'd freed myself. And then, stupidly, *"Peace, man!"*

Varnish snickered. I wanted to resist and didn't want to. What scared me was one thought. This was my chance to make up for the parking lot—for when I'd chickened out—when the weather and the people and my good-boy panic at the chance of getting in trouble gripped my heart and made me small. I didn't lick Michelle's pussy, and I lost her. So I'd do anything now. Anything.

"Tell me what you want me to do." Michelle's voice had shrunk to a whimper. "Tell me."

"Well," I said, my mouth dry as the cracks in Varnish's lips. "Well—"

"Well, shit!" Varnish whacked me again, this time knocking my forehead off Michelle's. Neither of us made a sound, too scared to say *Ouch.* "You think she's talking to you?"

"What?"

"You heard me. Sunshine girl's talking to *me.* Sunshine girl liked that taste of smack, didn't she?" We both regarded Michelle, who smiled back crookedly, her lower lip gone loose and drooly. Meat had begun to snore on top of her. She looked like a little girl peeping out from under a bear rug.

"Sweet thang," said Varnish, his voice growing hoarse. "Sweet, sweet thang."

The way he held me, at an angle, suspended over the car floor, I had to crane my neck sideways to see his face. The DMT had left me shaky but the heroin, I guess, kept everything coated in fur.

Look at me, I thought, and wondered what Tennie would say about the situation. I was being breathed on and squeezed. I was being dick-handled by a creepy hippie. My penis was semi-hard and out of my pants. And for good measure a girl I'd been pining for since preschool lay sprawled across a car seat, inches away, exposing her breasts and passing out, then coming to and blowing me weird kisses before nodding off again.

I didn't even know where we were. Once I'd puffed on that slider, sucked down that smack-and-DMT, I just went somewhere else. And when I came back the fucked-up Lincoln was parked in the dark. In nothing but trees. I could hear the whoosh of traffic. Maybe turnpike noise. But how far away? For all I knew we'd been air-dropped in the Black Forest. We could have been twenty miles from Mom's condo or twenty minutes from death.

I can't say I wasn't scared. It's just . . . it's like it wasn't happening to me. I remembered once, coming back from visiting my mother's big brother, Uncle Mitch, a jolly guy who'd made a fortune in electric fences, my mother drove into a highway divider on the Pennsylvania Turnpike. The thing of it is, I saw it coming. My mother, right before, was shouting at my sister to fix her hair. Bernice had taken to sleeping with empty Sunkist orange juice cans pinned to her head as curlers. For that bouffant effect. I thought it looked okay, but Mom accused her of looking like a puffwad, whatever that was. Mom said she was doing it just to embarrass her.

My father, who hated fights more than anything, had been trying to shut both of them up. When my mother ignored him, and Bernice broke into heaving sobs, he was so frustrated he began banging his head off the dashboard. Literally leaning forward, holding on with both hands, and conking his forehead on top of the glove compartment.

In the midst of this, holding my hands over my eyes, but peering through my fingers, I saw Mom veer left, saw her heading straight into the concrete divider. But (and I know this is hard to explain), but it *didn't matter*. I had gotten so good at willing myself out of family situations, at rendering whatever screaming drama was happening around me unreal, so as to keep from feeling it, that even when I saw the concrete rushing toward us—twenty, fifteen, ten yards away—I couldn't react. I could not break out of that space I'd spent so much of my life breaking into. The place I sealed myself when my house got crazy. Now, when we weren't even in the house, we were all going crazy *in the car*. But once I'd locked myself out of the present, there was no getting back in. Even if we were heading into a wall at forty miles an hour. This was the gift my father gave me: I knew how to disappear without leaving the room. I was better at it than he was.

I watched us carom into the concrete embankment, watched my dad slam his head off the plastic dash while my sister pulled her hair and my mother ranted. The car tipped and spun sideways, like the tilt-a-whirl in a carnival. But even facing backward and stalled, the hood popped open and pouring smoke, I felt the same furious peace I felt in the midst of all family maelstroms. *This isn't happening . . . I'm not here . . . None of this is real. . . .* All the trembling hexes I used to make the world inside my house go away—they couldn't be undone just because of some crunching metal and tractor-trailers barreling down the highway toward us. I remember hearing the deafening bleat of a truck's air horn.

Thinking it was beautiful. Thinking, just before impact, if I had one of these at home, I could drown out the screaming. . . .

When it was over, and we knew no one was dead or hurt, my mother began to curse. My sister started shrieking again, and Dad just sat with his fists on his thighs. I pretended I was in one of the cars full of Normal People who slowed to stare. "Looky-loos," my mother muttered, primping her hair in the rearview mirror, which was dangling by a wire.

By the time the State Police arrived, everybody else had piled out of the car. But not me. I was still in the backseat. *Humming.* I seemed so composed I heard a state trooper tell the ambulance lady I was probably in shock. But it wasn't that. I was not in shock. I just wasn't there. In my family, I survived by disappearing. Dad had his goingaways, but when they didn't work he'd start pounding his head. It was like he had two gears: insane frustration and insane calm. But I didn't like the frustration part. I stuck to calm. It's what I was best at. What he gave me. If the car exploded, I imagined myself sitting quietly, burning like a Buddhist monk.

So it was not just the lingering smack that let me handle things now. It was my whole life. I knew how to be here and not be here, to put myself in a movie so intense that watching it made me forget I was living what was going on. From the age of three, or, really, from as long I could remember, I'd known how to move sideways.

That's what I used to call it, in my nursery school brain. *Moving sideways.* When my mother gulped those Miltowns, grabbed me by the wrist, and screamed her Kent-breath in my face, *"Now you're gonna watch me die, mister! . . ."* When my father was alive and the daily fights got so frantic he'd crunch his skull through the walls, leaving his hair dusted white and knuckle-sized plaster chunks of red and green—from the roses-in-a-vase wallpaper that lined the house—graveling the carpets. . . . When the two of them, finally, retreated to different rooms, Mommy wailing and Daddy pounding. . . . When the downstairs TV did not turn up loud enough for the Three Stooges to drown out the shrieks, I'd simply crawl in the bathroom. I'd slip into the dirty clothes hamper and I would hug myself. I would hug and rock and repeat, *"Bobby go sideways Bobby go sideways Bobby go sideways"* until the drone of it took over and took me out. Later on I didn't even need the hamper. And though I was still there, still hearing Mom shout *"Let me die!"* and Daddy's strangled sobs as he tried to crush the rancid walls of our house with his skull, *even though,* I felt a kind of softness, a teddy-bear-fur barrier between me and the Bad Things going on all around me. The same softness, behind heroin, coated my nerve ends now. Scrunched by Varnish, trapped in a car, drugged up and lost and trying not to wonder, was I a faggot now? Was I a loser? Was I some freako lonely doomed to wander the earth with Jewy hair and sticky hands until they found me out and shot me? That softness made it all okay. Made it, in a dreamy-breeze way, almost pleasant. The Bad Things were still going on around me, they were just *different* bad things. Shame was what I knew how to do.

"Bobby, I really . . . love you," Michelle drawled, as Varnish eased his hand over my dickhead, shifting himself so now he was nearly under me, and I was nearly kissing distance from Michelle. Something made me turn, and I saw Varnish's glowing white face, his naked skin soaking through that fringed leather vest. He was grinning, breathing hard, moving his lips but not saying anything. I didn't realize he was crying, too, tiny tears squeezing out of his bloodshot blue eyes, crying and laughing, the way my mother used to do. It always scared me, because I didn't know whether she was happy or sad. I could have handled either—basked in her happiness or steeled myself to her grief—but the *not knowing*, the fear of feeling the wrong thing, that terrified me. And now—

"Kiss it, Bobby, kiss it!"

"Oh, Michelle. . . ."

A jet flew overhead. A whirring breeze shimmered the leaves outside the car. The air was ink-stained. A sonic boom rattled the Lincoln windows and Meat flinched awake, mumbled something like "truck bastards," and collapsed again.

I looked at Michelle, who looked back sweetly. I thought, *Stoned Bambi*, and fell deeper in love. I kept hearing her words in the Burger King. *"We had an invisible connection. . . ."* Was this it?

She offered her tiny breasts on her fingertips, inviting me, helping me focus there, to dream into her love-cups while below them, where I didn't dare peek, barely dared breathe enough to feel, Varnish eased his burning, clean-shaven face beside the shaft of my erect penis, just grazing me—barely *that*—the foreignness of it conjuring up hernia exams, Sharon Schmidlap, my dad showing me where to douse the Desenex.

"Kiss it," she groaned, but to which of us? "Kiss it," she sighed again, circling her thumb and forefinger around her left breast, holding it aloft with both hands. But thanks to anatomy—how to explain?—the second I lurched forward to suck her peach-colored nipple, Varnish dipped and wrapped his chops over the top of me, so that the more I leaned in to suck her, the further wrong I went in his mouth, up into the hot wet of it. Hating this: that I could feel my own dick swelling up, disobeying me.

When I took Michelle's tit between my lips, the skin like soothing velvet, like solid milk, I couldn't separate the pleasure of finally having her from the fleshy-gummed horror of being had. It wasn't just the sucking: the mouth of a man, and all that meant—but the big head, that solid block, the weight of Varnish's skull in my lap like a silky bowling ball. All this made me cringe as much as Michelle made me squirm, until I couldn't tell which was which. Repulsion was love was nausea was raw, fucked-up, squirrel-gnawing-my-heart desire. I wanted Michelle so much I bit her too hard. I forgot that what I gnawed was flesh and nerves. I made her scream. Made her hurt. Made her, I realized from the rolled-back whites of her eyes and her nails in my throat, *want me back.*

All this happening, and yet, in the thick of it—the seething man-on-my-dick, tits-in-my-face, car-rocking, grape-juice-colored nighttime thick of it—there was that niggling awareness, the one full-time druggies live and die with: *Pretty soon it will be over.* Pretty soon I'll be back. The twistoid, back-of-the-brain truth: Reality never disappears; it just hides out for a while.

Even if I hadn't done smack before (let alone DM—whatever it was–T), I'd done enough this and enough that to know the drugs *would* wear off and what I felt now I wouldn't feel later. And worse, in the case of heroin—that terminal soothe—what I didn't feel now I would feel later. Heroin spread that soft blanket over everything. But once the blanket was ripped off, it took a layer of skin with it, leaving nothing but nerve ends screaming in the breeze. All the bloody-eyed fear and panic and rip-your-own-flesh self-consciousness would not just come back—it would come back harder and worse. I'd seen Frank Sinatra in *The Man with the Golden Arm.* I'd seen my mother, how all her pain would blow away with enough booze and pills, and she would sing made-up lullabies to me and my sister: *"I love my girl, I love my boy, 'cause they're my special pride and joy...."* How she'd put her arms out and spin in the living room, her happiness terrible to watch. How she wanted to hold us, how she'd tell my sister she was pretty, so pretty, until Bernice, even knowing it wasn't how Mom really felt, knowing it wasn't real, knowing it was drug-love, still let herself believe, and whirled around the room with Mom, letting herself be held, be stroked and praised, as she never was at any other time, as she so needed to be....

Until, when the pills wore off, when the booze vaporized and Mom crashed, literally, into the coffee table or onto the carpet, we knew as we dragged her up to bed, we knew, the two of us, that Happy Mommy was gone, and when she woke—this never didn't happen—Normal Mommy would be back. Mean Mommy. And the first words out of her, in her daze, her two-P.M.-shades-down-terminal-headache, her first words would be for my sister: *"Bernice, can't you do something with that hair...? Are you still eating those greasy french fries...? My God, you look like a Polish lump in that dress."*

Then my sister's tears would come, tears that burned hotter than any other tears. Because for a moment, in Pill Time, Bernice let herself be seduced. She'd been lured up to the mountaintop, where love was—what looked like love, but was really euphoria, which was different—and when she got there, one more time, Mom had pushed her off. Each fall, for Bernice, was worse than the one before. She would cry, and run away; then it would be my turn. And in that croaking voice, her breath souring the air from across the bedroom, Mom would murmur, *"Bobby, cuddle..."* She'd whisper, *"Your mommy hurts so much. Bobby, please, just for a little while, just until it goes away...."*

That's what happened when the drugs wore off, I knew all about it. As a boy, I had to steal Mom's pills and hide them. I had to take them when *she* was on pills. Or off them. I knew the Domestic Algebra: if you felt nothing, you could take anything. And if you felt anything, there was nothing you could take. . . .

Without that junk-gunked marijuana, I'd have punched, kicked, writhed, invoked Siddhartha, to keep a man's paws off my cock. I would, at any rate, have cried and begged. Behind smack, though, it was all . . . *okay*. It was velvety. I'd have soul-kissed Lyndon Johnson if he hopped in the car and tickled my chin. Grim but true. Varnish sucking me was weird. It was *terrifying*. But weird and terrifying were pretty much fine in that satin moment. I'd never felt that fine before. Even after the rush, fighting the pukes and sweating ice water, fearing death, rape, shame, and my true love's deep disgust, I wished I'd had the stuff when I was three. "*Go ahead, Mommy, wipe my bummy and rub my nose in it. Just gimme some more of that clown powder. . . .*"

"Oh, Bobby, here," Michelle mumbled, jangling me out of my kiddy dope fiend reverie, bringing me back to the heinous here and now. "Bobby, help get him . . . off."

"Who?"

"Bobby ain't gettin' nobody off," Varnish snarled. He talked from the side of his mouth, around my penis, now clamped in his teeth like a fight promoter's stogie. By now it seemed normal. "Bobby's delicate. He's one of them sensitive types."

Michelle clucked her tongue, which seemed strange, considering. She was coming out of whatever she'd been in, her own private drug-fog clearing right up. "I'm not talkin' about Bobby, okay?" Biting her lips, she grunted and strained against Meat's leaden torso. Corkscrewing left, then right, then left again, she

perv—a love story

shouldered herself free from the out-like-a-light longhair. Meat did not wake up when she dropped his face on the cracked upholstery. Michelle just glared at him. Her attitude was back.

"How gross is drooling?"

She wiped at the wet splotch on her shirt, across Mr. Natural's mouth, making the stain even bigger. Finally she just pulled the thing off and tossed it on the steering wheel. Defiant and shiny-skulled, with that knotted ponytail, she looked like Yul Brynner in *Taras Bulba*. Moonlight drenched her scalp an iridescent ivory.

"That I like," Varnish announced, switching to manual labor, idly rubbing my penis while he rested his head on my thigh and gaped at the lapsed and ravishing Hindu-ette. He stroked mechanically. It felt all right, just not like sex. More like when you play with yourself because you can't sleep, when you're watching *Laugh-In* or reading *Archie and Jughead* and jerking off without knowing you're doing it. After a while my mind drifted. *On today's modern dairy farm, our farmer enjoys the latest in milking technology. . . .*

I pushed forward to kiss Michelle and for a second forgot Varnish altogether. When I came back, he was still at it, up-and-downing. Every time I inhaled, I smelled his hair. The DMT seemed to have tweaked my senses. Even in that nothing light, I could see between the follicles, to the buttery scalp. Scabs the size of pinpricks dotted the skin under his hair. He smelled like floor polish. Johnson's wax. The brand with those bragging commercials: *"BULLETS BOUNCE OFF!"* I thought, in the cracked-but-rational afterfuzz of dope and hallucinogens, maybe that's why he shampoos with floor wax—to repel lead.

"Coming through," Michelle giggled, and I couldn't tell if she was high or faking.

That's when she slithered over the top of the seat. Flopped right over into the back. Varnish let go of my flagging organ to break her fall, crying, "Whoa there!"

I tried to catch her, and got one of her legs hooked on my shoulder. The rest of Michelle slanted toward the car rug, sprawled partly across my attacker, partly across me.

I wanted to kiss her again, but Varnish wanted her pants off. "Help out," he barked, shoving his elbow in my throat so hard I gagged. "Jesus," I coughed, and then he slapped my dick. "Hurts good," he said, in a voice like the Lone Ranger. "Eh, Kimosabe?"

I couldn't even think about that. Michelle hadn't moved since doing her seat-flop, and I thought kissing her might be less important than artificial respiration. (I wasn't too sure of the difference.) Groping her throat, I searched for the pulse like I'd seen on *Ben Casey*, but Varnish slapped my hand away.

"Quit fucking around!"

"What?"

"We need ice cubes, man. Ice cubes in the furry valley, that's what we need. Don't you know nothin'? Shove some ice cubes in the valley!"

"Who has ice cubes?"

"Necessity is the mother-fucker of invention," he said, and popped open her hip-huggers. He peeled them over her slightly protruding belly all the way to her hips. What we saw shut us up. Michelle, of course, was no longer just bald on top. She'd gone whole hog and de-furred her pubes, too, rendering her sex as smooth and in-furled as an uncracked fortune cookie.

I knew I'd seen pubes at the mall. I remembered that champagne fur, sparse but silky. Between then and now—God knows how—it got shaved off. So much else had happened, why not that? Most likely, it occurred to me, when she was out cold Meat must have swiped her clean. It seemed like the kind of thing he'd do . . . For all I knew, Meat and Mr. Schmidlap attended the same barber college.

In spite of myself, however it happened, the sight got me hot. I could feel my cock throb to life again. I tried to hide it, to cover the organ with my hands. But Varnish grabbed my wrists. Then he wagged his finger at me.

"Tsk-tsk. We're all friends here, aren't we?" He smiled all the way to that gold tooth in back. "Dig it, Handsome, George Harrison said all you need is love. 'Course he's bi as the day is long. They all are. Mick Jagger swings three-sixty. Same with Sonny and Cher. And that's groovy. That's outasight. *Be here now!*" he chanted, uncoiling to inspect Michelle's interior like some kind of professional. He parted her labia and tapped something just left of her slit, a pimply bump that would, in normal girls, be covered by hair.

"Check it out," he snickered, indicating the pimple with his little finger. "What if they gave a wart and nobody came?"

"That's a wart?"

In my narcotic haze, curiosity drowned out the savage facts of this situation: that the man had just forced himself on my virgin engine, that I'd more or less given in. Every once in a while, that naked, nightmare fact leaked through and freaked me out, then sealed itself off again. For now we were a couple of cunt scientists. This marked the second time in my life I was excavating a vagina. Though the object here was not a missing Trojan. I was too terrified to think just *what* the object was.

Varnish screwed up his features and slid his ring and middle finger inside Michelle. He saw me blanch and grinned.

"Mellow out, Handsome. If I find a buried treasure, we'll split it."

He slipped his fingers out, slick and glistening, and before I knew what was happening he rammed them inside my mouth. Pulled them out again and sneered.

"Taste contagious?"

Without meaning to, I licked my lips. My mouth tasted pissy. Tart. But Varnish knew what he was doing. He must have— those double digits worked as well as ice cubes. Michelle looked like electroshocked. She looked that kind of awake, and it gave me a flash: if the doctors cut Mom off her Edison medicine, she could call Varnish and get a finger-jolt, something to shake her up and send her home happy and traumatized. I thought that, and thought right after, *I need to spray my brain with Raid.*

"Bobby," Michelle chirped, whether in shock or appreciation I couldn't tell. "Bobby . . ."

"Bobby what?" Varnish echoed, then backhanded me across the face so hard I fell against the door. "Bobby, get down here and eat my shaved tomato, that's what you want to say, isn't it, baldy-twat?"

The slap knocked the dope out of my system. For a second everything cleared up. I saw Varnish differently, saw he was older than any of the hippies I'd seen around. Saw how hard and un-peace-and-lovey he was. He might have been thirty.

"Yeah, Bobby," he mimicked, "get down there and do it."

"Don't hit him," Michelle whimpered. "Please, don't!"

"What?" Varnish raised his hand like he was going to smack

her, too, but she crumpled up. This seemed to calm him. " 'Where pain resides,' " he intoned, " 'joy lies sleeping in the corner.' Kahlil Gibran. You guys ought to read *The Prophet*, man. It's beautiful."

"I know *The Prophet!*" I blurted. "I read it on the Continental Trailways from Philadelphia to Pittsburgh."

"Did I ask you to talk?" Varnish shouted. He'd started to perspire badly. "No I did not. What I *am* asking is for you to eat some girl-pie. We're trying to have some fun here, okay? I'm trying to teach you how to behave at a love-in, so you don't get to San Francisco and act like Suzies when the other *flower children* invite you to party. Okay? I am doing you two a favor here. Show some appreciation."

Varnish sighed and contemplated the Lincoln's torn ceiling.

"Hey, Mother Teresa," he said finally, tilting his face toward Michelle, "you've got to help out here. *All we have is each other.*"

His tone had become gentle. *Sincere.* He'd switched to this loving, concerned manner so adroitly I found myself believing *this* was really him, that the brutal, bullying thing had all been an act.

"O Holy One," he went on, concerned as a guidance counselor, "we're going to let our boyfriend pray at the Fertile Crescent, aren't we? We're going to let him taste our puckered lotus."

Michelle didn't respond. She was still dangling there, pantyless, hyperventilating, her hip-huggers bunched around her scrawny ankles. Her hairless sex made her look like a little girl, a littler girl than she already was. This car, I thought, is the entire world. All the bad and all the good, right here. Then I got the barf-burps and swallowed them back.

"Buddha's delight," Varnish sighed, stroking Michelle lightly on the cheek. He eased her up off the car rug and onto the seat before me. "That's right, knees up. Page ninety-six of your *Kama Sutra*. Look it up some time, see if I'm not right on."

Michelle did as she was told. She was shivering now, and so was I. Varnish noticed and made a time-out sign. "What you guys need is more inspiration. That DMT *was* not my idea. DMT is Meat's thing. I like to keep it laid-back. I like to keep it on the ground where the grass grows, where you can feel the worms and birdshit between your toes. . . ."

As he talked, he worked his hand into his cowboy boot, coming out with a vial of white powder. He unscrewed the lid and tapped out a Hershey's Kiss–sized mound in the groove between his thumb and forefinger.

"All you need is love," he warbled. "Come on and love it up. It's okay, John Lennon does it."

I flashed on knocking the stuff out of his hand. My guess was he'd go for the drugs, try to save the smack instead of stopping us when we bolted. But then, I really *did* like the feel of that heroin. . . . I really did think that if I had another teensy bit, just a taste—I'd never do it again. I promised that to myself in a solemn oath: never. *Absolutement*, as Mom would say. But if I just had another snort, I could probably take whatever was coming, could even, without a doubt, get the strength to find a way out. I just needed some of that heroin first.

I whispered to Michelle, "Go ahead!" I tried to indicate over the top of Varnish's head that I had a plan. Tried to nod and wink in such a way that she'd see I had everything under control. She eyed me skeptically, but I knew she'd go along. I had a hunch.

perv—a love story

After the first hit of that laced-up joint, Michelle had changed completely. The fire went right out of her. She got nice. I could see where she'd be an easier person to be around when she was smacked out. Then I caught myself thinking that way—getting excited about it—and tried to squeeze the notion out of my brain. Just wring it out, like bad water from a squeegee. Squeeze it in the bucket and toss it out the door. *Only I couldn't.* I wasn't even sure I wanted to. After she took her dainty snort and I horned up mine, I fell back in a bliss of singing corpuscles, thinking, incredibly, *This is the best day of my entire life.* My body felt swathed in cashmere. Out of the ether, I heard Walter Cronkite, whisper, *You're a lucky little boy!*

After Cronkite, things get fuzzy. They get dark and they get fuzzy. Varnish told me to take my shirt off. I said okay. Then Michelle began to spasm. She rolled onto all fours on the scummy floor. Her ribs started juking up and down, like a cat coughing up a hairball. But Varnish wouldn't let her out of the car. Instead he opened the door and stuck her head out to puke. We both held her, me grabbing her naked rear and Varnish cradling her top half. The sick part, the part I wondered about, is that even while she was hoarking I could not stop staring. At her rear end, at her shiny pink vagina, the way the lips puffed out each time she heaved, as if they wanted to be fed. No cloud ever had a freakier silver lining.

I couldn't believe it! So much horrible stuff had happened: all that homo torture, those slaps on the head, the wondering whether we were going to ride to San Francisco or get chopped into chuck-roast by a two-man Manson squad. Not to mention, in the midst of everything, I was worried about my mother. Worried and guilty because I knew that *she'd* worry. She'd think something happened when I didn't come back from the library. She'd call them and lose it, maybe have some kind of breakdown, even though her next one wasn't due for another month.

All of *this*, fueled by pot, panic, and leftover DMT molecules, pounded through my mind. And nothing but this nakedly damaged girl could help me forget it. Could help me to lose myself. To blank out the world and all its creepy circumstance.

Stretched out like that, Michelle was my own private love-specimen. In real life, I hated biology. I just liked the squishy insides of things. When you were high, especially, nothing beat the color of a toad liver, or a worm under the microscope. What I hated was all that meiosis and mitosis shit. Who cared how cells divided, when your mother woke you up at three A.M. to bring her peaches and ketchup? If her cells divided, there'd just be more of her to scream at me.

That's why I didn't want to know anything, I just wanted to touch and ogle. The one bit of biology I remembered, staring at Michelle, was that baby girls were born with eggs. Millions of them. All stashed in their mini-wombs before they even made it out of their moms.

Little girl caviar. It was bizarre. But where was it? That was the question. Was there some kind of toddler egg locker? A secret room? The back of my brain shivered. The closest I'd come to hands-on vag-analysis was bobbing for Trojans in Sharon Schmidlap. But this was different. I was dying of different shame. My heart felt scorched. Everything that could save me in the world peeped up between Michelle's moist thighs. And she was still vomiting.

"Not on the car," Varnish kept yelling. "Puke'll eat right

through the paint job. Get it on the ground, bitch, the *ground!*"

Loud as Varnish hollered, it didn't make a dent in Meat. The other longhair's face was slung forward over the front seat like a moose head, the kind mounted over every barber chair in Pittsburgh. Between eruptions, Varnish bawled out Michelle for snorting so much. He warned that she could swallow her tongue, that Janis Joplin died from backed-up dope-sprat. . . . That's when I started to touch her.

I had one arm swooped under her belly when my right hand, all by itself, started stroking her sweat-damp rear. It drifted south to the backs of her thighs, down between them and into the bunched up sweet roll between her legs. The Mons Vanilla. I'd never seen it before. Not this willing. Not outside of Sharon and girls in Swedish magazines, but they had pubic hair. (I remembered, the first time I saw that term in a dirty book—*Wanton Widow*, by U. B. Hayve—I read it as "public hair," and thought that was what it was called in nudist colonies.)

Michelle's, being hairless, was completely exposed. Soft, but faintly bristly too, which made me wonder. Did girls who shaved down there get five o'clock shadows? Did some pussies have heavy beards, like little Richard Nixons? Mystery inside of mystery! But what really floored me were her labes—another porno term, what was happening to my brain?—how, up close, they appeared to be made from the same swath of peach-pit, wrinkly flesh as my testicles! It gave a man pause.

Months earlier, I'd read in one of Tennie's weirdo sex books about Christine Jorgensen, how when he became a she, the doctors used the scrotum to line his/her vagina. Basically, they scooped his nuts out and turned the sack inside out like a re-

versible car coat. Those were popular then—not inside-out scrotums, but reversible car coats: jackets that were plaid on one side,
red on the other, so you could mix and match. The scrote-sack/
cunt-lips situation was not the kind of thing Mrs. Cruikshank
covered in biology. If she had, I might have pulled down more
than a C-plus. Which, in fact, I only got because I copied off
Michelle. (What I couldn't figure were the doctors, and what
they did with Jorgensen's old balls. My guess was a key ring.
"Nice rabbit's foot, Fred, but check THIS out!")

"Meat scalped her!" Varnish hooted suddenly, tossing cold water on my reverie. That was the thing with these drugs: Whatever
you thought about felt like it was *actually happening*—just because
you were thinking it. Memory seemed like *right now*, and right
now seemed like it *wasn't happening at all* . . . When Varnish spoke,
I could feel his lips move on my thigh. "Meat's a smooth man
with the blade, Bob. He loves to scalp them Suzies."

"But when did he shave her?" I talked to the top of his head,
which I tried not to think about. "I didn't even see."

Varnish howled out a laugh. "You were temporarily *OUT*,
hombre. You were cryin' for your Mama's cookin'!"

Weirdness on top of weirdness. Each time she disgorged, Michelle bucked and wriggled. And while Varnish propped up her
head, I inspected her below. Examined her as closely as I
could. As closely as I wanted to, bending down to really peek
at the two different layers of lips, the purply-wrinklish outer
pair and the smooth pink conch shell walls inside; the ones,
when you splushed them open, you wanted to press your ear
to and hear the ocean. Except, when I slumped down further,
to take a more serious ogle, a once-in-a-lifetime, unimpeded,

perv—a love story

gyno-level eyeful, I could not just *look*. No! I couldn't stop there. Without planning to, I took a lick, a quick slurp from that pearly crease. And then, as though being instantly punished, I got a pain so sharp I didn't cry out so much as howl into Michelle's hairless cleft, *"He bit me!"*

It was that intense. I groaned and let Michelle drop. I couldn't believe it! Varnish bit me in the exact same spot that Sparky, our next door neighbors' collie, had taken a nip when I was two years old. That was the time Mom left me in our inflatable wading pool to answer the phone. People say you can't remember back that far, but *I* do. I do! I remember splashing frantically, crying for Mommy. Because I hated the wading pool, hated being left alone. And all that ranting must have startled Sparky, because next thing I knew the dog leapt in the pool, yelping crazily. The whole time, I kept thinking, *"But she looks like Lassie . . . why is she so mean?"*

Sparky poked her snout between my legs and when I whacked her she took a nip. Right through my soaking underpants. I didn't even have a bathing suit, just underpants. Sparky ripped right through the material, and the elastic got caught in her teeth. When she pulled away it snapped her back, which made her meaner. She took another nip. More than a nip. A bite. She chewed off a chunk the size of a jujube, right from the tip of my budding boy's penis. From that day on, I had a penile divot, a leathery pink dip, right on top of my organ. Thanks to Sparky, every time I took my pants off in front of a girl I'd have to explain. *"It's not VD, I swear, it's a dog bite. . . ."* A real aphrodisiac. Thank God, Sharon had been too busy to notice.

Half my angst over Varnish was that he'd spot my Sparky-scar and go off. I could already hear him, accusing me of leper-dick, syph, gonareeno . . . uglyitis. Shaft-shame was a fact of existence. In the showers at Hale, Tenny used to call me Scar-face. Or worse. *"Check out Mr. Lunar Log—he's got a crater on his gator!"* That kind of thing. A lifelong confidence booster.

On account of getting traumatized by Sparky, I grew up believing my unit was smaller than other guys'. As though, in its tiny peeny brain, it was afraid if it got too big it would be an easier target. I'd read on the back of a Fruit Loops box that the brontosaurus had a brain in its tail. So why not in my organ of procreation?

(For the permanent record, it was normal, except that it retreated under pressure. No doubt anticipating the return of Sparky, it took to hiding out. Packs of rabid Lassies nipped me in my dreams.)

All these thoughts flew in and out in an instant. The pain was insane. First I saw stars, then I grabbed myself and craned my head sideways to see Varnish with his lips pulled back, teeth clamped on the flesh just under my cockhead. Bad as the physical agony was the mental anguish. The grenade going off in my skull from that simple truth—now inescapable: *I am getting a blowjob, and it's not a girl down there* . . . Before that, I was distracted enough by Michelle's genitalia to deny what was happening to my own. To know but not think. But the pain cut through all that.

Now here it was, the sickening undeniable: some shirtless freak with Viking hair had his mouth around me. *And he was biting.*

"Cut it out," I shouted. "That hurts!"

I swung at the bobbing head. Cracked my knuckle off his temple. Nothing.

"Varnish, come on, man. . . . Get off!"

perv—a love story

For one bad second I flashed on infection, which was too frightening to contemplate. I couldn't handle another divot. One scar was explainable. Or almost. But two . . . *three*! I'd have to tell girls that I'd been caught on barbed wire, maybe tortured by Devil Worshippers. *"It was awful! They stuck it in a garlic press and made me praise Satan!"* After Sparky, I'd had to get rabies shots. What the fuck did they give you for hippie-bites?

Varnish was still holding Michelle by the pigtail. Just like the gods she said were going to pull her up to heaven. Except heaven wasn't where she was going. Not just now. She was so scared, her whole face quivered. But she was high, too. Every three seconds she'd stop looking terrified and giggle.

"You wah-ah play?" Varnish screamed at me. He shaped the words around my organ, which stung beyond belief. The sweat from his face made it worse. I pounded on his head and he still hung on. With his mouth occupied, he sounded like he had a speech impediment, but still managed to be mean and scary. *"You wah-ah I fuh yuh uh yo ath?"*

"What? No!" I yelled.

Varnish unclamped his jaw and spat. "Fucking asshole! Eating a chick while she's blowing chunks! Are you some kind of animal?"

"Me? You're calling *me* an animal? *Downer!"*

Varnish glared. He panted with his tongue hanging out, like a dog. Like Sparky, if Sparky'd passed on and come back as a vicious freak. The worst was, my cock throbbed so much I was tearing up, but I was afraid to touch it. A necklace of teethmarks dotted the head. By now Michelle'd finished purging and crumpled on the floor between us. She was completely naked, hugging her knees to her chest, jammed with her back against the front

seat below Meat's dangling head. She rocked herself, whimpering
quietly, a crooked, slack-jawed smile plastered on her lips.

"Fuckin' Meat should be filmin'," Varnish said, going all
friendly/normal again. "I had any more crank I'd get it into him,
but we left it in New York. All we got is scag."

"Sorry to hear it," I said, like things were normal, like we were
people in a car talking. "He does look really . . . tired."

"Who asked you?" Varnish growled. "Do you think you exist?"

Before I could figure that out, or how and when he'd climbed
out of his velvet bell-bottoms, down to a paisley bikini, he
grabbed Michelle's tail again. Still giving me stink-eye, he started
tugging her hair. With his other hand he tapped the seat. Michelle pushed herself up off the filthy car rug and crawled beside
him. Chewing her lip, she struggled to rearrange herself. This
was hard to watch. It was as if none of her body parts were
speaking to one another. Her left arm hung dead at her side.
She had to lift both legs with her right hand and tuck them
beneath her. We were all breathing hard.

"Power to the people," Varnish sneered. Then he let go of
Michelle's pigtail. He grabbed her by the ankles. He spread her
legs apart. Michelle cried out and Varnish slapped her fast. He
grunted and worked her thighs open even further. Snatching the
pot-leaf belt off the floor, he looped it around her wrists, pulling
tight and hooking her bound hands onto a bolt jammed into the
ceiling.

"What?" Varnish saw me staring and snapped. "I thought I told
you to get that shirt off. Go with the flow, dig it? The life force
is *here*. The life force is NOW. *Carpe diem*, Handsome."

In all this excitement I'd forgotten my tattoo. As soon as my
shirt was off, Varnish spotted it. Michelle looked, too. Her

perv—a love story

mouth crinked sideways, like some wise, sarcastic entity attached to her stricken face. *I know what's happening,* that mouth said, without a sound coming out of it. *The rest of me might look victimized, but I know the score.*

Varnish dropped his hand onto Michelle's pate. He scratched her without moving, fingers extending and retracting like a cat's claws. He turned away from me, toward the mumbling-in-his-sleep Meat, then swiveled and peered at my flowered pec. "Groovy rose. You surprise me, Handsome. Where'd you get it?"

He smacked me and something clicked in my head. I had a thought-storm. I flashed on Mr. Schmidlap and his flipper. On pockmarked Tennie Toad and sullen Farwell. On my street-cared father and electroshocked mom. All the stomach-clutchy, burning-eyed moments that crammed my brain like buried plutonium, a thousand feet under but poisoning everything above.

Jarred loose by that last wallop, it all came back: me curling up under my bed, hiding from my parents' shouts . . . fish-flopped on Sharon's carpet, watching my friends bail . . . sweating loser-stink while the headmaster eyed me like dog food on a plate . . . wanting to die while Mom keened in the mud in front of my father's coffin. Everything. Right up to Ned Friendly calling me Sissy-boy, to Laundry Room Dolly catching my face in her panty pad and Mr. Weiner-pronounced-Whiner weeping in the park. *Everything came back. . . .*

And the worst of it, the absolute worst moment in this Technicolor hell-fest, was me chickening out in the mall parking lot. I could still feel the heat of Michelle's disappointment, her heart-breaking, you're-not-a-man-but-I'll-find-one gaze when I passed up her pussy because I was afraid. *"OF WHAT?"* screamed the

Mommy-voice inside my skull. *"Of what, you dancing boy, you skeek, OF WHAT?"*

And what *was* I was afraid of? What was the real torment, underneath the namby-pamby dread of getting into trouble, the little-good-boy fear of getting busted, Mom-shamed and shipped off to some other school? The answer curled my toes: I was scared of *not doing it right.* I'd never licked a girl, except in wet dreams, and then it was always Janis Joplin. . . .

"I asked you a question, spaceman. Where'd you get the fancy tat?"

"Sing-Sing," I said.

Varnish coughed out a laugh. He held his face that way, frozen and open-mouthed, then laughed again. "You telling me you've done time? You've been *down?*" He reached past Michelle to thwack my shoulder. "You're trying to tell me you've been *inside?*"

"Juvey," I answered, tossing off a shrug, my voice gone flat and no-big-deal. "PA Youth Authority, Monongahela. They call it Little Sing-Sing."

Michelle stared but, thank God, didn't say anything. Varnish tilted his head sideways, doing the RCA Victor dog, then straightened up and sneered. "Don't con a con. You're fucking with my head, right? You're tryin' to blow my mind. Is that it? 'Cause you're pissing me off, Handsome."

"Ask me if I care," I said.

I was building for something, but didn't know what. I just knew I already felt stronger. *Badder.* An ex-con. *Go ahead and fuck with me, hippie motherfucker!*

"Okay, Jesse James, what did you do?"

I unfurled a long sigh, like I was thinking it over.

"Well . . ."

I avoided Michelle's eyes. Michelle who, trussed up and naked—I felt dirty admitting it—never looked sexier. Not even in
my sixth grade fantasies. Sixth grade was when she started showing up on my ceiling on a giant clamshell. In skin-tight gowns.
Like Rita Hayworth in *Gilda*, this flick I caught on the *Million
Dollar Movie* when I had the croup and jerked off in my rolled-
up Jethro Tull T-shirt. (I hated Jethro Tull, and just used the
concert T-shirt to wipe off.) I was afraid she'd speak up but pretty
sure she wouldn't.

"Well what?" Varnish said, either furious or amused. It was
hard to tell. I craned back and saw him sink a finger in his belly
button, like he'd lost something. He plucked out a nugget of lint,
examined it like a jeweler, and spoke up again. "You two on the
run? We got Bonnie and Clyde here? If you're packin', you must
have that piece pretty far up your butt."

"It was an accident," I heard myself say. "I didn't mean to kill
them."

The sneer died on his face. "Them?"

"These two Italian guys. At a bus station. I was—oh, forget
it," I said. "You're probably a snitch."

"*What?*"

I rolled my eyes. "I broke out, okay. I went over the wall."

I'd read the phrase in a biography of Legs Diamond, and
worked it in. It felt great so I kept going.

"I was dealing, see. Heavy weight. They tried to rip me off. I
stabbed the first guy and the second guy had a heart attack. I
didn't know he was old. He was like, thirty, but he had a wig
on. This longhair wig, so he looked like Wild Bill Hickok, but
Italian. Wild Bill Hickoni."

"Hickoni! Far out!" Varnish smiled and touched himself. He stared right at me and slid his hand into his paisley bikini. "Far out."

"That's nothing, man. Turns out the first cat was Wild Bill's son. When Daddy saw the blood he dropped to knees and fell sideways. But slow, really slow, like heavy syrup. I was doing eight hundred mics of Sunshine. The whole thing happened like we were soaked in syrup, the kind you drink out of the fruit cocktail can then throw out the fruit."

"Oh man!" Varnish rubbed himself more vigorously. "You stabbed him, huh?"

I still wasn't sure if he was making fun. Or if, for some creepy reason, it got him sexed up to hear me talk. But I was into the story, whether or not he bought it. I was starting to believe I was the kind of kid who could do the kind of thing I was describing. The more I talked, the more capable I felt. Anything was possible.

"The fuck!" I cried. "I had to stab him. I thought he was a narc. I catch a possession beef, I'm fucked nine ways to Sunday."

"Possession beef" I got from Lenny Bruce, *How to Talk Dirty and Influence People.* "Nine ways to Sunday" was Mom.

"My hero," Varnish snarled. He forgot Michelle and, before I saw it coming, went for me again. Pinned me to the back of the seat and jammed his tongue down my throat. He was a lot bigger than me, fatter in the muscle, but sinewy too. Like everything extra had been burned away.

"You been in the slam, you *know*," he snarled. "Free love inside's a whole other thing. I had you on my tier, I'd pretty you up. Put my baby in a red dress *toot suite.*"

I pushed against him but he pushed back, like he enjoyed the

perv—a love story

pushing. And then, in some twirly, spin-around jiu-jitsu thing I barely saw, he flipped me onto Michelle. Banged our foreheads again. And, just as fast, worked himself behind me.

His skin on mine felt scalding, drum-tight, like a chihuahua's belly. But Michelle's was cool. Her arms still bound overhead, she arched toward me. Her mouth found my mouth and sucked. She was shivering. Very turned on or very scared. Maybe both. Maybe something else I couldn't even imagine. It was all too schizadelic to tell.

I felt a whoosh, and my lungs twitched when those bikini shorts flew by my head.

Smashed between Michelle and Varnish—"*Sandwich,*" Varnish kept yowling in my ear. "*Sandwich, sandwich, sandwich!*"—I felt like the Hopping Moon Man. In third grade, Mrs. Mamulak, our Slovak science teacher, read us this myth from a picture book. On one side of the moon, it was so cold you'd freeze to death in a second. But the other side was so hot you'd fry. To survive, she read, you'd have to hop back and forth. Hop and spin. This was the lot of the Hopping Moon Man: ice on one side, flaming hell on the other. . . . Now I understood.

The pale effects of the dope kept me almost soothed, but the fear was still there. All smack did was make fear wait in the hall. I knew it was out there, pacing and furious.

But then—things went Sharon Tate. I felt the rubbery knob of his groin on my back. I screamed, "NO!" And Varnish screamed back louder, spewing out, "*You're mine! You're mine now!*"

Meanwhile Michelle was chanting. "*Om mane padme hum. Om mane padme hum. . . .*"

But I could barely hear anything. My heart banged against my ears. My lungs vibrated.

Shouting "I am the Lord!" Varnish stuck out his arms, Christ-on-the-Cross-style, and clamped his roach-stained fingers over my wrists. He pressed them into the rotten upholstery on either side of Michelle's collarbone.

Om mane padme hum . . . Om mane padme hum. . . . Om mane padme hum . . .

I didn't want to breathe. With every breath, it wedged into me, growing harder. More inescapable. Through the rear windshield, over Michelle, I thought I saw eyes, flashing golden eyes that turned out to be lightning bugs. It surprised me, in the middle of this, that the world was still out there. Trees and insects.

"Am I love?" Varnish ranted. *"Am I the Buddha-Fuck?* AM I JESUS CLEAVER?"

Each time he shouted, he forced his body against me, his erection smashed lengthwise up my spine. (*"Fleshpipe of death,"* Tennie called it. I closed my eyes, and I could hear him. His face leered out of a corner, in some vault behind my eyeballs, there and not there. An evil clown in a strobe light. *"You lak it, donchu! Fleshpipe of death. . . . You lak 'at shit!"*)

I tried to wriggle free, to crane my head and scream in his face. "YOU MOTHERFUCKER, I'LL STAB YOU! I'LL KNIFE YOUR FAGGOT GUTS ALL OVER THE CAR!"

I was howling at Tennie. Howling at Varnish. I hardly knew what was coming out of my mouth. *"YOU'RE GONNA HAVE TO KILL ME . . ."*

But, even screaming, words torn like bloody chunks out of my throat, things still felt so . . . unreal. Like a giant experiment. Like

I was watching myself. *Bobby go sideways.* The more I howled, the wider Michelle's eyes went in front of me. She'd been chanting this whole time. When she switched to talking, her voice came out spooky-soft. Weirdly sedate. *"You . . . can . . . do . . . it!"*

"What?" Hearing her brought me back. "Michelle, what did you say?"

I was trying to talk and shake off the beast. Because that's what it feels like, when you're attacked and can't see who it is. Even if you know, it's still the Beast. The monster who has you in its jaws. What you can't see is worse and not worse than what's really there.

"Michelle, what?" I panted again. This time, I couldn't believe it, she smiled. She opened her mouth and a string of milky blood quivered from her top lip to her bottom. Her voice came out ragged, like every word hurt more than the one before it.

"You can . . . do . . . it . . . Bobby. I want . . . you . . . to do . . . it . . ."

"Do what?"

This close up, Michelle smelled. She stank of vomit, of sweat and panic and strange, bad sex. That's when I realized, with genuine surprise, if you love somebody, you don't care. You can't care. It's them, whatever is wrong. That's who you love. And the wrong is what you love the most.

This is the truth: I kissed her. Closed my eyes and almost forgot where we were and what was happening. Almost. Until— that awful sound. Varnish hocking. Spitting on me. His saliva rolling down the groove of my spine. Then farther south. Into the crack of my ass. (Worse, if you have to know, than a tongue in the mouth.)

My spine tensed and I thought, insanely, *what if I'm not clean?* I could barely breathe. I died at the prospect of being told I was dirty *down there*. Of being exposed. A gift from Mom, this sick concern. Like being raped and wondering if your shoes are shined. I scrunched up. Slipped into pain-hallucinations. Saw burning corpses, enemas launched from Cape Canaveral, rubber bags circling my brain. (*"Don't force!"* my father used to yell through the bathroom door when he heard me straining. *"You force, you're gonna get hemorrhoids."* I pictured him watching me now, chewing his knuckles, pining for another streetcar to step in front of.) Varnish buzzed with glee.

"Gonna grease you up, killer. Gonna make your rose bloom."

"You—"

"Relax. I know how to handle a tighty. 'Course you probably had a few yourself. Up there at Sing-Sing, was it? Or was it Folsom? Or Q? I can't remember if you said Sing-Sing or Quentin."

I found myself sputtering, Mr. Weiner–style. "Just sh-sh-shut up, man! J-j-just fuckin' shut up." (Maybe *this* was what happened to Mr. Weiner, maybe he'd been BF'ed by smacked-out hippies in the back of a car, and it left him stammering.)

Varnish chuckled, a low watery chuckle. *Ya-huna, ya-huna.* His chest heaved like an asthmatic's. "Oh I know, Handsome. You're thinkin', 'Hey, Varnish, I'm a pitcher not a catcher.' Well, that's okay. It's all just . . . love."

"Krishna lives," Michelle whispered. *"Om mane padme hum. Om mane padme hum . . ."*

I stole a look, but her eyes were not her eyes. Something else peered out through the sockets. Something feral. Without blinking, she launched herself up and over me. Into position. Tit to mouth. Her breasts pushed into my face. I could have suffocated and died of love.

perv—a love story

"Michelle," I sighed, and got another slap.

"Shut up, Handsome."

Varnish whipped a hand down to my behind. He smeared the spit up and under. *Into me.* I gagged, though it wasn't my mouth he was probing. I wanted to die. Wanted to send my mind somewhere else. Go *sideways.* But I couldn't. Instead, I thought about *The Wild, Wild West,* my favorite show, where Robert Conrad escaped from ropes and wells and spiked walls that closed in while the music built.

But this wasn't TV. They didn't show this on TV. Jim West's enemies never came on like Varnish. I could not escape from Varnish. I couldn't even escape Michelle, the feelings that made me love what was she was doing and hate myself for loving it. I was hard and couldn't help myself.

"Bobby, *NOW!*" she cried. And still not blinking, one tear trailing from her eye, Michelle slid onto my involuntary boner. For a single, boiling second, I blanked out in the damp of her, the warm padding over all this pain. But then I came back, and I *knew.* This was what I'd fantasized about my entire life. I'd gotten what I wanted . . . but I got it the wrong way.

The Hopping Moon Man had to twirl or die two opposite deaths.

"You blow my mind," Varnish ranted. "You are a stud, Handsome. A little cherry-stud!" He bit me behind the ear and yelled. "*Bummer!* Smack makes my popgun go straight to Silly Putty. I get a stiff-on, then Puff the Magic Dragon. Gonesville! Not you, though. Not you, you fuck! You *shitbird!*" he squealed, in a hideous, begging tone. "I need me a jolt, man. I need to get my blood up." His voice changed again, going mean and dead. He sounded black. "I think I'm just gonna watch y'all make it. What do you think?"

"Fuck you," I said, like I had a thing to back it up besides stuttering rage. "F-F-Fuck you, I'm not doing it."

Varnish cracked up. "Whatsa matter, darlin'? You goin' romantic on us?"

While he sneered, I struggled to unpluck myself from Michelle. I squirmed back and forth, trying to pull out, even though every cell in my body wanted to stay inside her, to do it then and there.

Michelle just stared at me, wearing an expression I couldn't read. Then Varnish pulled my head back by my hair and, lurching forward, kissed her square on the mouth.

"Handsome's old-school," he said, speaking with his lips still puckered. Again, he'd begun to rub himself. I looked down, saw the tip of his dick poked out of his fist, the helmet swelling up, plum-purple. "Handsome don't go for that free-love stuff. Handsome wants it nice. Ain't that right, Handsome? You like it nice?"

I didn't answer. I couldn't. Michelle was still on top of me. We were stuck: two machines who'd collided and seized up. This wasn't sex. It was something else, something I didn't think there was a word for. No word I'd ever heard of. The only one that came to mind was *sacrifice*. But it wasn't that.

I aimed a gaze at Michelle and mouthed a single syllable: *No*. She smiled faintly back. And never taking her eyes from mine, like she knew, like there was a band of light flowing from inside her head to the inside of mine, she released me. I don't even know how. She didn't seem to move. One minute I was inside her, the next, I was throbbing in air. *Sacrifice*.

Varnish punched my neck and I hardly noticed.

"Our Handsome's kinda shy. Handsome wants a nice little hotel room. Handsome wants a nice little bed with nice little

perv—a love story

rosies on the sheets, nice little rosies to match his fairy tattoo. Pay attention, fuckwit!"

Varnish hit me again, then his body gave a twitching shiver. "Gotta lube up," he said, almost apologetically. He let go of himself, to spit in his hand, and that's when I saw: how tiny he was. No bigger than a gherkin. Below the bulb on top, his cock was no wider around than my little finger.

I couldn't believe it! When he was rammed in my back, I'd thought lead pipe, thought turkey leg, musket, Louisville Slugger. I'd thought, *I am going to be pole-axed.*

But now. . . . Michelle must have seen it, too, and we both burst out laughing. Me from relief, from gratitude: not just because I'd dodged the bullet—because I hadn't been raped—but because now I didn't have to die. If it *had* happened, if the worst occurred, I knew I would kill myself. Knew I could never face a living soul— my mother, bus drivers, every girl in the world—without thinking *They know. . . .* That would be my life. And death.

When Michelle and I caught each other's eye, we started laughing harder, as if we'd hit some pocket of mirth we'd over-looked in the first, hysterical wave. And inside that pocket was another, wilder joy. Beyond escaping rape, avoiding suicide, in-jury, and terminal shame, I was howling from the genuine kick of having found someone who made *me* look huge. Imagine!

What I felt at this moment was the opposite of shame. It was the power to shame someone else. . . . Here was someone who made *me* King Kong. In some cosmic, even-the-score way, this thrill made the nightmare worth it. Compared with my pinky-hung attacker, I was John Dillinger. I could feel the knowledge change my life.

Varnish backhanded me fast but I couldn't control myself. He jabbed me in the nose and I just guffawed. Michelle, too. We were close to sobbing, we were laughing that hard.

"I'm going to kill you," Varnish wailed, threatening both of us, or else threatening his penis. I knew how he felt. He tugged on his dwarf tool like he was mad at it. His face puffed up. Doughy veins swelled in his neck. But the more he pulled, the more it resisted, until the angry inch disappeared altogether, like a turtle retreating into its soft blue shell.

Varnish was livid now. He urged a low growl out of his throat, something below language. It sounded like "*Unnngggh. . . . Unnngggh.*" Then he hammered on his thigh and screamed "*SHIT!*" like he'd just invented the word.

But I didn't move. I couldn't. I was too spent. Even when he hurled himself back against me, trying to work himself in, it seemed more strange than dangerous. You can get used to anything. I wriggled, gripped by two sensations: Michelle's lashes fluttering on mine, and my ass-cheeks being gouged apart. The lashes were sweet. The other was gruesome. At first I felt his lumpen fingers, then came a weird breeze-feeling: air rushing where air had never been—followed by Varnish panting on my neck, trying to maneuver his smushed chunk of gristle. It felt, more than anything else, like I'd sat naked on a wad of bubble gum.

I was mentally counting to three, psyching myself to throw him off. Or try. When, out of nowhere—

"*Motherfucker!* You tried to dog me again. You motherfucker! You fuck! You *FUCK!*"

It was Meat, raving like a burn victim. Before I could even turn around I felt the thud. Saw the *Uh-oh!* look in Michelle's eyes.

Meat landed on Varnish's back, banged him against me and

knocked my head forward, throwing me against Michelle's breasts. The pair jostled behind us. I held on and caught an elbow in the head. It was like being in a car accident in a car that was standing still. I hugged Michelle and got another elbow. Tasted blood and saw hobbits. I wondered if Bilbo Baggins had ever escaped from evil wrestling hippies.

"You did me in Tulsa!" Meat screamed. "You did me in Biloxi! You did me in Kansas fucking City!"

Meat was giant, but he owned that high, thin voice. Like a cranky nine-year-old.

"I ought to off you now," he screaked. "What I oughta do, I oughta waste your nancy ass and feed you to chinks. They eat dogs like you."

"Try it," Varnish shouted back, his elbow, somebody's elbow, clanging my ear. Each accidental smack sent me harder onto the slung-up Michelle. I didn't care about moving now. It was over anyway. I used to daydream, when I was a kid, about being trapped in an airplane going down, the wing in flames outside my little round window. I fantasized about leaping on the starlet across the aisle. I'd get to do Jane Fonda before I died. Because why not, you were dead anyway . . . Then I heard Michelle, realized she'd been whispering while my mind was at two thousand feet.

"Bobby!"

"Mmmm . . ."

"Bobby!"

"Huh . . . what?"

"Bobby, undo me! My hands. *Do . . . it . . . now!*"

I heard her from far away. My hands were free, but wet cotton clogged my brainpan. Somebody's knuckle caught me in the temple.

"Now," she whispered, and I got it. Bouncing off the skull-punch, I flipped up and knocked her bound wrists off the bolt the Torture Hippies had rigged in the Lincoln.

This was Michelle being amazing: stoned and drooling and completely *on*.

"The belt," she said, very steadily, letting her head loll forward while, fumbling, stump-fingered, I struggled to undo the buckle and not get slammed sideways by the caroming fists of the junkies behind me.

"Now!" Michelle shouted, like we had some stragegy. "Bobby, *NOW!*" like we had a plan.

A boot jammed my chin and I reeled sideways, conking my head on the door. The Lincoln's lock jammed my ear and I thought, for one savage minute, *I've been impaled.*

"I am *bummed!*" Meat screeched, that pre-pube voice at horrible odds with his Mountain Man demeanor. *"I am bummed to the tits."*

"Fuck you," Varnish growled back. "I hadda wait for you to wake up, we'd still be on Avenue D."

Though Meat was bigger, the dope must have dulled his motor skills. He ended up in a headlock, sort of suckling Varnish, his rump upthrust and his bell-bottomed, cowboy-booted legs flailing behind him. It was his pointy toe that dimpled my chin.

"I hauled your smacked-out ass down five fucking flights!"

Varnish had canted down to yell at his friend's face, like Señor Wences talking to the man in the box. (My Mom saw the Beatles on Ed Sullvan and thought they were Jewish. Even Paul. *"Payess, no less..."*) Where was I?

I dislodged my ear and covered it. Meat grabbed for Varnish's crotch. He pulled a knife from his boot, reared back to swing it.

perv—a love story

The blade ripped through the ceiling, spilling glassine packets, and Michelle made her move.

"Bummer!" Varnish screamed. Keeping his squeeze around Meat's testicles, he wedged his wrist in his jaws, like a man training a dog. The ball-squeezing made sounds come out of Meat's throat, but the wrist muffled them. The wrist reduced them to low-end peeps and blips. Varnish actually smiled at me, like we were on his team. All part of the Let's Get Meat Club. Then Meat tried to tear off his nipple and they started up again.

I didn't know what Michelle was doing. But *she* did. She crawled into the front seat. Grabbed her yellow bells. Banged her fist off the dashboard while I scrambled to dodge Meat and Varnish and snatch up some of those glassine packets. Even in a luxury car, a barn-sized ride like a Continental, there's not much room when you're horizontal, when two killer junkies are marauding in the backseat, when you're trying to find your clothes, dress fast, scrape up fistfuls of heroin and figure out the locks on the suicide doors.

Michelle waggled her feet, parallel to the floor, like she was trying to swim her way out. "You fuckers," she hissed, but quietly, to nobody but herself. "You fuckers!"

"Michelle . . . hey!" I whispered. I wanted her to just leave, and tried to get her attention. "Pssst, Michelle!"

I don't know why I was whispering. It seemed unlikely either Meat or Varnish would snap out of their blood lust and remember whose lives they'd been destroying two minutes ago. By now the stench of them—stale drawers and B.O. and some foul, narcotic waft—had blended to a tear-making tang inside the tattered Lincoln. It smelled like frying meat, that plasticky-toxic reek when the handle on the skillet starts to melt.

I hadn't known how claustrophobic I felt until there was a shot at escape. Once there was a possibility we'd survive, the possibility we wouldn't sucked the air out of my lungs.

I couldn't say when I'd lost my boot, but just when I spotted it, Meat head-butted Varnish and a spray of blood doused my neck. I ducked down to grab the boot and found something hard under the passenger seat. Shivering up, I thought: gun, and slipped off the tracks. I went back to *Bonnie and Clyde*. Watched myself as Warren Beatty—Warren Beatty with Jew hair and a questionable complexion—blow the big boys away and earn Michelle-as-Faye Dunaway's eternal lust. For an instant, I got deep into that, slightly dope-dreamy and terrified. Then I pulled the thing out and saw what it was: a penis. A thick penis, long as a billy club, black as Sonny Liston, hard rubber etched on one side in Olde English letters: *YOU GOT IT COMING*.

The object galvanized me. I couldn't drop it. Could not stop looking at it, like some freak in a hurricane holding on to an heirloom while the roof blew off his house. Meanwhile, Varnish, heaving and bloody-lipped, had collapsed in Meat's arms, his Jesus hair spread out on that fullback lap, his eyes cast upward, a perv Pietà.

That fast, the cosmos had ricocheted from strange to dangerous and back again. I was still staring, could not stop staring, clutching the jumbo sex-toy and forgetting to breathe. Until Michelle, who'd clambered into the front, flew back over the seat-top as though shot from a cannon. All I saw was her

perv—a love story

face, blank and beautiful and fixed on something I could only guess at.

There was a flash of metal. A dime-blink of bright orange as she drove her fist into Meat's eye. It happened that fast: a kind of jellied hiss, then the moment froze. Meat's mouth formed a cartoon O! *You did this? To me?*

After that came shrieks and spume. Meat mashed his hands over his eye. Gurgling screams tore out of his throat.

Varnish, struck numb, just gazed at Michelle.

Meat swung blindly, all animal spasm, his lid melted into the burst eyeball, black-on-scarlet and still smoldering. He knocked into Michelle's fist and the shiny thing—the dashboard lighter—popped out of her grip onto the car rug.

Varnish roused and grabbed Michelle while Meat writhed and whimpered. *"My eye oh Jesus oh Jesus-fuck my eye!"*

That's when Varnish began to weep. Ranting through his snot, *"You bitch! You cunt! You stupid cunt!"*

Michelle stayed blank.

"You fucking Suzy! You piss!"

The lighter rolled to my bare foot. (A bee sting, charred carpet.) I picked it up and Michelle's eyes met mine. Right then I knew what love was.

Yes.

The air went dead. Varnish lunged. All I saw were fingers, throttling the one girl on the planet, squeezing her throat.

Michelle's gaze was calm.

I dropped the dildo. I had the lighter now. Still incandescent. An orange kiss making the dark darker.

"You slit! You cum-drunk whore! You fucking—"

"Varnish?"

My voice was easy, your friendly dentist saying, "Say Ah!" Varnish stopped to look and I took him, like a lover would, his penis going shy in my hand like it knew what was coming.

"Varnish?" I said again.

And tenderly, tenderly, I bowed close and planted the glowing circle on the very tip, pressed down until the flesh smoldered, until a thin and putrid stench insulted the air.

Varnish juked back, stunned. His hands slid from Michelle's throat and she pinned his arms to the car seat. There was wailing on top of wailing now. An orchestra of pleading. Then Michelle did something else.

Her eyes on mine, the seen-too-much-smile back on her lips, she lowered a hand between her legs and rubbed. She scooped into herself and brought her hand up glistening with her own juice. Then, shifting her gaze to the mewling hippie she'd nearly blinded, she smeared her wet palm all the way from Meat's forehead down to his lips, leaving him glazed. Scooping a second time, she moved on to Varnish. She clamped her sex-hand on his face, leaving a sticky film. Marking territory.

Varnish began to convulse. He shrieked and peed steam. Bloody urine dribbled from his burn-ruined organ onto his thighs.

"Michelle?"

I mouthed her name like a question. After what I'd seen, I needed to know she still was who she was. My teeth would not stop rattling.

But Michelle only smiled. "Now," she said for the second time. And, calm as a crossing guard, she plucked her hat and the rest of her clothes off the front seat. She even smiled.

Still twitching from what had just gone down—even more

perv—a love story

from what almost had—I fumbled for my own stuff and watched this miracle girl. Michelle was as happy as I'd ever seen her. It came to me, inside this unreal moment, that I'd never seen her happy at all, that this was why I loved her.

Awestruck, I observed her, in one balletic motion, jerk the car door open with her wrist and kick the automatic shift into neutral.

"No brakes," she said, with no affect whatsoever. She stepped out of the Lincoln like a girl going to her school picnic.

By now Varnish was in vibrating shock. Meat just scratched and babbled. He kept spitting in his hand, tamping his scalded eyeball. The thing had swelled to the size of a cracked egg, oozing bloody yolk.

The car was already rolling when I stumbled out. I had not even realized we were parked on a hill. Had not realized, for what seemed like forever, that there was any world left at all.

We stood on the deserted road, a tree-lined lane straight off a country calendar. Somehow, Michelle had turned on the Lincoln's lights. For a few moments, while we dressed, we watched the glowing red grow slowly smaller. The screams faded with the shrinking taillights. After the car disappeared, we laid down in the grass by the road and waited.

There were stars in the sky. Distant street-noise beyond the trees.

I said, "I wonder where we are."

Michelle looked at me. *"Why?"*

I thought about it, but couldn't come up with an answer. Then Michelle placed her hands on my face. Her fingers were still damp, and I breathed her in. She smiled. *My whole life.*

When we kissed, the explosion sounded very far away.

*   *   *

We stopped for a second, and I stared up at that black sky, thinking about all the people in my life. Maybe it was that last kick in the head, but each face filled a kind of floating circle, the way they sometimes showed the actors in old movie credits. (*And Tallulah Bankhead . . . as "Mom."*)

The odd thing was, I felt affection for all of them. Maybe more than affection. Some kind of honest wonder, which might even be love, because it had such warmth in it, down at the core. I pictured my mother, that very moment, in her usual blue haze, smoking her fifty-fifth filter-tip Kent and staring at the TV with the sound off. She may have called the police or she may, knowing her, have just doubled up on tranqs and staggered away from the problem.

My father, I always knew, never had that relief. He operated at a level of pain I could probably never understand. What I did get is that he couldn't find his way out of it. My sister was gone, his son was fucked up, and the woman he married was . . . the woman he married. He could find no sweetness in the world to complement his own. So he split one Sunday morning and waited for his streetcar.

Then I rubbed my tattoo and thought about Mr. Schmidlap. He did what he did, I think, out of scorched-soul anger. His rage was that way, you could tell: the kind that consumed everything, then got small and contrite when it was too late to matter. He loved his wife, and she died. He loved his daughters enough to shoot himself before he ended up shooting them.

This is, I believe, what happens when people take their own lives: They're not killing themselves, they're killing the world. Either to spare it pain or to cause it some, depending.

perv—a love story

"Were you scared?" Michelle asked, lying on her back beside me and breaking my trance.

"Scared? I don't know," I said. "Mostly, it was just all really *surprising*."

"You know," she informed me then, out of nowhere, her voice soft against the crickets and tree-breezes, "first grade was the best year of my life. After first grade, everything that happened was the opposite of what I wanted."

"First grade," I answered back, as if I was considering it, but really because the phrase "first grade" was so charged for me, so freighted with the weight of everything that kicked in then: my crush on Michelle, my secret—there's no other word—*devotion*.

Hearing her words now, with her taste in my mouth and her scent on my skin, made me think of a picture from my old *Golden Book Encyclopedia*, a picture I used to stare at for hours when I was a little boy. In a corner of the page, colored purple and set in a box, was an illustration of a Möbius strip. I could make the top of my head tingle by running my finger along the purple band, trying to find the place where the strip of paper in the drawing flipped over to the other side. Somehow, according to the encyclopedia, there *was* no other side. There was only one, even though you knew—and this is what made me tingly—even though you knew that there really was another side, even if we couldn't comprehend it, and everybody who lived over there knew there was a whole other world, as well, only they could only see theirs and they couldn't get to us.

I wondered, as I thought about it, and I knew that, in a way I could never articulate, I had crossed to the other side of the Möbius strip, the one you couldn't see. The one that didn't exist until you were there.

"I wasn't lying before," said Michelle, "back at the Burger King. I always knew you had a crush on me. I could tell."

"You really did?"

"I always knew about you, Bobby. Even in kindergarten. You're not exactly a boy for hiding things."

I thought about that—how the world you thought you were walking around in could turn out to be a different world entirely. The opposite of the planet you thought you were occupying. Maybe reality was always inside out.

"You never did anything about it," she sighed, plucking a long blade of grass and sliding it between her teeth. "But that was okay, 'cause everybody else did."

"Does that mean," I began, not knowing if I was being corny, but, for once, not caring, "does that mean you like me now?"

"Maybe," she said.

I looked at her, across the darkness, and saw the same girl I'd saved from fires in my nightly brain-movies, the girl I used to rescue in dreams.

Her hand slipped into mine almost without me noticing. As soon as it was there, it felt like it always had been. Like maybe, whatever it took to get here, this was exactly where we were supposed to be.

perv—a love story

epilogue
the petrified
florist

Twenty-five years later, I'm sitting in LAX with my five-year-old son, Malcolm, when I hear a voice I recognize but can't place. I swivel around, scanning the seating area at my gate, and still can't find the source. By chance, my eyes hit the TV, the ones they now have hanging from the ceiling and blaring whether you want to watch or not. I look up and, sure enough, there she is, the source of that voice, and it's Sharon

Schmidlap. Sharon Schmidlap! Unbelievable! Sharon Schmidlap with new hair, new clothes, and an on-air position—on the Weather Channel.

Needless to say, I'm floored. The last time I saw her she was sprawled on the carpet, spread-eagled, with her soon-to-be-dead dad shouting at her while I cowered beside her and wondered where my pants were.

It was twice as strange to see Sharon now, because now, as then, I was heading back to Pittsburgh. This time, though, I hadn't been thrown out of anywhere. It was my mother, in a manner of speaking, who was changing locations. She'd just died—of natural causes, if you consider weighing three hundred pounds, getting wedged in the shower stall, and having a massive coronary natural—and I was heading back for the funeral. Malcolm had only met her once, when I'd flown her to L.A. as a seventieth birthday present. But he was three at the time, and remembered her only as "the fat lady who smelled like an ashtray." Why that should make me so proud of the kid I couldn't tell you. Malcolm was the product of a short-lived union with his mother, an actress I met when she played "a virginal ho"— Shalana's description; she grew up in Bed-Stuy—in the first script I ever wrote that got made into a movie. Malcolm popped out within a year of our wedding. We split up, amiably enough, when Shalana took a role in a Brazilian action flick, and decided Rio was her kind of place. Malcolm doesn't remember her.

The whole flight, I couldn't concentrate. I couldn't even read USA Today, which is not a good sign. And it wasn't just from seeing Sharon. In truth, I hadn't thought about her in years. The sight of her now: anchor-haired, sensibly collared, with a pearl necklace and Leslie Stahlish articulation, actually cheered me up. I love when people beat the odds and make good, and in Sharon's case, I knew up close how grievous a hand she'd been dealt. All I could think, watching her pronounce "climatological" like a pro, was that once in a while, in this peculiar universe, something akin to justice actually reigns. (I planned to add TWC to my cable package the second I got back. . . .)

But it wasn't the Mom-thing that set me spinning, either. Her passing, if such a thing can be said without sounding malicious, could be seen as a blessing. She hadn't been happy. (What else was new?) And her doctor, with whom I'd been in touch off and on, informed me that, due to a fall the previous spring, the most she could do was shuffle between her bedroom and bath. Beyond that, she rarely moved. Except, apparently, to lift her hand to her mouth, as she packed in enough cheese and crackers to double her body weight and cement her arteries shut.

Toward the end, we spoke more or less regularly. By then my sister, God bless her, had come in from the cold and taken up residence with her new life-partner, Loretta, in a house down the street from the one we grew up on. Bernice is a Mom, too, having popped out a baby boy, Mahatma, now eighteen, by her pacifist boyfriend, who died in a bar fight in Manitoba the same week "Bernie" (her new moniker of choice) announced she was gay. Irony of ironies, my sister took care of Mom, right up to the end, claiming her last words to her, the day she died, were *Can't you do something with that hair!*

What had me spun, I think, was that for me, flying back to Pittsburgh packed a particular kind of dread. A journey home is always a journey back to the place you wanted to make it out

perv—a love story

of when you were there in the first place. And a part of me, irrational as it sounds, half feared I'd be tempting fate by entering that core shame-zone. One wrong move and I would never leave. I'd end up bunking with Herb Pazahowski, who was probably still slogging up the hill with his hairy-moled Mom for milk and lunchmeat on a daily basis. With Malcolm in tow, there'd be four us, so we could carry a lot more groceries. The horror!

My sense of foreboding was so profound, I actually considered calling the funeral home from two thousand feet to see if everything was all right. ("She's still dead," I can imagine the pinstriped smoothy on the other end informing me. At which point I'd say thank you and hang up gracefully.) As a rule, I'm not one of those people who dream of kidney beans, then wake up to a phone call informing them their Great-uncle Lucius has just died of complications from renal failure. But still, that psychic uh-oh feeling, above and beyond the inherent guilt-fest brought on by any parent's death, would not loose its grip from preboarding in L.A. to final descent into Pittsburgh International.

But it gets stranger. My plane touched down hours before the actual funeral. And, as I didn't feel like seeing people just yet, I figured we might as well cab straight to the mortuary. Which I did. Happily, Malcolm was not inclined, at five, to question the decision to head to a funeral home instead of his Aunt Bernie's house. (I was grateful that, despite her militant lesbian lifestyle, she hadn't insisted on "Uncle Bernard." She'd hinted at it, and it took me a minute to realize she'd been kidding. Coming out had given my sister something she'd never had before: a sense of humor.)

The funeral director, a Bill Murray-ish fellow named Howard

Teems, was somewhat hesitant about letting us in. He still had a napkin tucked in his collar, and a dab of eggy ketchup dotting his lip. But when I told him how far I'd flown, how I knew his son from high school (Tom Teems, as I recall, used to pee in the swimming pool during PE), and how anxious I was to "spend a few moments alone" with my mother, he reassumed his professional face and went back to Soothe Mode.

"Your boy is well-behaved," he said, striking the perfect balance between threat and observation. I assured him he was, and Mr. Teems ushered us into Mom's "viewing room," offering use of the "family salon" to "rest and reflect." He was so patently nasal and insincere, I could have listened to him for days.

Once in the chamber with Mom, who'd been rouged and lipsticked, apparently, by a mortician who apprenticed in Clown College (outside of Emmett Kelly portraits, I'd never seen cheeks so red), I left Malcolm on a couch in the corner, raptly coloring in his Batman coloring book, and sat down on a bench provided to wait for the requisite emotions to arrive.

None did. Neither grief, nor hair pulling, nor anything beyond a certain bemused awareness that, had she been alive to pay her own respects, Mom would be proud to finally have an occasion lofty enough to merit the sequined evening-wear she favored. This was my suggestion, offered when Bernie née Bernice informed me of our mother's passing: that she be buried in the most over-the-top item my sister could dig out of her closet. Which, as it happened, was a wine-colored, off-the-shoulder, plunging V-necked affair topped off with a heavy gold brooch in the shape of a bow the size of a milk bone.

"You look great," I said, careful my boy didn't hear, then

perv—a love story

flushed up with self-consciousness at behaving like someone with a camera on them. I didn't really feel like talking to my mother, even if she was dead. The moment had Movie-of-the-Week written all over it. So what I did, instead, was kiss her on the forehead—which smelled, mysteriously, like the "new car" scent they now can and peddle at low-end car washes—then grab Malcolm and drift out of the viewing room intending to walk the mortuary halls, maybe step outside to clear my mind. But first I had to pee.

"Where we going?" he asked me.

"To see a man about a dog," I said. He'd heard this nine thousand times, and it still cracked him up.

For a moment or two, with Malcolm assuming the position beside me, I perused the framed "inspirational" verse mounted strategically over the MU (Mourner's Urinal).

> *Dear Departed, Now that you're gone*
> *I wish you well, as you travel on*
> *Soon, perhaps, I'll see your face*
> *And join you there, in a Better Place*

Duly inspired, I washed my hands, made sure Mal washed his, splashed some water on my face, and headed back to the parlor's hushed interior. But my sense of direction, flawed in the best of times, failed me entirely under the strain of Mom's demise and dread over the approaching funeral. Rather than head for the exit, I found myself worming deeper into the mortuary's bowels. I was hoping to stumble into some back room, maybe catch the embalmers in a pot-addled round of strip pinochle. I arrived instead at a kind of central reception area.

"This is like the *Tyrannosaurus* place," Malcolm observed, referring to a topiary maze, with hedges trimmed to look like dinosaurs, we'd visited in San Diego the year before. I explained, as best I could, that this was actually where they kept my mommy, and other people's mommies, until they were buried. To which Malcolm, quite reasonably, replied that he'd just as soon not be buried at all, unless he could have TV and chocolate milk. Which made sense to me.

Before us, on either side of adjacent Viewing Rooms, stood a pair of mahogany podiums such as your average high school principal might prop his notes on while boring a hall full of teens to death on Career Day. On top of each was a large Guest Book, nicely bound, like a deluxe version of a five-and-ten photo album, with imitation brown leather cover and a black ballpoint on a chain attached to the spine—safeguard, perhaps, against grief-inspired kleptomania—for guests and loved ones to use in jotting down their names or thoughts.

I am, I may as well confess, an inveterate reader of obituaries. Not from any particular fear of death, but, on the contrary, from profound, disquieting wonder at the lives people led before they died. Confronted, say, with LEM BERKEY, 62, MANAGER OF 'ROSES ARE RED' FLOWER SHOP FOR THIRTY-SEVEN YEARS, I would experience a grateful shudder and think, *But how?*

I was petrified imagining even a month as a florist, and I *like* flowers. This was, perhaps, the last vestige of my brush with hippiedom. The straight world still put me off. Half the reason I turned into a writer is you didn't have to show up anywhere. You could work naked.

All of which should explain the guilty pleasure I felt at the prospect of whiling an idle hour or so in other people's memento mori—seeing what they did with their lives—prior to wending

perv—a love story

my way back to the viewing room and chapel where Mom's own service would kick off. In a little while we'd be piling into cars and shuttling off to the cemetery for the burial proper. Of course I knew that my sister would be waiting for word of me. That she'd be calling the airport, checking out the window every five minutes, and generally stressing herself silly over my delayed appearance. (Middle age had rendered her nerves not unlike my mother's—without the tranqs.) But all I wanted, in the grips of my strange foreboding, was to be alone a bit longer. To gather my thoughts in the relative sanctity of Howard Teems's labyrinth. Happily, Malcolm was a self-sufficient type, as I gather many only children are.

So it was, I spent some morbidly content moments escaping with MARIA GAROFOLO, BELOVED MOTHER OF CARLO, MARIO, ARTURO, ENRICO, PATRIZIO, THERESA, AND FRANK JUNIOR, WHO HAS JOINED HER BELOVED HUSBAND ANTHONY BY GOD'S SIDE.

The glossy photo, affixed to the inside cover, showed a svelte, radiant senior-ette with a lusciously coifed blond beehive, white teeth, and matching dimples. Producing a brood of seven had done nothing to diminish Mama Garofolo's good looks. She could have passed as Angie Dickinson's big sister.

Poring through the gilt pages of the Garofolo guest book was oddly enriching. A drawing, by one of her grandchildren, of a big flower with I LOOVE GRAMA on the blossom, actually made me stop and sneak over to hug my own chipper offspring. I felt close enough to the deceased to consider stepping into the Viewing Room and paying my respects. I could actually lean to my left and see the coffin, still open, flanked by an impressive array of standing floral arrangements and a large, gilt-framed picture of Maria herself.

I wouldn't say it was guilt that kept me from strolling in for a peek so much as squeamishness at the prospect of getting caught ogling a strange dead lady by Señor Teems or one of his minions. I could hear myself trying to explain that, in my grief. . . . my jet lag. . . . my confusion, I mistook Anthony's late missus as my own dead mother! (Though I was, admittedly, curious as to whether the late Mrs. G. would give off that new car smell, too. Or if, for reasons too arcane to fathom, only my mother packed that late-model Eau de Buick.) I didn't think they'd cart me off to mortuary jail, but it would, I suspect, have raised a few funereal eyebrows. No doubt I'd have to toss in a healthy tip as hush money above and beyond the hefty fee I was already shelling out for the proceedings.

Here, in any event, is where I made the decision, drawn like the fool in a Tarot deck who doesn't see the cliff at his feet as he capers toward it, to cross the hall to the other podium, to take a gander in the guest book of Maria's dead neighbor. In for a penny, in for a pounding.

"Where you goin'?" Malcolm called from his corner. He was always asking that. Not, I liked to believe, from any incipient "abandonment issues," but because he was genuinely curious about the world, and eager to come along and see it. "Where you goin'?" he asked again.

"Nowhere," I said, which didn't seem to satisfy him.

"That's impossible, Dad. Everybody's somewhere. Or else they're plastic."

I told him I agreed. And then it happened.

I knew before I even saw the name. That feeling of foreboding. . . . I knew in a second. A sleek helmet of black hair framed her face, a filigree of bangs across her forehead like a row of parentheses. The woman in the picture looked competent, wary, alive with a fierceness that begged the question, *How could she be dead?*

MICHELLE BURNELKA FRYE. BELOVED MOTHER OF SANDRA.

I could tell you I dropped to my knees and moaned. I could tell you I rent my hair, chewed my knuckles and sobbed on the carpet. But what went through my head, the moment it hit me, was something more mundane, possibly more damning. I thought, quite simply, *But she was a redhead*. Following which, without allowing myself another thought, I ran into the viewing room, all but crashing into the casket.

There were two simple flower arrangements. The coffin was ebony, the sheen off the wood no match for the gloss that came off the strange, severe helmet of hair encasing her tender features. But the lips had a pillowy fullness I didn't remember. Her skin, too, was different. She looked fit, tanned, as though she'd been swimming laps in Miami when tragedy struck. Unless it was some strategic rouging, womanhood seemed to have heightened her cheekbones. And her eyebrows, arched in repose, lent her an expression of loving irony. As if to say, "Live long enough, and look what happens." Still—and this was the important, the crucial thing—*there was no hardness in her face.* None of the pissed-off, suspicious, desperate-for-love-and-desperate-to-resist-it quality that marked our brief time together when we crossed the country and washed to the curb in California. Not that I actually *thought* any of this. These were flashes, bulletins that flared and sputtered in my brain as I clutched the bier, willing myself to maintain for Malcolm's sake, but reeling internally at the sudden, rug-pulled-out-from-under impact of what I'd stumbled onto.

"Michelle," I muttered, this time with no self-consciousness, no awareness of anything beyond the pounding blood in my ears and a sense that the room was tilting. My voice might have come from speakers in the vents. I leaned over and whispered, whether so as not to wake her, or not to attract the attentions of random mortuary staff I couldn't tell you.

"Michelle, what happened?"

There was so much I wanted to ask her. Not just about what happened to us, but about what happened to her since "us" stopped happening. By instinct, to keep from melting down, I checked on my son, still coloring his Batman coloring book out in the hall.

The sinking feeling in my heart dropped me three decades back. I remembered us stepping out of a VW bus in the Tenderloin, and Michelle asking a sallow man in a tuxedo how you get to Haight-Ashbury. I didn't understand that hollow look in his eyes until years later. "Follow the speed freaks" was all he said, before going back to the business of steering squares inside his strip joint for a peep.

Time stopped and I remembered. *Michelle in San Francisco* . . . The week we spent in Golden Gate Park before we ended in an actual crash pad. The night we both gulped horse capsules of chocolate mescaline, and I came to to find her gone, before wandering into the "living room" to catch her humping under a blanket with a Chinese dealer named Dove. The days after that when we fought, panhandled, snorted some bad crank, and fought some more. . . .

The whole time we hung out, Michelle and I had only messed

perv—a love story

around. We'd never actually gotten to the fuck stage. But after the Dove incident, faced with my constant whining—I hated myself, but felt such hurt, such a throbbing ball of shame, betrayal, rage, rejection, and woefulness in my gut that I couldn't stop—Michelle finally planted her hand over my mouth and explained things. "Fucking," she attempted to tell me, huddled under our sleeping bags one freezing dawn, "fucking is what you do when you want something from somebody. Love is something else. *And I love you.*"

Chinese Dove, as it happened, had given her a new army blanket and fifty hits of blotter we could sell on the street after she screwed him. But I didn't want to hear about it. I wouldn't let up. We were both sort of fluey all the time, staying up for days, sharing joints with people who ate out of garbage cans, when we weren't eating out of them ourselves. Everything had begun to look gray. And one night, when my nagging got too much for her, when, I suppose, I'd become so abject she either had to kill me or sleep with me, Michelle relented.

By then we occupied an overgrown closet on the top floor of a four-story dump just off the Haight, a ratty Victorian with more drafts than windows. We shared the attic with three speed freaks from Portland and an acid-burnout named God who never left his room. There were tears in Michelle's eyes as she led me down the hall to the bathroom. She ran a bath, and we got into it together. Michelle set up candles, plus some kind of incense the Panthers sold that smelled like burning fruit. After we soaped each other down, in a haze of fruit-smoke and Acapulco Gold, she pushed me back on the tub, got on top of me, and sang to herself the whole time.

After that, Michelle began to disappear. Sometimes for a

morning. Sometimes for days. Since I had nothing else to do, and hadn't made any friends, I spent the time she was gone hitting up tourists for change and haunting the streets. Sort of looking for her but sort of not. Mostly I wandered in and out of bookstores, shoplifting, getting high however I could.

Occasionally, when we were with each other, it was still nice. But I could tell I'd made a mistake by forcing things, even though I knew I'd have felt just as bad if I hadn't.

"As long as we know we're really together," she told me the last night we spent in our freezing room, "it doesn't matter what we do with other people."

I wanted to believe that. But free love, in my sixteen-year-old soul, didn't make me as happy as it was supposed to. I fucked a slightly overweight German girl named Franzy who showed up at the house for a couple of days and gave me crabs. But the whole time I was with her. I thought about Michelle. I couldn't help it. One time, on crystal meth, the three of us crawled into the same sleeping bag. Which was fun, but more like a science project. Making love to Michelle was making love. For everything else I had to close my eyes.

Finally, after she'd vanished for almost a week, I got tired of waiting for her. I got fucked up on some opiated hash and decided to call my mother, who said she had a razor blade in her hand that very moment—and she'd use it if I didn't hop right on the next plane and come home.

Of course, I didn't really believe her; I pretended I did. But two days after I arrived back at the condo, I already knew I'd made a horrible mistake, and loathed myself so much I could hardly breathe. That's when Michelle called up crying that she couldn't believe I'd left her.

perv—a love story

"Are you kidding?" I said, cupping the receiver so Mom wouldn't overhear. (When she wasn't listening on the other extension, she was usually hovering outside the door.) "I didn't even know where you were."

"So what," Michelle wailed, her words interrupted by loud, gasping sobs of a sort I'd never heard from her before. "I always came back, didn't I? *Didn't I?*"

That's the last part of the conversation I recall, and the last time we spoke.

"You're not coming back now," I murmured to the beautiful corpse in front of me. And realized, as I said it, that in some part of me I'd probably always been waiting for her to do just that.

I knew nothing of what happened to her in the intervening years: if she'd found happiness, or lost it, or achieved any kind of peace at all. I had to fight the urge to peel back Michelle's lids and peer in her eyes, as though maybe they could tell me. Instead, without thinking about it, I moved closer to the coffin and, resting one hand below the collar of her black dress, leaned in to plant one last kiss on the girl of my dreams. I lingered for a second, her neutral lips just brushing mine. Death had robbed her softness. But, closing my eyes, I could still see the scalped hippie chick reflected in the dress-shop window at the mall, the tiny, furious creature who stepped behind me while I ogled that platinum blond mannequin, the one in the white leather microskirt, the day we hit the road.

Accidentally, I'd let my hand slip south, to the modest breasts I'd watch develop from buds. I don't know if I felt a touch of lust—or if what moved me was nostalgia. Michelle and I had survived childhood, Pittsburgh, our families, not to mention the likes of Meat and Varnish (which, as far as I knew, left us linked in a double homicide, or something close to it), along with cops, Route 66, San Francisco, bad sex, and enough drugs to toxify an army of Young Republicans before we were seventeen.

I straightened up, felt the first sobs clutching my chest, and leaned in again. When, sharp as a shiv in the ribs, I heard that sepulchral "a-hem" behind me, and swung around to see a shrunken, tufted little lady in black lamb's wool bracing herself on a metal walker, glaring at me. Sure enough, it was Michelle's grandmother, Dolly. Last seen in the laundry room of Mom's condo.

For a second, when our eyes met, we were both horrified. Her at seeing me, and me, I suppose, at *being* me. I checked, out of the corner of my eye, to see that young Malcolm had raised his head in curiosity. He had a thing about wheelchairs, and probably thought walkers were even cooler. The kid just liked metal. He smiled his crooked smile, then went back to Batman.

"You!" the old lady exclaimed, her hunched-up spine rearing ramrod straight over the walker before caving forward again. All the decades had done was make her smaller, and curl her into a question mark. Her tongue seemed to be unaffected.

"Dolores!" I cried, hugely startled, and offered my lame condolences. "I'm sorry about your granddaughter."

The old woman. who must have been ninety-something, didn't bother to answer. For almost a minute she squinted through her glasses, making sure I was who she thought I was, then she worked her walker a few steps closer.

"You look respectable," she clucked. "What happened? What are you doing?"

"Well," I started to say, before she dismissed me in mid-sentence with a palsied wave.

"You weren't *sniffing*, were you?"

perv—a love story

"Of course not," I said, but flushed up as if I were, in fact, guilty as charged. The old lady just had that effect on me. "I was," I went on, hearing the catch in my voice and fighting it, "I was saying good-bye."

She eyed me suspiciously. This was a woman I couldn't help admire. Steely even in grief. Tragedy, I sensed, was her element. You didn't outlive a sex-bent, Rose Marie–crazed husband without a certain amount of grit. You didn't hang around dry-eyed over a granddaughter's corpse, either.

"You kept in touch with Michelle?" she asked.

"Not really," I said. "I'm here for my mother."

"Your mother knew her?"

Malcolm gave a me a little finger wave, getting his dad's back, and I waggled a finger back. I loved how he could just *be*. I still hadn't learned that.

"My mother died, too," I said, lowering my voice, afraid, insanely, of saying the d-word in front of Michelle, as if it were bad form mentioning death in front of the dead.

Dolores's blank look was magnified hugely behind her glasses. Either her eyes had grown larger as her form had shrunk, or her lenses, which had looked strong enough to see amoebae twenty-five years ago, had gotten even thicker.

"I mean," I explained, hearing myself speak louder, and easing back, "she died, and she's here. In this funeral home. That's why I'm here."

Outrage darkened the old lady's face. "You weren't coming to see Michelle?"

"No," I began again. "I mean, I am now. It's just, I didn't know about Michelle until I saw her. I was"—I gestured vaguely out the door and continued—"I was visiting my mother in another part of the funeral home, and I took a walk."

Again, I got a withering look. I didn't know whether to laugh or burst into tears. It was clear, no matter what I might accomplish in life—cure cancer, end hunger, snag a Nobel Peace Prize—I was destined to continue proving my moral turpitude to this old woman till the day I died. It was as mortifying as it was ludicrous.

"You take walks . . . in funeral homes?" Dolores clicked her tongue. She shook her tufted head and raised her eyes heavenward. "So why am I surprised?" she intoned. "Once a perv, always a perv . . ."

"It's not like that," I said. "My mother is dead. She happens to be laid out in another room."

Dolores was silent for a moment. "I knew your mother," she said, choosing her words. "She wasn't well."

"I know," I said.

I saw that Malcolm had fallen asleep, clutching his Batman book to his chest. He cuddled books the way other kids cuddled teddy bears. The old lady squeezed her eyes shut and took a long, difficult breath.

"Do you know what happened?" she asked.

"To my mother?"

"To this precious girl," she said fiercely, in a way that reminded me of her granddaughter.

I realized I was still stroking Michelle's hair, but left my hand there. In some strange way touching her gave me strength.

"I don't," I said.

"She got happy," Dolly declared. "That's what happened.

perv—a love story

Twenty years she knocks around from man to man. Different cities, different countries. She even has a baby, with some schlemiel she meets in a rehab and knows for five minutes. A *musician*. And then—an actual miracle—she meets a man. A wonderful man. He sweeps her off her feet. She sweeps him. Everything is perfect!"

"Who is he?"

I can't help myself. I feel jealous. Michelle, lying dead in front of me, and I'm stung all over to hear about Mr. Right. I try telling myself this is only human, but I'm not so sure.

"A doctor is who he is." Dolores beams, plainly grateful her pride and joy had finally done something right.

"A doctor," she says again, with a satisfied nod.

"Was she sick?" I blurt, feeling like an idiot as soon as I say it. But Grandma Burnelka is beyond noticing.

"Not *her* doctor," the old lady clarifies, with some impatience. "Little Sandy's. He's a pediatrician. The child went into Mercy Hospital, to have her tonsils out, and they met there. This man is a prince."

"A prince," I echo.

Real love, I suppose, is wanting the object of your ardor to be happy—even if they're happy without you. To my own surprise, this was my sentiment now.

"Six months ago, they got married. For their honeymoon, they go to *Canada*."

She threw up her gnarled hands, more, at this stage, like calcified claws than actual human extremities. I thought of Sharon's mom.

"This," she spits, "I will never understand. San Juan, Palm Springs. Bermuda, maybe. But no, he has a conference. *Acch!* So they go to Toronto for a week."

"Toronto," I repeat, like some kind of twitch. "But what . . . I mean . . . Something must have—"

"The flu," she explodes, outrage swelling her eyes. I know she hasn't noticed Malcolm, curled in his love seat in the corner. Unlike me, who bolts upright when someone sneezes three blocks away, Malcolm can sleep through a minor apocalypse. An asset when you live in earthquake country.

"The flu, the flu, *the flu*," she chants, only quieter now, one parched lip quivering, dabbing at the tears welling behind her glasses. Tears, I can't help believe, for more things than can be named in a single lifetime.

But I'm still perplexed. "You say the flu?" I inquire gently. "That's not usually—"

"It was *NOT the flu!*"

She stops, overcome, and slaps a palm to her forehead. Watching, I let a finger stray to Michelle's throat. This was always what I loved about her most. Her throat, and the back of her neck—still, I discover with relief, inviolate, pale to the touch, downy (if horrifically cool). Intact in its third-grade sweetness. We were children together. Virgins. Runaways. Criminals and lovers. The sentence, *I was in her*, blinks once in my mind. *And now she's dead.* That place, inside her, dead. Dead inside. Dead out. I want to cry for reasons I don't even know about.

"It was *not* the flu," Dolores sputters again, tearing up for the first time. "It was that men—that *meningitis*." Her face goes slack, then tough again. "They went to dinner. Who knows? It could have been an apple. A doorknob. She maybe forgot to wash her hands. He's fine. But not Michelle, not my Michelle. Trouble all her life, this one had. You remember that Krishna routine? *Oy!* So now, just when we think the trouble's over—*this*. The next morning, she has a fever. Brian gives her aspirin. He's a doctor, right? He knows what to do. By six o'clock, she's got a fever of one hundred three. At midnight, it's one hundred five. He calls an ambulance. They get her to the hospital. One-thirty, she's unconscious. They say her *brain* has swelled. Have you ever heard such a thing? By three in the morning—"

She doesn't finish. Doesn't have to. She just blinks at me and continues in a monotone.

"The hospital says if he'd brought her in earlier, she would have been fine. And Brian, *oy gott,* that poor man. Like a saint he's been. Like a father to Little Sandy. You'd think she was his. That's what I'm saying. But he's a doctor! He's a doctor, *and he didn't know.* Now he can't forgive himself. 'Meningitis,' he tells me over and over, 'Mama, meningitis is so easy to cure. One pill. One antibiotic. Gone. But you have to catch it early. Otherwise—' "

"He didn't know," I say, hearing myself defend a man I've never met, a man about whom I know nothing, except for his pain and his mistakes. I struggle not to let myself think *"waste."* Think *"tragedy."* Think *"God is a vicious bastard who should be hung by his thumbs and raped in the ass by frothing dogs for what he does to us."*

Only then, reversing everything I'd just thought about the Creator—if there is such a thing—in marches this little angel. A girl of five or so in a reddish bob, black satin dress, and white anklets with patent-leather Mary Janes and attitude for days. I can't believe what I'm seeing. The same hair. The same face, same eyes.

"Hi, Grandma," the girl says.

"Hi, darling."

"Daddy's crying," she announces. Matter-of-fact.

"He's what?" says Dolores, letting go of her walker, opening her arms up for a hug.

"He's crying. He has to go get some Kee-nex." That throaty voice.

My heart slips sideways. It's Michelle in kindergarten. Michelle incarnate. The first vision I ever had of her, and now the last.

Malcolm chooses this instant, mysteriously, to pop out of a deep sleep and gaze straight at this little beauty. The expression on his face is like nothing I've ever seen: curious, rapt . . . *totaled*. His mouth actually hangs open. I see him gaze at her and think: *Here we go.* History doesn't repeat itself, it just never stops.

Michelle's daughter, for her part, pretends not to notice. Little Sandy scoots behind Dolores, stealing glances at her admirer from behind her hips. The old lady and I exchange a look.

"Come on," I say to Malcolm. "We better get going. It's time."

I hold my hand out, but he just stays where he is, gaping past me. Transfixed.

I glance at Dolores, who turns her head from the little boy, to the little girl, and back again. I figure she's thinking exactly what I'm thinking: *For Christ's sake, let life turn out better for these two.*

Or maybe not. There's a glint in her eye that's none too grandmotherly. Maybe she's thinking something else entirely. Maybe, as I suddenly suspect, she's thinking, *"I don't care if he's only five, if I catch that little pischer sniffing HER panties, he's going to need his own damn coffin . . ."*

Dolly's grip on Little Sandy, I see, has grown raptorlike, as if she might swoop through the mortuary window and into the sky at any moment, just carry her off like a falcon with a mouse,

perv—a love story

making sure she raises the blood of her blood far away and un-
reachable by the blood of mine.

"It's okay," I say, "we're going back to California after the funeral."

But the old lady either doesn't hear me or doesn't care to.
Instead, she slides one gnarled hand over her granddaughter's
eyes, gesturing toward the door with a look that's hard to de-
scribe.

I nod, and, without another word, lead my boy away from
Michelle's prone body, toward his own strange destiny, and away
from mine.